I dedicate this book to future generations of children with disabilities who I hope will be able to embrace their disabilities, be more accepted in society, and someday be proud to not only advocate for themselves, but to also tell the stories of the many advocates that came before them.

THE MAGIC WITHIN

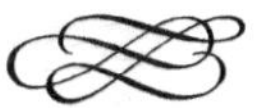

ALLISON M. BOOT

ISBN: 978-1-7321267-0-1

ACKNOWLEDGMENTS

Firstly, I'd like to acknowledge my guardian angels, which include my maternal grandmother, Maw-maw, my maternal grandfather, Papaw Hughes, my paternal grandfather, Papaw Lewis, my baby brother Luke Lewis, and many others whom I am sure have guarded me since moving onto the next life. Writing *The Magic Within* was difficult for me at times. It is one of the longest and most complex things I have ever written. There were many times I wanted to give up, but I didn't because your voices were in my head encouraging me not to give in to self-doubt and reminding me that this story was put in my heart because I was meant to tell it. I cannot thank you all enough for helping me through the writing process. I miss you all more than words can express and cannot wait to see you again, hug you, and read my books with you while we await loved ones at the Pearly Gates. Until then, I hope you smile and enjoy reading *Just the Way You Are* and *The Magic Within* each time one of our loved ones opens a copy.

Secondly, I'd like to acknowledge my loving husband, Dylan Boot. I know that my writing *The Magic Within* presented some unique challenges during the first couple of years of our marriage, but your support and your love for me never wavered throughout the writing and publishing process. I wouldn't be where I am today as a writer or as a person if it were not for your unconditional love and support. Thank you so much for going through this crazy journey called life with me ... ILYSMSM.

Thirdly, I would like to acknowledge my Nana Lewis, who inspired the Nana in this book. I know we don't see each other as much as we used to and that things are different now, but I hope you know that I will love and respect both you and Papaw until the end of time.

Additionally, I would like to acknowledge my older brother Josh Strong who inspired me to include a dragon as the villain in this book and write in a way that will hopefully appeal to boys and girls.

Last, but certainly not least, I would like to acknowledge my editors without whom *The Magic Within* would not be what it is today. The secret to great writing is good editing. I can't thank my editors enough for lending their skills and expertise to this book and for helping me to be a great writer.

CONTENTS

AUTHOR INTRODUCTION

Dearest Readers,

Writing *The Magic Within* has been a journey full of more highs and lows than I could ever have imagined. After I wrote my first book, *Just the Way You Are,* in 2015 I joined several disability and Cerebral Palsy specific Facebook groups in hopes of advertising the book to my target audiences. My Newsfeed morphed into something that disappointed me daily. I read post after post of people requesting miracles that would cure children with disabilities. I also saw article after article promising that new treatments or surgery had the potential to cure someone of his or her disability.

One afternoon I spotted an article advertising robotic onesies for babies who were unable to crawl and/or walk properly. To say that I became angry would be a gross understatement. The fact that someone had created something to make even babies "normal," and the fact that parents were being encouraged to use this equipment to get their children to conform to societal standards, left me outraged.

I wrote a Facebook post sharing the article detailing my feelings on the subject and, to my dismay, no one responded. After a couple of days, I decided to share my feelings on the subject with people in a different way and the idea for *The Magic Within* was born. Please don't misunderstand my feelings of anger. As someone with a disability who has experienced the pros and cons of both therapeutic and surgical intervention, I am not discouraging medical treatment. In fact, I would encourage both therapeutic and surgical intervention to treat someone with a disability when it is medically necessary. I just feel that surgeries and therapies should be seen and advertised as a way to allow those with disabilities to reach their full potential, instead of as a way to cure and/or allow them to achieve normalcy.

Any disability, and the unknowns that come along with that disability, can be scary. I can understand an adult who has acquired a new disability or a parent who has just given birth to a child with a disability striving to have and/or to give his or her child a normal life. When facing the unknown, a reaction like this is completely justified. I only wish that people could also look at the positive aspects that come with being diagnosed with or having a child diagnosed with a disability. For example, people with disabilities tend to be more resourceful and adaptable than the average person due to having to come up with innovative ways to complete even the most mundane tasks, such as pouring oneself a drink.

I don't have the dexterity required to twist the cap off of a gallon or two-liter jug. There was a time when I was so thirsty that I pulled a half gallon of lemonade from my fridge, used a small knife to poke a hole in it, and put two straws together so I could drink the lemonade straight from the carton. For any average person, this might seem crazy, but I was elated because I completed the task independently.

In addition to the fact that people with disabilities tend to be resourceful, we are also a part of an amazing history. The Disability Rights Movement, while still young, has a rich history full of accomplishments like the Americans with Disabilities Act (ADA) and the Individuals with Disabilities Education Act (IDEA), thanks to the tireless work of advocates like Ed Roberts and Judy

Heumann, who are known as the father and mother of the Independent Living Movement, a sub-movement of the Disability Rights Movement focusing on the rights of people with disabilities to live in the environment we choose, respectively.

Unfortunately, I did not hear about the likes of Wade Blank, who fought to make our transportation systems accessible; or Fred Fay, who fought for Section 504 of the Rehabilitation Act of 1973, which was a precursor, so to speak, to the ADA until I worked at a Center for Independent Living. When I first heard the personal stories and the accomplishments of leaders of the Disability Rights Movement, I wondered why I hadn't heard about them before. In time, I realized it was most likely because those people did not fit the definition of "normal" in society. I admit to knowing very little about the fight for disability rights outside of the U.S., but I'd venture to say that there is still little education about people with disabilities or our fight for equal rights around the world for the same reason.

Sadly, the disability rights advocates mentioned, as well as many others, are getting older or have already passed on. I fear that if society isn't able to move away from a world where people only accept those who are seen as normal, then someday when younger advocates like myself are gone, there will be no one to tell the stories of the incredible sacrifices others made when fighting for people with disabilities, just to be given basic human rights.

Worse yet, I fear that within a hundred years, thanks to technological advances and the societal belief that people need to be able-bodied to be healthy and normal, disabilities will be erased from this earth. I tear up when I think about the fact that someday there may not be anyone living with the unique perspective that having a disability gives. I have two degrees, a job, a house, and, most importantly, a husband whom I love very much. By societal standards, I am living a typical life, but some people don't always see it that way because I have a disability and require someone to help me get out of bed in the morning. Strangely, I find that I appreciate my accomplishments and blessings in life more than some able-bodied people would for that very reason.

My point is that people do not have to be cured of or have to overcome disabilities to achieve things in life. Additionally, if able-bodied people could look past the differences of people with disabilities, they would ultimately see that we are all just people. I hope that someday people with disabilities will be encouraged to achieve whatever they want in life while living with their disabilities, instead of being told that they will achieve more in life if they are cured of their disabilities.

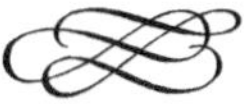

CHAPTER 1

*T*his kingdom really has come full circle, *Murlyn, thought to himself. I sat here with Natalie years ago. Now here I am with her granddaughter. Time has changed everything.—*

"Are you sure the land is ready for this, Murlyn?" Isabel interrupted his thoughts.

Murlyn nervously shifted on his two-and-a half foot frame, transferring his weight from one side to the other. Being a troll could be a real pain at times. Especially when dealing with humans like Isabel, who towered over him by about three feet and had the ability to make him nervous in a matter of seconds. He looked into her bright emerald, almond-shaped eyes, which were revered all across the land, and wondered what she was truly thinking. He had picked up on the trepidation in her voice as Isabel sighed. She had a huge decision to make and Murlyn could see she was struggling to come to terms with the implications. Her decision would change Cinder's Edge forever.

Murlyn cleared his throat, "I'm certain it is the first of many great things you will do for the kingdom, m'lady. But I think you need a bit more reassurance."

"I couldn't agree more Daddy," a cute little troll piped up in a squeaky voice. The little intrusion to the conversation was Missy, Murlyn's 50-year-old daughter. Middle aged by human standards, but Missy was merely around 5 years old for a troll. "That's why I invited Blaine and Natalie here to the castle." Missy, gave her father a smile and he ruffled her purple, sparkly hair.

"That's my girl," the bushy-eyebrowed troll smiled down at his daughter. "Is your Mama coming too?"

Missy looked at her father like he'd grown two heads, "Do you really think she'd miss a chance to spend extra time with us?" The smaller troll questioned, her tiny, high-pitched voice laced with sarcasm.

"Point taken," Murlyn nodded. "There they are now," Smiling brightly, Murlyn greeted the guests. "Out of retirement so soon?" He asked by way of greeting his old friends as they entered the throne room.

Blaine, a stocky, elderly man with thinning white hair and wiry eyebrows, that always looked a bit disheveled, threw back his head and laughed at the treasure troll.

"No way," he looked at his wife, Natalie, and smiled. "We are enjoying the peacefulness of our quiet, remote, little shack far too much. And to be honest, if it weren't for this one…"

Blaine flashed an even brighter smile at his significant other. "I don't think I would've ever left to come here. This part of our lives is over. So, we're just here to help our beautiful granddaughter and then we'll be on our way," the elderly man explained, his voice full of love and adoration as he looked at Isabel, his oldest granddaughter.

Isabel looked from her grandmother to her grandfather and back, smiling sweetly. "Hi Papaw. Hi Nana. Thank you for coming."

"What's wrong dear Isabel?" Natalie, a petite, silver-haired elderly woman with the same bright emerald eyes as her granddaughter, questioned sweetly.

"I am not sure the realm is ready for the change I wish to impart upon them," Isabel said, solemnly. "I'm reconsidering doing something so drastic with my first royal decree," she admitted apprehensively.

Shaking his head, Blaine looked his granddaughter in the eye. "Sweetheart, do not second guess your instincts. Your idea is magnificent and will do wonders for the kingdom," he said reassuringly. "We are all so proud of you, sweetie. Your Nana and I only wish that your beautiful mother, Madison, were here with your father to witness the wonderful changes you are about to introduce to the kingdom. Our lives all lost a little bit of light the day she became an angel."

Awww, Papaw, I miss Mama too. Dad is always reminding me that she is with us in spirit. I just wish I knew how she'd feel about what I am about to do."

"Sweetie, she'd love it," Blaine insisted. The whole kingdom will appreciate it. You're going to make the kingdom into what it should have been along. To be perfectly honest, I wish your Nana had thought of it years ago," he admitted quietly.

Natalie initially gave her husband a glare of disapproval, but her usual warm composure reappeared in seconds. "As much as it pains me to say this, your Papaw is absolutely right, Isabel. Your idea is ingenious and should have been thought of years ago. That's why you are the one running the kingdom now instead of me."

Shoulders slumped, Isabel sighed. "I appreciate all of the encouragement. But you of all people know how resistant this kingdom is to change. How do I know this decree will be received well?" Isabel's voice was slightly shaky as she folded her arms across her chest. Murlyn sensed the queen was anxious and hoped her grandparents could ease her concerns.

The treasure troll, who had been examining the interaction among his human friends, looked to Blaine and smiled. "What do you say we finally tell the beautiful, young queen how the kingdom became what it is today?"

"I've been telling 'em to do that for years," a pink-glittery haired treasure troll said, as she entered the throne room. "You can't really figure out where you are going unless you know where you came from."

"My beautiful wife has a point," Murlyn said sweetly as Rosie came to stand at his side. He flashed her a bright smile and gave her a quick peck on her cheek.

"Okay, okay," Blaine agreed. "But not here. It's—" he looked around the room, glancing from the sparkly-white cathedral style ceiling to the aged yet still impeccably shiny marble floor. "too much," he said finally.

"Papaw, what do you mean?" Isabel's eyebrows scrunched in confusion. "This castle is beautiful."

"Yes, sweetheart, it is," Blaine agreed. "A part of me will always consider it home, but the hut is where I feel most comfortable. That's why Nana and I retired there," he explained.

"If that's where you're most comfortable, Papaw, then we shall go there," Isabel said.

With that, the young royal stepped off her throne and climbed into her grandfather's lap just as she had done when she was little. The two hugged before Isabel's grandfather wheeled them in his wheelchair to the hut her grandparents called home. Isabel remained in his lap the whole time while Natalie and the trolls followed.

"Hey, Dylock, just the troll I was hoping to see," Murlyn said by way of greeting as the group ran into a green-haired troll with a four-leaf clover-shaped gemstone.

"Hey everyone, how's it goin'?"

"We're doing great. We are actually headed to the hut so we can sit comfortably and tell Isabel a little history about the kingdom. Would you like to join us? You'd bring an interesting perspective," the blue-haired woodland creature encouraged.

"That's for sure," Blaine agreed.

"Oh, wish I could, but I promised Bernie and some other trolls that I'd help clean their trees today," Dylock explained, his cheeks turning slightly crimson.

An awkward silence settled amongst Dylock and the others

when no one responded. *No troll I know has ever needed help cleaning anything. That's a definite lie*, Murlyn thought.

"Well, we'll miss you," Rosie said after a moment. "Don't work too hard."

"I won't. I'll see you all later," Dylock assured them, scurrying off into the distance.

"Well, that was weird," Isabel declared once the four-leafed-clover-adorned woodland creature was out of ear shot. "What's up with him?"

"You'll understand everything in time," Murlyn told the newly crowned royal, his voice calm and reassuring as he and the others continued the journey toward the hut.

SOME THINGS NEVER CHANGE, Murlyn thought as he and his friends began walking through the Forest of Wishes. Unlike a typical forest, full of richly green cypress trees, this particular forest was full of the tallest and most oddly colored ferns that ever existed.

"There it is," Murlyn smiled as the group approached a small hut nestled in the very back of the forest. This was where he had spent many hours with Blaine and Natalie. It felt like home. "This is my favorite place in the entire world."

Giggling, Missy studied the small shack. The walls were made of rough, aged, dark brown wooden planks covered in brightly-colored moss that matched the trees of the forest. They were haphazardly allowing sunlight to creep into the otherwise dark structure, highlighting its frailty. Touched by several of the ferns that towered above it, the moss-covered roof looked paper thin, appearing only slightly stronger than the warped, light brown, wooden door. The small structure looked as though it could cave in at any moment and become nothing more than dust on the path that sat before it.

"Daddy, how could this possibly be your favorite place?" Missy questioned, her squeaky voice colored with curiosity, "It's so modest."

"Well, I know it's not much in comparison to our beautiful trees," Murlyn chuckled. "But your Uncle Percy, a couple of other trolls, and myself helped Blaine's dad, Benjamin, to build it after we were sent into exile. Even though things are different now, this place is still near and dear to my heart," Murlyn explained, his voice quiet and thoughtful as he examined the shabby structure, placing a hand on the warped door as though it were the most delicate flower he'd ever touched. "Home sweet home," the troll whispered as he opened it.

Blaine entered after Murlyn. "Gather around the table and put on your listening ears girls," Blaine said, excitedly. "You are not going to want to miss a single word of our fantastic kingdom's history."

I AM ACTING *like such a scaredy little garden gnome right now,* Dylock shook his head, pacing frustratedly outside the hut. *He's going to start the story any minute. Why can't I just knock on the door, tell them I changed my mind, and go in there?* Sighing, he hung his head. *This is so stupid. They have to know I lied. No troll ever needs help cleaning anything. Seventy-five-percent of the wishes we grant have something to do with cleaning.* He chuckled at the thought. *This is absurd. Everything will be fine. I just need to face my past once and for all.* Taking a deep breath, he paused in front of the door of the hut and stopped just short of knocking on it. *I just can't.* Melancholy washed over him as he dropped to his knees. *What kind of treasure troll am I if I am this ashamed of my past?* He wondered, dropping his face into his hands.

Moments later, he lifted his head at the sound of faint voices from inside the hut. *I shouldn't eavesdrop,* he told himself. *Then again, maybe if I listen to my friends' pasts, it'll make it easier to face my own. Yes,* he decided. *If I can't face the past in there. I'll at least listen from out here.* Afraid that wasting another moment would give him time to talk himself out of the idea, Dylock rubbed his four-leafed-clover-shaped gemstone until a bright glittering green light swirled around the single window of the tiny moss-covered hut and said a spell.

> *"My friends are about to walk down memory lane.*
> *I am not brave enough to be near.*
> *Allow this magic to let me hear them without strain,*
> *so my past I will no longer fear."*

He smiled as the light dissipated and his friends voices instantly sounded as though they were standing right next to him. *Perfect. Now, I will be able to hear them as I face the inevitable,* he thought, settling on a patch of moss that had fallen just below the hut's window as Murlyn began telling tales of long ago.

"It's hard to know where to begin," Murlyn said before he, Rosie, Blaine, and Natalie also took seats at the table. "As Rosie and I were telling Missy outside, the treasure trolls and your family go way back." Chuckling, he gestured toward Isabel's grandparents. "As a matter of fact, the other treasure trolls and I were granting wishes for royals way before these two knuckleheads even came along."

"How can that be? You don't look half as old as they do?" Isabel asked lightheartedly, her voice colored with amusement.

"Hey, watch it, Isabel. Your Papaw is still young enough to put you over his knee," Blaine quipped, before flashing his granddaughter a grin.

"Not if I have anything to say about it," Natalie feigned anger as she shot her husband a look. A chorus of laughter erupted around the table.

"You know, your great grandmother, Elizabeth, had that same protective instinct," Murlyn explained as the laughter quieted. "Actually, two of your great grandmothers, Alexandria and Lizzie, did. They were the best of friends. I remember my first encounter with them as if it were yesterday."

As the treasure troll began talking about two of the kindest women he'd ever met, he couldn't help but remember how quickly and how much the two women had changed his life. Treasure trolls had guarded Cinder's Edge, a small kingdom nestled twenty miles west of the volcano, Mount Wishnik, and a mere three miles from the Forest of Wishes, for as long as Murlyn could remember. Trolls were selfless creatures by nature, but they had a darker side that was driven by a secret, which could make their motives not so pure at times. And that secret was a black diamond. The most powerful gemstone known to magic and mankind. It was the trolls main source of magic and was kept in the throne room of the castle. Guarding the black diamond was the sole purpose and the most important duty in Murlyn's life, until the day Alexandria and Lizzie found him in the forest. Murlyn thought back to that day and drifted off into his own joyful memories…

CHAPTER 2

On that fateful day, in the spring of the year 564, the last of King Samuel and Queen Sarah Crawford's reign, Murlyn had been busy working and was looking forward to a well-deserved rest. *Finally, a break*, he sighed, climbing into the dark blue sapling that was his home within the Forest of Wishes. *Time for a nap*, the treasure troll decided, slowly closing his eyes. But sleep was not to be, because suddenly there were two women under a purple fern about five trees down from him having a very loud conversation. *Ugh, so much for sleep.*

"Thank you for walking with me, Lizzie."

Murlyn looked down and saw a petite woman with long, auburn hair talking to another woman who had bright blonde hair in contrast to her companion.

"I just had to get out of there. Daddy's meeting with yet another suitor." The woman continued with a hint of sorrow in her voice.

"What do you think the odds are that he'll marry you off to this one?" Lizzie, asked jovially.

Murlyn watched grumpily from his tree as the two women settled in under the purple tree, making themselves comfortable amongst fallen moss. He was definitely not going to get his nap in now!

The sad, auburn-haired woman shook her head. "Lizzie…,"

Pet name, Murlyn thought when he heard the shortened term.

"…this isn't funny. I love this kingdom, but I don't want to be forced to live a life of unhappiness just to protect it."

"So, then don't, Alexandria," Lizzie said nonchalantly.

Murlyn raised his eyebrows in shock when he recognized the sad woman's name. This then led to him remembering where he had seen the woman before. She was a princess and lived in the castle that housed the black diamond he was charged with protecting. Murlyn moved a little to get a better view. The princess, Alexandria, had hung her head as if she were about to cry. "I wish it were that easy," she said somberly.

A silence settled between the two young women while Lizzie twirled her long blonde hair nervously awaiting the princess to resume speaking. But it wasn't Alexandria that spoke. "That's it!" Lizzie exclaimed excitedly after a few minutes, nearly causing Murlyn to fall from his perch out of shock. "You can make a wish!" She stood up, dragging Alexandria to her feet. Just to the left of them, was a hollowed out, brightly colored tree that Lizzie was now poking her head into, looking for something.

The young royal scrunched up her noes in confusion. "What do you mean? What're you doing?" Lizzie's head still buried in the tree.

Turning to face her friend, Lizzie giggled. "Think about it," she flashed a bright smile, scanning their surroundings. "We're in the Forest of Wishes. All we have to do is find a troll and all of this will go away."

Murlyn, stifled a loud gulp up in the tree and threw his hands up to his mouth to muffle any more involuntary sounds. The last thing he wanted to do today was make the princess's wishes come true. He was too tired for that.

"That's brilliant Lizzie!" the princess exclaimed, pulling her friend into a hug. "You're a genius. Let's go find a troll!"

Murlyn looked down at the two girls who were now hunting

inside any tree they could find for a troll. They were so loud traipsing around the forest, shouting at one another when they found another tree empty, that it was giving him a massive headache. He was desperate to sleep, and this was not going to happen unless he could get rid of the two women, who were as loud as a herd of elephants! He wondered if what he was about to do was a good idea, but he needed to sleep and so instead of thinking about it for too much longer and talking himself out of it, he poked his head out of the tree.

"I'll grant you a wish if you will just stop all that yelling," he said grouchily.

Both girls jumped out of their skins at the new voice. Murlyn had to stifle a giggle. Lizzie was the first to resume her composure though. "Oh, my gosh!" She shouted excitedly. "How cute is he?"

"So adorable!" The princess smiled and looked up at the treasure troll in the tree. "Can you really grant a wish for me, little guy?"

Rolling his dark blue eyes, Murlyn stuck out his hand. "I'm Murlyn. And you are?"

"Alexandria Antionette Crawford, Princess of Cinder's Edge," she shook his hand enthusiastically, pointing her head towards Lizzie. "And this is my best friend, Elizabeth, or as most of her friends call her, Lizzie."

"It's an honor to meet the both of you," Murlyn said sweetly before focusing on the princess. "Please don't worry about the black diamond, m'lady." He puffed out his chest to show his bravery and proudness. "My friends Percy and Rosie are protecting it in my absence," he assured her. "Now tell me, what wish is in your heart today, your highness?" He asked inquisitively.

"Oh, please," the princess chuckled nervously. "Call me Alexandria." Taking a deep breath, the young majestic begun in her soft and timid voice. "I wish that my father would understand that I want to marry for love and quit trying to marry me off to suitors that he feels would be good for the kingdom." Tucking her auburn hair behind her ear, the princess continued. "I wish my dad would put his love for me above his love for the kingdom."

Oh, great, the one wish she asks for is the one wish I can't grant. Typical. Murlyn thought. "My deepest apologies Alexandria. I should have told you before you asked that the one restriction on treasure trolls granting wishes is we cannot fulfill wishes that dramatically change fate without dire consequences," Murlyn looked at the ground not wanting to look the princess in the eye. "I'm afraid your wish would definitely impact fate and is, therefore, forbidden."

The princess sighed heavily. "Well, that's that," she said solemnly.

Lizzie shook her head. "Don't give up so fast, dear friend," she embraced the young royal once again, squeezing tightly. Turning to the troll, she smiled, her expression hopeful. "Murlyn, just because you can't stop the king from marrying off Alexandria, doesn't mean you can't grant other wishes, right?"

Murlyn nodded even though he felt a little apprehensive. "That's right. I can grant any wish that doesn't change fate or destiny."

"Great!" Lizzie exclaimed. "That gives me an idea." Smiling, she plucked Murlyn out of his tree.

"What're you doing? Put me down. Put me down right now!" Murlyn's cheeks turned bright red. *No one should ever pick up a troll without their express permission.* Murlyn was fuming. Even if she were a friend of the princess, if this woman didn't put him down soon, he would have to take matters into his own hands.

Ignoring Murlyn's squirms, Lizzie turned to her friend. "Let's go," she urged. "The three of us need to have a chat with your father."

Looking up at Lizzie, Murlyn's cheeks still crimson, he furrowed his bushy blue eyebrows. "What are you thinking?" he squealed with frustration. "I can't go anywhere. I have to guard the black diamond. Put me back in my tree!" Murlyn struggled even more, thrashing his arms and legs about to free himself, but Lizzie was having none of it.

Tightening her grasp slightly, Lizzie shook her head. "But you just said that your friends Percy and Rosie are guarding it," she pointed out, smirking mischievously.

Murlyn stopped struggling, knowing he was close to being

defeated and nodded. "Yes, but I need to relieve them after my nap so—."

"Sleep is for wimps," Lizzie joked. "You can relieve your friends as soon as we are done talking to the king," Lizzie assured the treasure troll, finally placing him on the ground. Looking from him to Alexandria and back, she smiled brightly. "C'mon, let's go."

"Okay, but you better take credit for whatever crazy idea you have," the princess warned lightheartedly.

"Don't I always?"

They started down the path toward the castle. But moments later, the princess noticed that Murlyn wasn't following. Sighing, she walked back to his tree. "Are you coming?" She queried innocently.

"It's not a good idea," Murlyn said matter-of-factly. He was not going to be cajoled by two women, even if one of them was a royal.

"I know we just met, but trust me when I tell you that Lizzie is always full of good ideas," the princess chuckled. "Please, come and see what she has up her sleeve. It would mean the world to me," she said sweetly and gave him a smile that ever so slightly melted his heart.

Who could resist such a kind girl? Murlyn wondered dreamily before reluctantly joining the princess and her best friend on the path to the castle.

King Samuel Crawford smiled at his daughter as she, her best friend, and a hesitant Murlyn, entered the throne room of the castle. Practically jumping out of his throne, the skinny, white-haired man with a prominent pointy nose and brown eyes, ran to her. "Great news, my dear. You are to marry Frederick Nordstrom in two short weeks," he announced, his voice coated with excitement.

Murlyn rolled his eyes and shook his head as he heard the King's news. *I cannot believe that I let these girls talk me into this. Coming here while on duty is one thing, but showing up as a surprise is a completely different thing entirely. And as the creature who is supposed to help the princess marry for love. This is not good.* Murlyn searched for a place to stay camouflaged. The sparkly white ceiling was incredibly high and instantly made him feel extremely tiny and insignificant, no matter how many times he walked into the room. *If it didn't house the black diamond, this would be no place for a troll... for cryin' out loud, the floor looks like it's never even been walked on.* He quickly hid behind a floor to ceiling burgundy colored curtain.

Alexandria cleared her throat, trying to gain her father's attention. The king glanced at his daughter and then at a red-haired troll who was just a couple inches shorter than Murlyn and had a red circular gemstone on his belly. The troll was standing to the right of the marble pillar positioned between the king and queen's thrones on which the black diamond was proudly displayed.

"Please give me a moment with my daughter, Percy, and take Rosie with you too." He addressed the two trolls. Murlyn hadn't noticed Rosie initially but as they scampered off together he was glad that both had been on duty as planned.

I hope they don't see me here before I'm supposed to be. Murlyn struggled to stay still behind the curtain as Percy and Rosie, who'd been standing to the left and right of the black diamond exited the room. Letting out a breath as the door closed behind them, Murlyn listened intently as the princess attempted to reason with her father.

"Daddy, I know you want me to marry Frederick, but—" she begun.

"No buts, sweetheart." Placing a hand on her shoulder, the king squeezed gently. "Trust me, Frederick is the perfect man for you. He will do a fine job of leading Cinder's Edge for years to come."

Sighing, the frustrated daughter turned to look at her best friend. "Keep trying. You can do this," Lizzie mouthed to her friend.

"Daddy, I hardly know Frederick. I know the future of the kingdom is important, but what about my future? I dream of a love like the love Lizzie and Benjamin share," Alexandria said.

So, this was why Murlyn had been dragged to the castle. The princess had seen her best friend fall in love and she wanted the same thing. Murlyn was truly regretting coming to the castle now.

Letting out a huff, the king pulled his daughter into the right-hand corner of the room out of her best friend's earshot.

I'll definitely be granting some wishes later, the woodland creature thought, his heart breaking a little, as he heard the sadness in their quiet voices.

"Sweetheart," the King started, as he always did with Alexandria. "Benjamin is a magician. I have no doubt that he and Lizzie will live a life of struggle. I don't want that for you. Our family has standards," the king whispered into his daughter's ear but loud enough for Murlyn to hear every word.

"Daddy, I 'm not saying that I want to be with someone like Benjamin. I just want a chance to be happy like he and Lizzie are. Can't you understand that?" The princess's eyes quickly filled with tears.

"You'll be happy with Frederick just like your mother is happy with me, my darling. Trust me, just give it time," he said, as he walked Alexandria back toward Lizzie.

"I trust you Daddy," the princess said solemnly, the tears now flowing down her cheeks. "I just wish there was a way to ensure that I'll be happy with Frederick."

"What if there was?" Lizzie asked meekly after a moment.

Turning to look at his daughter's friend, King Samuel smiled. "I've been trying for years to ensure happiness here in Cinder's Edge, Lizzie. Until Glomgurgle is eliminated, it can't be done,"

I wish people would stop talking about Glomgurgle. No one seems to understand that giving into the fear only gives him more power, Murlyn thought as he heard the king refer to the dragon who had been threatening to destroy the kingdom for years.

"Murlyn, please come out from behind the curtain," Lizzie called out, her voice shaking slightly.

So much for staying camouflaged. Murlyn hesitantly pulled back the curtain and walked toward them.

Clearing her throat, Lizzie glanced from the troll to the king and back. "King Samuel, this is Murlyn. As you can see, he is a treasure troll and we brought him here because we believe his wish granting ability is the key to Alexandria's happiness," she flashed a nervous smile at the king. "He can't make Glomgurgle disappear because he cannot grant wishes that dramatically change fate, but I have no doubt that he could help Alexandria be happy."

The princess looked to her best friend, eyebrows furrowed. "Lizzie, what're you doing?"

"Yeah, what's going on?" Murlyn echoed.

"Is that so?" The leader of Cinder's Edge queried, his tone skeptical.

Lizzie nodded.

Looking back at his daughter, Samuel smiled. "Make a wish sweetheart."

"Huh?"

"Make a wish. I want to see if this works." The king said.

Oh, here we go. I hope she doesn't wish for anything too crazy. Murlyn's heart beat faster than that of a hummingbird as he waited to hear the request.

"Remember, he can't grant any wishes that dramatically change fate," Lizzie said sweetly.

Letting out a breath, Alexandria considered her wish. "Well, if Daddy is going to insist I marry Frederick, then I wish to have the prettiest wedding updo the kingdom has ever seen."

Oh, good... that's an easy one, the treasure troll thought as he rubbed the blue, diamond-shaped gemstone in the center of his belly, preparing to grant the wish. Within seconds, the treasure troll's gemstone was glowing a bright blue.

"Interesting." The king said quietly, his voice coated with curiosity.

"Okay, Alexandria. I need you to kneel down and brush a few strands of your hair against my gemstone," the woodland creature instructed, his voice calm and quiet.

The princess looked down at the troll, her eyes wide and full of hesitation.

"Quickly, while my gemstone is still glowing," he urged.

As the princess fulfilled Murlyn's request, glittering light traveled from his gemstone and begun swirling around her head. Within seconds, her hair was styled into a perfect bun with gorgeous French braids on each side with tiny diamonds and purple and white wild flowers intertwined, "Oh, my gosh," Alexandria gasped as she spotted her reflection in the pristine marble floor. "It's perfect… absolutely perfect. You're awesome."

Murlyn waved a dismissive hand. "Thanks, but I'm just doing what I was meant to do. I'm no better than any other treasure troll."

"Sure, you are," Alexandria smiled brightly. "You were the first to be nice to me."

"Well, that settles it," King Samuel said after a moment. "You were the first troll to be nice to my daughter and you make her happy. If that's what it's going to take for her to marry Frederick and ensure the future of our kingdom, then I name you the official ambassador of happiness here in Cinder's Edge," he declared with authority.

"I beg your pardon, your majesty?" The woodland creature questioned. He had a bad feeling about this.

"Oh, Daddy! Do you really mean that? Can Murlyn really grant me and the other people of Cinder's Edge wishes to ensure our happiness?" Alexandria asked.

Clearing his throat, the troll tried to interject. "Uh, excuse me your majesty," he begun, his usually calm voice slightly shaky. "I have to help the other trolls protect the—"

The leader of the land eyed Murlyn, staring down at him. "This is not up for discussion," he shouted. "You should be honored to serve Cinder's Edge in any capacity."

"Yes, your majesty." Murlyn lamented quickly, his voice still trembling.

Ignoring the troll, King Samuel turned back towards his daughter and kissed her forehead. "Yes sweetie, as long as you agree to marry Frederick and be by his side as he governs the realm."

"Did that really just happen?" Murlyn questioned as the king stepped out of the throne room.

"It sure did. My hair looks amazing," Alexandria said, still admiring her reflection in the shiny floor.

Lizzie looked from the troll to her best friend and back, smiling brightly. "You're going to make a great ambassador of happiness, Murlyn," she said cheerfully.

"I don't think the other trolls will think so," Murlyn said, his voice laced with worry. "I don't know how I am going to tell them."

"Just explain that you were made ambassador of happiness by order of the king," Alexandria said. "They will have to accept that."

"It's not that simple," Murlyn explained. "We all keep a very busy schedule guarding the black diamond."

Eyeing the troll, the princess shook her head. "I understand that keeping the black diamond safe is of the utmost importance, but your position as the ambassador of happiness is just as important. Without you my life with Frederick will be miserable."

Lizzie, who had been listening, shook her head vehemently. "No, we've come too far. I am not going to let that happen. We're going back to the Forest of Wishes to have a discussion with the other trolls." Murlyn opened his mouth to object, but closed it quickly as both girls hurried out of the throne room.

"Okay, it's going to take a minute to gather everyone together," Murlyn explained as he and the two young women entered the Forest of Wishes.

"Uh, something tells me that's not going to be a problem," Lizzie said, pointing toward a multi-colored sapling, known as the Tree of Friendship where all of the other trolls were gathered around. This particular fern was special not only due to its variety of color but because it was littered with sweet, succulent blueberries and provided a place for the trolls to gather, talk, and have meals together.

Uh Oh, thought Murlyn. *I must have missed something important. Now I'll definitely be in trouble with everyone.* Forcing a smile, Murlyn tapped his love, Rosie, on the shoulder. "Hi. What's happening? Why is everyone here?" He whispered.

Turning to face him, the pink glittery-haired troll wiped a tear from her eye. "Myles and Minnie just got engaged right here at the Tree of Friendship. He gave her the prettiest engagement bracelet. It's double layered and made from quartz."

Murlyn looked back at his new friends, whose eyebrows were knitted in confusion. "When trolls get engaged, instead of rings, the guys give the girls something made of rock or gemstone as a source of further magic," he explained to Alexandria and Lizzie in a hushed tone.

"Isn't that wonderful?" Rosie said sweetly, glancing longingly at the happy couple.

Uh Oh, Rosie looks so envious. The subject of commitment is sure to come up again soon, Murlyn thought warily. He wasn't sure he was ready for marriage yet. His duty to the kingdom had come before his personal happiness for the last 594 years, and he wasn't sure that would ever change. "Yes, wonderful indeed," He finally mumbled. "So sorry I missed the big moment."

Giggling, Rosie eyed him. "I bet you are. Who are your friends?" She questioned, smiling nervously up at the girls.

"Oh, I'm sorry this is—" the dark blue-haired troll begun.

"My goodness," Rosie cried. "Now that I get a closer look. I know exactly who you are. My apologies, your majesty." Rosie's voice was high-pitched and full of anxiety as she knelt before Alexandria.

"Oh, my you're so cute," the princess gushed. "But there is no need to be so formal. Please call me Alexandria. And you are?"

"Rosie, your majesty," the pink-haired troll answered, holding her hand out toward the princess.

Grasping the tiny hand, the princess shook it gently and grinned. "It's lovely to meet you Rosie."

Likewise. What brings you to the Forest of Wishes?"

"Well, me and my friend, Lizzie, here wanted to come and help Murlyn deliver some exciting news."

"In that case, follow me," Rosie said, taking a hold of the two girls hands and walking them to the special sapling. "Hey everyone. Murlyn has big news. He even brought a special guest. Get ready."

"Oh, is that right Murlyn?" Myles, a dark-purple haired troll with a half-moon shaped gemstone piped up. "You got big news too? Are ya about to follow in my footsteps and make an honest troll out of Rosie?"

Murlyn felt his cheeks suddenly go hot with embarrassment. Glancing in Rosie's direction, he saw that her face had taken on a bright crimson color, too. *Oh, great. Just great!* "Help," he mouthed, eyeing Lizzie warily.

"Actually, Murlyn has some news that could impact all of you and not just Miss Rosie," Lizzie begun. "You see, Alexandria asked that Murlyn grant her a wish that would've impacted her fate, but he couldn't so—"

Rolling her eyes, the princess addressed her friend. "Oh, Lizzie, just let me tell them, will you?" Smiling, the young royal looked to the entire group. "My father, Samuel Crawford, King of Cinder's Edge, named Murlyn the official ambassador of happiness here in the kingdom," she announced enthusiastically. Despite the beautiful young royal's gusto, her announcement was met by numerous blank stares.

After a moment, Percy spoke. "What exactly does that mean princess?"

"Murlyn is now responsible for granting wishes for me and the other people of Cinder's Edge in order to ensure the overall happiness of the realm," Alexandria answered calmly.

While Percy and many other woodland creatures simply nodded, Dylock, argued. "What makes Murlyn so special?" He queried. "And what about the responsibility he already has to guard the black diamond? Are we all just supposed to pick up the slack?" The green-haired troll asked the group with a hint of irritation in his voice.

"Dylock makes a very good point," Myles agreed. "We are already spread pretty thin."

"Yeah, this isn't right," Bernie, a slightly chubby two-and a-half-foot tall treasure troll with a triangular gemstone agreed. "We need all the trolls we can get in order to guard the black diamond properly."

As more woodland creatures begun to voice agreement with Dylock, the typical tranquil atmosphere of the Forest of Wishes became chaotic as the chatter of several tiny, squeaky, frustrated voices filled the open space.

Oh, my gosh. This is crazy. Somebody has to reason with them, Murlyn thought, once again looking to Lizzie.

Taking a deep breath, the petite strawberry blonde-haired woman shouted with all her might. "Quiet!" Once silence was restored in the forest, she addressed the group again. "You guys all guard the black diamond in order to protect the people of the kingdom, correct?"

"Yeah," Myles agreed. "We don't want that overgrown lizard to come after anyone in Cinder's Edge."

"That's for sure. Protecting the realm is our number one priority," Percy said while the other woodland creatures nodded.

"As it should be," Lizzie agreed. "But don't you guys think that ensuring the happiness of the people of the land is just as important as protecting them?"

"This girl has a point," Minnie, a lavender-haired troll with a purple butterfly-shaped gemstone admitted after a moment.

"Yeah," Rosie said quickly. "I mean, c'mon, who really wants to protect a bunch of sad people? And besides we all know that Murlyn cares about the people of Cinder's Edge more than anyone else because he has lived here the longest. Why shouldn't he have the opportunity to ensure joy in the kingdom?"

Letting out a huff, Bernie once again addressed the group. "We all know that once girls get an idea in their heads there is no convincing them otherwise, so we will all just have to pull together and make this happen."

The princess, who had nervously been watching the exchange between her best friend and the trolls, smiled brightly. "Oh, thank you. Thank you! This is going to be great," she exclaimed, eyes sparkling with excitement as she looked to Murlyn. "C'mon, Murlyn, we've got a wedding to plan."

Oh, good lord. What have I gotten myself into? The dark-blue haired troll wondered, eyeing the cheerful royal as he followed her and Lizzie out of the forest.

⌁

"I'M SO EXCITED," the princess declared as the friends started down the path towards the castle. "I've been planning my wedding since I was a little girl."

"It's going to be perfect," Lizzie assured her sweetly. "Especially with a little help from Murlyn."

"For sure," the young princess nodded. "I've already made a list of things to wish for in my head. First the dress, then the flower arrangements, the cake, the—"

Stopping in the middle of the path, Murlyn threw up his hands. "I'm only one little troll," he shouted, gaining the attention of the chattering friends. "You ladies are going to wear out my gemstone before this wedding even takes place."

Eyeing the gemstone in the center of the woodland creature's belly, the princess scoffed. "Don't be silly. What you did with my hair was amazing," she encouraged. "Lizzie's right. You're going to help me put an amazing wedding together."

"Yeah," Lizzie agreed. "I'm always right. Besides, if you do need any help, I'm sure Rosie will lend a hand."

"That little pink-haired cutie really went to bat for you earlier," Alexandria smiled brightly. "What's the deal with you two anyway?"

"That, ladies, is a conversation for another day. Let's keep talking about the wedding. What sort of entertainment are you going to have for the guests?" He queried, casually deflecting the attention away from his own love life. Women were always so determined on marrying everyone off… besides, he would pop the question in his own good time.

"Wow," the princess chuckled. "Not only are you a master of magic, but you are also a master of the art of deflection," she joked. "I'll let you get away with that today, but don't expect to avoid the question forever. And entertainment is the one thing I'm not worried about. Lizzie and her husband Benjamin are going to do a magic show," the young royal said happily.

"Oh, good. I was hoping you'd ask us to do that for you," Lizzie said. *A magic show for entertainment? This should be an interesting wedding*, the woodland creature thought. "Look, there's Benjamin." Lizzie practically squealed with excitement, as a 6' 2" tall man with sandy blond hair, crystal blue eyes, and a crooked yet white smile, approached and enveloped her into a hug.

"What have you been up to sweetheart? I've been looking everywhere for you." Benjamin said. "We're heading to the castle to plan Alexandria's wedding. Are you up for the two of us doing a magic show at the reception?"

Smiling, the man nodded enthusiastically. "Anything for the princess," he flashed a smile at the young royal. "I didn't even know you were getting married. Is this little guy the groom to be?" He laughed, looking from her to the troll and back.

Lizzie giggled and introduced Murlyn to her husband. She also gave Benjamin a quick rundown of the events of their day.

"Jeez, I've missed a lot today, haven't I?" Benjamin questioned, wide-eyed. "Will you ladies give me a moment alone with Murlyn please? We're just going to have a chat, one magic man to another."

Why could he possibly be pulling me aside? Murlyn wondered. *We just met only five minutes ago.*

"Murlyn, I know we just met," Benjamin said as if he'd just read the woodland creature's mind. "But I am going to be perfectly honest with you. You're in for an uphill battle as the ambassador of happiness here in Cinder's Edge, so I am going to give you this," Benjamin pulled out a sparkly black cloth from his back pocket and presented it to the troll.

"What's this?" Murlyn asked, as he was examining the shiny black material. It didn't look like much to him and was way too girly for his taste, as well, but he didn't want to offend Benjamin when they'd only just met.

"It's an invisibility cloak," Benjamin explained. Murlyn looked up at him in shock. "You can drape it over yourself whenever you need a moment and I guarantee that not one creature will see you," Benjamin winked, flashing Murlyn a smile.

"We just met. You don't even know me. Why would you give me this?" Murlyn asked, completely bamboozled by Benjamin's generosity.

"It's really quite simple Murlyn. When my wife's best friend is happy, my wife is happy, so I'm gonna do whatever I can to help you in your new position. Besides, we magic men gotta stick together." Chuckling, he gave Murlyn another friendly wink.

Well, isn't that something? Maybe this ambassador of happiness gig will be a good thing after all, thought Murlyn.

s Murlyn continued describing memories of long ago, his thoughts quickly traveled to April 17th, 565. The day that marked Alexandria and Frederick's marriage, as well as the start of their reign as king and queen of Cinder's Edge. The grand ballroom of the castle was transformed into an exquisite rose garden with every shade of purple, fresh-cut roses imaginable for their wedding reception. The bright, fragrant atmosphere quickly got wedding guests talking, but everyone was stunned into silence the moment the newly-crowned queen walked in as a bride.

"I bet she looked really pretty," Isabel said, suddenly interrupting Murlyn's thoughts and bringing him back to the present. "What kind of dress did she wear?"

"Oh, yes, I will never forget how Alexandria looked when she entered the ballroom," Murlyn said as he thought back to that moment. "She wore a huge ball gown with a pearl encrusted bodice and lace roses on the bottom of the skirt," the troll said, his tone quiet and reminiscent. "She was absolutely beautiful, everyone thought so. Everyone but Frederick that is. He was whispering something to Alexandria during their first dance and as someone with the duty of keeping her happy, I felt obligated to listen in," he admitted solemnly.

"That couldn't have been too hard for you, Daddy," Missy said, her squeaky voice coated with innocence. "You've always been good at eavesdropping."

"Thanks, sweetheart. It's a talent I gained as the ambassador of happiness that I sometimes wish I didn't have," he said somberly.

Murlyn thought back to that day and remembered the conversation between Frederick and Alexandria as if he were once again sitting at a table in the reception hall, listening to it all.

"I cannot believe that I am now the ruler of the kingdom," Frederick whispered, his voice full of prideful arrogance. "Now, if I could just eliminate that stupid dragon everything would be perfect."

"Can we please not talk about *him* on our wedding day?" Alexandria said in a hushed, angry tone.

The groom shot her a look. "Don't you want to get rid of *him* and ensure the safety of the realm? I figured that you of all people would understand that. Your father spoke to me about your great love for Cinder's Edge."

Rolling her eyes, Alexandria let out a barely audible sigh. "Yes, I would love nothing more than to never have to think about that fire-breathing imbecile ever again," she whispered, looking up at him with eyes full of anger. "But I don't see why we can't enjoy just one day without thinking about all of this," she sighed again. "I know that you are just in this for power, but it is our wedding day regardless. This is some of the most beautiful music I've ever heard, our cake was prepared by the finest chef in the kingdom, and my very best friend and her husband are providing some of the finest entertainment around... can't we just enjoy it?" She questioned, her tone still hushed, yet slightly hopeful.

Ugh, Murlyn sighed. *This marriage is going to make my job ten times harder,* the troll thought as he realized that Frederick was eyeing Lizzie and Benjamin instead of listening or dancing with his new wife.

"Frederick... Frederick, you should at least look at me when we're dancing," the newly-minted queen insisted quietly.

After a long moment, the inattentive husband finally looked to Alexandria. "That's it!"

"What? What is it? Why did you stop dancing?" The bride questioned, her tone just above hushed.

"I need you to introduce me to your magician friends," the freshly-crowned king grinned mischievously.

"I introduced you to them just last night at the rehearsal dinner Frederick. What is this about?"

"I'm going to get Benjamin to make Glomgurgle disappear," he whispered just as the music for their first dance ended and the magician and Lizzie stepped onto the rose covered stage that had been built just for the royal wedding.

Ugh... magic cannot be used to manipulate fate or destiny. When will people get it through their thick heads? Murlyn got up from the table and rushed to the stage to warn Benjamin and Lizzie. Crouching down in front of the stage, Murlyn waved his tiny hands to get the illusionist's attention. "Psst... Benjamin... Benjamin—"

"Citizens of Cinder's Edge, may I have your attention please?" Frederick queried, his delivery loud and boisterous as he addressed the whole room.

Uh Oh... he's getting everyone's attention... this can't be good.

"My new wife has arranged for the amazing Benjamin Benson to entertain us tonight. How many of you have seen Mr. Benson perform before this evening?"

Enthusiastic cheers erupted from the crowd.

Frederick smiled and turned to face the magician. "Benjamin, since a number of the fine people attending this special day have already seen your amazing magic show, I was wondering if you may indulge me by granting a request?"

"Anything to make my Lizzie's friends happy," Benjamin said sweetly, his blue eyes twinkling with love as he glanced at his wife.

"Make your assistant disappear," Frederick said, his smile stretching from ear to ear.

"Ah that's easy," the magician smiled brightly. "I'm just going to put these on," he held a pair of white gloves trimmed in silver out to the audience, still grinning. "Lizzie, please step forward so each one of the lovely wedding guests can see you," he instructed in the same angelic voice.

Flashing a grin, Lizzie stepped onto the center of the stage. The light helped to show off her lavender, chiffon bridesmaid dress with a matching rose covered belt.

"Ah, you look as lovely as ever," Smiling at her, Benjamin addressed the crowd. "Doesn't she make a gorgeous bridesmaid everyone?"

The wedding guests once again cheered.

"It's almost a shame to make her disappear," the magician joked, winking at his wife. "But I'm going to anyway. And all of you are going to help me," he told the audience, his voice brimming with excitement.

Several members of the crowd cheered enthusiastically.

"Everyone simply say the word 'love' as I snap my fingers," he instructed, his voice laced with even more gusto than the crowd had.

Benjamin snapped his fingers and all of the guests shouted out the word 'love'.

The crowd erupted in applause as Lizzie was replaced by a puff of smoke seconds after they did as instructed.

Standing up, Frederick smiled from ear to ear and once again drew the attention of the crowd back to himself. "Incredible… wasn't that just incredible everybody?" He turned toward Benjamin. "You have a real gift there Benjamin and I bet you could use it to benefit the kingdom."

"I'm not sure I follow your majesty," Benjamin said. Murlyn could clearly see a look of concern on Benjamin's face.

"I believe you could use your power to make Glomgurgle disappear and ensure the future of Cinder's Edge." Frederick answered, his tone encouraging and confident.

Alexandria stood up quickly, her forehead wrinkled with worry.

"Frederick, are you sure this is a good idea?" She pulled at her husband's sleeve.

"Psst... psst... Benjamin don't do this." the dark-blue haired woodland creature whispered. "Remember that using magic to manipulate fate or destiny comes with a price."

At least Alexandria gets it, Murlyn thought as he struggled to get the illusionist's attention yet again.

"Uh... I've never thought about that before. I don't know if I could," Benjamin said hesitantly after a moment.

"Nonsense," Frederick shook his head. "You showed everyone here what you can do." He again turned to address the wedding attendees. "C'mon everyone, tell the amazing Mr. Benson what good he could do for our kingdom by making that stupid dragon disappear," he urged.

Words of encouragement erupted from the crowd.

With that, and before even helping his wife to reappear, the magician agreed he'd be the one to make Glomgurgle disappear.

UH OH, Murlyn thought as he walked into the foyer of the castle surprised to find a very solemn Lizzie with no sign of Alexandria. *The queen didn't mention that any guests were coming this afternoon, let alone that her best friend would need a little help from the ambassador of happiness, but it looks that way.*

"Lizzie, it's great to see you," the dark blue-haired treasure troll flashed the petite blonde a bright smile. "What brings you to the castle this fine afternoon?"

"Alexandria and I were supposed to have lunch, but she's over an hour late so I guess something came up again.," the young woman sighed. "I was actually just getting ready to leave."

"I'm sorry to hear that our newly-crowned queen missed your lunch date. She has been quite busy lately. I'm just here to fetch her a change of clothes. Apparently, the duties of the ambassador of happiness include that of a personal assistant," he chuckled. He had grown quite fond of the queen and was happy to do little chores for her.

Lizzie nodded. "I know Alexandria can work people, and trolls, a bit hard, but underneath that tough exterior of hers is a very kind heart." The young woman forced a smile. "I really should be going."

Uh Oh...that smile made my gemstone hurt. My good ol' treasure troll intuition tells me Lizzie is upset about far more than a missed lunch. She could use a little pick me up from the ambassador of happiness or at least a friend.

"Actually, I have a better idea. You must be hungry if you haven't had lunch yet, and I didn't get a chance to eat my berries yet today, so I'm going to have Percy take the dress to the queen and you and I can have a picnic and enjoy this beautiful afternoon. How does that sound?"

The moment Lizzie smiled in response, Murlyn knew he had made the right decision. And within minutes, the two were sitting under Murlyn's dark blue sapling enjoying a picnic of fresh blue berries, peanut butter sandwiches, and Lizzie's favorite drink, sweet tea.

"This forest really is beautiful," Lizzie said after taking a bite of her sandwich.

"Yes, it is. The other trolls and I have done our best to nurture it. It's unique in that it's the only forest within five hundred miles that has a direct path to a castle or any other landmark."

"Even with the direct path, the castle sometimes feels a world away from the rest of the kingdom. I just wish Alexandria could understand that." the young woman said wistfully, staring off into the distance as she chomped away on a blueberry.

Ouch. There goes my treasure troll intuition again, Murlyn thought as his gemstone begun to throb. "Well, unfortunately that is a wish I cannot grant. But I may still be able to help you. What's on your mind?"

"I've lost my husband to Glomgurgle," she admitted, her voice quiet and fretful.

Eyebrows furrowed, Murlyn shot his lunch companion a questioning look. "Come again?"

Biting into another blueberry, Lizzie contemplated her answer. "I feel so selfish even bringing this up," she admitted sheepishly after a moment. "It's just that Alexandria becoming queen and getting married has changed a lot of things for me. I have only seen her twice over the past couple of months because she's so busy with her royal duties." Pausing, she took a bite of her peanut butter sandwich then continued. "I understand that the first year of her reign is crucial, but I wish she'd make more time for me. Especially now that my husband has become obsessed with making Glomgurgle disappear thanks to her husband. I'm lonely and miss my best friends," she said solemnly.

Looking Lizzie straight in the eye, Murlyn flashed an encouraging smile. "I'm certain Alexandria misses you too. She'll come around. Just give her time to find a little balance. And I hope you don't think I'm overstepping when I say that it sounds to me like you and Benjamin need to spend some time together, so you can turn up the romance a little bit."

Giggling, Lizzie eyed the woodland creature. "Awww...that's so sweet," she said, continuing to chuckle.

"I'm serious," Murlyn insisted. "Quality time together is an important part of any relationship. Rosie and I have been together for five years now and with my busy schedule the reason we've lasted so long is because we take the time to spend an evening together once a week."

"My mother always said that the way to a man's heart is through his stomach. I could make him his favorite dinner."

"Then I guess I'm going to have to help you prepare a romantic dinner for Benjamin," the woodland creature smiled.

"Sounds like a plan," Lizzie agreed. "But first, what's the deal with you and Rosie?" She questioned before finishing her peanut butter sandwich. "Why don't you want to marry her?"

"I, uh..." the woodland creature begun. *This is getting awkward.*

"C'mon Murlyn," Lizzie persisted after eating another blueberry. "I opened up to you. Now it's your turn."

Looking toward the pink sapling that Rosie called home, the blue-haired treasure troll contemplated his answer. *If I'm gonna tell anyone the truth I suppose I might as well tell a human.*

"It's not that I don't want to marry her," he confessed after a moment, still looking towards Rosie's fern "I would marry her tomorrow if life allowed, but I was busy before becoming the ambassador of happiness so now..." His voice trailed off as he turned to face the petite blond. "I don't want her to be a wife who sits at home waiting for her husband. Rosie is wonderful and deserves to have someone devoted to her instead of the kingdom or the black diamond," the troll explained, his voice resolute and solemn.

"I see." Lizzie took a sip of her sweet tea. "Take it from a wife who has been waiting for her husband a lot lately. It's better to have someone to wait for then to have no one at all."

Murlyn nodded. "Very profound. Are you sure you weren't a troll in another life?"

Lizzie considered her answer, smiling. "Maybe," she said after a moment.

Laughing so hard that the gemstone in the center of his belly shook, Murlyn looked straight at the young woman. "I think this is the start of a beautiful friendship Lizzie."

SMILING AT BLAINE, the dark blue treasure troll continued his story. "That was indeed the start of a beautiful friendship with your mother which, to this day, continues in its own way. And I'm happy to say that my suggestion of a date night improved things between your parents to the point that you came along about six months after Natalie. You were the cutest baby I'd ever seen," he flashed the silver-haired woman a bright grin. "I knew right away that your bright, emerald eyes were windows into the soul of someone very special," he said, his voice full of love and adoration.

"Awww...thank you Murlyn," the well-respected royal said kindly. "You're so sweet."

"You were always the charmer, Murl," Blaine flashed a mischievous grin at the treasure troll. "I can hardly remember what I ate for breakfast yesterday morning," he joked. "How do you remember my wife as a baby?"

Rolling his eyes, the troll placed his hand over Natalie's and addressed her directly. "With all due respect to your mother, I was the one who often fed you, clothed you, and otherwise cared for you." *That was one of the happiest times in my life*, he thought, chuckling softly. After a moment, the troll continued, his tone reminiscent. "Alexandria always said that my most important duty as the ambassador of happiness was to keep her little princess happy. I did my best to care for you and enjoyed every moment of it." Pausing, Murlyn took a deep breath before once again speaking to everyone around the table. "Things became infinitely more complicated when Blaine came along. It has been over 75 years, but I recall the events of that day as if it were yesterday. I can say with absolute certainty that what happened will haunt me as long as I live."

As the treasure troll once again begun describing past events, he felt like he was back in the year 566, one of many marked by turmoil during the reign of King Frederick and Queen Alexandria, reliving the whole experience again.

It's nice to be out of the castle, but I miss that sweet little baby, Murlyn thought as he knocked on the door of Benjamin and Lizzie's old, but rather welcoming cottage with Rosie in tow. The structure, made entirely of dark red brick and surrounded by fragrant honeysuckle was modest yet very beautiful. *I can't wait to watch kids play here*, he thought as a pregnant Lizzie opened the door. "Good morning,

Lizzie." The treasure troll flashed a bright smile. "How are you and baby doing?" He queried sweetly, walking into the house.

"Forgive the intrusion," Rosie said kindly as she walked in behind Murlyn.

"Don't be silly. You two are always welcome here," Lizzie assured her friends, closing the door behind them. "Baby is doing well," the young woman's soulful blue eyes lit up as she spoke of her future child, patting her tummy affectionately. "He or she has been kicking all morning." She sat at a small, circular wooden table in the dining room and motioned for the trolls to join her. "I, on the other hand, have seen better days," she said solemnly.

Murlyn nodded. "Alexandria thought as much after she spoke with you last night. She asked that we come this morning and cheer you up. After all, I am the ambassador of happiness," he said joyfully. "So, what wish is in your heart today, Miss Lizzie?" Murlyn watched the many emotions that flitted across Lizzie's face as she contemplated her answer.

"Well, I keep trying to get Benjamin to go on a picnic or do something else with me since it's such a beautiful day, but he walked to Mount Wishnik instead to think through his newest strategy." Glancing down at her growing belly, the mom-to-be sighed, her voice solemn. "I'm worried," she admitted quietly. "Benjamin really wants to eliminate that horrible creature before the baby comes. Over the past couple of months, he's become even more obsessed with the task. I'm afraid if he doesn't conquer Glomgurgle soon this baby will grow up without a father and, to be honest," Lizzie's eyes welled up with tears. "I'm worried about my own fate too. I have this strange feeling I won't be able to raise my baby the way I want to."

"Oh, Miss Lizzie, please don't cry," Rosie said, her tone sweet and quiet as she placed a hand on her friend's shoulder and squeezed gently. "Everything will be all right," she assured.

"Rosie is right," Murlyn agreed. "As soon as Benjamin lays eyes on the baby, I'm sure he will be able to think of nothing else."

Lizzie smiled weakly. "I hope so, but just in case I'm right, I wrote the baby a letter," she carefully retrieved a piece of parchment from the pocket of her dress. "If ever I'm not around and the baby needs my guidance, will you give this to him or her please?"

"Of course," the blue-haired woodland creature said, his voice calm even though the thought of anything happening to Lizzie was sending him into his own kind of turmoil. "But don't worry too much. It's not good for you or the baby," he advised.

"What should I do? How do I keep myself from worrying too much?"

"Well, as you know, even though I'd love to make this problem disappear I cannot. But I do have an idea," he said excitedly and nearly kicked himself for not thinking of it sooner.

"What's that?" The girls asked simultaneously.

"Just follow me," Murlyn said encouragingly.

The blue-haired treasure troll breathed a sigh of relief as he, Rosie, and Lizzie found Benjamin halfway between the cottage and Mount Wishnik. He hadn't liked the idea of having to go all the way to Glomgurgle's lair to find the man.

"Sweetheart, what're you doing out here?" Benjamin questioned as he spotted his wife.

"I'm tired of being cooped up in the house," Lizzie admitted. "It's such a beautiful day and, besides, Murlyn said he has something in mind to cheer me up," she explained, her voice laced with anticipation.

Benjamin kissed his wife. "Is that so?" Grinning, he looked down at the woodland creatures. "Hey there, Rosie," he flashed her a sweet smile then focused on Murlyn. "What do ya have in mind my friend?"

"Well, as you know, Frederick needs an update on your quest to rid the kingdom of—" the troll lowered his voice to a whisper, so as not to frighten any passersby. "Glomgurgle," his usually smiling mouth twisted in disgust. "He and Alexandria are going horseback riding through the kingdom this afternoon and I thought maybe you could give him an update while the two of you joined them."

"Oh, I love that idea," Lizzie exclaimed. "I haven't been riding in a month. And I've been meaning to tell Alexandria that I had another dream about the babies getting married. She's going to be so excited," she said cheerfully. "We're both hoping my dreams are a sign that the kids will fall in love someday."

"You're seven-and-a-half months pregnant sweetheart. I don't really think horseback ridin' is a good idea," Benjamin cautioned. "Can't you just tell Alexandria about your dream the next time you two have lunch?"

"Nonsense," Lizzie shook her head. "I've been riding since I was a kid. I'll be fine."

"Yeah, she'll be okay." Murlyn agreed. "Rosie and I will tag along to watch over her. In fact, how about I give you a little reassurance?" The treasure troll questioned rhetorically. Before any of the humans could object, he rubbed his gemstone until it was glowing bright blue. "Lizzie, quickly put your hand on my gemstone," he whispered.

"Oh, I see what you are doing," the expectant mother said, her voice laced with excitement as she placed a hand on the center of Murlyn's belly.

Grasping her fellow troll's hand, Rosie grinned. "Go ahead," she urged.

"Our friend is about to go on a horseback ride.

> *Tiny troll legs can't compete.*
> *Allow this magic to give Rosie and I the strength to equal*
> *   their stride*
> *so if a problem arises we may help them in a heartbeat."*

Within moments, a glittering blue light surrounded the trolls and Lizzie, leaving them with nothing, but smiles as it disappeared. "That was awesome, Murlyn. I feel at peace now. Better than I have been in days," Lizzie said excitedly.

"See? She's going to be fine," the dark blue-haired troll insisted.

Sighing, Benjamin lamented. "Guess I'm out-voted then."

The treasure trolls and the happy couple proceeded to walk to the castle and explain that they would be joining the royals for a horseback ride through the kingdom that afternoon.

"Are you sure that's a good idea?" Frederick queried. "Couldn't riding a horse be dangerous for someone in your..." the ruler of the realm paused while searching for the right word before finally finishing, "condition."

Lizzie's husband smirked. "Frederick, trust me, king or not, you don't want to go there. Ya won't win."

Alexandria looked from her husband to Benjamin and back. "I managed to dance the waltz at The Ball of Wishes one week before giving birth to Natalie. Lizzie and I are both strong women," she reminded them. "We've been riding horses since we were kids. I'm quite sure she'll be just fine."

Smirking, Benjamin looked to Frederick. "See what I mean."

I sure hope Alexandria and I are right. Lizzie looks really uncomfortable on that horse, Murlyn walked alongside the pregnant horseback riding enthusiast so he could keep a close eye on his friend. As concerned as the troll was for his dear friend, a conversation between her husband and the leader of the kingdom soon stole his attention.

"How's the quest to eliminate you know who going?" Frederick whispered as he waved hello to citizens that had gathered in the streets to catch a close-up glance of the royals.

"Slow but good," Benjamin admitted quietly, tightening his grip on the reins of his horse. "I think I've made some progress wi—"

Benjamin was stopped by a loud scream coming from behind them. "AAAAAHHHHH!"

The next few moments lasted an eternity yet passed in a blur for Murlyn as he watched Lizzie fall off of her spooked horse after a horse-drawn stagecoach sped past. He watched as she fell to the ground in seconds, powerless to do anything. *Oh, god ... no ... please let her be okay.*

"Oh, my god Lizzie!" Benjamin quickly dismounted his horse and rushed to her side. "Murlyn she's unconscious... do something!" He shouted, his voice frantic and thick with emotion.

"Yes, do something!" Alexandria echoed.

The troll's dark blue eyes filled with tears. "I can't," he said solemnly. "Remember…trolls can't impact fate or destiny without dire consequences." Tears rolled down Murlyn's cheeks as he felt helpless for the first time in his life.

"But what about the spell you did? Alexandria insisted, tears rolling down her cheek. "You're supposed to protect us."

"I wish that what Murlyn said wasn't true, but he's right. We can't protect you from this," Rosie reiterated, tears also streaming down her face.

"A doctor … we need a doctor!" Frederick shouted, taking control of the situation.

Murlyn could once again do nothing but watch as a petite woman with long brown hair and hazel eyes made her way through the crowd, kneeled next to Lizzie, and quickly examined her.

"I am an obstetrician." The woman explained. "We need to get that baby out as soon as possible if there is any hope," she said with quiet authority.

Benjamin shook his head. "No, no, it's too early," he cried. "Are you absolutely sure?"

"Isn't there anything else that can be done?" Alexandria queried, her voice thick with worry.

"What are your credentials, miss?" The king questioned, echoing his wife's concern.

Finally, something I can help with, Murlyn wiped away his tears and addressed his human friends. "I know this is scary, but we are wasting precious minutes. The best thing we can do is trust the doctor and get Lizzie and the baby to the infirmary as soon as possible."

Time once again became hazy for the treasure troll as a stagecoach arrived and rushed Lizzie and Benjamin to the infirmary. He, Rosie, Frederick, and the queen arrived minutes behind them, having traveled as quickly as they could on horseback, only to find Benjamin pacing nervously, alone, outside of the infirmary.

"I-I'm so glad you guys are here," Fighting back tears, he pulled Alexandria into a hug and squeezed tightly. "They wouldn't let me go in with her, but the doctor promises to be out as soon as she can."

What's going on in there? Is the doctor ever going to come out? Murlyn wondered as he waited with the others to hear the fate of Lizzie and the baby. *I hate feeling so powerless,* he thought. *I've never wanted to be able to influence destiny so badly. Has time actually stopped?* The blue-diamond-adorned treasure troll wondered to himself a while later as they continued waiting. He opened his mouth to question how long it had been, but closed it the moment the doctor walked outside. *Oh, no,* Murlyn's chest tightened as he noted her sorrowful hazel eyes and solemn expression. The exaggerated sigh and apology that followed were all it took for Murlyn to realize that Lizzie had passed away. As the words sunk in it felt as if someone had punched him in the stomach. But as quickly as he felt sorrow, he suddenly felt joy and an incredible lightness wash over him as he heard Lizzie's voice.

Murlyn, I need you to do something for me, she called out, her tone quiet and angelic. Murlyn watched as his soul floated out of his body and followed her voice. They met, one soul to another, and he was reunited with his dear friend within mere moments.

"Wow!" the woodland creature breathed as he spotted Lizzie wearing a beautiful, flowy, white dress. In typical Lizzie fashion, not one blonde hair was out of place and her blue eyes sparkled with love, but the white, luminescent glow surrounding her added a gorgeous quality she'd never had before. The troll struggled to focus on her words rather than her incandescent quality as she spoke. It was nearly impossible to tear his eyes away from the beautiful light surrounding her.

I can only speak with you for a moment. Please tell Benjamin, Rosie, and Alexandria that I'm sorry I had to go and I love them, but most importantly protect my baby boy... my Blaine whose soul I got to hold before he came into the world. Tell him to live life to the fullest and that, no matter what his magician of a father might say, love is the most powerful form of magic there is.

Shaking his head, Murlyn pleaded with her. "Please come back Miss Lizzie. We all need you. A boy needs his mother. Please, please, come back."

I must go, but don't be sad. Blaine will still have me... you all will, she assured him. *For I am now and always will be a guardian angel.*

Speechless, the treasure troll watched as Lizzie's beautiful soul turned and walked into a bright white light.

"Murlyn... Murlyn... are you okay?" Rosie questioned.

As Lizzie disappeared into the light, the treasure troll's soul heard different voices calling his name and followed them. Moments later the woodland creature's eyes opened as his soul reentered his body. Alexandria and Rosie looked down at him, their tear-stained faces wrinkled with concern.

"Murlyn, are you all right?" Rosie asked again. "You passed out," she explained, her voice thick with a mixture of sadness and apprehension. Bending down to his level, the queen held out her hand.

Accepting her assistance, the troll stood up slowly. "Yes, I am okay," he assured them. "How's Blaine?"

Worry wrinkles in the young woman's forehead deepened. "How's who?"

"How do you know the baby's name?" A distraught Benjamin questioned, wiping moisture from his tear stained face. "Lizzie and I decided to name him after my great grandfather if he were a boy, but we hadn't mentioned it to anyone."

Taking a deep breath, the treasure troll told them about his out-of-body experience and how Lizzie had revealed the baby's name. Knowing that she was at peace seemed to give Alexandria, Benjamin, and Rosie some solace, but Frederick was a bit more skeptical. "Just how hard did you hit your head?" He eyed Murlyn cynically.

Shaking his head, Murlyn dismissed Frederick. "Blaine is what matters. How is he?"

"He only weighs three pounds," Benjamin explained, his voice was that of a man who felt utterly defeated. "The little guy's lungs aren't fully developed so he has to stay in the infirmary for a few weeks." Fresh tears were running down his cheeks. "The doc says that there's only a twenty percent chance the little man will make it." Benjamin hung his head and sobbed.

"I don't believe that," the treasure troll said defiantly after a moment. "He's going to be fine. His mother will make sure of it, you'll see," he insisted.

Four pairs of sad, uncertain eyes fell upon him. At a loss for what to do, the treasure troll walked into the infirmary to tell the tiny baby about his sweet, beautiful, guardian angel of a mother.

CHAPTER 4

"Papaw, you never told me that you only had a twenty percent chance of survival at birth," Isabel exclaimed, wiping tears from her cheeks.

"Don't cry, sweet girl," Blaine said thoughtfully. "Everything turned out great for me."

Sniffling, the loving granddaughter looked to Murlyn. "Did everything really turn out well? What happened next?"

"The weeks following the death of your great grandmother were some of the saddest weeks of my life. We were all heartbroken, but no one more so than your great grandfather," he said solemnly. "The only thing he would do in the weeks after Lizzie's death was visit his son at the infirmary." Sighing, Murlyn looked to Blaine. "Your father became more like his old self when he brought you home, but that didn't last long."

As Murlyn continued to talk about the past, he once again felt like he'd traveled through time and was back in Benjamin's cottage watching little Blaine and Natalie.

"Hey, Murl, thanks for watching the little guy today. How'd it go?" Benjamin asked, grinning at his little boy, who was happily chewing on a rattle as he lay on a cot next to Natalie.

"He's as smiley as ever, but to be honest, I'm concerned," Murlyn admitted solemnly. "The little guy is eight months old today and he's still not crawling or sitting up."

Sighing, Benjamin eyed the troll. "Murlyn, we've been through this before. Blaine was born early. It is going to take him some time to catch up. But he's a Benson. He'll be fine," he declared.

The treasure troll shook his head. "But Natalie sat up at four months old and crawled by the time she was Blaine's age. I'm worried that—"

"Is Natalie the benchmark that all babies are compared to?" Benjamin questioned through gritted teeth.

"Well no. But—"

"Exactly. Stop comparing them. Better yet, stop worryin'. Blaine may need a little time to catch up, but he's gonna be fine." Letting out a huff, the caring dad picked up Natalie and handed her to Murlyn. "Go on back to the castle."

Holding the tiny princess against his chest, the woodland creature shielded her somewhat. "No," the troll's usually calm, quiet voice was just as insolent as Benjamin's had been moments before. "I told Lizzie that I'd protect that boy," pausing briefly, he smiled at Blaine than looked back to Benjamin. "So that's what I am doing. I don't see any harm in at least talking to a doctor about my concerns."

"But he's—"

"No Benjamin," Murlyn said. "You must understand that getting your boy looked at by a doctor doesn't mean he's not going to be fine or that you're giving up on him. It merely means you're protecting him like his mother would want you to," the troll insisted.

"I'll never give up on my boy," Benjamin glanced lovingly at his son. "I suppose we can get him looked at," he lamented. "You're right. It's what my Lizzie would've wanted."

"I'm really glad to hear that because Dr. Steinman is waiting right outside. He's the finest pediatrician in the kingdom," Murlyn explained.

"He's here now?" Benjamin shifted his weight from one side to the other, his voice suddenly coated in anxiety.

"Yes." Laying Natalie back down on the cot, the treasure troll ran outside to get the doctor.

Oh, no, this is not going to go well, the woodland creature thought as he watched Dr. Steinman, a skinny man with thinning gray hair, dark brown eyes, and wiry glasses, and Benjamin size each other up.

Looking over his glasses, the doctor studied Blaine. "Is this the child with developmental delays?" He queried after a moment, his voice serious and strangely nasally.

"Yes," the troll explained. "This is the child that we want you to take a look at."

"He's not just any child," Benjamin said angrily. "He's my son, Blaine."

Dr. Steinman looked to Murlyn. "This one is a bit of a papa bear, huh?" He asked pointedly.

Rolling his eyes, Benjamin became angrier. "Just do what you need to do and examine my boy,"

An awkward silence fell over the cottage as the doctor examined Blaine and took notes simultaneously.

Why is he taking the little guy's toy? Murlyn wondered as he watched the doctor take Blaine's rattle and encourage him to reach for it.

Grunting, the tiny boy gave his best effort but couldn't reach the toy.

"Just as I thought," Dr. Steinman mumbled.

"What's going on?" Benjamin queried, his tone quiet and fretful. "What're you thinkin'?"

Ignoring the loving father's questions, the doctor arranged pillows on either side of Blaine and sat him up on the edge of the cot.

"Posture and muscle tone are consistent," the physician whispered.

This really isn't looking good, Murlyn thought. *Please give us the strength to get through this Lizzie.*

"What was the nature of Blaine's birth?" Dr. Steinman questioned, once again ignoring Benjamin's query.

"His mother fell off a horse at seven-and-a-half months pregnant. The impact caused both of them to be in distress, so a doctor had to deliver early. Only he made it," the loving father said solemnly.

The pediatrician nodded. "Well, there is no way to sugarcoat this," he begun, his voice tentative.

"Just come out with it doc," Benjamin urged.

"Yeah," Murlyn echoed. "Just tell us what's going on with the little guy and how we can fix it."

"You're going to need to get a second opinion to confirm diagnosis, but from what I can tell, Blaine's poor posture, muscle tone, insufficient motor skills, as well as his medical history are consistent with a disability called Cerebral Palsy," he explained, his voice quiet and nonchalant.

Oh, no... I never should've suggested that Blaine get checked out. What was I thinking? Murlyn struggled to listen to the physician and not become lost in thought.

"What exactly does that mean doctor?" Benjamin wiped beads of sweat from his forehead and looked Dr. Steinman straight in the eye.

"Well, in his case, it means that he will likely spend his life in a wheelchair. It's probable that your son will have some intellectual deficits and never be able to walk or talk," the physician explained, his tone still casual.

"Whoa, whoa, whoa," Benjamin shouted, his face suddenly bright crimson with rage. "Ya looked at my son for ten minutes. Where do you get off sayin' all this?"

Uh Oh, Murlyn thought as both Natalie and Blaine begun bawling. *He's scaring the babies.* As the troll searched for their pacifiers, in hopes of soothing them without magic, the soft crackling and gasping sounds that can only belong to a crying baby filled the cottage.

"Mr… uh…" Dr. Steinman begun.

Benjamin glanced at the troll. "Hush those babies, Murlyn!" He shouted before turning his attention back to the pediatrician.

"Benson, the name is Benson." A vein bulged out of Benjamin's forehead as it turned a deeper red. "Now explain yourself," he insisted through clench teeth.

Easier said than done, Murlyn thought as both babies spit their pacifiers out at him. Still listening to the doctor, he attempted to calm the children a second time with a bottle and sippy cup.

"Mr. Benson, I'm only trying to explain the reality of the challenges Blaine is bound to face in life. You have some options. You can send him to a home for special needs children in our neighboring kingdom of Stalagmiteville or, if you choose to keep him here with you, therapeutic and surgical intervention should give him a decent quality of life."

"How dare you suggest I not keep my boy? Do you think I'm some kind—"

"Mr. Benson, I'm only saying—" the physician begun, his voice shaking slightly.

Still furious, the caring father leaned forward so he was nose-to-nose with the doctor. "Get out of my cottage and never step foot near me or my boy again!" He shouted, the vein in his forehead bulging so much it looked as though it may pop out at any moment.

In mere seconds, the doctor stumbled nervously out of the cottage.

Slamming the door behind him, the protective father looked at Murlyn who was still attempting to mollify the crying babies by checking their diapers. "You are gonna fix this," he said matter-of-factly.

The treasure troll hung his head. "Benjamin, you know I would if I could," Murlyn said solemnly. He laid Natalie and Blaine, who were finally content, back on the cot. "But I can't. It's a part of your little guy's destiny."

"Oh, don't give me that crap," Benjamin said angrily. "This is all of your fault anyway. You're the one who talked his mother into going on that horseback ride."

I knew he was going to do this. Humans always need someone to blame. Glancing toward the babies, the troll avoided eye contact with his friend. "The little ones are finally tuckered out," he said after a long moment. "Why don't we talk outside?"

Benjamin shrugged his shoulders. "I ain't got nothin' else to say. This is all of your fault so you're gonna fix it," he reiterated.

Without another word, Murlyn opened the door of the cottage and walked outside. Moments later, Benjamin followed. As the two stood across from each other, a tense, awkward, silence that not even the sweet, calming smell of honeysuckle could help dissipate settled between them.

"Ya said you wanted to talk outside," Benjamin said after about five minutes. "What do ya have to say?" The frustrated father's voice was calmer than it'd been in the cottage but still had an edge to it.

Murlyn's heart began beating so fast he could hear it in his ears. *You can do this. Just breathe.* "Okay, but please don't respond until I am finished," he said firmly.

"I'll respond whenever I want."

Taking a deep breath, Murlyn looked his friend in the eye and begun. "I realize that Blaine's diagnosis is difficult to process and that right now you're grieving the life you wish he would've had. Regardless of that, you have no right to ask me to change his destiny." The troll cleared his throat and continued, his tone a bit more serious. "We trolls succumb to dark magic if we use light magic to manipulate destiny or fate. I cannot use magic to cure Blaine of his disability for that reason, but I can make you a promise." Pausing, Murlyn furrowed his bushy, dark blue eyebrows, considering the right words. "I told Lizzie that I would protect Blaine and I stay true to my word. I promise you that I'll use magic whenever necessary to protect Blaine and to ensure that he has as happy of a life as possible while having a disability." *Why isn't he saying anything?* Murlyn wondered as a silence settled between them.

After another five minutes, no longer able to stand the quiet, the treasure troll spoke "I suppose I should be getting Natalie back to the castle soon," he said quietly before turning to go back into the cottage.

"Wait," Benjamin called out.

"Yes?" The woodland creature questioned, turning his attention back to his friend.

"Just because you can't use magic to fix my boy's disability doesn't mean I can't, right? I got to thinkin' that maybe if I transfer some treasure troll magic into a pair of pants, like we did for the white gloves I wear in my magic shows, then my boy could wear 'em and walk."

Oh, my gosh. How many times do I have to tell this man that magic cannot be used to manipulate destiny or fate? The treasure troll wondered. *I doubt he's ever going to understand.*

Sighing, Murlyn tried to reason with his friend yet again, "Benjamin, I know this is hard for you, but you must understand that magic should not under any circumstances be used to impact fate or destiny."

Benjamin nodded. "I know, I know, but—"

Holding up a hand, the treasure troll interrupted, his voice quiet and very serious. "Magic always comes with a price. When it is used in a selfish manner that price can be particularly dire. For me, it would be succumbing to dark magic. In your case, well... lord knows what it may be, but you have a little boy to think about. Do you understand what I am trying to say?"

"I *am* thinkin' about my boy, Murl," Benjamin insisted, his eyes suddenly sparkling with excitement. "Ah yes, by the time I'm done my boy won't just be walkin'... he'll be runnin'. I'm goin' to go get started right now," he said enthusiastically. "Watch the little guy a bit longer for me, will ya? Take 'em to the castle. I'll be by later."

"But, Benjamin, I don't think—" Murlyn begun.

"See ya later, Murl," Benjamin yelled as he sprinted down the path toward the castle.

Can't say I didn't try, the treasure troll thought as he went back into the cottage to check on the babies.

"OH, MY GOSH, PAPAW," Isabel exclaimed, interrupting Murlyn's story and bringing him back to the present. "I'm so sorry. Why didn't you tell us your father didn't accept your disability?" The adoring granddaughter asked, her voice a mixture of anger and sadness.

Reaching out, Blaine took his granddaughter's hand and squeezed gently. "Sweetie, your great grandfather's legacy, our family's legacy, is not what you think. Keep listening. Trust me, it'll be worth it," he assured her.

Blaine is so good with that girl. His father would be so proud to see him now, the treasure troll thought as he watched the two interact.

"I agree," Rosie tilted her head towards Murlyn. "This old troll is a long-winded story teller," the glittery-haired woodland creature chuckled. "But he always makes it worth it to listen through to the end."

Nodding, Natalie took her husband's free hand. "Rosie is right," she said as she looked at her granddaughter. "They both are. Your great grandpa was a very eccentric, extremely sweet man who loved your great grandmother more than life. From the moment I met him, I was certain of that and, after hearing Murlyn speak today, I'm even more confident of that." Looking to the blue-haired treasure troll, she smiled brightly. "Sorry to interrupt your story, old friend. Please continue."

"I couldn't agree more," he smiled at Blaine and Natalie. "You know you two have something just as special as what Benjamin and Lizzie had. In fact, you two have had something since you were kids. I can still remember when I first came to that realization. You were both about two and Blaine wasn't even speaking yet, but the two of you already had a special connection. While it took Benjamin, the other trolls, and myself a while to make sense of the grunts Blaine used in place of words, you had no problem. It was almost as if the two of you had your own language."

"That's funny," Blaine chuckled. "Sometimes I could swear we speak different languages," he joked.

Rolling her eyes, Natalie looked to her granddaughter and chuckled. "Luckily for your Papaw, we connect on more than just a verbal level."

"That's true. Your Nana is the very reason your Papaw started using a wheelchair," Murlyn explained.

"What do you mean?" Isabel questioned, eyebrows scrunched in confusion.

"Well, when they were two years old, I decided to take advantage of how rambunctious they were in order to keep my promise to Benjamin that Blaine would live a full life with his disability."

As he continued to tell the story, Murlyn remembered the day he created Blaine's wheelchair and drifted into the memory...

CHAPTER 5

Okay, Lizzie, I think this chair is perfect for your Blaine, he thought, as he stood in front of the Tree of Friendship examining the manual wheelchair, complete with extra-large tires that would allow Blaine to better navigate the paths of the forest. Murlyn had used his magic from his gemstone to conjure it up. *The question is how do I introduce it to him without impacting his destiny?*

Moments later, as if on cue, the troll heard a piece of wisdom from his dear old friend Lizzie. *If it is his choice to use the wheelchair then you will not impact my boy's destiny.*

"Oh, my gosh," he whispered looking up to the sky. "That's brilliant."

Smiling, Murlyn pushed the chair to Benjamin's cottage where, sure enough, the kids were already playing outside. *Well, isn't that a pretty picture,* the troll thought, having spotted Natalie chasing Rosie through the honeysuckle field surrounding the cottage. "Hey there, little one, what are ya doing?" He asked happily.

"Playing tag," Natalie giggled.

"That looks like fun," he said as he parked the wheelchair near a blue blanket which Blaine was laying on. Looking from the little boy to Natalie and back, the troll's smile widened. "Don't you think that looks like fun Blaine?" he queried, his voice full of hope and encouragement.

Turning his head toward Murlyn, the little boy spotted the wheelchair.

Before the troll could say anything in response, Benjamin stepped outside. "What the heck is that?" His voice full of urgency.

After taking Benjamin into the cottage, the treasure troll explained why he'd made the wheelchair and that it had to be the child's decision to use it.

"I don't like this," Benjamin said angrily. "Why would you do this when you know that I am making the pants?"

"C'mon Benjamin, you and I both know that your boy can't spend his time scooting around or laying on blankets for much longer. That's no life for a child. Besides, I know that I'm always saying this, but the wheelchair is what Lizzie would've wanted for Blaine… for sure."

Shaking his head, Benjamin raised his voice slightly. "I don't believe that. I don't believe my Lizzie would want our boy to have something that shows the world he can't walk."

"No, no, no. A wheelchair will do nothing of the sort. It will just give him more independence while you work on the pants. And I know it's what Miss Lizzie would've wanted because she told me herself.

Hanging his head, Benjamin sighed. "Not this again," he mumbled, his voice full of disdain.

"Yes," the treasure troll insisted before explaining that he was still very connected to Lizzie and occasionally heard from her spirit, as he had the day she died. "She is the one who told me that it has to be Blaine's choice to use the wheelchair since I can't use magic to convince him to do so."

Benjamin nodded. "That sounds like my Lizzie. Throughout her pregnancy, she was always talking about wanting the baby to have choices because her parents didn't give her much freedom growing up."

Murlyn nodded. "Ya know, a little encouragement from you

when it comes to the wheelchair might go a long way. It wouldn't mean that you were making the decision for him and it wouldn't involve magic, so—"

"Okay, okay, I'll do it," Benjamin's voice was full of annoyance. Even though he was agreeing to this, Murlyn knew Benjamin wasn't exactly thrilled with the idea. "On three conditions. First, you stop talking. Second, you widened the paths in the Forest of Wishes. I know that you sometimes bring the children there to play and those things are far too thin for a wheelchair. My boy's safety is the first priority. Finally, you must understand that I'm not gonna stop makin' the pants. That son of mine is going to walk someday, even if making him do so is the last thing I do," Benjamin said, his voice full of determination.

"As you wish my, friend." *I know this has to be Blaine's choice, but please be with us right now, Miss Lizzie. We could use your guidance,* Murlyn thought before heading outside.

THIS JUST MIGHT WORK, the dark blue-haired troll thought, feeling incredibly calm as the sweet smell of honeysuckle wafted into his nostrils.

"What's that?" Natalie questioned, pointing at the shimmery black contraption.

"It's a wheelchair sweetie. Murl made it to help B get around," Benjamin said cheerfully.

"Really?" the tiny princess asked, her voice full of excitement.

"Yep. What do ya think my boy? Ready to give this thing a try?"

The tiny boy smiled as his father lifted him off the blanket he'd been laying on.

"I'll take that grin as a yes." The caring dad chuckled, before gently sitting Blaine down in the wheelchair.

The moment Blaine's butt hit the wheelchair the tiny boy begun to throw a fit, his face bright red, as tears escaped his eyes and he thrashed his legs about.

"Guess that grin wasn't a yes," Benjamin said before quickly laying his son back on the blanket.

Letting out a huff, Benjamin eyed, Murlyn who'd been watching intently. "What do you suggest we do now?"

Lizzie, it's time for that guidance I asked for. I know this has to be your son's choice, but as his mother, will you tell us how to encourage the choice that is best for him?

Calm once again washed over him as he heard Lizzie's answer moments later. *My boy is scared and cannot yet communicate his fear properly. Perhaps he needs to see someone else try the wheelchair before he does.*

Eyebrows furrowed, Murlyn considered the words of his old friend. *Perhaps someone else...* "Natalie!" As Benjamin and the tiny girl shot him questioning looks, the troll's eyes lit up with recognition. "Have Natalie try the chair. She can help encourage him," he said excitedly.

Benjamin looked to the little girl. "What do ya think, sweetheart? Ya wanna give this shiny thing a whirl?"

"Miss Rosie and I like anything glittery," she said as she smiled at the pink, glittery haired troll, her tiny, high-pitched voice full of sweetness as she sat in the chair.

"You look good sweetie. Now use your arms to push the wheels," Benjamin said encouragingly.

Natalie giggled before pushing the chair toward Rosie. "Tag, you're it."

Soon a chorus of giggles erupted as Rosie and the princess played a game of tag. "B, this is fun," Natalie said after a few minutes.

"It is fun, isn't it?" Benjamin questioned. "Do you think B should try it?

Natalie nodded and looked to her friend. "Try it... play with me."

Benjamin smiled at his son. "What do you think, my boy? Ready to try again?"

Grinning from ear to ear, Blaine studied Natalie.

"Hop down, little lady," Benjamin said after a moment. "It's Blaine's turn."

"Play with us, B… it's fun," the princess said before doing as instructed.

"Here goes nothin', my boy," Benjamin whispered in his son's ear before, once again, placing his son in the wheelchair.

"You're it, B… come and get me," Natalie said, her voice cheerful as she hit him on the shoulder.

With that, the little boy begun chasing the princess around the beautiful field of honeysuckle surrounding the cottage.

Well, isn't that something? Murlyn thought as he watched the kids play. *The little guy looks like he was always meant to be in that chair. I guess mothers really do know best.*

"Murl, keep an eye on the kids for me. I'm gonna keep workin' on the pants. I don't want my boy stuck in that thing for his whole life," Benjamin said before running off into the distance.

"This is really something, isn't it?" A sleepy sounding Rosie asked sweetly, smiling as she approached Murlyn.

"Yeah, it is," he agreed.

Now, if only we could get Benjamin to understand and accept Blaine's destiny, the troll thought wistfully.

He will in time my friend. He will in time, Lizzie assured him as he continued to watch the kids chase one another through the honeysuckle field with a tired, yet content, Rosie by his side, happy to have found peace for the moment.

"OH, my gosh! That's so sweet," Isabel gushed. She looked from her grandfather to her grandmother and back. "How come you guys never told me that story?"

Natalie giggled. "Sweetheart, we were really young. We don't remember some things as well as Murlyn.

"Yeah," Blaine agreed. "I don't really remember much at all before I learned to speak."

Isabel shot her grandfather a questioning look. "Hmm?"

"I still remember the exact day you started speaking or, rather, reading because it was one of the happiest of my life," Murlyn explained.

"Oh? Do tell," Isabel urged.

Smiling, he looked to the newly crowned royal. "Your nana wouldn't shut-up for anything," he joked. "Whereas your papaw typically used a mixture of grunting and pointing to communicate, although he was very observant, always listening and taking everything in." Murlyn explained, his tone lighthearted.

As the treasure troll recounted one of his favorite memories he soon found himself back in the throne room of the castle with Blaine in tow.

Wow... this floor is as shiny as ever, the treasure troll thought as he saw his reflection in the tiles.

"B!" A happy three-year-old Natalie with bright emerald colored eyes, auburn pigtails, and freckles covering her cheeks exclaimed, running to hug her friend as Alexandria led her into the room moments later.

Smiling from ear to ear, the little boy, a contented three-year-old with a captivating smile, a mop of wavy blond hair, and deep, soulful blue-gray eyes, who spent most of his days now in his new wheelchair, hugged the princess back.

"Murl, it's so great to see you," the queen said as she spotted the treasure troll.

"It's great to see you too," he echoed. "Are you staying for the reading lesson today?"

The beautiful royal shook her head. "Wish I could, but the family has a public appearance in an hour and I have to go get ready. I'm sorry, I'm just so busy. I must go," she said, her tone solemn, before rushing out of the room.

That's been her go-to response since Lizzie died, Murlyn thought sadly.

"Hi Natalie, are you ready to read today?" The troll questioned, his voice sweet and quiet, as the kids continued to embrace.

Finally, freeing Blaine from her grasp, the tiny royal smiled at the woodland creature.

"Can B and I sit in my mommy and daddy's special chairs?" The little girl queried sweetly, pointing towards the thrones. The troll glanced at the tall, jewel crested chairs that had been carved from the finest oak in the kingdom.

If only she knew how much time she'll be expected to spend in those special chairs when she's older..., the troll thought as he quickly spit-shined the black diamond that was inlaid in a prominent spot on a pedestal between the thrones.

He flashed the little girl a smile. "Of course, little one, you two are special people after all."

He walked with them to the chairs while Blaine pushed himself in his wheelchair.

"Okay, Miss Natalie, remember to sound words out as we go along," he encouraged after propping both kids up on the thrones with pillows.

Smiling, he held an index card with a picture of a feline out in front of the kids. "What does this card say?"

The young girl was silent for a moment as she looked at the card, her nose slightly scrunched.

"Sound it out," the troll urged, his voice coated with encouragement. "One letter at a time."

"C-ca," the princess begun hesitantly.

Murlyn smiled brightly. "Good job Natalie," he encouraged. "Keep going."

Studying the second letter, nose still scrunched, Natalie looked to Murlyn. "Aah like apple, right?" She questioned, her high-pitched voice coated in the sweetness only a toddler can possess.

Giggling, the treasure troll nodded. "Yes, sweetheart. That's exactly right. Now sound out the last letter."

The tiny majestic did as instructed.

"Great," the woodland creature praised, his voice full of pride. "Now put all three sounds together, little one."

"Ca-aah-" Natalie begun.

"Ca-aah-t… ca-aah-t… ca… aah-t," Blaine said suddenly, putting the sounds together faster each time until he finally said 'cat'.

"Yes sweetie. That's—" Pausing, Murlyn looked to the little boy, wide-eyed. "Did you just…" The treasure troll shook his head. "No, that can't be."

Either I'm hearing things or he really just read the card. Oh, Lizzie, please tell me this is happening.

"B stole my word," The princess cried, confirming the troll's suspicion.

"Yes, he did little one," the treasure troll agreed, looking from Natalie to Blaine and back. "How about we play a little game? Let's see who can sound out the next word the quickest, okay?"

The princess nodded while Blaine stayed motionless.

Please don't tell me it was a fluke… please, Murlyn thought as he held up a flashcard that featured a crying little girl.

"What does this card say kiddos?" the treasure troll questioned eagerly. "Sound it out."

"Sss-aah," Natalie begun excitedly.

"ss-aah-ddd… sad," Blaine said quickly.

"That's exactly right little man," Murlyn praised, smiling from pointy ear to pointy ear. This was really happening and Murlyn couldn't contain the excitement that was bubbling up inside him.

"Murlyn, B stole my word again!" The young royal whined, sticking out her lip as she folded her arms across her chest.

Just as Murlyn opened his mouth to comfort the tiny royal, Blaine put his tiny arm around her shoulder and squeezed. "It's okay," he soothed, his tiny, high-pitched voice full of reassurance, "you read next."

"You read two words," the tiny royal whined. "I wanna read two."

※

Missy giggled as Murlyn imitated three-year-old Natalie's whiny voice, bringing him back to the present. "You're so funny, Daddy."

"Natalie is the funny one, not me," Murlyn smiled affectionately at the queen before continuing, looking to Isabel. "I was amazed as I witnessed your grandparents having their first real conversation. The more your nana groaned at the fact that she couldn't sound out the words, the more your papaw comforted her. That was the moment I knew they had something special, even though they didn't know it yet."

"That's one of the cutest stories that I've ever heard," Rosie said. "It must've been amazing to watch."

"It certainly was. It was as if something clicked that day, and from then on not only could Blaine speak, he couldn't get enough of reading books."

"That's for sure," Isabel said. "To this day, he has a book with him everywhere he goes."

"There is nothing wrong with being an avid reader, sweet girl," the elderly man said kindly. "Books can transport people into an entirely different world."

"It's interesting that you say that," Murlyn said. "For you, I believe, books have always provided..." the troll paused for a moment, searching for the right word, "...an escape," he said after a moment.

As Blaine nodded in agreement, Missy and Isabel exchanged a confused look.

"What do you mean?" The newly-crowned queen asked.

"As the years continued to go by, your great grandfather became more and more obsessed with curing your papaw's disability. He became so fixated with the task that he started neglecting other duties, like making Glomgurgle disappear or taking care of your papaw. I became so busy taking care of your grandparents that I eventually pushed your papaw to be more independent," he explained, chuckling softly.

~

As he listened to Murlyn continue the story, Blaine was transported back through time to the morning of the year 574 of King Frederick and Queen Alexandria's reign. He was eight-years-old, and he woke to find Murlyn about to head out the door. "Morning, Murl, where you goin'?" He asked sleepily.

"It's okay, Bud," Murlyn reassured, looking down at his feet. "I have to get to the workshop. I told your Papa I'd help him today."

"But I'm hungry," Blaine protested, frowning.

"Your chair is right there, bud. I left your clothes at the end of the cot here and there is some oatmeal ready to be cooked on the stove outside. I figured you could make your own breakfast this morning seeing as I'm so busy." Murlyn gestured toward each of the items as he rushed out the door.

Am I dreaming? Blaine wondered, sitting up slowly. Pinching his wrist, he tested the thought. "Ouch." *Well, looks like Murl really did leave me alone. I guess I'll go back to sleep until he's done working.* He thought, quickly laying back against his pillow. *Ugh, how is a kid supposed to sleep when he's so hungry?* Blaine placed a hand on his rumbling stomach. *Wait, didn't Murlyn say something about oatmeal?*

Sighing, Blaine pulled his wheelchair even closer to the cot and put on the brakes. *What did I read about wheelchair transfers?* Closing his eyes, he thought back to the many books about living with a disability that Murlyn had snuck in with other collections that he'd wished for. *Okay, I remember. I got this. One step at a time,* he told himself as the instructions he'd once read filled his mind. Without giving it another thought, he rolled onto his stomach, slowly lowered himself to his knees, turned around, and then using his elbows and upper-body strength, climbed into the chair. *Oh, my gosh, I did it! I got into my wheelchair all by myself!*

Amazed and exhilarated by his new accomplishment, Blaine bent down and grabbed his clothes off the cot. *How should I put these on?* He wondered, studying the pair of brown fleece pants intently. *It's so much easier just to wish my clothes on.* Sighing, he carefully slid his feet into the pants then pushed up, bracing himself up against his footrests, wiggling his pants up to his waist in the process. *Wow...*

I'm pretty good at this, he thought, pulling his long-sleeved black t-shirt over his head before pushing his arms through their corresponding holes. *Time to brush my hair and teeth. At least I am used to this part.* "Personal hygiene is far too important of a matter to leave up to wishing," he said, in a perfect imitation of Murlyn's voice.

Moments later, as he was finishing up combing his hair, his stomach growled again. Sighing, he grabbed onto the string Murlyn had put onto the door of the hut, opened it, and made his way outside. *That thing looks more ominous than usual*, he eyed the campfire stove warily. *I think I'll find someone to help with breakfast*, he decided before heading out into the Forest of Wishes.

After a few minutes, the boy saw his red-haired friend. *Oh, there's Percy. I'll bet he'll help with breakfast if I offer him some*, he thought excitedly, as he spotted the crimson-headed woodland creature and wheeled himself over to Percy as quickly as he could.

"Hi, Percy, how are you?" He questioned, flashing a cheesy grin.

"Oh, hey Bud, you're looking sharp. Did you pick out your own clothes today?" The red-haired troll asked by way of greeting.

Blaine's grin widened, stretching from ear to ear. "No, but I did get myself dressed. Wanna come and cook me some breakfast to celebrate?" He asked, his tone anxious and hopeful at the same time.

Percy shook his head. "Sorry kid. Wish I could." Glancing around, he made sure no one else was within earshot before adding, "I'm just sneakin' some berries."

"C'mon," Blaine grinned mischievously. "I bet those berries would taste real good in some oatmeal."

"Sorry, Blaine. I have to get back before anyone misses me or my magic, but don't worry, you got this, bud," he encouraged, scurrying toward the workshop. "Just use what you know."

Use what you know? What does that mean? I've never cooked. I'm just a kid. When I'm hungry I make a wish and Murl cooks something up using magic.

"That's it… magic!" Blaine whispered. Smiling, he rushed toward the Tree of Friendship.

Approaching the special tree moments later, the boy let out a breath he hadn't realized he'd been holding, relieved to see that no trolls were out enjoying berries. *I sure hope this works. Otherwise, I'll go hungry.* Shaking his head, he dismissed the thought, picked a handful of berries from the lowest branch, and rushed back as fast as his arms could push him. Once inside the hut, he placed the berries on the table and contemplated his next move. *Ugh, I'm so hungry I could eat a horse,* he thought as his stomach rumbled once again. "That's it," he realized, suddenly inspired as the perfect spell came to him. *You can do this. You'll be eating oatmeal in no time.* Taking a deep breath, Blaine gathered the berries, headed back outside and carefully positioned his wheelchair in front of the campfire stove. *Here goes nothing.* Leaning forward, he squeezed the berries as hard as he could over the pot of uncooked oats Murlyn had left that morning. As the crushed berries begun to fall into the pot of oatmeal, Blaine closed his eyes and said,

> *"I am so hungry I could eat a horse.*
> *Let the magic of these berries cook this for me.*
> *For, I've never read a cook book or taken such a course.*
> *And if I don't eat soon, I'll turn into a banshee."*

Opening his eyes, he smiled from ear to ear as a puff of blue smoke, matching the color of the berries, swirled around the pot and disappeared within seconds. *Oh, my goodness. It worked. It actually worked!* Excited at the sight of the pipping-hot oatmeal, he rushed inside, grabbed a spoon, and wheeled right back, proceeding to eat it right out of the pot.

"Well, look who got himself dressed and fed in just under two hours." Murlyn said, his voice full of mischief, as he, the other trolls, and Benjamin approached.

Eyebrows scrunched together, Blaine eyed Murlyn. "Wh—what're you guys doing here? I thought everyone had to help Papa out in the workshop today."

"Well, ya see, this—" Murlyn begun, his usually calm voice slightly shaking and coated in nervousness.

"Oh, just spit it out already." Rosie shouted at Murlyn. "And when you do, be sure to tell him I had nothing to do with it," her tiny high-pitched voice edged with frustration.

"Sweetheart, he's getting older and bigger. He has to gain some independence eventually," Murlyn insisted through gritted teeth.

"Not like this though," retorted Rosie.

"What's going on?" Blaine questioned, cutting Rosie off. "Are you guys fighting? I thought you and Rosie never fought?"

LAUGHTER ERUPTED throughout the small hut, bringing Blaine back to the present moment. Murlyn was describing the shock that had come over Blaine's face when he heard that the morning had been a plan to help him become more self-sufficient.

"It's good that my mom was there, huh?" Missy asked, her voice sweet and quiet. "You definitely needed a friend."

Blaine nodded. "I sure did. And your mom was there for me," he looked to the pink, glittery-haired woodland creature and smiled. "No one could ever take the place of my mother, but you offered me a friendship like no one else could. If it weren't for you, lord knows how many bones I would've broken those first few years in my wheelchair."

Giggling, Rosie nodded. "That's for sure. You would've broken every last bone ten times over."

"What are you talking about, Mama?" Missy questioned, her sweet voice colored by curiosity.

"Murlyn, sweetheart, you've been telling the story up to this point. Would you like to fill her in?" Rosie asked.

Smiling, Murlyn tilted his head and contemplated where to begin. "Hmmm... how can I put this and allow Blaine to keep his dignity?" He winked at the old man. "As soon as he could speak,

Blaine made it his mission not only to make Natalie smile, but to impress the heck out of her, too."

Murlyn was once again immersed in his memories as he spoke. Within moments, he was back in the throne room, standing to the right of the black diamond as he and Percy filled their daily guarding duties simultaneously.

❧

CAREFULLY RUBBING the black diamond with a silver, silk cloth, Percy did his part to polish it. "So, how're you doing—" he begun.

Before Murlyn could speak, they both heard a sound. "AAAHHH —stop, stop—" A squeaky, high-pitched voice yelled moments later.

Standing up on his tippy toes, Murlyn looked to his red-haired pal. "Was that Rosie?" He asked warily.

"Sure sounded like her," Percy agreed. "Go ahead. I got this."

Following the sound of the scream, Murlyn found Rosie in the kitchen of the castle glaring at Blaine and Natalie, her eyes full of fear.

"What in the name of wishes are you screaming about?" Murlyn questioned, looking from her to the children and back.

Eyeing him, the pink, glittery-haired troll let out a huff. "Can't you see?" Her voice full of irritation.

Scanning the room, Murlyn noted the sleek, professionally designed, granite counters, stainless steel appliances, spotless utensils on hooks, and the gentle swish of the dishwasher. After a moment, he shrugged his shoulders. "The kitchen seems fine."

"The kitchen… you think I'm worried about the kitchen?" Rosie queried, disbelief dripping from her words. "Do you not see the milk crates stacked up here?" She gestured toward the milk crates between Natalie and Blaine.

Smirking slightly, the woodland creature looked at his pink, glittery-haired friend. "I still don't see the problem," he admitted.

The star-adorned troll shook her head, a scowl on her usually smiling face.

"She's mad cuz I'm poppin' wheelies," Blaine mumbled quietly, his arms folded across his chest.

"It's far worse than that," Rosie argued. "These two stacked up three milk crates and somehow built ramps on either side of them. I don't know for sure, but I'm guessing Bernie—"

"Sweetheart, the boy needs ramps to get around," Murlyn chuckled, interrupting her.

"Not if he's going to jump off them," the pink-haired troll argued. "He could get hurt."

"He's a really good jumper," Natalie said.

"Yeah, I won't get hurt," Blaine insisted.

"You two are trying my patience—"

Oh, my lord. What did I walk into? Murlyn wondered. *This is crazy.*

Compromise... Lizzie's voice filled his ears *...is key, dear friend. Allow the children to play as they wish, but make sure they are safe while doing so.*

That's it, the troll thought. *We just have to ensure the little guy's safety.*

Flashing a bright smile at the kids, he interrupted their argument with Rosie. "Hey kiddos, I have an idea!"

"You do?" Rosie asked pointedly.

Winking at his glittery-haired pal, Murlyn answered confidently. "Safety gear."

Rosie's pink eyes sparkled with realization. Murlyn could see she was on board with his idea. "That's a wonderful idea, Murlyn. Elbow pads, knee pads and a helmet should do the trick," she said happily.

Natalie and Blaine looked at each other, not sure what the two trolls were up to.

Smiling, the glittery-haired troll looked to the young boy. "Hey little man, do you wish you had something to help keep you safe when you do jumps or pop wheelies?"

"Yep, but I'm good. I'm not gonna—"

The moment she heard Blaine's confirmation, Rosie rubbed her gemstone vehemently until it was glowing bright pink. Within moments, the bright pink light shot out of her gemstone and surrounded the little boy and his wheelchair.

"Wow, cool!" Blaine exclaimed, examining the matching metallic blue helmet, elbow, and knee pads that appeared on him moments after the bright light dissipated.

~

"It sounds like Blaine was really excited, Mama," Missy said sweetly, once again bringing Murlyn back to the present.

"Indeed, he was, sweetie. Indeed, he was," Rosie agreed.

Blaine nodded. "Yes, I'd had wishes granted before, but that was the first time one had been granted to protect me personally. It was the first time I felt a motherly type of love and it was amazing."

"Your father did his best to make up for your mother being gone," Murlyn said, "but he was convinced that making the pants was the best way to show his love and, no matter what I said, it was impossible to convince him otherwise. I still remember one attempt to reason with him in particular…"

CHAPTER 6

$\mathcal{M}$urlyn sighed, as yet another sad memory emerged from the recesses of his mind and transported him back through time. Within moments, he found himself in Benjamin's cottage caring for Blaine and Natalie, who were about five years old at the time. It was well past nightfall but neither child was eager to find slumber.

"But, I'm not sleepy yet," Blaine protested, as Murlyn tucked them into their beds.

"Yeah, I'm not either," Natalie whined, sitting up in the bed.

Looking from Blaine to Natalie and back, Murlyn smiled, "I understand you're not sleepy yet, little ones, but it's late and you must rest. How does a bedtime story sound?" Murlyn queried, touching a hand to his mouth to stifle a yawn.

"Let's read *Marmoset's Bad Hair Day!*" Natalie exclaimed, handing the troll a copy of her favorite book about a monkey with crazy hair who lived in the tropical rain forest and used the help of a wise old toucan to tame his style.

Rolling his eyes, Murlyn sighed. "We've read that book dozens of times, kiddo. How about we let Blaine pick tonight." Looking to the little boy, he smiled brightly. "How's about it B? What do you want to read tonight?"

"When will my Papa be home?" Blaine asked, his voice full of a mixture of curiosity and hope.

Here goes... I can't believe I have to disappoint the boy yet again. Please give me the right words, Lizzie. "He is not going to be home until morning, little man."

The little boy frowned, looking to his tiny, royal playmate. "My daddy's never home," he said solemnly.

"It's okay B," Natalie said sweetly. "My daddy's not home much either because being king is a lot of hard work. But he loves me and wants to keep me safe. He says I come first. That's why he gave Murlyn the job of protecting me and my friends."

"That's right," Murlyn agreed. Smiling, he focused on Blaine. "Remember that your Papa is going to be home in the morning. The sooner you go to sleep, the sooner you can see him," he explained, just as there was a knock at the door. "That must be Percy. Why don't we get him to read your bedtime story tonight? Wouldn't that be fun?" The troll asked.

"Yay!" The princess exclaimed. "He does the voices much better than you."

"Yeah, the toucan is my favorite," Blaine agreed.

Rolling his eyes once more, Murlyn opened the door of the small cottage. "Oh, my gosh! What happened to you?" The troll asked, as he saw his friend and fellow woodland creature had spots of black soot all over his body, as though he had been singed several times.

"Are you okay?" Natalie asked, having spotted Percy from behind Murlyn.

"What happened to you?" Are you hurt?" Blaine asked, his small, quiet voice suddenly fretful.

Oh, shoot! Why do these kids have to be so nosey? Stay calm, the wise, old treasure troll told himself. Taking a deep breath, he turned to face the children, feigning a smile. "Uncle Percy is just fine," he assured them. "He and I are going outside for a moment and then he'll be back to read you your bedtime story, okay?"

"We never get to hear the good stuff," Natalie said grumpily.

Murlyn left the hut and went to examine his soot splattered friend as they walked into the moon light. "What in the name of wishes happened to you?" Murlyn queried, his voice colored with disbelief.

"What do you think happened?" Percy queried in a sarcastic tone. "Why do you think Natalie is here instead of at the castle?"

Murlyn shrugged. "The princess is always here when I am here. What does that have to do with anything?"

The red-haired troll's voice dropped to a whisper. "Alexandria had her dropped off here to ensure her safety. Glomgurgle came after the black diamond."

"Oh, my gosh! Did you stop him? Is everyone okay? What did Frederick say?" The wise, old woodland creature was suddenly frantic. As he waited for his old pal to answer his questions, all he could hear was the sound of his heart pounding in his chest, but then suddenly he heard Lizzie's voice.

Take a deep breath. It's going to be okay. Just remember I'm watching over all of you. I'll protect you.

The troll begun to relax as he followed the advice of Lizzie's spirit.

"That stupid fire breather somehow flew to the perimeter of the castle unnoticed," Percy said. "But as soon as Bernie and I realized what was going on, we gathered up everyone and formed a large circle around the diamond. Thankfully, together, we had enough light magic to combat that scaly imbecile's dark power, but, well..." Pausing, Percy searched for the right words. "Let's just say that I'm not the only one who looks like this."

"Oh, my gosh! How bad is it? Is Rosie okay?" The treasure troll asked frantically as his heart pounded yet again.

Looking down at his toes, Percy avoided the question.

"Just tell me," Murlyn insisted.

The red-haired troll sighed. "Her hair is not quite as glittery tonight as it usually is," he admitted after a moment. "But she is going to be fine. We're all going to be okay," Percy assured him.

Murlyn nodded. "You haven't said anything about Frederick yet. On a scale of one to ten, how irate is he?" Murlyn found his mouth suddenly dry, as his nervousness continued to increase.

"About a twelve. He's doubled detail around the black diamond and has asked that we treasure trolls tell Benjamin that if he doesn't make the dragon disappear within a month, there will be dire consequences. The other trolls and I were talking and, well…" Percy hesitated before continuing. "Our gemstones have been throbbing, so we think our treasure troll intuition is telling us that Glomgurgle is going to try again and we were hoping that, since you weren't around to help earlier, you would be the one to tell Benjamin."

"Of course," Murlyn assured him. "It's the least I can do. Go get yourself cleaned up and come back to read the children a bed time story. I'll take care of everything else."

Nodding, Percy started down the path toward the castle. "Oh, and one more thing," he stopped and looked back at Murlyn. "Just to be on the safe side, we put a protection spell on the black diamond, but it is very powerful and should only be activated under the direst of circumstances," he warned.

"Completely understandable," the slightly taller troll agreed. "Hopefully, no one will need to use it at all." With that, he stepped out onto the path between the forest and the kingdom, determined to find Benjamin and save the people of Cinder's Edge from whatever fate Glomgurgle may have in store.

Oh, thank goodness, Benjamin's here. Hopefully that means he's already hard at work making that scaly monster disappear, Murlyn thought, as he found Benjamin sitting just outside of Mount Wishnik.

Looking up from a pair of pants he'd been examining, the magician spotted the treasure troll. "Murl, what are you doin' here? Is my boy okay?"

"Blaine is perfectly fine. I'm actually here to see you, but I don't want to disturb you, so I—"

The magician waved a dismissive hand. "Nonsense, I'm just here keepin' up appearances while I finish up these pants for my boy," he said proudly. "What's on your mind?"

Lizzie, please give me the words and wisdom to motivate Benjamin. The future of the realm depends on it.

As the troll opened his mouth to answer, the smell of sulfur came from the volcano and it made his stomach churn. *Ugh... I better say what I have to say before I toss up the berries I ate for lunch.* Murlyn stepped further away from the dragon's lair and took a deep breath. "I know that you care about your boy and you want to do what is best for him. Trust me, I understand that more than any creature in the realm because I care for him too." The treasure troll let out a nervous chuckle before continuing, "It's time that you start doing more than just keeping up appearances. It looks—"

Benjamin shook his head vehemently, irritation etched throughout his features. "For cryin' out loud, Murl, what're ya gettin' at? Just spit it out. I ain't got all day."

Dropping his voice to a whisper, the woodland creature looked Benjamin straight in the eye. "You know who attempted to seize the black diamond today. Percy and the other trolls were able to harness enough of their light magic and stop him, but their treasure troll intuition is telling them that he is going to come back... and soon." *I cannot believe that I just uttered those words. Especially so close to the dragon's lair.* As the mere thought of Glomgurgle overwhelmed him, the troll's stomach continued to stir and his throat tightened. *We are in so much trouble here, Lizzie. I feel it. I can just feel it. Please give me the right words. The words to make Benjamin understand the gravity of this.*

"That's it?" The eccentric magician asked, his voice colored by disbelief. "That's what you're worried about? Well, don't fret, buddy, I'm gonna make the overgrown lizard disappear in no time. I got a plan," Benjamin reassured, before Murlyn could even utter a response. "Ya see, it's all up here in the ol' noggin'," the illusionist grinned. "I just need a little more time to perfect my boy's pants first."

Hanging his head, Murlyn let out a frustrated sigh, his bushy, blue eyebrows furrowed, unable to hide his irritation. "No, no, no, Benjamin, you don't understand. You have to make good on your word… now. King Frederick has said that if Cinders Edge is not safe within a month you will face dire consequences."

Benjamin scoffed, quickly dismissing the idea. "That's all talk. Frederick's not gonna do anything to me. My Lizzie was his wife's best friend and Natalie practically lives at my cottage."

"That's right," Murlyn interrupted. "Frederick's daughter practically lives at your cottage where I am essentially raising her and your son. It's time that changed. It's time that you stepped up as a parent. And the first way you can do that is by doing what you set out to do long ago and ensure the future of our kingdom.

"How dare you!" Benjamin shouted, his face turning a mixture of red and deep purple. "How dare you tell me to step up as a parent when all I've been doing for the past five years is trying to better my son's life?" Pausing, Benjamin let out a breath then continued, his voice and demeanor calmer, but still very firm. "Why do ya think I work so hard? Why do ya think I've put everything else aside in my life, including what I said I'd do at that wedding? I'll tell ya why. It's because I'm a good parent and I want what's best for my son. And what's best for my boy is a normal life." Proudly holding up the pants he had been examining earlier, Benjamin showed them to the troll. "These pants could give him that," his voice full of excitement. "They could give him a life without disability. And for me, as his father, there's nothing more important than my boy having the opportunity to live a happy, healthy, normal life."

Murlyn stared at Benjamin, not knowing what to say. Then a familiar voice sounded in his ears. *Tell my Benjamin that the magic that will lead to what he wants for himself and our baby boy is already within him... within all of us.*

"You're right. I apologize," Murlyn begun. "Perhaps I was out of line. However, something tells me that the magic that will give you everything you want, everything you hope for, is already within you. Just know, there will not be enough time to find or utilize it unless you do as you promised Frederick you would all those years ago. It may be the only way our kingdom has a future," Murlyn warned, his voice full of caution, before turning to walk back to the cottage.

Looking up to the sky, the treasure troll did the only thing he could to help ensure the future of the kingdom... he pleaded to Lizzie. *Please be with Benjamin tonight, Lizzie. Remind him of how important it is that he listen to me. The future of Cinder's Edge may very well depend on it, so please protect us as well as the entire kingdom.* The woodland creature's heart ached for his dear old friend as he entered the place that had once been her home hoping that she could hear him and would encourage Benjamin to take his warning seriously.

~

"WE ALL KNOW what happened after that," Missy said, her tiny, squeaky voice once again bringing her father back to the present.

"Yes, indeed, and those of us who lived through it remember the events as if it happened yesterday," Murlyn said solemnly.

The dark blue-haired woodland creature had no desire to even think about Glomgurgle but, in that moment, while telling the story, he couldn't help but relive what would end up being a defining day in the history of Cinder's Edge.

"Ugh," Murlyn sighed, as the rising sun shone into the hollow of the dark blue fern tree that he'd once considered to be his home. He spent more time looking after Natalie and Blaine that his little home was just somewhere to sleep. "How is it time to get up already?" He questioned rhetorically. "It took hours for the princess to fall asleep last night," he groaned, wiping sleep from his deep, dark blue eyes.

Sticking his head out of the hollow of his red sapling, Percy nodded. "Little Blaine didn't go easy on me either," he chuckled weakly. "But a troll's work is never done. We're both on guard duty this morning. Want to grab a quick bite first?"

Nodding, Murlyn reluctantly climbed out of his tree and followed Percy to the one multi-colored tree in the forest.

"Whoa…" Dylock, said by way of greeting. "You guys look rough." Smiling, he plucked a few berries from the sapling and held them out to his fellow trolls. "Have some breakfast. It'll help get your energy up."

Eyebrows furrowed, Murlyn accepted a berry and examined it. "This is a blackberry not a blueberry. What changed?" He questioned warily.

Don't eat the berries, Lizzie's voice warned him as he continued inspecting the magical fruit.

Dylock shook his head. "Don't know. Just found them here this morning. Pretty tasty, if you ask me," he smiled and plucked more berries from the tree.

Percy yawned as Dylock continued to chomp on the new-found berries. "Goin' to save any for the rest of us there, Dylock?"

"Hey, I'm not the only one enjoying them," Dylock exclaimed, glancing back at a group of six other trolls who sat enjoying the berries to the point that their lips were stained purple. Sighing, Percy picked a berry from the sapling and opened his mouth to eat it.

Carefully breaking open the berry he'd been inspecting, Murlyn was horrified. "AAAAHHHH… SPIDERS!!!"

Wide-eyed and horrified, the troll watched as three spiders crawled out of the crumbled berry and scurried up the Tree of Friendship.

Murlyn's vision blurred as he watched the other treasure trolls spit remnants of the berries out of their mouths, increasing the number of spiders crawling around the forest by hundreds in mere minutes. *After all these years, are spiders really going to be the source of darkness to do us in?* The troll wondered as his knees buckled and he fell to the ground.

Just as she had time and time again since she crossed over into the next life, Lizzie offered him words of encouragement. *Don't give up, dear friend. All you need to counteract dark magic is light magic and treasure trolls have an abundance of the most powerful form of magic there is.*

Inspired by his departed friend, Murlyn picked himself up and sprang into action. "Listen up everyone!" He shouted getting the attention of his fellow trolls. "It's going to be okay. We can fix this, but I'm going to need everyone to trust me and each other, okay?"

Weak mumbles of agreement came from the other woodland creatures.

"Everyone gather around the Tree of Friendship and hold hands," Murlyn grabbed Percy's hand, his voice steady, despite the increasing number of creepy crawlers still scampering around them.

Quickly forming a large circle around the tree, the other trolls linked hands, following Murlyn's lead.

"Great," Murlyn said after a moment. "Now, I need everyone to think of the thing, person, or troll that they love most. Let your love fill your body until it overflows," Murlyn thought about his love for Blaine. *That kid has become quite the reader in just a couple of years. He makes me so proud,* Murlyn smiled as he thought about Blaine and his affinity for books. *The only thing he seems to love more than reading is Natalie. Who can blame him?* Murlyn wondered. *She's so cute and—*

In that moment, as all of the treasure trolls were focused on thoughts of love, a burst of positive energy emanated around their circle, restoring the Tree of Friendship, as well as the rest of the Forest of Wishes, to its former glory.

Cheers of celebration filled the forest as the trolls hugged one another rejoicing in their victory. Murlyn's joy ended the moment Rosie approached him frowning.

"Murlyn," she whispered, her tone fretful.

"What's wrong?" He asked quietly. "You should be celebrating."

"I can't find Dylock," she told him in a hushed tone. "I went around to make sure everyone was okay and I can't find him. He could be anywhere and he's still under the influence of dark magic," she said worriedly.

I miss the days when all I had to worry about was guarding the black diamond, Murlyn thought as he discreetly left the joy-filled forest in search of Dylock.

IF I WAS *under the influence of dark magic where would I go?* Murlyn wondered as he walked down the path between the forest and Cinder's Edge. Moments later, as the answer dawned on the troll, his stomach begun to churn. In spite of his discomfort, the woodland creature ran down the path and up the hill to the castle as quickly as his tiny legs could carry him. Panting, he rushed inside and headed straight to the throne room without stopping to catch his breath. Upon opening the door, the treasure troll's worst fear was confirmed as his eyes landed on the empty pedestal between the two thrones. Knowing that there was no time to waste, Murlyn ran out of the castle and toward Mount Wishnik.

Please give me strength, Lizzie. The kingdom will never recover if Glomgurgle gets to the black diamond before I do. "You can do this," Murlyn said out loud, interrupting his thoughts about the dragon "You have to, and you will, for all of the trolls and citizens of Cinder's Edge," he whispered to himself firmly.

Empowered by his love for the kingdom, the treasure troll continued to run and made it to the outskirts of the volcano in minutes. *Oh, no...this can't be,* Murlyn thought, as he spotted a troll with hair as dark as coal and, instead of his normal gemstone in his belly, there was the outline of a spider with red eyes. This troll was standing just outside the dragon's lair holding the black diamond. *It's far, far worse than I ever imagined,* a lump forming in his throat.

Lizzie, thankfully, invaded his thoughts... *Stay strong, dear friend. Remember that light magic conquers all.*

Looking up to the sky, Murlyn nodded. "Thanks for the reminder."

Feeling slightly more confident, the troll swallowed his emotions and shouted to get his fellow woodland creatures attention. "How the heck did you capture the black diamond by yourself? Bring it back right now!"

Jumping slightly at the sound, Dylock scoffed as he realized it's origin. "Duh, I used dark magic to shrink it, you fluffy-haired dummy. There is absolutely no chance of you getting it back. Go home, treasure troll. You're NOT welcome here!"

Folding his arms across his chest, the dark blue-haired troll eyed Dylock. "We can make this easy or we can make this really difficult. It's your choice," Murlyn assured, his tone serious and unrelenting. "But I am not going anywhere without the black diamond."

"You want the black diamond?" Dylock asked, holding the diamond out toward his fellow troll. "You want it?" He asked again, his tone serious and spiteful. "Then go and get it," he taunted, throwing the black diamond straight into the dragon's lair.

"Noooo!" Murlyn cried as he ran into Glomgurgle's lair without giving it a second thought.

The air in the volcano was thick and so filled with soot that Murlyn could only see about two feet in front of him. "What the..." the troll whispered as he felt coal dust hit his cheek. Looking up, he literally stumbled backward at the sight of long, sharp stalactite hanging just a few feet above his head. *Oh, my... there must be dozens,* the treasure troll thought, stomach churning as the smell of sulfur assaulted his nostrils, making him feel nauseous. Squinting, he struggled to see through the smoke ahead of him. *This is most definitely Glomgurgle's lair. I don't know how I am going to do this...* Shaking his head, Murlyn dismissed thoughts of self-doubt. "You can do this," he whispered to himself. "Just find the black diamond and get out."

Taking a deep breath, he pushed through the nausea and took a step forward, only to feel intense heat on his ankle. "Ouch," Murlyn yelled, glancing downward to examine the source. Wide-eyed, mouth agape, his knees buckled as he realized the source was a crater full of hot, bubbling lava.

"Pretty amazing, isn't it?" Dylock called, his tone still condescending.

Jumping at the unexpected sound, Murlyn responded through gritted teeth. "Show yourself."

"Why would I do that?" Dylock queried. "I'll just show you this instead." He teased as the hot, smoke filled space lit up, revealing more lava-filled craters scattered around the volcano floor.

Oh, for the love of all that is magical... more lava? How the heck am I going to find the black diamond, let alone get out of here, without practically being turned to ash?"

In moments, the troll heard Lizzie's voice so clearly that it was as if she were right there next to him. *Don't let him see you rattled, dear friend. You can do this. Remember that you have light magic inside of you.*

Inspired by Lizzie's encouragement yet again, Murlyn cleared his throat and said, "Enough is enough. Hand over the black diamond now!"

"Can't do that," Dylock's voice taunted. "If you want it, you have to find it."

Oh, I'm going to find it all right... and then I'm going to find you and show you enough love to knock the dark magic right out of you. Letting out a huff, Murlyn looked to the sky. He opened his mouth to talk to Lizzie, but closed it as he spotted the black diamond suspended in the air above the space between two of the bubbling lava craters. *Oh, thank goodness, the other trolls put that protection spell on the diamond. If it weren't for that I... wait... that's it! The protection spell!*

Rubbing his gemstone, the treasure troll looked directly at the black diamond. *Little does that misguided soul know that there is a protection spell on the black diamond that can only be felt and activated by those who wield light magic. Please let this work.* Within seconds, his gemstone started glowing, and he continued to focus on the black diamond.

> *"Light magic conquers dark.*
> *Before lava leaves its mark,*
> *remove the black diamond from this space,*
> *and return it to its rightful place."*

Murlyn watched, smiling from pointy ear to pointy ear, as the black diamond instantly disappeared.

"What just happened?" Dylock questioned warily. "What did you do?"

"Don't worry, Dyl, I'll be back for you," Murlyn said, his voice full of excitement as he raced out of the volcano.

The black diamond has to be on its pedestal… it has to be. I just know it, the troll thought as he ran down the path to the castle with a bit more pep in his step than earlier that day. Entering with gusto, the treasure troll held his breath as he slowly opened the door to the throne room, peeking inside.

Slowing and exhaling deeply, the troll spotted the black diamond sitting proudly on its pedestal and Murlyn smiled brightly. "Yes, yes, yes!" He shouted excitedly, a feeling of pure elation and happiness washed over him as he celebrated. Still grinning, he looked at the castle ceiling. "Lizzie, we did it. We saved the black diamond," he whispered, his voice full of a mixture of joy and gratitude.

"Murlyn, what are you doing here? Shouldn't you be with the other trolls?" Katherine, a maid at the castle who had long black hair, olive colored eyes, and dimples, asked.

"What do you mean?" He questioned, the elation he had been feeling suddenly being replaced by anxiety. *Oh, No! Dylock!*

"My apologies, Katherine. I must go," Murlyn called out before practically bursting out of the castle.

CHAPTER 7

Thick, dark smoke clouded Murlyn's vision the moment he stepped outside. Within minutes, the troll's eyes felt as if they had been stung by half a dozen bumble bees and his chest burned as though he'd just eaten ten hot peppers. *Oh, lord. There's only one thing that could cause this much smoke... an attack by Glomgurgle.* A chill traveled down the troll's back as he realized just what that meant. *Oh, no... this must have happened while I was in his lair. He used Dylock and the black diamond as a distraction. How did I not see it?* Murlyn thought angrily. *It didn't even occur to me that he would've been here. How could I be so stupid?*

Lizzie intruded on his thoughts. *Now is no time to be angry at yourself, dear friend,* her voice quiet and sweet.

You're right, Lizzie, the troll thought, struggling to breathe through the soot-filled air. *Please give the entire kingdom strength to get through this, Lizzie,* he prayed whole-heartedly as he maneuvered through the remnants of the kingdom, unable to believe his eyes, as the smoke slowly begun to dissipate. In place of sturdy buildings stood beams of wood, blackened from flames that had recently devoured them. Charred ash with slightly glowing embers filled the path between the castle and The Forest of Wishes up to the woodland creature's knees, but the adrenaline coursing through his tiny body kept him from feeling it

Oh no, I don't see any humans nor trolls, Murlyn realized, as he carefully navigated through the debris. *I must get to the cottage now.* The further down the path he traveled, the more the burning sensation in his chest intensified. *Keep going. You promised to always protect that little boy and treasure trolls always keep their promises.*

Remembering his promise to Lizzie gave Murlyn the strength to make it to where Benjamin's cottage had once stood. "Wow," Murlyn whispered, realizing that the cottage, once the home of his dear friend, had suffered a fate far worse than the rest of the kingdom. While there were charred remains of other homes and buildings around it, the space where the cottage had once been was completely empty, aside from a singed outline of Glomgurgle's footprint on a large piece of burnt parchment.

Tears filled Murlyn's intense dark blue eyes as he looked from the empty space to the burnt parchment and back. *No, this can't be. This just can't be,* Murlyn thought as he fell to his knees, giving into sobs. "I'm so sorry that I didn't keep my promise, Lizzie," he whispered, looking up into the still, smoke-filled sky. "I'm so, so sorry I failed you," he added, tears still streaming down his cheeks. Were Benjamin and Blaine really gone? Had they lost their lives due to Murlyn's inability to protect the realm? After a moment, he spotted Percy approaching and wiped the wetness from his eyes.

"Murl, what are you doing here?" Percy queried, his voice fretful. "There is no time for tears," he urged before Murlyn could answer. "We need to get to the forest, now! King Frederick is livid."

Can't a troll have a minute to grieve for his old friend? Sighing, the treasure troll stood up slowly. "Frederick is the last person I want to see right now," he mumbled.

Placing a hand on Murlyn's shoulder, Percy squeezed reassuringly. "I get it. Today has been a tough day for all of us. But, look at it this way, the sooner it ends, the sooner we can start to rebuild." Percy started down the path to the forest.

Rebuild? How am I supposed to think about rebuilding anything right

now? Murlyn wondered as he followed his fellow troll down the path to the Forest of Wishes. The bright saplings, home to many of the treasure trolls, stood in stark contrast to the blackened remains of the kingdom. The magical place gave Murlyn some comfort. *Light magic is indeed stronger than dark*, he thought, as he approached the leader of the realm.

"It's about time you showed up," King Frederick shouted, looking down at Murlyn as though he were a bug that needed to be crushed. "I wasn't sure which one of you cowards would show up first…" he said sarcastically, his face turning a deep red. "You or your magic-obsessed buddy."

Murlyn could feel his heart rate beating slightly faster than it had a moment before. *Stay calm*, he told himself. *Don't let him see you sweat.* Shifting his weight from one foot to the other, the woodland creature cleared his throat and said, "With all due respect, your majesty, treasure trolls are not cowards. I understand that you're angry, but—"

"I'm far more than angry. I'm irate," the leader of the realm lowered himself to Murlyn's level so the two were nose to nose. "You are the worst kind of coward. You're a traitor. You betrayed this kingdom and now you'll pay the price," he shouted, his voice full of pure hatred for the little troll.

Suddenly, other trolls throughout the forest gasped as footsteps approached the king. "What's with all of the yelling, Frederick?" Benjamin queried innocently. "You're scarin' my boy."

Jumping at the familiar sound of Benjamin's voice, Murlyn spotted Blaine sitting in his wheelchair directly behind his father and rushed over. "Oh, my gosh! It's so good to see you little man. I thought you had both perished in the fire. Where have you been?" He asked, as he embraced the little boy tightly.

"Murl, give my boy a chance to breathe, will ya? What're ya babblin' about?"

"I'm just so happy to see you guys," Murlyn explained, wiping fresh tears of joy from his eyes. "I thought neither of you had survived the attack."

"I'm happy to see ya too, Murl. I took the boy over to Embersville to buy some new fabric and came back to this. What's going on?"

"What do you think is going on, you imbecile?" Frederick shouted. "Glomgurgle burnt down the kingdom because you didn't do your job and make him disappear like you said you would." Frederick was so angry that spittle landed on Benjamin's cheek, his face ten times more crimson than it had been moments before.

Wiping his cheek, Benjamin tried to defend himself. "I feel awful. I've just been so focused on helpin' my boy—"

Letting out an exaggerated sigh, Frederick screamed at Benjamin again. "I'm sick of you using your cripple of a son as an excuse. You're just as useless as the traitorous treasure trolls," he looked Benjamin straight in the eye and paused as if considering what to say next. "I'm sentencing you, your boy, and the trolls into exile here in the Forest of Wishes," the king said after a moment, his voice considerably quieter, but still very serious.

"What?" Murlyn and Benjamin questioned simultaneously.

"You are no longer welcome in Cinder's Edge," the angry King clarified. He looked from Benjamin to Murlyn and back again. "You are hereby stripped of your citizenship as well as any titles you hold within the realm."

"What? You can't do that," Murlyn exclaimed, his voice full of a mixture of surprise and outrage. What about the black diamond? We trolls have to guard the black diamond.

Sneering, Frederick shook his head. "This is my kingdom. I can do whatever I want," he said in a smug tone. "I'll just instate a royal guard to watch over and protect the black diamond. I don't know why you're worried about this anyway. It doesn't look like you can provide much protection anymore."

"What is that supposed to mean?" Murlyn asked, feeling like he had been punched in the stomach. "Just because you took away my ambassador of happiness title doesn't mean I'm going to stop using magic to protect the people of Cinder's Edge and to make them happy."

The king scoffed and eyed the troll's belly.

Following the kings gaze, Murlyn gasped as he looked to his belly. Instead of his usual gemstone proudly on display, there was an empty space.

WIDE-EYED AND MOUTH AGAPE, Murlyn rubbed his empty stomach as though doing so might make his gemstone reappear. "How can this be?" He asked his voice coated in disbelief.

Frederick scowled at Murlyn. "You of all creatures know that magic comes with a price. You should have come to me when the blackberries appeared in the forest this morning, but instead you put the interests of your kind ahead of the kingdom and took matters into your own little hands."

"I was thinking about the realm the whole—" Murlyn wasn't able to finish his sentence. He was in total disbelief at all that was happening.

"That doesn't matter now. It seems like both the universe and I are making you pay the price for your selfishness." Grinning mischievously, the king looked around before finally addressing Benjamin. "If you, your boy, or any of these creatures ever step foot in Cinder's Edge again, every last one of you will meet a fate far worse than being exiled to this forest, is that understood?"

Benjamin, who up until that point looked as though he'd been stunned into silence, spoke up. "To tell ya the truth, I'd rather my boy and I live out here with the trolls than in any kingdom you rebuild anyhow," he admitted. "But can the kid at least say goodbye to Natalie? He's been missin' her all day and now he's worried."

"Yes, can we at least say goodbye to Alexandria and Natalie?" The trolls echoed.

Shaking his head vehemently, the ruler of the kingdom disagreed.

"No, he may not. None of you can speak a word to my wife or child ever again. In fact, I plan to hire a hypnotist to remove all knowledge of any of you from their memories. Now, if you'll excuse me, I have a kingdom to rebuild," Frederick announced before turning to leave the forest.

This is terrible. Me paying the price for magic is one thing, but Natalie paying for it, too, is an entirely different matter. This can't happen, the dark-blue troll thought as he watched the leader of the realm walk away. *We have to do something and quick.*

"Rosie, we—" Murlyn begun, as he walked toward her tree where she stood trying to comfort Percy and some other trolls.

"Everything is going to be ok—" Murlyn heard her say. He shook his head.

"We can't let this happen," he said, interrupting Rosie.

The glittery-headed troll eyed him. "Now is not the time to think about what we can't do, Murlyn. We must focus on what we can," she encouraged.

"I know," Murlyn agreed. "That's why I need you to come with me," he urged, grabbing her by the arm.

"Ahhh… Murlyn what're you doing?" Rosie screeched as he pulled her toward his tree.

"You need to go with Frederick and protect Natalie," he explained upon making it to his sapling. "Stay hidden and make up a story about what kind of creature you are after the hypnosis. Protect the princess and make sure that she knows she is not alone. I'll come and find you both when the time is right," he assured her.

The pink-haired troll studied Murlyn for a moment, looking at him with total confusion. "Have you lost your mind?" She asked, her voice colored by a mixture of sadness and disbelief. "I love that little girl as much as anyone else, but I cannot do that. King Frederick will have my head."

Shifting his weight from one side to the other, Murlyn let out a huff. "Rosie please. We have no other option. The princess loves you and she needs you. Someone needs to protect her. Just think of how sad that little girl will be without any of us around."

Rosie sighed. "Why did you have to go and put it like that?"

"Don't worry everything is going to be fine Rosie. "I have a plan. I want you to use Benjamin's invisibility cloak to hide yourself."

This plan has to work. Lizzie, please let it work. Please watch over Natalie and the rest of the kingdom in the days to come, Murlyn thought, handing the shiny, silky, black cloak to the only treasure troll he'd ever imagined sharing a life with.

"Okay," Rosie said, hesitantly accepting the cloak. "But if I am invisible, how are you ever going to find me?" She asked.

Looking down at his toes, Murlyn again shifted his weight from one side to the other. *How do I tell her the next part of my plan?* He wondered. *She is really not going to like it. What should I do, Lizzie?*

Lizzie's voice sounded in his ears. *Just be honest. Honesty is always the best policy... especially when it comes to speaking to those you love.*

Murlyn looked up at Rosie and flashed a nervous smile. *Oh, Lizzie I hope you are right.* "I was thinking we could split your gemstone," he admitted, his voice full of apprehension.

In that moment, Rosie 's eyes opened so wide that they practically fell out of her head. "Give up my gemstone... are you nuts?" She screeched, her voice full of anger and disbelief.

"I am not asking you to part with it completely," Murlyn assured her. "I'm only asking you to share it for a while, so we can stay connected. I'll give it back as soon as I find you guys. I promise."

Murlyn watched as Rosie mulled the idea over in her mind. He hoped that she was coming to the right decision. "Oh, all right," the pink glitter-haired woodland troll huffed. "Just do it fast before I change my mind."

Taking a deep breath, Murlyn looked straight at the pink star-shaped gemstone of his fellow woodland troll, grasped her hand, and said,

> *"Split this gemstone in two,*
> *so that no matter how far we go,*
> *we always know that the other is safe and true."*

Within seconds, the spell took effect and half of Rosie's

gemstone traveled to the center of Murlyn's belly. *Why does it have to be this way?* Murlyn wondered to himself as a silence settled between the two of them. *Oh, Lizzie, please help me get through this. I just can't imagine not seeing Rosie or sweet little Natalie every day.*

Lizzie whispered in his ear. *Don't worry, dear friend. We are only ever separated from those we love temporarily, and I will watch over Rosie and the princess to ensure their safety.*

"You chose an interesting spell," Rosie said after a moment, breaking the silence between them. "Why did you choose my gemstone to split in two?"

Looking down at his feet, Murlyn contemplated his answer. After a long moment he hesitantly looked up at her, his eyes full of tears. "Things are about to change for us, Rosie. I chose that spell because, regardless of the changes coming, I want us to be true to who we are as treasure trolls."

Sighing, Rosie looked at him, eyebrows furrowed. "Murlyn, have you and I ever really been true to who we are... or rather what we are... to one another?" She queried, her squeaky voice coated in sadness.

"We can't worry about that now," he said solemnly. "If you don't leave soon then there is no hope."

Rosie nodded, wiping tears from her cheeks. "Stay true to who you are, Murlyn, and I will stay true to who I am." Rosie said somberly before draping the invisibility cloak around herself and disappearing from his sight.

How am I going to go on without Rosie? Murlyn wondered, as tears welled up in his dark blue eyes. *I always thought I would tell her my true feelings someday, but now I don't even know when I'll see her again.* Wiping the moisture from his eyes, the troll looked to Blaine and realized that the boy was just as upset. Not only would Blaine not be allowed to see Natalie again, he was going to lose Rosie too.

Pull it together and be an example, Murlyn told himself as he walked over to the little boy. "Hey, little man. I know this is scary, but it is going to be okay. We are going to make the Forest of Wishes a great home for you and your papa."

"What about Natalie?" Blaine sniffled.

What can I possibly say that won't disappoint this little guy? Murlyn wondered as he looked into the boy's tear-filled eyes. *Oh, Lizzie, please be there for your son right now and give me the proper words to comfort him.*

Lizzie's spirit spoke to Murlyn. *Make a special place for my special boy.*

Flashing a weak smile, the woodland creature placed his hand on the little boy's shoulder and squeezed gently. "Natalie's daddy took her back to the castle, but don't worry because we are going to make a place just as special as the castle for you, right here in the forest."

"A place just for me?" Blaine asked, a sudden hint of excitement in his voice. "Can it have ramps for wheelies and jumps?"

Leave it to this kid to be worried about wheelies and jumps, Murlyn thought. *At least he's good for a laugh.* Chuckling weakly, the troll nodded. "You can have as many ramps as your heart desires, as long as you wear your helmet. Just go to Uncle Percy and wish for your special place."

The little boy opened his mouth to say something but closed it as a loud thud stole his attention. "What was that?" Blaine asked, glancing in the direction of the noise.

Following the little boy's gaze, Murlyn searched for the source of the sound. "Stay here," he said anxiously.

The little boy shook his head. "I have to find Papa."

Sighing, the blue-haired troll lamented. "Stay behind me then and do as I say."

Don't let anything else bad happen today Lizzie. I can't take any more. Blaine can't take it either, the troll pleaded as the two ran toward the sound. "What in the name of wishes is going on here?" He questioned, eyeing a yellow fern tree that had fallen to the ground. Bernie sighed gesturing toward Benjamin.

"Papa, are you okay?" Blaine asked.

"Yeah little man, I'm just building our new home. Don't worry, we're going to be just fine here... we will be just fine." Benjamin whispered, as though he were trying to convince himself just as much as his son.

Bernie, the orange-haired troll, turned to Murlyn. "This guy has decided he wants to build his new home without using magic. Is he crazy?"

Chuckling, Murlyn looked to Blaine. "Now that you know your Papa is all right, go with Percy and do what we talked about, okay?"

After he was certain Blaine was out of ear shot, Murlyn addressed Benjamin. "Why the heck would you cut down a beautiful tree instead of using magic? You know how special the trees are here in the Forest of Wishes and you're a magician for cryin' out loud."

"Exactly," Benjamin agreed. "Magic got me into this mess so, aside from makin' my boy's pants, I'm never gonna use magic again."

"But magic is a part of who you are," Murlyn argued. "Are you saying you are not even going to do magic tricks for Blaine anymore?"

Benjamin shook his head. "Nope. Now, if you'll excuse me, I have work to do."

Maybe he's right, Murlyn thought. *Perhaps magic did get us into this mess.* Looking down at the partial pink, star-shaped gemstone adorning his belly, he chuckled. *I'll give this no magic thing a whirl. After all, it would have been my destiny had Rosie not been generous enough to share her gemstone. Oh, how I miss her already.* Shaking his head, Murlyn dismissed the thought and focused on the task at hand. "Fair enough," Murlyn said. "The least I can do is help. Let's get to it."

With that, Murlyn, Bernie, Benjamin, and Lilly, a troll with yellow hair and a matching circular gemstone got to work building the hut. Just as they begun discussing how wide the door needed to be to accommodate Blaine's wheelchair, they heard the little boy scream.

Murlyn ran as fast as his little legs would go and found Blaine in a clearing. *Oh, thank goodness, he's okay,* the blue-haired troll thought, relieved to see that Blaine was not screaming but instead squealing with delight as he and the others approached.

Benjamin studied his son who was happily eyeing a purple sapling. "What's going on here?" Benjamin asked.

"Percy finished my treehouse. It's awesome!" Blaine exclaimed. "Watch this!"

I really hope your idea pays off, Lizzie, Murlyn thought, watching the little boy in anticipation.

Taking a deep breath, Blaine looked straight into the hollowed-out trunk of the purple fern and yelled the magic word, "Alakazam", his voice dripping with excitement.

The moment the magic word left the little boy's lips, the sapling took on a life of its own. The hollowed-out portion of the trunk expanded to three times its normal size, as branches lowered simultaneously, providing ramp access to the inside. "Isn't it great?" Blaine said. "I am going to get so good at jumps in my wheelchair. And did you guys see these?" He pointed upward.

Looking up, Murlyn spotted four metal rings hanging from thick, purple ropes that looked to have been made from the sapling itself.

"Watch what I can do." Blaine smiled from ear to ear as he approached an eight-inch-tall ramp.

"Don't even think about it, young man," Benjamin warned, speaking for the first time since entering the tree house. "You don't have your helmet on."

The little boy's shoulders slumped. "Okay Papa," he sighed. "I'll show you later. Did you see what we did for my books? It's my favorite part!" he motioned toward a three-tiered bookcase with a ramp on either side of it.

"That is awesome, little man," Benjamin said happily. "This whole place is, but you have to promise that you will always be safe while you play in here."

"Yes," Murlyn agreed. The last thing they needed was for Blaine to seriously hurt himself. "You can start by wearing the helmet and gear that Rosie gave you," Murlyn said, pointing to the safety gear, which was hanging from a handcrafted hook to the left of the bookcase.

"I will, I promise. Papa, if you like my special place, then you're really going to like your special place," the little boy said excitedly.

Benjamin glanced at his son with a questioning look. "Huh?"

"I wished for you to have a special place, too. Come see."

"This should be interesting," Benjamin whispered before he, Murlyn, and the other trolls followed Blaine to the Tree of Friendship.

"Percy, why did you use this tree?" Murlyn questioned as Blaine used the word 'love' to open the trunk of the tree, just as he had with the other sapling.

Sighing, Percy glanced at the little boy. "He insisted his daddy's special place should be in the biggest tree in the forest." *Whoa. I have never seen so much stuff in my life,* Murlyn thought, as he looked up and saw shelf after shelf of different types of fabrics ranging from suede to silk in every color imaginable.

"Is that the SewSmart 3000?" Benjamin asked, looking at a jewel encrusted sewing machine, his voice coated in amazement.

"Yep, but Percy added gemstones," Blaine chuckled.

"I can see that," Benjamin said, continuing to scan his surroundings. "Wow, that's a beautiful desk, my boy," the loving father commented as his eyes landed on a beautiful mahogany roll-top desk.

"Look closer, look closer," the boy urged, flashing a bright smile. *There's almost as much thread as there is fabric. How can that be?* Murlyn wondered, wide-eyed, as he watched his friend pull various colors of thread, sewing needles, a pair of scissors, and a seam ripper out of the various compartments of the desk. *Uh oh, something is wrong,* Murlyn thought, suddenly noticing that his friend was tearing up.

"Where did this come from little man?" Benjamin, was holding up a picture of a very pregnant Lizzie.

Looking down at his feet, Blaine looked to Percy. The red-haired troll sighed. "I found the picture on the floor of the cottage the other day and gave it to the little guy. Today, he insisted I put it on your work desk. I apologize if I have overstepped my bounds," Percy looked to the floor.

Blaine frowned. "Please don't be mad, Papa. I thought you'd like it."

Shaking his head vehemently, Benjamin looked to his son, "I don't like it. I love it. I thought we'd lost all pictures of my Lizzie in the attack." More tears flowed down Benjamin's cheeks.

"Do you mean it Papa? Do you really love it?" The young boy queried, his tiny voice full of a mixture of hope and longing.

"Yes, yes I do." And, with that, Benjamin leaned forward to embrace his son. Looking over his shoulder, he winked at the photograph of his late wife. "We have a wonderful son, my love… absolutely wonderful," he whispered, squeezing the boy tightly.

CHAPTER 8

*I*t's ironic that the need for the black diamond and its power led to my friends rebuilding their lives here in the forest, but ruined my life. To this day, I can't believe the price I paid for losing it. It seems so unfathomable now, but I will never forget as long as I live. As resistant as Dylock was to face his past, he soon found himself so engrossed in the memory of the day that changed his life forever that he couldn't help but relive it. He soon found himself back in Mount Wishnik contemplating what to do in the wake of Murlyn stealing the black diamond back from him.

"A protection spell. A protection spell... I can't believe that blue-haired imbecile screwed up everything for me with a freakin' protection spell," Dylock muttered angrily. "The master is gonna—"

"Where is it?" Glomgurgle said. He was a twenty-foot-tall dragon, covered in thick, dark red scales that looked sharper than any of the stalactites inside of the volcano could have hoped to be. He looked more threatening to Dylock than ever before, as he stepped into the light that shone into the entrance of the volcano. "Where is the black diamond?" The dragon questioned, his eyes turning from coal black to fiery orange.

Dylock cringed, looking away from the dragon. He felt his

gemstone throbbing at his belly. "One of the treasure trolls got it back," he cowered below the giant creature, his voice trembling. "He used a protection spell."

"The black diamond was the key to everything, you idiot troll," Glomgurgle huffed, causing a puff of black smoke to explode out of his nostrils.

"I'm sorry, Master. I—I failed."

"I should kill you," the dragon growled. "But, instead, I am going to make sure you suffer a much worse fate."

Dylock quivered in front of the dragon, his knees starting to knock together whilst Glomgurgle carried on with his rant. "Until you devise a plan to once again retrieve the black diamond, you will not be able to use light magic, dark magic, or any magic at all," the dragon bellowed.

"No, no, no. Please don't take my magic away," Dylock pleaded.

Ignoring the troll's plea, the dragon stared at Dylock's gemstone; the fire in his eyes more intense than ever before. As the flames turned from orange to bright red, he bellowed:

> *"This troll embarrassed me in the worst way.*
> *Let this puff of my breath strip him of his magic so it won't*
> *   happen twice.*
> *Miserable is how he will stay after paying the ultimate*
> *   price."*

Seconds later, he took a deep breath and let it out directing a cloud of smoke at Dylock's gemstone.

"AAAAHHHH…" A piercing scream left Dylock's lips as the smoke hit his gemstone, making it burn and throb worse than ever. For Dylock, this was a fate worse than death, as he watched the jewel in the center of his belly disappear along with the smoke. Frowning, Dylock fingered his bare belly. It was gone.

"Stop frowning," Glomgurgle growled ferociously. "You'll get your magic back when you have a plan. Now get to work!" The dragon's roar was so loud the volcano shook as he turned and made his way to his lair.

As the pain in the center of Dylock's belly subsided, a funny sense of freedom washed over him too. What that stupid dragon didn't know, was when he took Dylock's magic away, it also took away the control Glomgurgle had over him. But, now that he was free, he didn't have any intention of going back to his troll home. Oh, no. He was going to show everyone how strong he was and that the creatures of Cinder's Edge should respect him. But how was he going to get the diamond for himself? What could he do to get them to give him the black diamond? And then it came to him… Natalie. If he went after Natalie, they would do anything to get her back.

The growl of Dylock's newly bare belly interrupted his thoughts. Chuckling, he went in search of food. While in the Forest of Wishes, he'd gotten bored with eating blueberries. He was sure the scaly, winged bully was hiding food in the volcano somewhere. He would find it and eat it, because the dragon had ruined his life and he didn't care anymore. Dylock promised himself that he would destroy Glomgurgle.

Suddenly, as he focused his thoughts on Glomgurgle, the troll recalled something the dragon had said after declaring him his minion. The words muddled around in his head *"The northwest side of the volcano is off limits. You are to stay to the west, where I can always keep an eye on you. Wander anywhere near the northwest side and you won't take another breath."* Throwing his head back, Dylock chuckled as he remembered how much the threat had scared him. "I'm not gonna let that scaly, firebreather intimidate me anymore," he whispered, before scurrying to the forbidden corner, without remembering to cover his tracks.

Darker and colder than the rest of the volcano, a chill in the air sent shivers down the troll's spine. "Whoa, it's freezing over here," he whispered to himself, walking further into the dark space. He wondered why this end of the volcano was forbidden. It was much colder, that was for sure. But just then, a glow in the distance interrupted his thoughts. As he walked closer to the light, he saw that the source of the glow was a mushroom. Bending down, Dylock examined the incandescent mushroom. "Whoa," he said, reaching out to pick it. "This may be just what I need to capture Natalie." And he popped the mushroom into his mouth. Just as he was about to bite down on it, he heard some rustling on the northwest side near to the dragon's lair.

"What's going on?" The dragon growled, quickly approaching the northwest side. "I know you've been in the corner. Your stench and footprints are all over the place. Explain yourself or prepare to face dire consequences!" Glomgurgle bellowed, bringing himself so close that Dylock feared the dragon's smoldering, red eyes would catch his hair on fire.

"I-w-was just looking for a source of magic," the troll admitted sheepishly. "I'm not giving up just because you took mine."

"If you're so desperate that you'd defy me, you are even more pathetic than I thought," Glomgurgle snarled.

"I only wish to please you, Master," his voice still meek as he feigned anxiety. "I won't stop until the black diamond is back in your possession. You have my word."

"A troll's word is nothing, the dragon growled, eyeing the troll as if he were the most pathetic creature that ever existed. Take your pathetic self to the southeast wing and gather up the leftover blackberries before I change my mind about turning you into charcoal."

I'll eat my own toenails before I eat another blackberry, Dylock thought, scurrying out of Glomgurgle sight. *That scaly idiot actually believes I am on his side. Revenge will be so sweet. Now to capture Natalie.*

Once back in his usual corner on the southeast side of Mount Wishnik, Dylock scanned his surroundings to ensure he was alone. Seeing no sign of Glomgurgle, he retrieved the glowing mushroom from his hair and tried to think of the perfect spell.

As much as I wish I could transport that annoying little princess here right now, I have to be smarter about this, he thought. *I have to make her come to me. But how? She's surrounded by royals around the clock.* Cringing at the mere thought of such togetherness, the troll shook his head, attempting to clear his thoughts. *Get it together,* he told himself. *This isn't your first spell. Just think.*

That's it, he realized after a moment. *Her thoughts. If I figure out what she's thinking and what's going on around her then I can easily manipulate and capture her.*

Dylock suddenly became aware of his heart as it pounded against his chest cavity. Not wanting to let the nerves get the best of him, he quickly chomped down on the mushroom and swallowed it. Moments later he said the following spell,

> *"Give me insight into what the princess is thinking*
> *so I can learn how to convince her that my friendship is*
> *genuine*
> *before bringing her to her ultimate end."*

Within moments, a puff of black smoke appeared causing the troll's vision to blur. *This is it,* he thought. *The beloved princess is going to help me bring down the kingdom and doesn't even know it.* Taking a breath, he closed his eyes for a moment then reopened them. *What the heck?* He wondered as he opened his eyes, saw a rainbow, and was transported through time back to a long-ago day in the Forest of Wishes.

"Code brilliance everyone," Murlyn declared, his voice full of excitement as he stood at the Tree of Friendship, looking up at the sky. "I repeat code brilliance this is not a drill. I have spotted a rainbow and the colors are indeed brilliant. We must go to the throne room now."

A chorus of excitement erupted in the forest.

"Is this really happening?" Rosie asked, her tiny squeaky voice full of disbelief. "I never thought I'd see the day," she peered up to the sky, her eyes full of awe.

"Yes sweetheart. I cannot wait. It's going to be absolutely wonderful."

"I don't get it," Dylock said, reluctantly following the other trolls down the path from the forest to the castle. "What's so special about rainbows?"

Stopping in the middle of the path, Murlyn eyed Dylock, eyebrows furrowed. "Have you been living under a rock for the last 500 years?" Murlyn queried, his voice colored by disbelief. The magic of rainbows has been rumored to increase the power of magical creatures and objects by up to 100 times. All we have to do is—"

Murl stop gabbin'. We've got to hurry. The rainbow is already starting to fade," Percy urged.

Glancing up at the sky, Murlyn's eyes widened. "You'll just have to come with us and see," he said urgently. Quickly everyone, he declared, addressing the group. "We must get to the castle." Taking the dark blue-haired trolls words to heart, the trolls were gathered in the throne room in minutes. *What am I witnessing... a synchronized dance or something?* Murlyn wondered, as he watched the other trolls open the curtains in the room and form a circle around the pillar holding the black diamond, as if they had done so a dozen times.

"Dylock, quick, come stand next to me," the blue diamond-adorned treasure troll urged, his voice full of excitement and anticipation.

"Yeah get over here. We need everyone to say the spell," Rosie insisted.

Letting out a huff, Dylock reluctantly joined the other woodland creatures in the circle. Before he could prepare himself for the spell, the voices of the other trolls filled his ears.

> *"A rainbow is one of the world's greatest magical sources.*
> *Allow its light to strengthen the magic in this land*
> *so that whether we work alone or join forces*
> *every citizen can trust that we will be his or her right hand."*

Within minutes, the colors of the rainbow became a hundred times better, temporarily blinding the trolls as it shown onto the black diamond. *Oh, thank goodness,* Dylock let out a breath, as the rainbow disappeared restoring his sight.

"Ugh, why do I feel so different?" Dylock groaned, "What the heck just happened? I feel awful."

"What're you talking about?" Murlyn asked, eyebrows furrowed. "I feel great. The best I've felt in years."

"Me too," Rosie agreed, smiling from pointy ear to pointy ear. "I feel all warm and fuzzy inside. It's wonderful."

I have got to get the heck out of here now. All this happiness is gonna make me puke. Scurrying out of the throne room, he kept his head down, avoiding eye contact with the other woodland creatures.

"Dylock..."

Dylock, suddenly startled, the woodland creature recognized Glomgurgle's thick and raspy voice. *Oh no, I was dreaming.*

"Wake up you little leech. I can't sleep when you're snoring like a dump truck. Shut your trap before I come in there and shut it for you," the dragon bellowed angrily.

Rolling his eyes, the troll became extremely angry despite feeling all warm and fuzzy inside. *Mushroom or not, I swear I'll conquer that scaly bully and show Cinder's Edge who the real threat is. The stupid mushroom did nothing but make me feel all warm and fuzzy. What the heck am I gonna do?* Dylock groaned as he pondered the question.

THE SOUND of Missy crying startled Dylock enough to bring him back to the present. Touching his belly, he made sure his gemstone was still intact. *Oh, thank god.* Letting out a breath, he glanced into the window. *I hope Missy is okay. I love that little purple glittery-haired troll so much. I hate to hear her cry.* Looking to Murlyn, Dylock saw that his fellow troll looked to be as startled as he had been moments ago. *Seems like Murlyn is having a hard time reliving his past too. One can only hope that Missy won't think badly of either one of us after hearing about the past. Time will tell I—*

The sound of footsteps approaching the window pulled Dylock

out of his thoughts. *Uh oh, I better hide before anyone seems me.* Lowering himself onto the moss, he moved from the window seconds before Natalie looked through.

"I guess we're imagining things because there is nothing there," the former queen said.

Oh good. She didn't see me. Now, I can get back to listening. He thought, once again making himself comfortable on the mossy patch.

"I AM SO SORRY, Daddy. You must have been devastated when Mama left," Missy said, her tiny, high-pitched voice thick with sadness.

Murlyn sighed. "Indeed, I was, sweetheart. But the hardest part of being in exile for all those years was not the sadness I felt from being separated from Rosie, but the unhappiness I witnessed in Blaine, who could not stand being apart from Natalie. Despite being separated from her at the tender age of five, he never forgot about the princess. One afternoon, when he was about ten years old, the knucklehead missed her so much that he decided to take matters into his own hands," Murlyn chuckled, as he remembered what Blaine had done.

The treasure troll continued to tell his story to the others. He couldn't help but smile as he remembered the determination Blaine had the day he'd spotted the boy trying to leave the hut, with nothing but the clothes on his back and a brown satchel full of cookies on the back of his wheelchair. "Whoa, there little man, where do you think you're going?" Murlyn had queried, as the young boy was headed toward the door.

"I am going to find Natalie. She was in my dreams again last night. I want us to play together in my treehouse, so I am going to find her," the young boy announced, his voice full of resolve.

Murlyn sighed, stepping between the young boy and the front door of the hut. "I know, little man. I miss her too, but don't worry. We'll see her again someday. I promise you that."

"I don't want to wait for someday. I want to see her now." Blaine whined, his eyes filling with tears. *Oh, I hate to see him cry. Lizzie, please give me the right words to comfort your sweet boy and make him understand.*

"Come sit at the table with me, little man. It's time we had a talk," Murlyn pointed his head toward the handcrafted table and chairs in the center of the room.

Rolling his eyes, Blaine reluctantly pushed his chair up to the table to sit across from the troll. "Weren't you supposed to be helping Papa in his workshop today?" Blaine questioned when Murlyn only stared at him and didn't say a word.

Murlyn laughed and eyed the boy. "Don't try to distract me, bud. Besides, I am sure your father would agree that helping you is more important than whatever is going on in the workshop."

"You really think so?"

Uh oh, I shouldn't have said that, Murlyn thought warily. *It's clear that Benjamin loves his boy, but his priorities are so mixed up that even Blaine is starting to wonder where they lie. Oh, Lizzie, what should I do?* Focusing on a slightly warped spot on the wooden table, Murlyn avoided eye-contact with the boy, anxiously waiting for an answer to come.

Eventually, Lizzie spoke to Murlyn. *The truth will set you free, dear friend.*

Ugh. Murlyn huffed, *why does the truth have to be so complicated?* Sighing yet again, he finally focused on the little boy. "Of course, you are your father's number one priority." Murlyn smiled at Blaine. "Do you know what exile means, little man?" Murlyn questioned, his voice calm and casual as he changed the subject.

Frowning, Blaine nodded. "It means we can't enter the kingdom."

"That's right. If anyone were to see either of us in the kingdom then everyone back here in the Forest of Wishes would be in a lot of trouble."

"I know that." Blaine mumbled, his voice whinier than it been just moments prior. "But why can't we sneak in to go see Natalie anyway? You have Papa's invisibility cloak, right?"

I knew this day was going to come. But I was hoping to be able to avoid it for a few more years. Lizzie, please give me the right words. "Bud, do you remember Rosie?"

"Sure," the little boy frowned again. "I miss her, but she was your best friend, so I know you miss her more than anyone else in the forest."

Nodding vigorously, Murlyn agreed. "I miss her every day, but I know she is right where she needs to be."

"What do you mean? You told me a couple of weeks after the attack that she moved to Embersville."

Here goes, Murlyn thought. *I hope he understands that I only told him that to spare his feelings.* "I know, bud," Murlyn agreed. "But Rosie didn't actually move to Embersville. The truth is: I only told you that because I didn't want you to know that I gave Rosie the invisibility cloak and sent her off with Natalie."

The little boy stared at Murlyn, his face turning red. "Natalie was my best friend! How could you not send me with them?" He shouted, his voice full of anger and disbelief.

Murlyn placed a hand on Blaine's shoulder and squeezed lightly. "I am sorry little man, but I just couldn't risk it."

"I don't see why not," the little boy said defiantly, practically spitting the words out at the troll.

Letting out an exaggerated sigh, Murlyn looked upward. *Lizzie help me. Help me figure out what to say.*

Lizzie whispered: *Remind my boy how important it is that he be with his father.*

Taking a deep breath, the troll focused on Blaine and followed the advice of his long-departed comrade. "In all honesty, I didn't even consider it because I knew your father would say no. You belong here with us where we can protect you."

"I belong with Natalie. How can I trust you to protect me when you lied to me?"

"I'm sorry—"

"Don't!" Blaine shrugged Murlyn's hand off of his shoulder and took off, wheeling himself out of the hut in tears.

Oh Lizzie, I am so sorry to have disappointed your boy. I am so sorry. Hanging his head, Murlyn began to cry. *When are things going to get better?* He wondered as he scurried to his blue sapling where he allowed himself to cry tears of sorrow.

~

"MIND TELLIN' me what my boy is so upset about?" Benjamin asked, approaching Murlyn's sapling a couple of hours after his argument with Blaine.

Poking his head out of the sapling, Murlyn spoke, his voice full of trepidation. "I am so sorry, Benjamin. Your boy is really missing Natalie. I tried to explain to him why we can't go see her, but then he brought up the invisibility cloak."

"So?"

"Well, he got really upset when I told him that I sent your invisibility cloak with Rosie. He's wondering why I didn't send him with her."

Benjamin nodded. "I see. Say no more. I'll handle this with a good ol' father-son talk." Benjamin walked away from Murlyn's personal sapling and toward Blaine's treehouse with a determined expression on his face.

Murlyn wasn't sure Benjamin would be up to the task and so he jumped out of the tree to go and help. *Lizzie, please go and be with Benjamin right now and give him the right words to say.*

Murlyn watched the father kneel to his son's level. "Hey, my boy, can we talk for a minute?"

Blaine was sitting with *Marmoset's Bad Hair Day* open on his lap as the tears continued to flow down his face. Blaine nodded. "What do you want to talk about?" He mumbled, sniffling as he looked up from the book.

"Well, Murl just told me that you're a little upset that you didn't get to follow Rosie to the kingdom."

"Yeah that's right. And now I want to see Natalie. She is my best friend and I miss her," he said.

"I know, son. I miss her too. But you can't just run off to go see her. It's too dangerous. You could get into so much trouble."

Rolling his eyes, Blaine let out a huff. "I know. I know. Because we're in exile."

"Correct, but there is another, even more important, reason. Do you know what that reason is?" The little boy shook his head.

"People in Cinder's Edge aren't used to seeing people like you son. Chances are, if you went into the kingdom today it wouldn't even be accessible. People with disabilities are not seen as equals in Cinder's Edge. Trust me buddy, you're much safer here where Murl, the other trolls, and I can protect you and make sure you have everything you need."

"What about Natalie? Are you saying that I can never see her again?" Blaine asked, as fresh tears started welling up in his eyes.

Benjamin shook his head vehemently. "No, no, no, my boy. I've been working on a special pair of pants that will give you the ability to walk."

A smile graced Blaine's lips for the first time that day. "Really, Papa?" His eyes were suddenly sparkling with excitement.

"You betcha. I'm this close," he explained, holding his thumb and index finger an inch apart from each other. "The next time you see Natalie you'll be able to wear them, and it won't matter that Natalie was hypnotized. But for now, you need to stay here where I know you're safe. Is that understood?"

"Yes Papa, but—" Blaine begun to protest.

"No 'buts'; you stay here and keep readin' and I am gonna get back to work on those pants so we can get you up and walkin', okay son?" He asked before standing up and kissing his little boy on the head.

Leaning forward, Blaine smiled and briefly hugged his father's legs. "Get to work Papa," the little boy said sweetly before turning his attention back to *Marmoset's Bad Hair Day.*

～

WELL THAT WASN'T SO bad. Blaine looks happy, which is the most important thing.

"Murl, I know you've been listening in. You can come out now," Blaine called out.

"I'm sorry Blaine. I just wanted to hear what your father had to say and make sure that you were okay."

"I am," the little boy nodded. "Sorry I got mad at you. If I ask you something about what my father said, do you promise to tell me the truth?"

"I'll do you one better. I promise to never lie to you ever again."

Smiling brightly, the little boy shook his head in agreement. "Sounds good to me. Now, will you please tell me what does hyp-Hypno-" Blaine begun.

"Hypnosis?"

"Yeah that. What does hypnosis mean?"

Of all of the questions this kid could have thrown at me, why did it have to be that one? "Hypnosis is a way of encouraging people to relax, open their minds, and resolve their problems." Murlyn explained.

"That sounds complicated."

The woodland creature shook his head. "Just think of it as a way of getting someone to do or stop doing something he or she normally wouldn't. Sometimes, people know they're being hypnotized. Other times they don't. Does that help answer your question?"

"Yes, but what did Papa mean when he said Natalie was hypnotized?" The boy pressed.

The difficult questions just keep on coming. "Well, the truth is, little man, that hypnosis can be used to help people remember or forget something or someone. Natalie's dad hypnotized her and her mom to make them forget about you, me, your Papa, and the other trolls."

"So, if I see Natalie, she won't remember me?"

"Not if the hypnosis worked," Murlyn admitted sadly. "But look at it this way, bud, someday you'll have the pleasure of becoming friends with Natalie all over again."

"I guess that's a good way to see it," the little boy glanced from his book to Murlyn. "Want to read with me?"

"Sure, why don't you read out loud to me?"

Nodding, Blaine opened his mouth to begin reading, but closed it as the trunk of the sapling began to open, allowing his father to enter.

Benjamin lifted Blaine out of his wheelchair and squeezed him, smiling from ear to ear. "Our talk earlier must have brought us some good luck my boy. The pants I have been making for you are finally ready. Come try them on," he said, as he placed the boy back in his wheelchair.

"What do you mean the pants are done?" Murlyn asked. "I had no idea. Don't you think you should…" Murlyn didn't get to finish his words. Blaine was too excited.

"You mean it Papa? Am I really going to be able to walk?" He asked.

"Hopefully. Come and give 'em a try," he said, as he wheeled Blaine to the trunk of the sapling.

"Wait," Murlyn called out.

"What is it Murl?" Benjamin queried, an edge of frustration to his voice.

"May I speak to you privately for a moment please?"

"No, there is no time to waste." Benjamin exited the sapling with his son in tow.

"Ouch." the troll whispered as the partial gemstone in the center of his belly begun to throb. *There goes my treasure troll intuition. This is not going to end well. What the heck is Benjamin thinking? He should have come to me first. Blaine is so excited. When this doesn't go well, he is going to be crushed. Lizzie, be with your son and wrap your arms around him a little tighter than usual today,* Murlyn pleaded as he scurried into Benjamin's workshop, following closely behind the father and son.

❧

"WELL, how's about that son? They fit like a glove," Benjamin said, happily. "Grab my hands and I'll pull you up."

"Are you sure Papa?" Blaine asked, his voice full of trepidation.

Sighing, Benjamin looked to Murlyn. "Do me a favor and call the rest of the trolls in here, will ya?"

Moments later Percy, Bernie, Lilly, and the rest of the trolls piled into the workshop. "Wow, this place looks like a tornado just ran through it." Percy whispered as he settled in next to Murlyn.

"Yeah it does," Murlyn agreed quietly, scanning his surroundings. The collapsed work desk, crooked shelves, and scraps of denim, silk, and suede were scattered about, but it was the pair of denim pants walking freely around the workshop holding a pair of scissors that really shocked him. "Are you seeing what I am seeing?" Murlyn whispered to his red-headed friend as the pants walked by them for the third time.

Percy chuckled softly. "Let's find out." Clearing his throat, he got Benjamin's attention. "Benjamin, buddy, have you noticed anything other than trolls running around this place?"

Benjamin shook his head, clearly not interested and turned to his son.

"See my boy? We're all here. Just give it a shot," he encouraged.

Taking a deep breath, the little boy grabbed his father's hands.

"You okay there, little man?" Benjamin asked calmly after pulling him up out of his chair and into a standing position.

"I th-think so."

"Okay, now you need to activate the magic in the pants, so I need you to picture yourself walking and wish as hard as you can for it to happen, okay?"

"I don't know if I can do that Papa."

"Just try, my boy. Just try," the hopeful father urged. "We're all here for you." Letting out a huff, Benjamin looked to the trolls. "C'mon, guys. Give my boy some encouragement."

"You can do this Blaine," Percy encouraged as the woodland creatures begun to clap. "We're all here for you."

"Here goes," the little boy whispered, attempting to take a step forward. Smiling nervously, Blaine tightened his grip on his father's hands as his legs started to shake.

"That's it son. Keep coming," Benjamin encouraged.

Oh no... here we go, Murlyn thought as he watched the little boy fall to the ground following his third step. Gasps filled the air as Murlyn rushed to the crying little boy.

"What hurts little man?" Benjamin asked, his forehead wrinkled with worry as he examined his son for bumps and bruises.

"S-Something in my knee snapped," Blaine cried. "It really hurts."

Benjamin looked to Murlyn. "Get that quack Dr. Steinman. He's the best doc in the kingdom, right?" Benjamin's voice was full of panic.

"Yes, he is, but Benjamin, aren't you forgetting that we have been exiled?"

"It hurts so bad," the little boy sobbed, fresh tears welling up in his eyes. "Just do something!"

Oh, Lizzie please give me the strength to get through this and help your boy. His crying is breaking my heart. Murlyn examined the still crying child and saw that his right knee was slightly kinked and already swollen. *That's what Frederick's knee looked like when he dislocated his kneecap years ago,* Murlyn realized suddenly. Knowing there was no time to waste, he addressed the others. "Calm down everyone. Please calm down. I can fix this. Everyone just needs to focus on helping Benjamin keep Blaine calm while I tend to his knee."

"What do you mean tend to his knee? What are you going to do?" Benjamin asked frantically.

"The little man's kneecap is dislocated, so I am going to reset it. I need everyone to form a circle around him and think positive thoughts." Within moments, the trolls had done just that. "Here goes nothing." Murlyn whispered to himself. "Hey little man, what was the name of the book you were going to read to me earlier? You know the one that you and Natalie used to love to read?" Murlyn asked causally after a moment.

"Marmoset's baaaaaa-" The boy screamed.

Without waiting a moment longer, Murlyn pulled at Blaine's knee, putting the kneecap back in place. "You're all set bud. You'll be good as new soon enough. We just need to make sure you rest up, okay?"

Nodding, the still emotional little boy looked at his father. "Papa, will you stay with me while I rest?"

"Of course, I will! Then, as soon as you're better, I will get back to working on the pants."

"Oh my gosh, Papaw." Isabel said. "I can't believe your father was that focused on making you walk even after you dislocated your kneecap trying,"

"My father had the best of intentions, sweetheart," Blaine said sweetly. "He was just a bit misguided. It took both of us some time to figure that out."

"Indeed, he was," Murlyn agreed, looking to Isabel. "After the incident your Papaw was too scared to get out of the wheelchair, let alone try and walk, but that did nothing to deter your great grandpa." The troll's gaze traveled to Blaine. "I will never forget the fear in your eyes when your father suggested trying yet another pair of pants, just six weeks after you dislocated your kneecap," he said solemnly.

Blaine nodded. "I still remember how frightened I was," he admitted. His quiet, nonchalant, voice did nothing to hide the hurt he felt as he thought back to the memory. Murlyn could see the pain in his friend's eyes and he was transported through time, yet again, as he looked into them.

CHAPTER 9

*S*ounds like Blaine became as frustrated with his father making
magic pants as I did with finding a source of magic years ago. I
was almost as obsessed with that as I was with conquering Glomgurgle. He
chuckled at the thought. *How did I ever think that little ol' me was going
to defeat him?* Thinking back, he pondered the question. After a few
moments of intense thought, it was as if he had traveled through
time and was once again experiencing his search for a source of
magic in the midst of his quest to defeat Glomgurgle.

"If only snails were sources of magic," Dylock grumbled before
biting the head off of one of the tiny creatures.

The ground shook under his feet as Glomgurgle laughed and a
sound akin to a clap of thunder rolled through the volcano. "You are
beyond pathetic. I could have killed you a thousand times in the
past five years and gone after the black diamond myself, but I would
rather witness your misery."

Shaking his head, the troll spoke, his voice meek and hesitant as
he disguised his hatred for the dragon with feigned fear. "You'll s-
see v-very soon, Master. W-we will ha-have the black diamond
before you know it," he stammered.

"Keep telling your pathetic self that. I'm going after my next meal." Letting out another roar of laughter, the dragon left, eyeing a baby goat that was innocently grazing outside of the volcano.

Finally, I thought he'd never leave, Dylock thought, quickly sneaking into the forbidden corner of Mount Wishnik as he had each day since he'd first discovered the mushrooms. *Is that what I think it is?* He wondered aloud, having spotted an incandescent light. Another mushroom is the last thing I need, scoffing he headed back to the southeast side of the volcano.

"Ouch", he cried out as a sudden stabbing pain shot through his belly, nearly knocking the wind out of him. "Stupid troll intuition," he groaned. I thought once my gemstone was gone that would be gone, too. Reluctantly listening to his body, Dylock walked back to the northwest corner and gathered up the mushrooms before Glomgurgle could catch him. Once back in the privacy of the southeast side of the volcano, he studied the mushrooms, relieved to feel the pain in his belly subsiding.

Why is my intuition telling me to use this magic when it didn't work years ago? He wondered, tossing the mushrooms toward a lava crater behind him. Tilting his head back, he scoffed. *Dang, I missed.* Within seconds, a stabbing pain once again radiated through his core, knocking him to his knees. Instinctively grabbing his stomach, Dylock fought back tears. *Okay, okay, I get it. I'll use the mushrooms,* he whispered, a single tear trickling down his left cheek as he turned around and retrieved the fungus. *I can't let this pain take me down. I gotta do whatever it takes to get my hands on that black diamond. Heck I'll even eat two mushrooms,* he thought before doing so. Grabbing his stomach again, Dylock took a deep breath, let it out, and said the following spell:

> *"Give me insight into the life of the beloved princess of*
>   *Cinder's Edge.*
> *Allow me to see what makes her vulnerable,*
> *so I can convince her that my friendship is genuine*
> *before bringing her to her ultimate end,"*

Within moments, a cloud of smoke surrounded him, blurring his vision just as it had years prior. However, this time after his vision cleared he found himself alone in front of the Tree of Friendship. After five years in the cave with only Glomgurgle, he'd become no stranger to being alone, but the loneliness he felt in that moment, standing in front of the Tree of Friendship with not one friend standing beside him, left a hollow feeling in the pit of his stomach. Shaking his head, Dylock tried to dismiss the feeling. "I don't need any friends, he told himself. I will have everything I need once I get my hands on that black diamond." Excited by the prospect of finally being all mighty and powerful, the troll reached for some of the succulent blueberries he'd missed for so long from the tree. *What the heck?* His eyes widened in disbelief as he watched the tree evaporate into thin air the moment he tried to pick a berry, leaving in its place the words friends equal life. *I ate two mushrooms for a freakin' optical illusion?* Dylock wondered as the words disappeared just as quickly as the tree of Friendship had moments earlier.

Letting out an evil laugh, the troll considered the results of his latest spell. *Friends equal life... what does that mean anyway? Magic is life. I'm gonna show the royals, the trolls, and all their little friends—wait that's it. Friends. If I include the princess's friends in the spell, then it will encompass the entire kingdom.* Elated by his epiphany, Dylock turned and grabbed the four remaining mushrooms. *The black diamond is about to be mine!* Smirking, he lifted a mushroom to his mouth.

"What the hell is going on here!" Glomgurgle bellowed, reentering the cave.

Startled, Dylock dropped the mushrooms. He sighed inwardly. *The overgrown lizard has perfect timing, as always.* "I am just preparing a spell to get the black diamond," Dylock hid the mushrooms behind his back, feigning innocence.

"Do you actually think I don't know what you've been up to?" The dragon questioned, his pupils glowing fiery red as he eyed the woodland creature. "This is my volcano," he snarled, a smug quality to his raspy threatening voice.

"Then you know how hard I've been working. Like I said before,

I'm not going to give up until the black diamond is back in your possession," Dylock persisted.

Small smoke rings escaped, the dragon's nostrils as he snarled again. "Remember what I said about torturing you?" He queried, before expanding his wings and flying over the troll's head. "It's one of my life's simple pleasures," the dragon growled. Before Dylock could respond, the giant creature took a deep breath and let it out, shooting fire directly at the troll's hands.

Biting down on his lip, Dylock stifled the urge to cry out.

"Your burns will heal in time, but the pain will return to your hands and radiate through your entire being any time you step foot into the northwest corner. Now, get back to work," Glomgurgle growled, flying off toward his lair within the volcanic cave.

As Dylock watched the dragon disappear into the distance, a profound sense of hopelessness washed over him. It was in that moment that the warm and fuzzy feeling that had disgusted him since he cast the first spell had been replaced by the sense of emptiness he'd felt after casting the second. *Buck up*, he told himself. *Nothing worth doing is ever easy and all this struggle will be worth it once that winged bully and Cinder's Edge are conquered once and for all.*

"You all right there, bud?" Percy questioned, bringing Dylock back to the present as he walked by.

"Hmm? Oh yes, yes, I'm fine." The stunned four-leaf clover adorned woodland creature answered making it a point to sound casual.

Nodded hesitantly, Percy placed a hand on Dylock's right shoulder and squeezed gently. "It's okay if you have the occasional setback. You spent many years in that volcano. We are here for you no matter what. Treasure trolls stick together, remember?"

Dylock flashed a smile. "I wouldn't be here if it were not for that, but please don't worry about me. I'm fine. I promise."

Percy nodded again. "Good. Try to get some rest and I'll see you at the ceremony later," the red-haired troll said before scurrying away.

Dylock let out a breath as he watched Percy leave. "Whew. That was a close one. I'm so glad he didn't ask where my head was. That would've been so embarrassing."

As he struggled to get comfortable yet remain unnoticed near the window, he considered what his red-haired friend had said. *Percy's right, treasure trolls do stick together. I hope I can eventually think of a way to show my fellow trolls that I will never betray them again. For now, I suppose I must continue to explore the past.* Sighing, he lied flat, positioned some moss under his head, and continued to listen to his friend talk about days gone by.

AN INSTANT after Murlyn looked into Blaine's eyes, he found himself back in year 576 of King Frederick and Queen Alexandria's reign, his fifth year of being in exile with the Bensons, struggling to make ten-year-old Blaine follow his father's orders.

"But I don't wanna try on another pair of pants for Papa," Blaine whined. "My knee just got better," he mumbled as he pushed his chair up to the table in the center of the hut.

Climbing onto the least wobbly of the chairs, the troll brought himself to the young boy's level, placed a hand on his shoulder, and squeezed lightly. "I know, little man, but all of the other trolls and I will be there. We'll make sure that you are just fine."

"Yeah, that's what you said last time."

I should've seen that response coming. This kid is as stubborn as his father. What am I going to do?

Lizzie's sweet voice floated into his mind… *Remember, my boy has to know he's safe.*

Murlyn racked his brains and then it came to him. "Perhaps you can wear the gear Rosie gave you, just to be on the safe side."

"Safety gear won't make any difference, Murl. I haven't told Papa or anyone else, but the pants he makes aren't comfy and Rosie's extra gear will just make it worse."

"Fair enough, bud. Go to the workshop and keep your Papa occupied. I'll go talk to some other trolls and see if we can come up with another way to keep you safe while wearing the magic pants." With that, Murlyn climbed out of the chair, scurried to the red sapling that Percy called home, and explained the problem he was trying to solve.

Percy reluctantly poked his head out of his fern, "C'mon, Murl, short of building a new bubble-wrap-coated floor, there is no way we can keep that kid from getting hurt when wearing the pants Benjamin makes."

Letting out a huff, Murlyn shook his head. "Percy, get serious. Blaine is too scared to even try another pair of the pants Benjamin is making. You and I both know that won't go over well. We have to figure something out."

Percy opened his mouth to respond, but closed it as Bernie walked up.

"Hey guys, I couldn't help but overhear and, personally, I think Percy's idea just might work," the orange-haired woodland creature said confidently.

Murlyn looked from Percy to Bernie and back. "What in the name of wishes are you two thinking? We have to be serious about this."

"I am being serious," the orange-haired troll argued. "I mean, I know we can't cover the floor in bubble wrap, but I like the idea of the floor protecting the little guy from a fall." Pausing, the chubbiest of woodland creatures considered his thought. "Maybe we should make him something to walk on."

"Okay, now I understand where you're going with this," Murlyn nodded.

"Yeah," Percy agreed. "We can make a magic carpet."

"Yeah, but if we start using magical materials or thread, how is that any better than using it to make the pants?" Murlyn questioned.

"At least our carpet would help Blaine instead of just reminding him of something he can't do," Bernie mumbled under his breath.

What should I do Lizzie? How are we going to help your boy through this?

Think outside of the box, dear friend, Lizzie's sweet voice advised moments later. *Magic materials don't just exist in my Benjamin's workshop. There is magic throughout the entire forest.*

Murlyn contemplated Lizzie's words. *Hmm... magic is all over the forest, so...*

"Uh oh, why did your eyes just light up?" Bernie questioned warily.

"I've got an idea," Murlyn said excitedly. "Come with me fellas."

With that, Murlyn led his fellow woodland creatures to the bright pink fern that had once been Rosie's home and explained that they were going to use the branches and needles to make a magic carpet for Blaine.

"Are you sure you want to do that, Murl?" Percy queried, his voice full of skepticism. "I mean, with this being Rosie's home and all."

Shrugging his shoulders, Murlyn looked down at his feet and considered the question. *Is this a bad idea? Would Rosie be upset?* As if on cue, his half of the gemstone that he shared with Rosie begun to glow bright pink.

"Something tells me our glittery pink-haired friend wouldn't want it any other way," Murlyn said. "Besides, it's not like we're destroying it or anything, we're just borrowing some materials. Now stop worrying and grab a branch."

After gathering up the materials, the three woodland creatures stood in front of the sapling, linked hands, and focused their thoughts on Blaine and his wish to be safe while trying on the magic pants. Within moments, three bright lights traveled from their gemstones to the pile of branches.

"That's beautiful," Murlyn said breathlessly as the bright lights around the tree dissipated to reveal the branches had been woven together into a gorgeous carpet with red, blue, orange and bright pink stars throughout. "It definitely has Rosie's touch."

"How do we know it's going to work?" Bernie asked.

There's only one way to find out," Murlyn said. *I really hope this works. Lizzie, be with us and protect your boy this afternoon,* Murlyn pleaded as he led his friends to Benjamin's workshop.

~

"WHAT IN THE name of wishes took you so long?" Blaine asked as Murlyn, Percy, and Bernie stepped into the workshop.

"You've been around trolls for too long, little man," Murlyn chuckled.

"Ain't that the truth?" Benjamin said, looking up from the SewSmart 3000 at his work desk. "He wouldn't even try on the pants until ya'll got here. Now that they are here can we get to it Blaine?"

"Help me," Blaine mouthed toward Murlyn.

"It's funny you ask that." Murlyn winked at the little boy. "These guys and I actually made a carpet for the little guy to walk on." The dark blue-haired troll held the carpet out in front of himself for all of them to see.

"Cool," Blaine said, examining the carpet. "Look, Papa, it's got stars on it."

"What'd you go and make that for?" Benjamin asked, ignoring his son's excitement. "My boy's gonna be just fine. He don't need no fancy carpet to walk on," he said defiantly.

"But Papa, I want to use it," Blaine insisted. "Murl says it will keep me from getting hurt again."

"Is that so?" Benjamin said with a hint of skepticism in his voice.

"Mm hmm," Murlyn nodded nervously. "Just watch and see." *Lizzie, I really hope you're with us right now because this has to work,* he thought, stretching the carpet out in preparation for Blaine's steps.

"Are you sure it's safe?" Blaine asked.

"Would I make anything for you that would be unsafe?" Murlyn questioned. "Just try it. Everything will be fine." *I sure hope I'm right*, the troll thought, nervously glancing from his fellow woodland creatures to the carpet, waiting for Benjamin to help his boy into the pants.

"Okay, my boy, are you ready to give these pants a whirl? I have a real good feelin' about 'em."

Glancing from the pants to the magic carpet, the little boy nodded hesitantly. "Let's give this a shot."

Please let this work, Murlyn thought, holding his breath as he watched Blaine grasp his father's hands, slowly stand up, and take a hesitant step onto the magic carpet.

"That's it son, take another step," Benjamin encouraged, smiling brightly.

"But, Papa, something doesn't feel right."

"I'm right here son. You're gonna be fine. Take another step."

Letting out a quiet sigh, the little boy reluctantly did as he was told, only to fall onto the magic carpet.

"Wow, the carpet definitely works." The dark blue-haired woodland creature whispered as the magic carpet safely lowered Blaine to the ground the moment he fell.

"Papa, I told you something didn't feel right," the young boy whined, looking up at his father.

"So sorry, my boy. I think I need to go back to the silver silk and matching thread. I'll get to work straight away."

"Don't you think you should at least get me up first?" Blaine asked, his tiny voice full of frustration.

"Oh yes, of course," Benjamin assured before helping his son change and transferring him back into his wheelchair. Before the little boy could even fasten his seatbelt, his father was back at his work desk tinkering with the sew machine.

"Wow, great grandpa had some serious tunnel vision," Isabel said, her eyes wide and full of disbelief.

"Indeed, he did," Murlyn agreed. "I wish I could tell you it didn't last, but that's not the case. As the years rolled by, your great grandpa only became more and more determined to help his son walk. The more determined he was, the more resistant your Papaw became.

As Murlyn spoke, the years once again disappeared for Blaine. Within moments, he found himself back in year 589 of King Frederick and Queen Alexandria's reign, being rudely awakened by his father on the morning of his eighteenth birthday.

"Wake up, my boy. You're an adult now. You can't be sleepin' in all day." Benjamin called out.

"C'mon Papa," Blaine groaned, barely lifting his head from the pillow on his cot. "The sun only rose an hour ago and it's my birthday. At least let me sleep in a little bit."

Rolling his eyes, the caring father sighed. "Fine, but like I said, don't be all day. Me and the trolls have some gifts for ya and Murlyn conjured up a cake. I was thinkin' we could do lunch."

"Sorry, I can't... I have plans."

"Very funny, son. I will see ya at lunch," Benjamin said, before heading out the door.

Ugh, why did Papa have to wake me so early? Blaine wondered as he tossed and turned, struggling to go back to sleep. *Screw it,* he thought after a few minutes. *I'll just get up and go now. It's probably best that I get a head start anyway. Today is the day,* he thought as he pulled his chair over to the cot and transferred into it effortlessly. "I am an adult now and it's time I start acting like it," he whispered to himself. Completing his morning routine in record time, Blaine ripped a corner from a page of *The 411 on Feng Shui*, scribbled the words *back by dinner*, tossed it on the table, and headed out the door.

"Hey there, Blaine. Happy Birthday. What brings you out this way?" Bernie questioned, stopping him when he was halfway to the edge of the forest.

"Thanks Bernie. I just thought I'd venture out for some fresh air," Blaine explained, trying to keep his voice casual.

"This is definitely a good day for it," the orange haired troll nodded. "What are your other plans for your birthday?"

"We're having a special dinner tonight," Blaine explained, placing his hands onto the wheels of his chair. "I hate to be rude, but if I want to be back by then I really should be going."

"Okay, but before you do, I was wondering, have you ever read anything about what to do when a troll's hair starts falling out?"

Letting out a huff, Blaine eyed the troll. "Your hair looks as crazy as ever. It's not falling out. Now, if you'll excuse me, I—"

"But my hair *is* falling out," the triangle-adorned woodland creature insisted, "Look!" Bending down in front of Blaine, the troll parted a section of hair. "It's receding, can't you see?"

At this rate I won't get anywhere until night fall, Blaine thought. Sighing, he looked the treasure troll straight in the eye. "Give it a rest. Your hair looks fine. A little receding wouldn't hurt if you ask me," Blaine said before wheeling past him.

"W-wait. There's one more thing," Bernie called out.

While he found it easy to ignore Bernie's pleas, Blaine stopped the moment he heard his father's voice. "Hey there son, where ya goin' so fast?" The loving father queried as he approached.

Turning to face Benjamin, he flashed a smile. "Can't a guy take a long walk without facing the inquisition?" He asked innocently.

Shaking his head, the caring father shot him a look. "Ya never were a good liar, son. Why did ya bother to leave this note if you're just taking a walk, huh?"

"I just, uh—"

"C'mon Blaine. My gemstone has been throbbing since the moment I saw you. My troll intuition is telling me something's up. I'm sure the other trolls would agree if they saw you. And your father knows something is going on, so just come clean," Bernie pleaded.

Sighing, Blaine lamented. "Fine. If you must know. I am taking control of my own destiny. I am an adult now, so I've decided to go into Cinder's Edge, talk to the king, and convince him to let us out of exile."

Benjamin's response was instant. "You can't be serious," he said, his voice laced with disbelief.

"I'm very serious. I am an adult now. That means I can make my own decisions so if you'll excuse me, I'll be going." Turning back, Blaine continue down the path toward the edge of the forest.

"Son, please, think about this. The kingdom could be dangerous for someone like ya. It's not accessible and even if you could find your way around, Frederick is a very stubborn man. Adults make responsible decisions. Is it responsible for ya to go somewhere ya could be in danger?"

Blaine sighed yet again. *I knew Papa was going to be like this. Why must he be so stubborn?* "Papa, I know your scared, but you've got to let me do this. I need to make a decision about Cinder's Edge for myself.

Benjamin nodded urgently. "I understand that my boy, but if you could at least wait until I make another pair of pants ya'd—"

"Papa this is my decision. I am going now." Blaine said defiantly before once again continuing down the path.

"You leave me no choice my boy," Benjamin declared before turning his attention to Bernie. "Bernie, the wish on my heart today is for you to stop Blaine from going to Cinder's Edge."

Turning his head, Blaine spotted Bernie placing a hand on his gemstone. "No!" He shouted angrily.

Bernie looked at Blaine, his orange eyes full of apprehension. "Sorry," he shrugged.

> *"This young man thinks his idea is courageous,*
> *but his father feels it is outrageous,*
> *so allow light magic to keep him from jumping off a*
> *metaphorical ledge*
> *and venturing into Cinder's Edge."*

I cannot let them stop me from taking control of my destiny, Blaine thought, backing away from the light that shone from the troll's gemstone. Despite his resistance the glowing orange light was surrounding Blaine and his wheelchair moments later. As the light disappeared, Blaine shot his father a look. "Nice try Papa, but this is my destiny and magic cannot be used to manipulate destiny," he declared, turning his attention back to the gravel path. Taking a deep breath, he pushed his wheelchair forward only to have an invisible forcefield send him right back to where he started.

Benjamin smirked. "Looks like the little trip you planned wasn't part of your destiny, my boy. Why don't you come back to the hut and we'll open your gifts?"

"No thanks, like I said, I'll be back by dinner." With that, he headed to the one place in the forest that he knew he could blow off steam… his treehouse.

Since the day it was created, Blaine's treehouse had been his sanctuary. Initially, it consisted of various eight to ten-foot ramps and a few rings hung from the ceiling, but over the years many curved-shaped, pyramid-inspired, and dome-like ramps of various sizes had been added. *Time to fly*, Blaine thought as he put on his helmet and safety gear. With practiced ease, he made his way to the top of a 20-foot ramp, using only a knotted rope and momentum to pull himself up. Leaning forward slightly, he went down the ramp. *Here it goes*, he thought, using his abdominal muscles to tuck himself into a ball and get enough momentum to spin in the air and land solidly on the platform of the ramp.

Yes, nailed it, Blaine's lips broke into a genuine smile for the first time that day. *Landing jumps makes me feel so free. Why can't everything be this much fun?* He wondered as he continued performing effortless jumps and wheelies from every ramp. Soon, sweat dripped into the young man's eyes and he found it difficult to catch his breath, but he kept going, chasing the adrenaline rush. *I should just stay here*, Blaine thought, once again at the top of a ramp ready to jump. *I feel like I can do any—*

Suddenly, a loud whooshing sound startled Blaine from his thoughts as the tree trunk expanded and opened.

"Oh, hey Murlyn," he said by way of greeting. "What have you been up to?"

"I should be the one asking you that question."

Blaine shrugged. "I was just blowing off a little steam."

"A little?" The troll chuckled. "You've been cooped up in here all day. It's nearly dinner time."

"Did you hear about this morning?" Blaine brought himself down the ramp to meet Murlyn at ground level.

"Yes, and if you tell Bernie, your father, or anyone else I said this I'll deny it, but I wish they had let you go to Cinder's Edge. I am proud of you for trying."

"I really thought it was part of my destiny but here I am. I don't get it," Blaine said solemnly.

"Don't lose hope, bud," Murlyn encouraged. "If going to Cinder's Edge becomes part of your destiny then neither man nor magic will stop you from going. If you ask me, your destiny is greater than you can even imagine. You just need to find your purpose before you can achieve it."

Tilting his head slightly to the right, Blaine considered the thought. "I hope you're right," he said after a moment.

"Trust me," Murlyn assured as they headed out of the treehouse. "I know all about destiny."

If a purpose is what you need to find an order to achieve your destiny, I'm not going to stop until I find my purpose, Blaine thought as he headed back to the hut with a proud, hopeful Murlyn by his side.

～

"So, Papaw, how many times do you think you had to tell great-grandpa that you didn't want to try on anymore pants? Isabel asked, stunning Blaine back to the present.

"It seemed like I said it countless times over the years, but, it wasn't until the eve of our twentieth year that I got what I thought was the smart idea to do something about his tunnel vision," he explained, chuckling at the thought.

I can relate, Dylock thought as he listened to his friends talk about the tunnel vision Blaine's father had. *I definitely had a one-track mind when it came to finding mushrooms and conquering Glomgurgle. Heck, I even ventured into the northwest corner knowing I'd burn to a crisp. Sure, it was partially due to my troll intuition, but I had tunnel vision nonetheless.* Thinking back once again caused a time warp for Dylock and he soon found himself back in Mount Wishnik searching for mushrooms.

"Ouch," he whispered, as a sharp pain gripped his bellybutton. *Troll intuition strikes again. My intuition tried to tell me something about the mushrooms years ago, but I ignored it. Well no more. If the scars on my hands mean anything, it's that the mushrooms are key to my getting out of here. I'll find them and another spell to get the black diamond if it's the last thing I do,* Dylock told himself as he walked towards the forbidden corner of the volcano after Glomgurgle left in search of sustenance.

What the heck? Dylock wondered out loud as light hit his bellybutton, instantly making the pain he felt disappear. Ignoring the warning Glomgurgle had given him years earlier, Dylock ran to the northwest corner. *I knew it. I just knew the mushrooms had to be here.*

"AAAAHHHH," Dylock cried out the moment he reached for the mushrooms. Instantly, the woodland creature felt as though bubbling hot lava had exploded inside his chest and was coursing through his bloodstream, but he pushed through the pain until each small bit of fungus was securely hidden within his hair. Running to the safety of the southeast wing as quickly as his tiny legs could take him, he let out a breath as the pain he felt inside dissipated as quickly as it appeared.

Yes, I got 'em. There's no way I'm gonna let that scaly overgrown lizard get in my way. Carefully, freeing the mushrooms from his dishelved hair, he smirked. *Now to work a little magic.* Lifting a mushroom to his mouth, he stopped short of biting it, having noticed black dots all over it. *What in the heck?* He wondered. Hesitantly sniffing the mushroom, he examined more closely. "This is tainted!" He shouted angrily. "That's scaly bully thought he could actually pull one over on me by poisoning these mushrooms with dark magic. Letting out a huff, he studied the mushroom and contemplated his next move.

Light magic conquers dark. But where is a troll like me going to find a source of light magic? he wondered. *Maybe I could go after some blueberries or—.* A loud growl stole Dylock's attention. *Is that overgrown lizard back already?* Quickly hiding the mushrooms in his hair, he followed the sound. Stepping just outside the volcano, he discovered the source. *Oh, it's just a wolf about to eat a rabbit,* he thought, turning to go back inside. *Wait, that's a baby rabbit,* he realized. *Baby animals are pure. I could use it as my source of light magic.* Excited by the mere thought, the troll turned on heel and faced the wolf. "Hey buddy, how about I give you a few strands of my hair in exchange for that rabbit? I need it for a spell, but don't worry because the magic in my hair will allow you to catch any other animal you'd like," the lie practically flew off his lips.

Eying the troll intently, as though he were sizing him up, the wolf let out a dry chuckle. The four-legged creature looked muscular even from a distance. White fur as shiny as the first snow of the winter season blanketed his entire body. Many other animals in the forest envied the wolf's pristine appearance and he carried himself in a way that let them know he knew it. "The name's Tobias and we are not friends," he growled. "Animals around the land talk. I know that you no longer have magic. I find the fact that you would lie just to get this rabbit rather pitiful. I am just going to give it to you, so you'll leave me alone," the wolf growled before giving him the dead rabbit carcass. "I hope that whatever spell you're doing puts some life back into you because you look so sad and just plain empty," Tobias declared before scampering back into the forest.

I can't believe that stupid wolf. I will show him and every other creature in the forest how not sad I am once I capture the princess and get the black diamond. Bet no one will take pity on me then. Empowered by the idea of absolute power, Dylock retrieved the tainted mushroom from his hair and held it in his left hand. After securing the baby rabbit carcass in his right hand, he quickly recited the following spell:

> *"Light magic conquers dark.*
> *Allow the pure light magic within this baby rabbit's heart*
> *to function like a dart*
> *and from this mushroom completely remove dark magic's*
> > *mark."*

The white-haired woodland creature's eyes widened as a puff of pink smoke swirled between the rabbit and mushrooms and disappeared in mere seconds, leaving only the rabbit remains and pure white mushrooms in its wake. "Oh, My God...it worked!" Smiling from pointy ear to pointy ear for the first time in years, Dylock studied the mushroom as his heart pounded in his chest. *This is it. After I do a spell and capture the princess, the black diamond will be mine.* Just thinking about total power over the realm made the tiny troll tingle from head to toe. Unable to stand the anticipation, Dylock lifted the mushroom to his mouth but stopped short of eating it when he heard stomping in the distance. *The scaly fire breather must be back. World domination will have to wait. For now, I'll just dream about the sweet, succulent taste of revenge.*

"Now is my chance," Dylock whispered to himself as the cold settled into the volcano that evening and the dragon begun to snore. Once the woodland creature was certain that he'd figured out the perfect wording for the spell, he reached into his dishevled hair for the mushrooms. "What the—AAAAHHHHHH!" Dylock couldn't help but scream as a colony of bats swooped into the volcano and stole the mushrooms from his messy hair.

Moments later, the sound of thunder rolled through the cave as the dragon exploded with laughter. "I should be angry with you for defying me, but I can't be. Your misery is so much fun to watch," Glomgurgle snarled.

As the reality that the mushrooms had been stolen sank in, the troll realized he was going to have to start over and felt completely defeated. "I don't get it," he shouted after a moment. "If you want me to get the black diamond back for you so badly then why do you keep torturing me?"

"Like I said before, I torture you because I enjoy it. Now get back to work and be quiet so I can sleep!" Glomgurgle bellowed angrily.

I'll show you what real torture is as soon as I get my hands on that black diamond, Dylock thought to himself deciding in that moment to not only get revenge, but to kill Glomgurgle in the most torturous way he could as soon as possible.

"You look much better than the last time I saw you," Tobias said, once again bringing Dylock back to the present.

"Thank goodness for that," Dylock whispered, standing up to talk to the wolf. "You look just the same. Haven't aged a day."

"What's with the whispering?" Tobias queried, his growl matching the woodland creature's auditory level.

Instantly frowning, the troll hung his head. "I don't want anyone in the hut to know I am out here," he admitted sheepishly.

"If that's the case, then why are you here?" Tobias growled.

In that moment, as Dylock considered his answer, a bit of the hatred he'd felt toward the four-legged creature years ago returned. Finally, he said, "I could ask you the same question. The area around Mount Wishnik is your territory."

Tobias let out a low underwhelming growl. "Fair enough. I didn't see you, you didn't see me. I'll leave you be but, before I go, I have to say this new persona of yours would be more believable if you'd stop acting like a creepy stalker."

Maybe I haven't changed as much as I'd like to think, Dylock thought, his hatred of Tobias increasing a little more as he watched the snowy-white wolf leave. Dismissing the thought just as quickly as it came, the treasure troll shook his head. *No, the wolf's just trying to get to me. I learned not to trust him a long time ago. I can't falter now. I won't. I need to focus on the point of my spell,* he reminded himself as he lied back down in the moss beneath the window and tried to focus on listening to Murlyn's calm yet very serious voice.

CHAPTER 10

As his friend continued speaking of long ago, Murlyn found himself drifting through his memories to the day in the year 591, the final year of King Frederick's and Queen Alexandria's reign over Cinder's Edge, that Blaine told him something that would change their lives forever.

"Okay, but this is the last time," Blaine insisted as he looked at the newest pair of pants his father had created. "In fact, I'm taking this with me as well." He placed a book called *How to Easily Hypnotize* on his lap and opened the door of the hut.

"Since when have you been reading about hypnosis?" Murlyn asked.

"Since I decided to hypnotize Papa so that he will accept my disability and no longer make any more of those awful pants."

"W-wait," Murlyn called out as he followed the young man out the door. "Blaine, please don't do this," the troll begged as he continued to follow the young man. "Trust me. You'll regret it. Nothing good will come from taking such drastic measures."

Letting out a huff, Blaine stopped in his tracks and turned to face Murlyn. "If I can't take drastic measures then what can I do? I'm so sick of this. I just want him to accept me as I am."

"I know, bud," the troll shook his head. "The thing is, your father loves you and only wants what is best for you. Someday, he'll realize in his own time that his acceptance is all you need. I am sure of it."

Blaine chucked weakly, "I used to think that too, but it's been twenty years. Is there anything we can do to speed up the process?"

Oh, Lizzie, I am tired of not knowing how to answer your boy's hard questions. I could really use your guidance right now. What do I say?

Lizzie spoke loud and clear… *Perhaps now is the time to seek Rosie's help.*

Yes, of course. Why didn't I think of that? Murlyn's heart suddenly started pounding in his chest.

"Your eyes just lit up. Let me guess?" Blaine chuckled. "Ma just gave you an idea?"

"Hey, don't mock me. Your mother's guidance has gotten me through some tough times."

"Is her guidance going to help us through this?"

"Only time will tell, but I am hopeful. We need to head to the workshop before your father starts to worry. Don't do anything drastic. Just humor your father as always and I'll handle the rest," Murlyn winked at Blaine.

"Okay, but if whatever you have planned doesn't work, I will take matters into my own hands," Blaine warned.

"There ya guys are," Benjamin said by way of greeting as Murlyn and his son entered the workshop. "I was beginnin' to think ya'll ran away."

"That's not such a bad idea," Blaine mumbled.

Benjamin looked at his son. "What was that, my boy?"

"Nothing Papa, come help me."

"You're lookin' dapper as always, son," Benjamin encouraged moments after helping his son into the pants.

"Thanks Papa, can you lay out the magic carpet now?"

"Of course, my boy. Of course." Benjamin quickly rolled out the star-covered carpet in front of his son's wheelchair.

Here we go again, Murlyn thought as he watched Benjamin help his son into a standing position for what seemed like the millionth time. Yet, Murlyn still encouraged the young man. "You can do this. Your father and I are right here with you."

Taking a deep breath, Blaine slowly stepped forward.

"That's it son, take another step," Benjamin insisted.

The young man sighed. "Don't rush me, Papa," his voice edged with frustration as he slowly took three more steps.

Wow. Lizzie, your boy has actually taken four steps this time. This might actually work... Suddenly the magic carpet lowered Blaine to the floor. *Uh oh, no such luck,* the troll rushed toward Blaine. "You okay, Bud?"

Benjamin hurried to get Blaine up and back into his wheelchair. Shaking his head, the young man frowned "Something has got to give," he whispered, quickly fastening his seatbelt.

"Sorry about that, my boy," Benjamin said. "But you took four steps this time, so I think we're getting closer. I am gonna work on it till it's perfect and you're up and runnin' around. I promise."

Letting out a huff, Blaine eyed the treasure troll. "Figure something out," he mouthed.

Nodding quickly, the troll turned his attention to Benjamin. "Before you get too busy working on the pants again, will you look around and see if you can find some of the material you used to make that invisibility cloak you gave me?"

"What're you askin' about that for, Murl? I thought you gave it to Rosie years ago. If I recall correctly, this guy here was pretty upset about it." Chuckling softly, the loving father pointed his head toward his son.

Murlyn nodded, "Yes, indeed. That's exactly right. But lately my treasure troll intuition has been telling me that an invisibility cloak might be a good way to entertain the younger trolls, so I was going to make another."

"Well, if there is any of that material left, it will be on the shelf off to the far right, above my work desk."

Blaine chuckled, eyeing the partially broken, disordered workspace. "You mean what used to be your work desk. How do you even know where anything is in this place, Papa?"

"Don't underestimate the power of organized chaos, my boy," Benjamin mumbled.

Those two are going to be distracted for a while. Now's my chance. He glanced over his shoulder at the father and son. *Lizzie, please let this work. This plan has to work.* Murlyn carefully climbed onto the half broken, unorganized shelf in search of the familiar shiny black material.

"Got it," he whispered after a moment having found it between piles of suede and denim material. "I'll see you guys later."

"Wait, Murl—" Benjamin called out as Murlyn ran out of the workshop. *I've got to do this quick before someone foils the plan. Please give me strength Lizzie,* the woodland creature thought, running as quickly as his tiny legs would take him to the crimson fern that his red-haired friend called home.

Taking a deep breath, he frantically knocked on the tree trunk. "Percy, are you here?" He called out. After a moment, the red-haired troll stuck his head out of the sapling.

"What in the name of wishes are you yellin' about?" Percy asked, his voice laced with irritation. "Can't a troll get some shut eye while he's not helping that crazy magician?"

"So sorry, Percy, but this is important. Here is a piece of the material Benjamin used to make his invisibility cloak. I need to use magic to make a second cloak, using this material," he explained, his voice full of urgency.

"Did you fall and hit your head?" Percy questioned, as he looked Murlyn up and down like he'd gone mad. "We have been stuck in exile with the same beings for the last twenty years, why do you need an invisibility cloak all of the sudden?"

Letting out an exaggerated sigh Murlyn whispered his plan to Percy.

Wide-eyed, mouth agape, Percy silently studied his friend once again. "Now I am more than certain you have fallen on your head. How can you even think of going into the kingdom? How many times have you told Benjamin that magic cannot be used to manipulate fate or destiny? Have you lost your mind?"

"This isn't about me. It's about everyone. I know it's risky, but it could benefit the greater good."

Percy let out a sarcastic chuckle. "Are you forgetting about what happened to you the last time you used magic to benefit the greater good? What am I supposed to do if my gemstone disappears and you're off gallivanting in Cinder's Edge?"

Lizzie... why doesn't anyone understand how ingenious this plan is? Please be here with me as I try to convince him. Taking a deep breath, Murlyn reasoned with his friend. "I, of all creatures, know that magic comes with a price, but when it comes to Blaine and Natalie, I'm willing to pay whatever the price. Can't you understand that? You practically helped me raise them for cryin' out loud."

"I can't believe you actually went there. You're not going to let this go, are you?"

"Not until you use a little magic." Murlyn insisted, pushing the shiny black material at his friend.

Letting out a huff, Percy grabbed the sparkly cloth, placed it over his gemstone and spoke, a slight edge to his usually calm voice.

"This cloth once had the power to make someone invisible.
That magic is needed once again,
so I enchant it to make the goal reachable for my friend."

"Seriously that's never going to work? You didn't even use the full power of your gemstone." Murlyn said angrily. "How...?" irritation suddenly gone, he smiled from pointy ear to pointy ear, as the shiny cloth begun to glow.

"See? All it takes is a little bit of magic my friend."

"Thanks, Percy. I promise you won't regret it." Murlyn called out, while quickly pulling the material from his friend's stomach and rushing off. *This is going to work Lizzie. I can feel it. It's going to change everything.* And with that, Murlyn made his way to the Tree of Friendship.

TAKING A DEEP BREATH, Murlyn focused his thoughts on Rosie. He rubbed his half of the gemstone he shared with her as hard as he could. The moment it started glowing he spoke, his voice crystal clear and full of hope.

> *"I share this gemstone with an old and loyal friend.*
> *The time has come for us to reunite.*
> *Please bring her location to light*
> *so our long separation can finally come to an end."*

Moments later, the woodland creature smiled brightly as the gemstone lit up like a crystal ball and revealed that Rosie was sitting in the throne room trying to comfort a very solemn-looking Natalie. *It looks like they need me as much as I need them.* Sighing, he waited for the image of his old friend to disappear, threw the newly-made invisibility cloak over himself, and ventured onto the path toward the kingdom.

I COULD'VE USED an invisibility cloak while searching for fungus all those years ago. Then again, I was so lost back then that nothing could've helped me. When I think back to those years it almost seems like I was a different troll. Why did I take Tobias's advice? What the heck was I thinking? As Dylock contemplated those questions, he once again got lost in memories of the past. In mere moments, he found himself in the volcano searching for mushrooms yet again.

WHERE THE HECK are those mushrooms? Where could that winged bully have hidden them? Those thoughts and questions swirled around in Dylock's mind as he walked around Mount Wishnik in search of mushrooms unable to find them anywhere. *This is pointless.* The emptiness he'd felt inside for years intensified as he realized that he'd walked through every inch of the volcano and there were no mushrooms to be found. Letting out a huff, Dylock ventured outside the cave. *That wolf mentioned years ago that animals in the forest talk. Maybe they'll know something.*

"You look even worse then you did years ago," a familiar voice said just mere moments after he'd stepped outside the volcano.

Sneering at the wolf, Dylock nodded. "Yeah, yeah, whatever. I look awful. I know. You seen any mushrooms lately?"

Tobias eyed him intently. "Seems to me, if you want to get out of that volcano as much as it looks like you should then I am not the one you should be asking," he growled pointedly.

Dylock sighed. "Can you help me or not?"

"I just did," Tobias insisted, growling louder. "Confront that idiot dragon. Prove to him once and for all that you're not intimidated by him unless... you're not scared of him, are you?" The wolf questioned, growling warily.

Scoffing, Dylock shook his head vehemently. "That's absurd. Of course not."

"Go prove it," Tobias urged.

"Oh, I'll do more than prove I am not scared of him. I'll conquer him," Dylock declared before heading off to do just that.

"Where have you been?" The dragon bellowed as Dylock entered Mount Wishnik.

Unleashing his anger and frustration, the woodland creature yelled at the top of his lungs.

Where are the mushrooms? Where did you hide them!?"

"Quit screaming," Glomgurgle growled. "I have no idea what you're talking about."

"Don't play dumb. Tell me! What have you done with them?" Dylock shouted, his voice brimming with frustration.

"I destroyed them in the hopes of sending you on a fruitless search today," Glomgurgle growled. "I can't believe you actually went to talk to a wolf? Could you be more desperate?" The dragon questioned, thunder rolling though the cave as he laughed. In that moment, the emptiness that Dylock had felt for years was finally replaced. His empty soul was filled with pure hatred for Glomgurgle, Tobias, and any creature that might dare cross his path. *Oh, what is this feeling in the pit of my stomach?* He wondered as the hatred inside of him bubbled more than the lava in the craters of the volcano. *Power... I feel powerful*, he realized as a cloud of thick, black smoke, swirled around him and disappeared in seconds. *Oh my God. Was that...* the troll tentatively touched his belly and felt his spider-shaped gemstone in the center. *Yes, my dark power is back. Now, I'll definitely be able to get my hands on the black diamond.*

"Someone got his magic back," Glomgurgle snarled sarcastically. "Now things should get real interesting," he growled before sulking toward his lair.

Throwing his head back, Dylock let out an evil laugh, feeling strong and optimistic for the first time in years as he scurried to the southeast corner of the cave. *That overgrown lizard has no idea what's coming to him,* he thought as he fell asleep that evening hoping to dream of days to come.

A SLIGHT SHAKE of Dylock's shoulder woke him. "You okay bud?" Bernie asked, his forehead wrinkled with worry. "Percy asked me to come check on you and I'm glad I did. You were whimpering in your sleep."

"Was I?" The green haired woodland creature queried.

Bernie nodded. "Seems odd that you'd fall asleep after casting a hearing spell. You must be tired. Why don't I take you to your tree so you can rest more comfortably?"

Dylock shook his head. "No. I have to stay here," he said. "I'm fine. I promise. Besides, the spell I cast is important," he added, his voice laced with urgency.

"Okay," Bernie sighed. "I don't know what you're up to, but I'll let you off easy on this one. Just be careful and make sure you get some rest before the ceremony tonight, will you?"

"Of course," the four-leafed-clover-adorned troll assured.

I know I should be happy that my friends keep checking up on me, but it's annoying. I wish I could just finish facing my past and know once and for all how to prove that there is goodness inside of me. I just can't stop trying. I never will. I have to make the other treasure trolls see that I've truly transformed, he thought as he once again turned his attention to Mulyn's voice.

CHAPTER 11

"The moment I saw Rosie again after all our years apart was one of the happiest of my life and a moment that I am certain will stay with me forever." Smiling, Murlyn reached for Rosie's hand and continued to describe the happy moment. As he spoke it was as if years melted away and in instant he was experiencing the pure joy of reuniting with Rosie after years apart.

Wow... Rosie hasn't aged a day, he thought as he spotted her hiding behind the curtain in the throne room of the castle. *She is as beautiful as ever. Where do I even begin after all these years? What do I say? What will she say to me?* Holding his breath, he removed his invisibility cloak and tapped Rosie on the shoulder.

Murlyn's worries all disappeared the moment his old friend jumped into his arms and embraced him tightly.

After hugging Rosie for a long moment, Murlyn draped his invisibility cloak over the two of them and led her into the hallway.

Glancing to the left and then to the right, Murlyn made sure that they were alone and then removed the cloak.

"I can't believe you're really here," Rosie exclaimed. "I mean, my troll intuition told me you were coming, but I didn't believe it. What brings you here after all this time?"

Murlyn explained how Blaine missed Natalie terribly and was at his wits end with his father's attempts to make him walk.

The pink glittery-haired troll nodded. "The princess misses Blaine, too. The poor thing dreams of him, but of course she doesn't realize it's him due to the hypnosis," Rosie said solemnly. "And the queen lessons don't do much to help matters either."

"Queen lessons?" Murlyn asked, completely confused by Rosie's words.

"Alexandria is teaching Natalie how to be a proper queen while Frederick hunts for an appropriate suitor for her. Speaking of which, we should get back in there."

Grinning, Murlyn once again draped his invisibility cloak over the two of them. "Let's go, shall we?" He asked as they walked back into the throne room.

You were right, Lizzie, I already feel so much better being back with Rosie. Now if we could only help Blaine and Natalie. As he listened intently to the princess and her mother, Rosie leaned in close to him and did the same.

"Natalie... Natalie...," Waving a hand in front of the young woman's face, Alexandria, a slender fifty-something-year-old with long gray hair and deep amber colored eyes, got the girl's attention.

"My apologies, Mama," the young woman sighed. "I don't see why I have to have queen lessons. It's not like Daddy would ever let me reign over the kingdom independently anyway. Finding an appropriate suitor for me has practically become an obsession for him."

Placing a hand on both of Natalie's shoulders, Alexandria pulled her into a hug. "Your father is only trying so hard to find you a husband because he loves you and wants to secure your future. Which reminds me, he set up another dinner date for you tonight. This time it is with Sir Franklin Blackford of Stalagmiteville. You are to meet with Margret in an hour to refresh your hair and make-up, and then meet Sir Blackford in the dining room, so there is no time to dilly-dally. Now, as I was saying, a proper curtsy is completed by putting one foot behind the other and—"

"No mother, this is ridiculous. I'm almost twenty-five-years-old. I've watched you and daddy for years. I know how to do a lot more than curtsy. I don't need queen lessons and I don't need Daddy to set me up with Sir Blackford or anyone else. I'm not dealing with this anymore," Natalie declared, her voice shaking slightly.

"Do you care about Cinder's Edge?" Alexandria queried pointedly.

Natalie sighed once again. "Mama, you know I do. I'm confident that I—"

The older woman shook her head. "If you truly care about this realm then you will do as your father and I wish."

"But, Mama—"

"No, you listen to me young lady. Every female heir born to the throne of Cinder's Edge has had a strong, intelligent king, who was chosen by her father to stand by her side. I don't care how old you are or how confident you feel you are. You are not reigning over this kingdom alone. You will be no exception, is that understood?"

"Yes, Ma'am," the dutiful daughter muttered meekly.

The apple doesn't fall far from the tree, does it? I remember Alexandria saying something very similar when she was about Natalie's age. Murlyn continued to listen in.

"Don't worry, sweetheart," Alexandria continued. "Your father and I have grown quite fond of each other over the years. I'm sure that you and whichever suitor your father chooses will be blessed with the same good fortune. Now, let's get back to curtsy practice, shall we?"

What has happened to Alexandria? Doesn't she understand that a partnership is about far more than fondness? Murlyn was shocked at how much the queen had changed and watched as she explained the art of the perfect curtsy to her daughter. *Rosie and I must introduce Natalie and Blaine to each other again. But when? And how?*

Two hours later, Murlyn was still pondering over his questions while he and Rosie followed the princess into the dining room. Sitting at a table was a heavyset, nearly bald man with a thin moustache and a large reddish-brown mole on his nose; Natalie's dinner date, Sir Franklin Blackford.

Standing up as the young royal approached the table, her dinner companion extended his hand. "Natalie, if you don't mind my saying so, you look ravishing," he flashed her a crooked smile.

"Why thank you," she hesitantly offered her hand in return. "That's very kind of you to say, Sir Blackford."

What the heck is this guy thinking? Can't he see the disgust in her eyes? Murlyn watched the potential suitor kiss Natalie's hand in lieu of shaking it.

"Why don't we address one another formally until we become better acquainted?" The princess suggested quickly ripping her hand away. *That a girl. Show him who is boss.*

"As you wish, your majesty," Sir Blackford said, his voice full of anxiety as he took a seat at the dining room table and gestured for her to do the same.

I hate that Natalie looks so sad, Murlyn thought as the beautiful young royal obliged and sat across from her dinner companion.

Natalie had covered all standard small-talk topics before the first course even arrived. She asked about his family, hobbies and what he appreciated most about Cinder's Edge, whereas he only questioned her age and level of familiarity with his family tree.

The princess breathed a sigh of relief as Theo, the castle butler, placed Caesar salads in front of each of them.

"This is delicious," Sir Blackford said as he finished his initial bite of the salad. "Do you have any influence over the recipes used here in the castle?"

"No, unfortunately, I don't have a lot of time to cook or go through recipes. I wish I could learn, though."

Shaking his head, her dinner companion let out a slow breath. "That's a real shame." Taking another bite of salad, he continued, his mouth full of leafy greens. "Royal or not, any wife of mine must know how to cook. It is a woman's duty to care for her husband and family, is it not? Speaking of which," he said after finally swallowing, "how many children do you want?"

How can this man sit across from the princess and act so high and mighty when he has the manners of a child? Murlyn, watched the princess stifle a laugh as she spotted a blob of Cesar Dressing dripping down Sir Blackford's chin.

I can't take this anymore, and with that, Murlyn snuck up behind Sir Blackford and removed the invisibility cloak. Natalie's eyes met his own and she did her best not to make it known that they were being watched.

"It was nice to meet you Sir Blackford, but this just isn't going to work out," the princess said.

Eyes widened in surprise, Sir Blackford stammered. "W-w-well, that's a—"

"Let me guess… a real shame? Something tells me that we will both recover perfectly fine. Feel free to finish your salad." Natalie then got up from the dining room table and sprinted out of the castle, Murlyn and Rosie chasing close behind.

"SWEETHEART, WHERE ARE YOU GOING?" Rosie called out, as Natalie ran off in front of them.

"Away," the princess shouted angrily. "I have to get out of here. I can't believe Daddy tried to set me up with that jerk. What was he thinking? And who is this?" She asked, pointing toward Murlyn. "Didn't you tell me you were the only gnome around here?"

Murlyn looked at Rosie, confused by the princess's last comment. "Gnome?" He whispered to Rosie in disbelief.

"So not the time Murl," she whispered back as she looked to the princess. "Yes, I did say that, but that's not exactly the case sweetheart," the pink glittery-haired troll admitted sheepishly. "This is my friend, Murlyn."

"You've always told me that you're the only one I can trust. Why did you lie to me?" Natalie asked, ignoring Murlyn's tiny extended hand.

"It's a long story, sweetheart. I'm—"

"Perhaps, we should just show her," Murlyn suggested.

"Take her to the Forest of Wishes?" Rosie questioned.

"Where is this forest?" Natalie asked.

"It's about three miles west of the kingdom. The path starts just up that way," Murlyn answered, gesturing toward it.

"Well, what are we waiting for? Let's go," she said firmly, starting for the path.

The moment they arrived in the Forest of Wishes, Murlyn could tell, based on Rosie's bright smile, that she was pleased to be back. He also watched the way Natalie's eyes sparkled with curiosity as she admired the beautiful, brightly-colored saplings.

"What is this place?" Natalie asked, in awe of her beautiful surroundings.

Rosie looked to the young royal. "This, sweetheart, is where I used to live. It's called The Forest of Wishes. The bright pink fern over there was my home for many years." As Rosie pointed at the tree her eyes narrowed in confusion. "Wait," she looked to Murlyn, "It looks different. Are there fewer branches?"

"Oh," Murlyn's eyes widened. Looking from Rosie to the tree, he shifted his weight from one side to the other. "I've been meaning to talk to you about that—"

But before Murlyn could explain, another troll appeared. "Oh, Rosie, is that really you?" Minnie asked excitedly, running toward the three of them. "I never thought I'd see the day!"

"Did someone say Rosie?" Bernie queried, his voice full of excited anticipation.

Word of Rosie's arrival quickly spread throughout the forest and, within minutes, her fellow trolls were gathered around her and the others, shouting things like, "It's great to see you" and "is this little Natalie?"

"What in the name of wishes is going on here? I'm trying to read," Blaine shouted as he burst out of the hut a few minutes later.

"Natalie and Rosie are back!" The woodland creatures shouted happily.

Murlyn noticed that a mixture of fear and happiness colored

Blaine's features the moment he heard Natalie's name, but, to his surprise, Blaine looked to the pink-glittery haired troll first. "Oh my gosh!" He exclaimed happily, "It's so good to see you, Rosie!"

Hopping on to Blaine's lap, Rosie threw her tiny arms around his neck. "It's great to see you too, young man. I'm delighted to see you looking so well."

"Rosie, what's going on?" The princess asked, placing her hands on her hips. "Who is this guy? Where did all of these other gnomes come from?"

"What are you going on about?" Percy questioned, glancing up at the young royal. "We're not gnomes. We are treasure trolls and proud of it."

Natalie let out a huff, her hands still on her hips. "Rosie, explain this!"

"Sweetheart, this is Blaine. He's an old friend of mine and an avid reader, just like you."

Blaine finally looked to Natalie, grasped her hand, and shook it gently. "It's nice to meet you," he said, his tone apprehensive yet sweet.

That's my boy, Murlyn thought, quietly observing the exchange. *You can do this.*

The troll smiled as he saw familiarity flash in Natalie's eyes. "Likewise," she said. "What you got there?" She questioned, tilting her hand toward the book on his lap.

"Nothing," he quickly shut the book and placed his hands on the wheels of his chair. "It's just a boring book about hypnosis. Come on in and we'll take a look at my other books."

But, just as Blaine started to wheel himself into his home, Natalie gave out a loud yelp.

"I'm so sorry, your highness," Blaine said fretfully, as he looked down to see that the wheel of his wheelchair was on top of the princess's foot. He turned bright red with embarrassment and backed off her foot.

The princess shook her head. "Please, don't worry. It only hurt for a moment, and please call me Natalie." She smiled, blushing slightly. "I've worn heels that are two sizes too small for years. These days, I can hardly feel my toes. Trust me, I'm fine," she assured him as she walked into the hut.

"I'm glad," Blaine smiled. "Please come and sit." He motioned to a chair that he'd pushed away from the table for her to use.

Smiling, Natalie sat down and looked to the lone bookshelf in the far-left corner. "Wow, you've got a lot of books."

"Yes, I have quite a variety of books. Including everything from *The Anatomy of Treasure Trolls* to *Marmoset's Bad Hair Day*," Blaine chuckled as he picked up the children's book which featured a monkey with disheveled hair on the cover and showed it to her.

"Oh, my goodness," she exclaimed, taking the book from him. "I haven't seen this book in years. I used to read it all the time as a child."

"Me too. I used to read it with you," he said quietly.

"I'm sorry? I don't know what you mean."

Rosie and Murlyn, who were sitting on Blaine's cot quietly watching their human friends interact, shot him wary glances.

"What would you like to read today?" Blaine asked, quickly changing the subject.

Natalie studied the bookshelf more closely and considered her answer. "Oh my gosh… is that *Gluttony Versus Guilt* by the Bonnett sisters?" Her voice colored with a mixture of excitement and amusement.

Fidgeting in his chair, Blaine looked from the book to the princess, his cheeks slightly crimson. "The Bonnett sisters are a guilty pleasure of mine. I actually just started reading *Love & War*," he admitted sheepishly.

"I totally get it," she said excitedly, smiling from ear to ear. "The Bonnett sisters are my all-time favorite authors. Their *Eternal Opposites* series is amazing. Maria can make even the most mundane of love stories sound eloquent and purposeful. And Anita can make the lamest of arguments sound like the greatest of verbal sparring matches. Anyone who reads their work will completely understand—"

Loudly clearing her throat, Rosie reminded Blaine and Natalie of her and Murlyn's presence. "As much as I would love to hear the rest of what is sure to be a scintillating review of the writing ability of the Bonnett Sisters, I'd like to suggest another topic."

"What topic did you have in mind, Rosie?" Natalie asked. "I do hope it was worth interrupting our conversation," she said pointedly.

"Indeed," the pink glittery-haired troll nodded. "Sweetheart, it's time you knew the true history of Cinder's Edge. Blaine, why don't you tell her why you, your father, and the trolls here in The Forest of Wishes were sent into exile?"

Blaine shook his head. "Oh no, I'm not the right person for that, Rosie."

"Yes, you are, my friend. You are precisely the right person." Rosie insisted.

"Oh yes," Natalie said. "Blaine, my parents have always been tight lipped about the history of Cinder's Edge. Please tell me what you know."

She might think I am crazy after I tell her everything. Blaine thought, flashing her a sweet smile. "Okay, but let's go outside, shall we? A little fresh air will make this easier."

Natalie nodded and followed everyone outside to a large purple fern tree with a small red blanket underneath. "We can sit here. This is my favorite reading spot," Blaine rolled onto the blanket. "It provides just enough shade from the sun," he explained, pushing the brakes of his wheelchair forward, locking it in place. "And it's quite beautiful if I say so myself." Smiling, he unfastened his seatbelt and grabbed onto the right armrest of his chair, preparing to turn slowly and lower himself onto the blanket.

Placing a hand on his shoulder, Natalie stopped him. "Blaine, I don't mean to be rude, but rather than stalling, please tell me whatever it is you know about Cinder's Edge that I don't know."

Buckling his seatbelt again, Blaine took a deep breath and considered where to begin. *I guess there's no way to avoid this. Here goes nothing.* "Natalie, have you ever heard of Benjamin Benson?" He queried after a long moment.

"No," she shook her head. "That name doesn't ring a bell."

"Well, he's my father. Years ago, he was a beloved magician in Cinder's Edge. He spent his days amazing audiences by cutting people in half and then putting them back together or by making them disappear. Somewhere along the way he met my mother, who volunteered to be his assistant and the two fell in love."

"That's so sweet. But, what does it have to do with the history of my family's kingdom?" Natalie asked.

She's so cute when her nose does that winkling thing, Blaine thought. "I was getting to that," he said sheepishly, as he caught another whiff of Natalie's perfume, which reminded him of chocolate covered strawberries. He suddenly felt heat on his cheeks. *She smells so good. I-*

"You look a little flushed. Are you all right?" Natalie asked, putting a hand to his forehead to check his temperature.

Blaine nodded quickly, her touch stunning him out of his thoughts. "Where was I?"

"I think you were about to tell her about your mother," Murlyn, who had been studying the two of them, answered quietly.

Blaine nodded. "Thanks, buddy."

Smiling, he looked back at Natalie, and began to tell her all about the history, as well as the friendship their mothers had and the deal their fathers had made at her parents wedding. "Life was great for a while, but then my father experienced a tragedy," he said solemnly as tears pricked his eyes.

"Oh no," she said, her voice suddenly solemn. "What happened?"

Sighing quietly, Blaine told her about his mother's untimely death and his disability.

"But that's not the worst of it. My Papa became so consumed with guilt that he spent all of his time and magic-related skills trying to develop a pair of pants that would allow me to walk."

"Are you saying that your father didn't make Glomgurgle disappear because he was too busy developing pants that would allow you to walk?" Natalie questioned, bewilderment coloring her features.

"Exactly. When Papa didn't make good on his promise, the dragon was able to capture about half of the treasure trolls and burn down the kingdom. Thanks to Murlyn's quick thinking most of the trolls escaped the dragon's influence. Sadly, during one of the dragon's earlier attempts to destroy the kingdom, one troll by the name of Dylock fell under the influence of dark magic long enough for Glomgurgle to essentially make him into his minion."

"Oh, my gosh," Natalie whispered, wide-eyed.

"Your father was so angry that he sent my father, me, and the remaining trolls into exile, saying that we could no longer be trusted. We've been here ever since."

"Blaine, I don't know what to say. I am so very sorry. I should go. Thanks for showing me your books. My apologies to you, as well, Murlyn." She looked from the troll to Blaine and then back. "Thank you both for making sure I know the true history of the kingdom. I must go," she said as tears filled her eyes.

"Miss Natalie, please don't be upset," Murlyn said sweetly. "I never could bear to see you cry."

Reaching out, Blaine gently grabbed the princess's arm. "Natalie please don't cry. I didn't tell you any of this to get an apology. I'm sorry I even mentioned it. Please stay. We'll read."

"I'm sorry. I must go," she insisted, before quickly backing away and running toward the path to the castle with a solemn Rosie in tow.

CHAPTER 12

"Why did you make me tell her?" Blaine shouted as he headed back into the hut with Murlyn trailing behind.

"She deserved to know the truth about why we were sent into exile," Murlyn said. "Maybe now," he paused before continuing, "she'll do something about it."

Turning his wheelchair quickly, Blaine faced Murlyn, eyes full of frustration. "There's the truth!" he cried. "You only wanted me to tell Natalie about the past so you could get out of exile. How dare you—"

"Whoa there, son, what's with all the yellin'? I'm readin' here," Benjamin, said, as he looked up through his reading glasses, which were now a permanent fixture due to old age.

"The princess came by here today and Murlyn made me look like a complete imbecile," Blaine shouted, his face turning more and more crimson by the minute.

"Master Blaine, it was never my intention—"

"Oh, don't you dare 'master' me, Murlyn. What you did was selfish and did nothing but shock and hurt Natalie. Did you not see how she ran out of here? She probably thinks we are all awful."

Putting down his book, Benjamin looked from the treasure troll to his son. "Blaine, my boy, you've never cared what people thought about you before. What's going on here?"

"Nothing," Blaine shook his head. "It's just that Nat—I mean, the princess, visited the forest today and Murl kind of ruined it for me."

Benjamin smirked. "Ah. Murl ruined it for you, huh? Now we are getting somewhere." He looked to the treasure troll, his voice suddenly quiet and coated in a sadness. "Murl, it's time you go get him the letter."

"Yes, of course. I'll be right back." Nodding, Murlyn quickly scurried out of the hut.

After the treasure troll left, a silence settled between Blaine and his father until, after a long moment, Benjamin spoke. "Son, it's time we talk about love."

Oh, here we go... Blaine looked around, searching for dishes to wash, clothes to fold, books to straighten, or anything that could possibly serve as a distraction, but the small, sparse hut was immaculate. *Darn those trolls for keeping this place so clean. Here goes nothing.* "Papa, you don't need to—" he began.

"Love sneaks up on you when you least expect it, Blaine. And, when it does, you have to seize it because you might not get another chance. You and I both know how short life is."

"Papa, Natalie and I just reunited today. It's not like that."

Smiling, the older man opened his mouth to say something then reconsidered.

Blaine sighed. "Just say what you want to say Papa."

"Ya might not love her yet, but ya care about her. I can tell by the way ya yelled at Murlyn today."

"C'mon Papa, I'm not saying that's true, but even if it is the truth, is caring about someone a crime?"

"No, my boy. It made me so happy to hear ya become so emotional about her."

"Good, I'm glad to hear that. Now, may I please go read? I'd really like to dig into some of Natalie's favorite books so that, on the off chance she does come back to visit, we'll have something to talk about."

"Son, the thing is, when it comes to matters of the heart, you normally don't put yourself out there because of your…" The loving father paused, as he searched for the right word, "situation."

"For Pete's sake Pop, just say Cerebral Palsy. Saying the words isn't going to kill you."

Rolling his eyes, Benjamin sighed. "The point is, my boy, I don't want you to be afraid or reluctant to pursue Natalie because of your special circumstances."

And he avoids saying the name of my disability yet again. Ugh. I'll never understand why he acts like the words are going to set his lips on fire. "Again Pop, just say Cerebral Palsy or at least CP. For cryin' out loud, this goes against everything you've ever told me." Pausing, Blaine took a deep breath and slowly let it out. "You've always told me that us being in exile is for the best because the people of Cinder's Edge are ignorant and won't accept me. Now, all of the sudden, you're telling me to pursue the freaking princess, whom I just reunited with today. C'mon Pop, it makes no sense."

"I am aware, but there's somethin' you don't understand son."

"What's that?"

Benjamin was about to speak when Murlyn arrived waving a piece of paper in his hands. "I have the letter," the woodland creature said.

"Good. Maybe you can help my boy understand," the caring father said.

Hopping into the chair across from Blaine, Murlyn begun. "I don't think it's a coincidence that Natalie showed up here today. When it comes to the two of you, I think greater forces may be at play."

"What are you babbling about, Murl?" Blaine asked, a hint of frustration in his voice.

Sighing, Murlyn handed him the letter that Lizzie had made him promise to keep safe years ago. Tears welled up in his eyes before he continued. "Your mother always had high hopes for you and

Natalie. She and Alexandria mused from time to time about sharing grandchildren. Your mother even had dreams about the two of you being together," he said solemnly.

Uh oh... it's official. Murlyn has spent too much time around Papa. He is going bonkers, too. He eyed the troll "Murl, I know you like to think that Ma watches over us and she probably does, but—"

Benjamin shook his head, looking his son straight in the eye. "No buts, son. Put yourself out there and go with the flow 'cause, if I didn't know any better, I'd say your gorgeous mother is doing a little match making from her spot up at the pearly gates," he managed a weak smile in spite of the tears in his eyes.

Blaine laughed curtly, dismissing the idea. "The two of you have always said that Ma is an angel. Well, if angels up in heaven have magic, I can think of a few ways I'd prefer she'd use hers rather than play matchmaker," he said heatedly.

Benjamin nodded. "I have some of my own ideas as to how your mother and our savior could help us too, son. Is there anything you want me to ask your mother next time I pray to her?"

Yeah, ask her to use a little magic to help you accept my disability. Shaking his head, Blaine dismissed the thought. "No, Papa, I just want a little peace and quiet, so I can read, okay?" He asked, his voice edged with frustration, as he turned his attention to the books he planned to discuss with Natalie.

"Aww, that sounds like something your father would say," Natalie said sweetly, bringing Blaine back to the present moment. "Why didn't you ever tell me that he urged you to pursue me?"

Laughing, Blaine looked to his wife. "You and I both know that I didn't do a good job of putting myself out there in the beginning."

Chuckling, Natalie nodded. "That's for sure."

Isabel looked from her grandmother to her grandfather and back, eyebrows furrowed. "What do you mean?" She queried, her voice colored by curiosity.

As Natalie answered her granddaughter's query, it was as if time once again melted away, transforming her from a silver-haired, wrinkled woman full of wisdom to a fresh-faced, auburn-haired, young lady full of hope for the future.

Soon she found herself in the Forest of Wishes, knocking on the door of Blaine's hut, wondering if he wanted to see her as much as she wanted to see him.

"Queen lessons are driving me bonkers," she explained as Blaine opened the door of the hut, smiling sweetly. "May I hide out here for a bit?"

"Of course, you're welcome here anytime."

"Thank you so much." She stepped inside and handed him her coat. "For the past three days, I've had everything from the proper dinner etiquette of a queen to how a queen crosses her legs when sitting practically drilled into my head. I can't take it anymore." The princess let out a heavy sigh.

"Sounds to me like you need to scream," Blaine suggested, his tone very matter of fact.

"Huh?"

"Scream," he said again. "It's cathartic. It'll help you feel better."

"Oh no," the princess shook her head. "I wouldn't want to scare anyone."

Shooting the young majestic a questioning glance, Blaine smirked slightly. "Natalie, we're in the middle of a forest. Papa and the treasure trolls are busy working. You're not going to scare anyone, and it will help you feel better. Trust me."

"Will you scream with me?" She asked.

He nodded and counted to three.

Together, they let out a loud, long scream: "AAAAAAAAHHHHHHHHH!"

"Feel better?" Blaine asked.

"You know what?" The princess grinned. "I do."

"Great. Come and sit."

As Natalie sat down, Blaine noticed a beautiful diamond-studded bracelet on her wrist. "Your bracelet is just as beautiful as you," he said, his voice sweet yet full of anxiety.

"Oh, thank you," Natalie said, her cheeks turning slightly pink. "So how far did you get into *Love & War?*"

"Last chapter." He reached for the book and opened it. "Want me to read aloud?"

Natalie couldn't help smiling to herself whilst he read. She felt safe with Blaine and she loved his calming, deep, soothing, voice. *I really do feel better. I've never met another guy like him. Most men I meet only seem to care about the kingdom, but Blaine cares enough to make me feel better and he is so smart, considerate and—*

"Natalie... Natalie... are you still listening?" Blaine asked, stunning her out of her thoughts.

"Yes, of course. I'm sorry it's just the story is so good. I got lost in it," she fibbed.

Blaine shook his head and smiled. "I totally get it," he said sweetly. "Just making sure you are still with me because I am on the last paragraph."

Leaning in closer, the princess flashed him a grin. "I'm all ears."

Blaine let out a breath and then continued, doing his best to imitate a female voice whenever he read the thoughts of the book's conquering heroine. "A distraught Sarah walked through the battlefield of deceased and injured soldiers. *I know Leonard is alive. I can feel it. I must find him.* Closing her eyes, Sarah prayed as hard as she could to find the love of her life. *Am I hallucinating?* She blinked as she spotted her loving fiancée on horseback in the distance. *Oh my God. My prayers have been answered.* Running to him, she smiled brightly. The moment Leonard saw her, he wordlessly pulled her up onto the horse and kissed her passionately as they rode off into the sunset." Smiling, Blaine closed the book. "Wow... that wasn't quite the ending I anticipated."

"I couldn't agree more. I love the book, but the ending was horrible. I mean she doesn't even describe the kiss and she—"

"How would you describe it?" Blaine questioned, grinning.

"Huh?"

"How would you describe the kiss?"

"Oh well, I suppose I'd write something like he slowly leaned in, closing the space between them, and kissed her with an intentional tenderness." *I wonder what it would be like to kiss Blaine.*

"Is someone an aspiring writer?" Blaine queried a hint of surprise in his voice.

I love how he actually takes an interest in me. Every book written by the Bonnet sisters says that love goes far beyond status and looks. Not that his looks are bad. I love how his hair is kind of wavy and his eyes are so expressive.

"Earth to Natalie," waving a hand in front of the princess's face, the young man stunned her out of her thoughts once again. "Sorry, what did you say?"

"Do you want to be a writer?

"What gave it away?"

"I don't know many people who know how to kiss someone with 'intentional tenderness', much less use the phrase," he laughed.

Is he flirting or just trying to be funny? She wondered. *Is this his way of hinting that he is wondering about kissing me too?* Chuckling nervously, Natalie tucked her hair behind her ear. "Do you know how to kiss with intentional tenderness?" The princess teased before she could stop herself.

"There are not many girls—"

Cutting him off, Natalie leaned forward and kissed him lightly on the lips. Overwhelmed by the warm softness of his mouth, it took her a moment to realize that he was kissing back. *This must mean that taking things into my own hands was a good idea,* she thought. A moment later, Blaine stopped kissing her and broke away.

"Why did you do that?" He questioned.

"I thought—"

Letting out an exaggerated sigh. "You know what? That doesn't matter. Just go."

"But I—"

"Just go," Blaine persisted, quickly handing the princess her coat.

With that, Natalie walked out of the hut and into the forest with her head down, feeling utterly crushed.

~

"OH, THANK GOD," Margret, the princess's lady in waiting, said the moment Natalie walked into the castle. "Malcom Morrison, the Duke of Embersville, is here to have dinner with you." She explained, while adding blush to Natalie's blotchy, tear stained cheeks. "I can tell you're upset princess, but try to smile through whatever is bothering you. Your parents are entertaining the duke right now, but if you don't hurry you'll be late and your daddy will blow a gasket." Margret applied lipstick to the princess's lips. "And no one wants that."

"Of course not," Natalie agreed. "Thanks for the warning but, I got it from here," she ran to meet her parents and the potential suitor.

"There she is," Alexandria said sweetly as her daughter walked into the castle's formal dining room. "Right on time." The queen eyed her and mouthed, "luckily," before turning towards the duke.

Following suit, Natalie held out her hand. "Duke Morrison, it's lovely to meet you."

As the duke shook her hand, Natalie glanced at her parents. "Mama, Daddy, will you be joining us for dinner this evening?"

The king shook his head. "No, of course not. We want you and Malcom to get to know one another privately."

"That's right," the queen agreed. "Have fun and enjoy your dinner."

As her parents said goodbye to Malcolm, Natalie took in her surroundings for a moment. A mahogany table took up most of the room. The table was adorned by a white cloth with a delicate rose design woven in silver along the edges. Two tall silver candelabras served as a centerpiece, holding two smooth, white candles whose wax never dripped. The matching silver cutlery was polished to perfection and sparkled beneath a chandelier that hung in the center of the ceiling. At each place sat an empty wine glass and a beautifully folded silver cloth napkin to match the accents on the table cloth. *This is a far cry from the wooden table and chairs in Blaine's hut,* she sighed. *I wish he would've talked to me about what happened this afternoon,* shaking her head the princess dismissed the thought. *Ew, salmon and broccoli... mama must've approved the menu again,* Natalie decided after finally taking note of the meal being served that evening. Sighing again, the young royal pulled out a chair and reluctantly sat across from the duke, a pudgy, bald man with a double chin, dark-brown eyes, and age spots on his neck.

Eyeing the fish, Malcom cringed. "Does your kitchen have a blender? I prefer my food puréed."

Wow... it's going to be a long night, the princess bit the inside of her cheek to keep herself from wincing.

Malcom chuckled. "I was only joking, miss," tucking his napkin under his chin he grinned at her.

"Oh," Natalie giggled. "I'm sorry. I guess I'm a little distracted."

"You don't really want to be here, do you?"

Natalie flashed him a nervous smile. "Of course, I want to be here," she said sweetly. "It's just—"

The elderly man reached out and patted Natalie's elbow. "It's okay." Leaning in closer, he whispered, "Don't tell your parents, but I'm just here for the pleasure of your company and a free meal."

"Sorry?"

"Don't get me wrong, you're beautiful," he assured her. "But an old man like me could never do you or this kingdom justice," he cut into his salmon and took a bite.

"So, then why are you here exactly?"

The elderly man opened his mouth to say something then hesitated, taking another bite of salmon. "I lost my wife three years ago and tend to get lonely every now and again."

"I'm so sorry to hear that, Duke Morrison,"

"Please call me Malcom." Smiling sweetly, the pudgy man looked straight at the princess. "What about you? Who has your heart?" He asked, his voice full of curiosity.

An image of Blaine smiling appeared in her mind. Shaking her head, the young majestic did her best to ignore what she already knew was stirring in her heart.

"Excuse me?" Natalie questioned, not wanting to tell this man about her feelings for Blaine.

"Miss, with all due respect, you don't have to play coy with me."

The princess shot Malcom an angry look.

"My apologies miss, I didn't mean to speak out of turn. It's just that your enthusiasm, or lack thereof, about this dinner tells me you have no interest in me, which is completely understandable. Furthermore, the way your parents were whispering earlier about how you had been gone all afternoon tells me that you don't have an interest in any other suitor that they may have in mind. I can assume, based on the way you blushed when I questioned who has your heart, that your heart is already spoken for."

Natalie's expression softened as she stared at him, speechless. *How does he know so much?*

"With age comes wisdom princess," the elderly man said as though he were reading her thoughts.

"At this point, the only thing I can tell you honestly is that I hope for love." Natalie explained as she finished the last of her salmon.

Malcom nodded. "Show me a twenty-something-year-old woman who doesn't," he chuckled. "Again, with all due respect miss, I sense that there is something you are not telling me."

"There may be a particular person at the center of my hope for love," Natalie admitted shyly. "But things are complicated and I am not sure he reciprocates my feelings."

"I see," Malcom nodded, considering what to say next. "As someone who has experienced and lost a great love, the best advice I can give you is to tell him how you feel because if you don't take a chance, you might miss out. Life is short; too short to live without love, in my opinion."

"Thank you, Malcom. This has turned out to be a lovely evening."

If you don't take a chance you might miss out on a great love. As the princess tried to sleep that night Malcom's words ran through her mind. *I'm going to go to Blaine tomorrow and tell him my true feelings,* she decided, finally drifting into slumber.

~

"OH MY GOSH, Papaw! How could you send her away?" Isabel cried, stunning Natalie back to the present. "That's so awful." The newly crowned queen looked to Missy. "Tell him that what he did was appalling," she urged.

Biting her lip, the purple-haired woodland creature considered how to respond. "Sorry, I have to agree with Isabel on this one. Sending a girl away right after she kisses you is just plain cold."

Frowning, Blaine nodded. "I know. I felt awful," he said sincerely. "But I had my reasons."

"Which were?" Isabel asked, her voice coated in disbelief.

"Yeah, what exactly were your reasons?" Natalie asked, chuckling faintly.

As Blaine opened his mouth to answer the question he couldn't help but remember the first time he'd been asked about the kiss. Surprisingly, it wasn't the princess who had come to him with the query, but rather Murlyn.

CHAPTER 13

Murlyn had burst into the hut without knocking, his usually kind and gentle eyes full of worry. "What in the name of all that is magical has been going on in here?" The tiny woodland creature questioned, climbing into the chair directly across from Blaine.

Sighing heavily, the young man hung his head. "Murl, this really isn't a good time."

The troll shook his head, causing his messy hair to sway in all directions.

Eyeing the troll, the usually mild mannered young man bit down on his bottom lip, his cheeks turning bright red.

Murlyn let out a huff. "If you don't tell me what's going on then I'll tell your father why you have been studying hypnosis."

Letting out an exasperated breath, Blaine shook his head yet again. "If you must know, Natalie kissed me and I sent her away." The redness of his cheeks deepened as he spoke.

"After what your father and I told you the other day, how could you possibly send her away?" Murlyn looked at him wide-eyed.

It's official, the treasure trolls have spent too much time around Papa and lost their marbles. Picking up *The 411 on Feng Shui*, the avid reader ignored Murlyn.

"You can't pretend to read to get out of this one Blaine. Answer the question," Murlyn insisted, a slight edge to his tone despite the somber quality.

Firmly closing the book, Blaine who was suitably embarrassed, and angry considered his response. "Do you want to know what I really think?"

"I sense an avoidance tactic coming on, but go ahead. Tell me what you think."

"Despite what my father has been able to convince himself, you, and the other trolls, there is no way that my mother is up in heaven playing match maker. Honestly, the idea is just ludicrous."

"What other explanation do you have?" Murlyn queried, his voice still coated in melancholy.

"Isn't it obvious? Natalie kissed me out of nothing more than pity. Why else would she want someone like me?"

Rolling his eyes, Murlyn sighed. "With all due respect, Blaine, I will never understand you."

"What is that supposed to mean?"

"You are constantly telling your father that you don't want to be able-bodied because your disability is a part of who you are, but now I see the real reason you don't want to be able-bodied. It's because your disability is something you hide behind."

Blaine looked Murlyn straight in the eye. "You're one to talk. Isn't there something you've been meaning to tell Rosie all these years?"

"This isn't about me," the troll said dismissively. "Blaine please—"

"Get out," the young man shouted.

Sighing, Murlyn hopped off the chair and walked out of the hut, leaving Blaine alone.

NODDING, Murlyn let out a curt laugh, stunning Blaine out of the memory. "I remember that argument as if it were yesterday. I've never been so mad at a human," he admitted quietly. As he went on to recount his own memory of that afternoon, once again Murlyn found himself angrily pacing the forest, as Blaine's words echoed in his mind.

～

"How dare he call me out! How dare he disrespect me!" The troll muttered angrily.

Although he wasn't directing his thoughts or words toward Lizzie, the troll quickly heard his dear friend's response. *Can you truly expect my boy to be honest with you or himself if you're not honest with yourself?*

"Why do I always have to be the one to show Blaine right from wrong?" He wondered out loud. "For cryin' out loud, I'm not even his father. I'm merely a troll. Why do I have the responsibility of showing him how to be a good and honest man?"

Within moments, Lizzie's beautiful spirit responded. The calm voice of reason as always. *No, dear friend, you're not Blaine's father, but he cares for you and you love him. Whether he admits it or not, he looks up to you and always has. You've been a great influence on my boy up to this point, so why change that now when you have a real opportunity to shape the man he will ultimately become?*

Slowly letting out a breath, Murlyn felt his anger dissipate as the words of his dear departed friend sank in. "You're right Lizzie. I haven't set a good example," he whispered tearfully, looking up to the sky. "This is just all so complicated."

Everything is complicated when it comes to matters of the heart, dear friend.

"That's for sure," Murlyn agreed.

At that moment, Rosie entered the forest, her eyes full of alarm. "What's wrong?" She questioned, her voice full of worry. "Why are you so angry? You never get upset. What's going on?" The more questions the pink glittery-hair troll asked, the more breathless and anxious she became.

Grasping her shoulders, Murlyn squeezed gently. "Rosie, take a breath. I'm okay. Blaine and I had a moment and I got mad, but I'm fine now. What are you doing here? How did you know?"

"My treasure troll intuition of course,"

Murlyn chuckled nervously. "Oh, yes, of course. I should have known."

Stay calm, dear friend. Now is as good of a time as any to be honest with yourself and with Rosie.

"Well, regardless of the reason, I'm glad you're here Rosie. We haven't had nearly enough time together since we were reunited. I haven't even given you your gemstone back. Let's get that taken care of now, shall we?" Murlyn placed a hand on his half of the gemstone the trolls shared.

"No, stop!" Rosie cried, a sense of urgency in her tiny, high-pitched voice.

Murlyn looked at her, eyebrows furrowed. "You don't want your gemstone back?"

Rosie's cheeks turned slightly pink. "I love having such a special connection with you," she admitted sheepishly. "Besides, I can't bear the thought of you having no magic at all."

Murlyn smiled. "In that case, I'd love to continue sharing a gemstone. Let's take a walk. I'd love to hear more about your years in the kingdom with Natalie."

Smiling, Rosie took his hand and obliged. As the two walked through the beautifully colored forest, she spoke about everything from Natalie's first debutante ball to her recent queen lessons.

"Sounds like you had your hands full," Murlyn chuckled.

"I sure did, but it was worth it. She has grown up into a beautiful, kind, intelligent woman."

"She sure has," Murlyn agreed, smiling. "Is it safe to assume you have been too busy to venture into another kingdom and meet someone yourself?" He queried in a nonchalant, slightly teasing tone.

Stopping in her tracks, Rosie looked at her fellow woodland creature, her eyes full of moisture. "How could you even think I'd try to meet someone else," she cried, a tear falling down her left cheek.

Uh oh... I made her cry. This definitely isn't going well. What should I do Lizzie? How can I make her feel better?

Lizzie spoke... *Just take a deep breath and follow your heart, dear friend. Love is the most powerful form of magic in the world. If you act with that as your intention, everything will be fine.*

"Rosie... sweetheart, please don't cry. I can't bear it. I haven't thought of anyone else since the day we were separated. I'm pleased to know you haven't either." Looking down at his feet, Murlyn tried to avoid eye contact with her. "You were right all of those years ago when you said we hadn't been true to ourselves."

"What are you saying, exactly?" Confusion was etched into her sad expression.

"I put my duty to this kingdom and my friends ahead of you all those years ago, but no more. We have a second chance to be together now and I want to take it," he explained, his voice still apprehensive but slightly more confident.

"Murlyn, I—"

Wrapping his tiny arm around his fellow woodland creature's waist, Murlyn pulled her in, closing the space between them. "I love you."

Rosie smiled brightly, her eyes sparkling with happiness. "I lo—"

Kissing her tenderly, Murlyn cut Rosie off once again. After a moment, he reluctantly pulled back. "Sorry to cut you off again," he chuckled. "It's just that I've waited years to do that."

"I'm not sure what's gotten into you," Rosie giggled. "But, it's refreshing."

Grinning from pointy ear to pointy ear, Murlyn took her tiny hand. "An old friend reminded me that it's important to be honest about your feelings with yourself and others."

"An old friend, huh?" She questioned knowingly. Lizzie always did give great advice. I am so happy to know that she watches over us." Looking up to the sky, Rosie's smile widened as a tear fell down her cheek. "Thank you, old friend, for being our angel," she whispered.

"Don't cry, sweetheart." He embraced her, squeezing tightly. "This is our second chance. Everything will be different. I promise," he assured, finally pulling back.

Nodding, the pink glittery-haired woodland creature smiled through her tears. "I believe you. And I couldn't be happier, really. But, Blaine and Natalie need us now, more than ever before. And we're still in exile, even though I have the cloak. I'm not sure we can overcome all of that."

"Sweetheart, Lizzie also reminded me that love is the most powerful form of magic there is. I believe that our love is strong enough to conquer anything. As long as you believe in that too, everything will be fine," he assured her, pulling her into another hug.

"Of course, I do," Rosie returned his embrace.

Be happy with yourself and the one you love, dear friend. It is the best way to be a good example for Blaine and Natalie, Lizzie whispered to Murlyn as the trolls watched the sunset in the Forest of Wishes.

"Murlyn isn't the only one who got some help from my dear ol' mom that night," Blaine said quietly after Murlyn had finished describing his memory.

"Oh, tell us more, Papaw," Isabel urged. "How did great grandma Lizzie help you?"

Smiling, Blaine obliged his granddaughter's request and continued his story. Within moments, he was his 25 year-old-self once more, alone in his hut reading a book.

"Any idea why Murl didn't want to help out in the workshop this afternoon?" Benjamin asked Blaine as he stepped into the hut moments later.

Blaine shrugged, pretending to read. "Sorry…" Looking up from the book, he flashed a smile. "No idea."

"You never were a very good liar, kid. Why don't you just tell me what's goin' on?"

Blaine shook his head. "Papa, I don't want to talk about it. Just go back to your workshop."

"I am not going anywhere until we have a discussion," Benjamin said sternly. Taking the seat that Murlyn had sat in moments before, Benjamin frowned. "Son, please talk to me."

Blaine leaned across the table, looking his father straight in the eye. "Papa, Murlyn was way out of line. That's all there is to it. There is nothing more to talk about."

"I see." Benjamin chuckled. "If that's the case, then why have you been reading the same page for the past five minutes. Could it perhaps be because you know that Murl wasn't so out of line?"

"What're you getting at, Papa?"

"Murlyn told me what happened between you and the princess earlier, my boy. Why didn't you put yourself out there like I told you to?"

"Because, Papa, regardless of what you and the trolls believe, Mama is not orchestrating my love life from heaven and, even if she was, a beautiful woman like Natalie would never be with a cripple like me."

The older man studied his son for a moment. "If that's really how you feel, then why are you so against me using the magic of the trolls to help you walk?" Benjamin paused before continuing, "I'm so close to perfecting the pants… I can feel it," he added excitedly.

"Papa, I love you. You know I do. But the chances of the pants allowing me to be able to walk are about as high as the chances of Mama playing cupid from the streets of gold."

Benjamin stayed silent for a long moment as his eyes filled up with tears. "I am so sorry, Blaine. I'm so sorry that I let my guilt and grief prevent you from seeing and trusting in the true magic of this world." A single tear rolled down his left cheek. "I'm going to say one more thing before I leave you be. Son, I worked as a magician for years. I have it on good authority that the love that exists between soulmates is the most powerful form of magic in this world. If you deny it, you will also be depriving yourself and Natalie of the deepest form of happiness in the world."

Rolling his eyes, Blaine sighed yet again. "Papa, how many times do I have to tell you that we have no way of knowing whether Natalie is actually my soulmate or not."

"Son, did you ever read the letter from your mother?"

Blaine shook his head. "It's under my pillow."

Carefully, removing the letter from Blaine's cot, the loving father handed it to his son. "Read it. Hopefully it will provide the clarity you need," he said, his voice solemn as he turned and left.

Letting out a breath, Blaine opened the letter and read it.

My dearest child,

I am not sure if it's the curse of being a magician's wife or just plain old mother's intuition, but I sense that, for whatever reason, I may not be able to teach you all of the important things a mother should teach her son before he becomes a man. Your father says I am being silly, but just in case I'm right, I am going to give you a few pieces of motherly advice...

Be brave. The best men are. Follow your father's example. He is the bravest man I know.

Be kind. As I am sure you will find out, the treasure trolls that live with us in Cinder's Edge are some of the nicest creatures that have ever lived. Unfortunately, the same cannot be said for many people in this kingdom. Do your part to change that by always being kind to others.

Most importantly, always put yourself out there when it comes to love because, as I am sure your father will tell you, love, particularly the love between soulmates, is the most powerful love there is.

Lastly, be sure to live the greatest life you can, little one. I can't promise that your life will be perfect if you follow my advice, but I can promise that I will do my best to help you be happy no matter what.

Love, Mama

Blaine looked up at the roof of the hut, still clutching the letter. *How did you know the exact words I needed to hear, Mama?* When he didn't get the sort of response Murlyn had spoken about, he looked up and whispered, his voice full of determination. "I am sorry I've disappointed you, Mama, but I'm going to fix it."

CHAPTER 14

*A*s darkness fell over the Forest of Wishes, Blaine did something he had never done before and traveled outside of the forest. *I wasn't stopped when I left the Forest of Wishes so this must be part of my destiny, but something still doesn't feel right,* he thought, eyeing the castle warily. "I really hope I am not making a mistake here, Mama," he whispered, looking up to the sky, before continuing his journey. "A sign would be nice."

Moments later, Blaine felt something under the wheel of his chair. Backing up slightly, he looked down and saw the small white-gold, diamond-studded bracelet Natalie had worn the day before. "Thanks, Mama," he smiled.

He was about to continue on down the path when he was startled by the sound of sobbing in the distance. *Could that be Natalie,* he thought, his heart suddenly thumping in his chest as he rolled closer to the sound. "Natalie, is that you?" He called out.

"Blaine?" Sniffling, the princess walked into the moonlight, her shoulders slumped.

"It is you... what's wrong? Why are you crying?" He asked.

"I came to apologize to you today, but then I couldn't even bring myself to knock on the door," the young royal explained between sniffles.

"Natalie, I—"

"On my way back, I lost something very special. I can't go back to the castle without it, so I've been here ever since," she explained as fresh tears streamed down her cheeks.

Smiling sweetly, Blaine took the bracelet out of his pocket. "Is this the something special you are talking about?" He held the bracelet out into the moonlight. "I remember you wearing it the other day."

"Oh, my gosh!" She exclaimed, wiping away her tears. "Where did you find that?"

"I found it in the forest while on my way to see you."

"Thank you so much," she took the bracelet and clasped it around her wrist. "This was my grandmother's bracelet. It's very special to me."

"I'm glad I could find it for you, but that's not why I came to see you."

"Then why were you coming to see me?" The princess asked. "If it was to tell me not to visit anymore, don't worry I won't."

Hanging his head, Blaine sighed. "That would be a shame, Natalie. I really have enjoyed your visits. I came to tell you that I was a jerk yesterday."

"You can say that again. I just don't get why."

"I freaked out when you kissed me because… well, I don't have much experience, being in exile and all. And, well, I don't know how someone as beautiful as you could be interested in someone like me."

The princess studied him, her nose scrunched in confusion. Chuckling, she questioned him. "Why wouldn't I be? You're handsome, smart, nice most of the time, and we have a history. Even though I don't remember it, you often seem familiar and provide me a sense of comfort."

"Yes, indeed, but what about my wheelchair?"

"What about it?"

"Can someone like you be with a man in a wheelchair?" Blaine asked pointedly, still smiling up at her.

"Do you really think I am *that* shallow?"

Shaking his head, Blaine disagreed. "No, no, of course not. I think you are a beautiful woman who is going to make a great queen someday. I just don't want to hold you back."

At that moment, Natalie surprised Blaine by putting her feet onto the footrests of his chair and gently climbed onto his lap. "I'm tired of letting other people tell me how to live my life, so let me tell you how this is going to work." Looking him straight in the eye, she took a deep breath then continued. "I like you and you like me, so we are going to continue enjoying each other's company with the understanding that neither one of us is going to hold the other back, understood?"

"Yes, your majesty," Blaine answered, smiling brightly.

"Good. Now kiss me."

Laughing, Blaine happily obliged until they were giggling together.

"Great, now read this book," smiling, she broke their kiss and placed a copy of *Romance & Conflict*, the sequel to *Love & War* onto his lap.

Grinning excitedly, Blaine picked up the leather-bound book and examined it, fingering the spine carefully. "Were did this come from?"

"A lady never reveals her secrets," Natalie said, lightheartedly.

"Some ladies are also apparently very bossy," Blaine said, jokingly.

"Just read."

The two spent the rest of the night talking, reading, and enjoying each other's company under the moonlight.

REACHING FOR BLAINE'S HAND, Natalie squeezed it and smiled. "That was a lovely night," she said wistfully. "One of many." Natalie winked at her pink glittery-haired friend and let herself revel in happy memories as she continued to talk about days long ago. In no time at all, she was once again her young self and walking into the Forest of Wishes with her longtime woodland friend.

"ARE we crazy for coming to this forest all the time Rosie?" Natalie asked.

The troll shook her head. "No, sweetheart. We're just following our hearts."

The princess sighed. "Yeah, I just hope we're doing the right thing."

"Sweetheart, it is never wrong to follow your heart. In fact, it's extremely important that you always follow your heart and stay true to who you are if you want to be an excellent queen someday."

"That's an excellent piece of advice if I have ever heard one," Murlyn said cheerfully as he approached them.

Rosie looked at him. "Awww, thanks. You're so sweet," she said, her eyes sparkling with love.

Looking from Rosie to Murlyn, Natalie giggled. "I'm going to head to the hut and leave you lovebirds alone for a while."

"Oh, Blaine is not in the hut right now. I think he just headed to his treehouse." Murlyn explained whilst looking longingly into Rosie's eyes.

"His what?" Natalie asked. Murlyn pointed to the purple fern that served as Blaine's treehouse.

That doesn't look like any treehouse I've ever seen, Natalie thought, walking towards the tree which, unlike any other she'd seen in the forest, had a ramp leading into its trunk.

Cautiously walking up the ramp, she stepped inside before the ramp disappeared and the trunk of the tree closed in behind her. "Wow, that was awesome." she reached out to feel the tree trunk, tracing the part that had just closed behind her.

Jumping at the sound of her voice, Blaine smiled. "Hey, beautiful, what're you doing here?" He spun on one wheel at the top of a twenty-foot ramp.

"Murl told me where you were. I hope it's okay that I'm here. What is this place?" She questioned, her eyes scanning her surroundings before falling upon a three-tiered bookshelf. "I can't believe you have more books in here. You've been holding out on me," she teased.

"Nah, I just needed to make sure that you were a book nerd like me before showing you my full collection," he joked, speeding down the ramp. Rolling toward her, he leaned in and kissed her gently. "Of course, it's okay. I've had this treehouse ever since we were sent into exile. Nowadays, it's where I come to blow off steam."

"Uh oh," Natalie's forehead wrinkled with worry. "Why are you blowing off steam today? What's up?"

Blaine hung his head and let out a slow breath. "It's nothing," he mumbled.

"If it's nothing then why can't you tell me about it?"

"It's my Papa. I haven't seen him in two days because he's in his workshop making yet another pair of pants."

"Well, at least he is keeping himself busy. That's a good thing, right?"

Blaine shook his head. "Not when it comes to trying to cure me. Why won't he just give up and accept me for who I am? Is it really that important that I walk? I mean, I think I've turned out pretty well, considering that we've been exiled from our home for the past twenty years. I mean, I guarantee that I'm more knowledgeable than ninety-five percent of the people in Cinder's Edge because of all the books I've read." Letting out a huff, he pointed toward the bookshelf and shook his head, more irritated than he had been, just moments before. "And, despite being in this chair, I bet I'm in better physical shape than most of them. I mean, look at this place, I've been pulling myself on those metal rings since I was five, for cryin' out loud. I mean… c'mon, do you see these muscles?" He asked, flexing his left bicep.

I hate seeing him so upset. There has to be something I can say or do. I, of all people, know what it's like to have parents who don't accept you. Smiling, Natalie decided to try and lighten the mood. "If it means you flex your biceps when you get angry, you should get angry more often," she joked.

Letting out a weak chuckle, Blaine lowered his arm. "Natalie, what should I do? I'm so tired of my father trying to make me into someone I'm not." Sadness etched across his face.

Natalie smiled sweetly and climbed onto his lap. "Don't let him. Don't let your father or anyone else change you. Just be true to who you are, because you're great." She placed a gentle kiss on his lips. "Now, show your fellow literary nerd your reading collection." After a brief moment of surveying, she suddenly exclaimed, "Oh, my gosh, I can't believe you have a copy of *Love & Lust*! That should definitely our next read."

"You're so cute when you get excited," Blaine chuckled. "Yes, that is another great book by the Bonnett Sisters."

Natalie nodded. "I just love their books. I wish I could describe characters the way Anita does or write dialogue the way Maria does."

"I bet you could do even better. Have you ever tried?"

If only it were that easy. Natalie's cheeks turned pink at the thought. "I really wish I could, but my life was pretty much planned out from the moment I was born," she said solemnly.

Nodding, Blaine opened his mouth to say something then closed it.

Tucking her hair behind her ear, the princess flashed a nervous smile. "I can tell there's something on the tip of your tongue. Spill."

"You only live once Natalie. You shouldn't let your parents keep you from pursuing your passions."

"My mama has always said that a future queen should not engage in frivolous activity and I am pretty sure she'd say writing was frivolous."

"So?" He asked rhetorically. "You have to live your life sweetie, not anyone else's."

Ugh, why doesn't he understand? Natalie let out a huff, unable to hide her frustration. "You don't get it. You don't have a mother like mine." *Oh my gosh. What am I saying? He never even got to meet his mother.* "I'm so sorry. I shouldn't have said that," she admitted, her cheeks suddenly hot.

"You're right Natalie, I don't. And that's why I understand more than most people how short life is. It's important for you to pursue your passions before you have the weight of the entire realm on your shoulders."

I hate that he's so right, Natalie let out a slow breath. "I'm so sorry, Blaine. Again, I shouldn't have said that. It's just that things are so complicated. Speaking of which, my parents are expecting me home soon, so I should get going."

"Sure, I am sorry if I spoke out of turn. I only want what's best for you because..." he hesitated, his cheeks instantly turning bright red. "Be—because I love you."

A CLAP of thunder suddenly brought Natalie back to the present. She looked at her granddaughter. "Sounds like a storm is brewing, should we head to the castle and continue this tomorrow, sweetheart?"

Shaking her head, Isabel objected. "No, I want to hear more. I want to know everything before I sign the decree."

Chuckling, Blaine took Natalie's hand and looked her in the eye. "Sweetheart, don't worry. We are safe here and I am sure other citizens and trolls have already headed to the throne room for the ceremony. Let's finish the story. We haven't even gotten to the good part yet."

Smiling sweetly, Natalie nodded. "You're right." Taking a deep breath, she looked to Isabel and continued, "I expressed my love for your grandfather that evening as well. From that night on, we were together whenever we could be. I would feign being sick in order to skip queen lessons or I would just sneak away at night."

The newly crowned royal stared at her Nana. "You snuck out of the castle?" She asked, her voice full of disbelief.

Natalie smiled. "Many times," she chuckled sweetly. "It was always worth it." She looked to Blaine. "You were always so thoughtful."

Blaine chuckled with his wife. "Have you totally forgotten about our first fight?"

The elderly woman smiled. "I could no sooner forget my own name," tucking a few strands of hair behind her ear, she took another deep breath and began recounting her first argument with Blaine.

"Are you excited for your birthday next week?" Blaine asked after he and Natalie had spent an hour finishing the novel *Love & Lust* just a week after they started it.

What?" Natalie questioned, eyebrows furrowed. "How did you—"

Closing the book, the young man grinned mischievously. "Rosie confirmed it today," he admitted. "But I'm happy to say I remembered the date from when we were kids. And, boy, do I have a surprise for you!" He declared, his voice full of excitement.

"Oh," Natalie blushed. *Awww, he made plans. How cute is that? Too bad I've already spoiled them.* "I have actually been meaning to—"

Suddenly, Benjamin burst in, full of excitement, interrupting the princess.

"I've done it, my boy. I've done it. The pants are nearly finished!" Benjamin shouted. "All I need is a little love. I was gonna get it from Murl, but Natalie will do much better."

Rolling his eyes, Blaine let out a huff. "Papa, can we do this later?"

Eyes wide, Benjamin stared at him. "Blaine Edward Benson, did you not hear what I just said? The magic pants are finished! Come to the workshop now and bring your lady friend," he declared triumphantly before heading back to the forest.

Letting out a nervous laugh, the young man watched as his father disappeared and then looked back at Natalie. "So... that was my father," he said after a long moment.

"Yeah, I gathered that," Natalie giggled. "Let's head to his workshop."

Shaking his head fervently, Blaine was quick to object. "No, no. We're not going to humor him. Besides, the workshop is the epitome of chaos with all the machines, the trolls, and the—"

"The trolls? Is that where they have all been hiding since the first day Rosie and I came?" She questioned, her eyes bright with excitement. "What are we waiting for? Let's go." Smiling brightly, the princess ran out of the hut.

"Wait, no! Natalie... wait!" Blaine shouted as he left the hut. "Why are you moving so fast? You don't even know where you are going,"

"Your father seemed pretty adamant and besides, I'm anxious to see Percy and the other trolls again." She insisted, still running.

"Natalie, I really don't think—"

"Take me to the workshop or I will just keep running through the forest until I find it." Natalie demanded.

"Okay, I'll show you my father's workshop. Just understand that you must never speak of it to anyone outside of this forest," he cautioned. "It's like nothing you have ever seen before."

Natalie beamed, "I cannot wait to see it!"

Shaking his head, Blaine forged on in front of her and led the way. Within minutes, the two stopped at the Tree of Friendship.

"Wow, this is a beautiful tree," Natalie whispered, eyeing the myriad of brightly colored branches.

"Yes," Blaine agreed. "It is, it reflects the beauty and love that make up this forest," he smiled sweetly, watching her facial expression the moment the password 'love' left his lips.

"Ooh... something's happening!" She exclaimed, a spark of excitement in her eyes as the trunk of the tree spread open while some of its branches came together to form a ramp for Blaine.

"Whoa… wha—" Natalie began, her voice shaking slightly as she watched Blaine push his chair onto the newly-formed ramp,

Laughing, Blaine waved her into the tree trunk. "C'mon," he urged. "It won't stay open long."

Taking a breath, the beautiful majestic flashed a nervous smile and grabbed onto the back of Blaine's chair, allowing him to lead her into the workshop. The floor shook slightly as the tree trunk closed behind the couple moments after they made it inside. *Uh oh… Maybe this wasn't such a good idea*, Natalie thought, squeezing Blaine's wheelchair a bit tighter. "Wha… what's happening?"

"Don't worry. We're safe here."

"That's right," Percy agreed, flashing a smile as he spotted Natalie. "Our magic will protect you."

"Percy!" She exclaimed. "It feels like it's been forever since I've seen you." Crouching down to the woodland creature's level, the princess hugged him, squeezing tightly. "Is this where you've been hiding?" Glancing over her shoulder, Natalie's mouth dropped open in disbelief. *Blaine was right when he said this place is the epitome of chaos*, she thought, scanning her surroundings. Several trolls looked to be avoiding working on the numerous, sewing machines that were covered in vibrantly-colored glitter and shined as brightly as any diamond ring she'd ever seen. They ran around holding screwdrivers and scraps of brightly colored fabric. "Whoa… what's going on around here?" The princess queried, as a black pair of pants holding a hammer walked swiftly passed her.

Smirking, Blaine whispered, "The pants are Papa's past failed attempts, now they work here right along with the trolls."

Smiling, Benjamin looked at Natalie. "This, young lady, is magic at its best," he held out his hand. "Ya probably don't remember me, your highness, but I know you," tilting his head toward Blaine, the older man smiled. "I'm Benjamin Benson… this knucklehead's dad. Sorry for being so rude before. I'm just so darn excited."

Chuckling, the princess shook his hand. "Don't worry about it, sir," she smiled brightly. "Please call me Natalie. I'm so glad I'm in your workshop. This is just amazing!"

"Well, then drop this sir business and call me Benjamin," smiling wider, he looked at her intently. "Do ya want ta' see somethin' real amazin'?"

"Sure, I would love to—" Natalie smiled nervously, eyeing the sewing machine over his shoulder.

Blaine, who had been quietly watching the exchange between them sighed heavily. "Papa, I'm sure she doesn't—"

Shaking his head vehemently, Benjamin cut off his son. "Stop gabbin' and let the lovely lady answer for herself son."

Giggling, Natalie shot Blaine a look. "Yeah, I'll speak for myself," she insisted before turning her attention back to his father. "Yes, I'd love to see something amazing."

"What're you doing?" Blaine whispered, his voice coated in anxiety.

"Stop worrying and just smile," Natalie whispered back as Benjamin led them to the only sewing machine in the workshop that was not covered in glitter. "You look super annoyed."

Letting out a huff, Blaine flashed a forced smile.

Unlike the other machines, the one Benjamin led them to was gold, shiny, and covered in gemstones. "You're here to do more than just see the workshop, young lady. I need you to sew the last stitch into this pair of pants."

Natalie looked from Benjamin to the sparkly machine and back. "This doesn't look like any sewing machine I've ever seen. Are you sure it's okay for me to use it?" She questioned, her voice tentative and full of anxiety.

"That's cuz it's not just any sewing machine, little lady. It's the SewSmart 3000. The gemstones add a bit of magic, which you are gonna finish stitchin' into the pants for my boy. It'll be great. You'll see. Now, take a seat and start sewin', little lady."

Glancing at Blaine, Natalie noted that his forced smile had turned into a full grimace. *I don't get why he looks so nervous. Whatever happens can't be that bad, right? His dad seems hopeful.* After considering it for another moment, she shrugged her shoulders, took a seat at the dilapidated work desk, and sewed the final stitch into the pair of pants.

Seconds later, the tree and everything in the workshop begun to shake and rattle. "Whoa... what's happening?" Natalie asked, running to Blaine's side, her eyes full of fear.

Gasping audibly, Benjamin could not contain his excitement. "You've done it!" Smiling from ear to ear, the excited magician cautiously picked up the pants and examined them, carefully tracing over the stitching with his forefinger. "Excellent! I have a really good feeling about these, son. Ya wanna know what the best part is? I don't have to put them on you like in the past. All you have to do is tap your knee three times, look at the pants, say Alakazam, and the pants will put themselves on. Why don't you try it? I have your magic carpet ready," he urged, his voice full of anticipation.

Blaine eyed the silver pants warily, his forehead scrunched in worry. "Uh... I don't know, Papa. Maybe later. Natalie and I really should be going."

Benjamin hung his head and let out a breath. "Okay, son."

Awww... they both sound so sad. I have to fix this. "Don't be hasty," Natalie said. "All we were gonna do is go back to the hut and read. Take a minute and try out the pants."

"Listen to your girl, my boy," Benjamin urged. "She's a good one."

Sighing, Blaine shot his father a look. "Papa, give us a minute, will you please?"

"What are you doing?" Blaine whispered once his father and the trolls had turned their attention back to the pants. "You know I don't want to try on the pants. You and I both know I'm not going to be able to walk in the pants, so humoring him is pointless. It will only encourage him."

"I don't see any harm in trying them on to make your dad happy." Natalie admitted in a hushed tone. "You never know, these pants might be different."

Blaine studied Natalie for a moment. "We talked about this. I thought you understood my point of view. Why do you want me to try the pants on so badly?"

Natalie sighed. "I was going to tell you before your father interrupted us that I want you to come to the castle for my birthday and meet my parents. I was thinking that maybe if the pants give you the ability to walk and you wear them to the castle, then Daddy will realize that he made a big mistake sending you guys into exile," she confessed quietly.

"So, all that stuff you said about how I should stay true to myself was a lie then, huh?" Blaine replied angrily.

Shaking her head vehemently, Natalie defended herself. "No, of course not. I just thought maybe if Daddy could see that your father's efforts weren't for nothing, then maybe he'd let you guys back into the kingdom and we could be together."

"Now the Forest of Wishes isn't good enough for you? We have to live in your kingdom even though I won't be accepted?" Blaine's anger increased by the minute.

"What are you talking about? I never said that," Natalie cried, her eyes filling with tears.

"No, but you've said enough. You should go," he said through gritted teeth.

"No, please. We need to—" she begun, tears streaming down her cheeks.

Ignoring her, Blaine looked to Percy. "Hey bud, Natalie's ready to go home. Show her out, will ya?" He turned around and sped away.

"Blaine... Blaine, where are you going?" Natalie called out, still crying.

What just happened? Doesn't he see I just want what is best for everyone? Grasping Percy's hand as the tree trunk begun to shake and once again formed a ramp she walked out to the Forest of Wishes.

"Don't cry, Miss Natalie. Whatever is troubling you will work itself out," Percy said kindly as he walked to the path leading to the castle.

I sure hope he's right, Natalie thought, slowly walking down the path toward her home.

A STILL TEARFUL Natalie described her argument to Rosie once the two were in the privacy of her bedroom that evening "I never expected him to get that upset, Rosie," She mumbled solemnly.

"Sweetheart, you guys had a fight. All couples have fights. Just give him time to cool off. I'm sure everything will be fine."

"I wish I was as confident as you are," the princess said, reluctantly crawling into her bed. Tossing and turning, she struggled to get comfortable. "I never should've encouraged Blaine to try on the pants."

"You had the best of intentions, Natalie. Blaine will understand that eventually. Trust me, you two are meant to be together," Rosie yawned. "It's getting late. You should really get some sleep. It will help you feel better."

Sitting up in her bed, Natalie shook her head. "I can't sleep at a time like this. I don't know how I ever found peace in here." Letting out an exasperated huff, she threw off her covers.

"What do you mean?" Rosie questioned sleepily, "Your room is so beautiful."

The room was indeed fit for a princess. The walls were a deep amethyst that pulsed in the light, sprinkled with framed photographs of the royal throughout her childhood. A mahogany desk, littered with wadded-up pieces of paper and various quills, stood in the right-hand corner while a wardrobe made of the same wood sat in the left, across from a marble vanity. This vanity matched none of the other furnishings but had sentimental value because it belonged to her grandmother. "I know, but it has way too much stuff. I'm really missing Blaine's hut right now. Being in such an uncluttered place really helps to free your mind. I could really use that tonight."

"I think you miss more than the hut right now, young lady. If you can't quiet your thoughts, why don't you try writing them down?" Rosie handed the princess a piece of parchment and a quill from her mahogany desk.

"Oh no, I couldn't." The young royal shook her head, her eyes wide and full of apprehension.

"C'mon, it might help. Besides, Blaine's been encouraging you to give in to your passion for writing, hasn't he?"

"How did you know that?" Natalie questioned, her cheeks suddenly a little pink.

"Murlyn's got a bit of a big mouth and, besides, your desk kind of gives it away," Rosie giggled, tilting her head toward the mess. "Go on sweetheart, give writing a shot. You may not be able to sleep, but my eyes are starting to feel heavy. I'll be able to sleep much better knowing that you're occupied and channeling all of those feelings into something useful," the troll urged, pushing the parchment and quill at Natalie again.

Taking the writing materials, Natalie groaned. "All right. I'll try. You might as well sleep in my bed. I'm not going to get any rest tonight anyway."

What should I write? How do I convey my feelings? Natalie stared at the blank parchment on her desk. *I'll express my feelings through characters,* she thought after a moment. *I'll write Blaine a story. He'll love it.* Taking a deep breath, Natalie reveled in her new-found confidence and inspiration as she began writing with furious determination. *Regardless of whether I'm able to make a difference in the kingdom, once I become queen, at least I wrote this.* Natalie started writing feverishly as the hours ticked by. Before she even realized what was happening the story was finished. *That was crazy,* she thought, blinking as she looked down at the words. *I can't believe how quickly the words came to me.* Letting out a breath, she sat at her desk and read with nothing but the sound of Rosie's quiet snoring in the background. *Wow... it's almost like writing is what I'm really meant to do. I just hope that the story can do what it is meant to do and convince Blaine that I don't want to change him, because I love him just the way he is.* Suddenly exhausted, she lay her head on the desk and quickly drifted off to sleep.

~

"Ugh, why does the sun rise so early?" Natalie shielded her eyes as the light poked through her curtains the next morning, waking her up.

Wiping sleep from her eyes, Rosie blinked at the beautiful majestic. "Oh, my goodness, have you been there all night?" she asked, a mixture of surprise and alarm in her voice.

"Judging by the pain in my neck I'd say so," the princess groaned, lifting her head up. "But I don't remember why," she said sleepily, finally opening her eyes.

Rosie chuckled, pointing to the large stack of parchment on the young woman's desk.

"Oh yes, yes of course," Natalie gathered the story and stood up at her desk. "This needs to get to Blaine ASAP. Will you take it to him for me please?"

"Don't you think I should help you first, sweetheart?" Rosie asked, her voice coated in concern. "Seems like you could use a wish to relieve the pain in your neck."

Natalie shook her head vehemently. "No, no, don't worry about me. Just get this to Blaine. And hurry," she urged, practically pushing the book pages at Rosie.

"Okay, okay… I'll go now." The pink glittery-haired troll assured her before scurrying out of the room.

I really hope the story serves its purpose. Natalie thought, crossing her fingers as she watched her friend leave to deliver her book to Blaine.

CHAPTER 15

I'm sure glad the storm blew right by the forest. It definitely would've ruined my spell, Dylock thought as he listened to Natalie talk about her writing. *Poor Natalie had no idea what events she set in motion by sending the story to Blaine that day,* he thought solemnly. *I thought things were going to be so much easier once I got my magic back.* Laughing, the troll shook his head. *That couldn't have been further from the truth.* The more Dylock was brought in and out of memories of the past, the more he dreaded even thinking about it. Still, he couldn't bring himself from going back in time to the night his dark magic returned. Within moments, he was his dark self, sitting in the southeast corner of Mount Wishnik, extremely agitated by the fact the Glomgurgle had yet to retire for the night.

THE SUN WENT down hours ago. I bet that idiot drake plans to never sleep now that I have my dark magic back, Dylock thought angrily. *No matter how long it takes, I'll be ready. Even a gargantouous creature like him has to give up sometime.* Finally, as the sun rose the morning after the woodland creature got his magic back, the floor of the volcano shook as the dragon begun to snore.

Time to give the ol' spider gemstone a whirl, Dylock stayed in the safety of the southeast corner of the volcano, ensuring that there was no chance that the dragon or other creatures who may walk by could see or hear him.

Glancing down at his belly, he smiled, rubbed the gemstone in the center of it, and said a revised version of the spell he'd developed long ago:

> *"Give me insight into the lives of the princess of Cinder's*
> *Edge and her friends.*
> *Allow me to see what makes them most vulnerable,*
> *so I can convince them that my friendship is genuine,*
> *before bringing them to their ultimate ends."*

The woodland creature's eyes widened in disbelief as he finished the spell and no smoke, light, or any sign of magic appeared.

What the heck? It's not working. Why isn't it working? He wondered, rubbing his gemstone harder. Despite his increased effort, Dylock still wasn't able to conjure up any magic.

Maybe I should repeat the—

A stabbing pain in his gemstone jarred the woodland creature from his thoughts. "Ouch," he shouted, grabbing his stomach instinctively.

Just when I thought I was going to get off the hook and figure out a way out of here, stupid troll intuition strikes again. Guess it's back to searching for mushrooms for me. The question now is how do I keep the dragon from once again getting in my way?

After pondering for several minutes, he could think of no solution. *This is hopeless,* he thought. *I am no better off then I was the day that blue-haired imbecile activated the protection spell and stole the black diamond.* "That's it," he whispered. "I can do a protection spell on the area of the ground where the mushrooms usually grow and then when they pop up in a few years Glomgurgle won't be able to touch them." *Why didn't I think of this years ago?* He wondered as he tipped-toed to the northwest corner in hopes of not waking the sleeping dragon. The closer he got, the more the ground shook. *Yes, the winged bully is still sleeping.* Smirking, he finished the trek to the stop where the mushrooms grew. "In the name of all that is magical, please let this spell work," he said in a voice just above a whisper. Gathering up as much of the dry soil as he could in one hand and rubbing his gemstone with the other, he quickly recited the following protection spell:

> *"Allow my dark magic to protect this soil and its fruits.*
> *Block the powers of Glomgurgle as well as the powers of*
>   *other creatures,*
> *so I an claim the black diamond from its roots, take control*
>   *of Cinder's Edge,*
> *and bring the kingdom to a boil."*

Dylock's heart pounded faster than a cheetah on the first day of hunting season as a cloud of thick black smoke formed around the soil he'd gathered. *It's working!* Energized by the thick smoke, the troll let out a roar of evil laughter.

Awaken by the sound, Glomgurgle snarled, poking only his head out of his lair. "Stop that laughing before I come in there and give you a reason to cry," he bellowed.

"I am s-sorry M-master," the troll stammered, turning to face the dragon. "I'm just excited about having my magic back."

"Magic back or not, I can still crush you like the larva you are," he growled before retiring to his lair for slumber.

My revenge toward that overgrown reptile is going to be so glorious. I'll bask in it for years. Smirking he glanced back at the soil he'd just protected. *Yes, indeed. I'll have my revenge. It's only a matter of time.*

~

SUDDENLY, a blue swallowtail butterfly landed on Dylock's nose, startling him back to the present moment. "Hey there, little guy," he whispered. Flying away as quickly as it had landed, the polka-dotted insect tickled his nostrils with its delicate wings as it took off effortlessly. Giggling, he watched it fly off into the distance. *Creatures like that are proof that no matter how crazy this world gets, it will still be beautiful. I am just so grateful that I'm able to see the beauty in this world now. No matter how often I try to forget, I'll always remember being blinded by the darkness,* he thought. *Now that I am as free as that butterfly, it's hard to believe that I once almost paid the ultimate price for freedom. If only I'd been more focused on finding freedom than conquering the dragon.* As Dylock's mind continued to reel with regrets of the past, he couldn't help but recall not putting a stronger protection spell on the mushrooms. Within mere moments, he was fully immersed in the memory and reliving the consequences of the spell.

"HOW DARE you put a protection spell on *my* mushrooms you measly little worm!" Glomgurgle growled, startling Dylock awake the morning of his twentieth year in the cold, drafty volcano.

Yes! Even after all these years my spell guarded the mushrooms. Adrenaline coursed through his tiny body as he ran to the northwest corner uninhibited. *Now's my*—Dylock stopped dead in his tracks when he spotted not the dragon eyeing the mushrooms, but a wild boar with coarse black fur that looked to weigh around 300 pounds and had a very hungry look in his eye.

Thunder erupted through the cave as the dragon approached. "I can't believe you thought you could pull one over on me. You may have protected the mushrooms from magical powers other than yours, but you didn't think to protect them from hungry wild animals," he snarled, a vindictive quality to his thick raspy voice.

That two-ton imbecile is right, Dylock thought angrily. *Why didn't I do a more inclusive protection spell? I am such an idiot. If I can't even get my hands on those mushrooms then I'll never be able to get my hands on the black diamond. I might as well just sacrifice myself*, he decided, quickly diving in front of the boar to cover the fungus.

A spell to make the mushrooms invisible to the naked-eye popped into his head at that moment. Quickly gathering them, he turned to face the wild pig. "You want the mushrooms?" He taunted, his voice coated with hatred.

The pig snorted.

"Of course, he does," the dragon snarled. "Give up, you pathetic little cockroach. You lose again. I may never get the black diamond back, but I am sure I'll find another way to conquer Cinder's Edge, and until then I'll keep torturing you," he growled.

"I wouldn't be so sure about that," Dylock declared before throwing the mushrooms as hard as he could.

The moment his enemies turned their backs, the troll rubbed his gemstone and quickly whispered the following spell:

"Make the mushrooms I just threw visible to only my eye.
Allow them to settle in the southeast corner where they can
    easily be found,
so the dragon I may defy,
before ultimately bringing Cinder's Edge to the ground."

Minutes later, the drake stomped back into the northwest corner sans the boar.

"What did you do?" He growled. "How did a creature as stupid as you get rid of the mushrooms so quickly?"

"I have no idea what you're talking about," Dylock said, feigning innocence. "The boar must've gotten them."

"You're a horrible liar you miserable little berry lover. Know that this doesn't change anything. I still expect you to get the black diamond back and *will* come up with different ways to make your life miserable. I am going to go find the boar and teach him a lesson for leaving the cave so rudely. I'm sick of you and your little games. Have a plan to get the black diamond back by the time I come back or else!" He bellowed, flying out of the volcano in moments.

That spell worked out better than I thought. Revenge is so close I can taste it, Dylock thought, smirking as he watched the dragon fly off into the distant sky.

～

WASTING NO TIME, Dylock gathered the mushrooms from the southeast corner of the volcano, popped them into his mouth, rubbed his gemstone and recited the only spell he could, his voice the quietest of whispers:

> *"Give me insight into the lives of the princess of Cinder's*
> *Edge and her friends.*
> *Allow me to see what makes them most vulnerable,*
> *so I can convince them that my friendship is genuine,*
> *before bringing them to their ultimate ends."*

Within seconds, a cloud of thick, black smoke formed around the troll. *Oh, thank god, it actually worked this time,* he let out a breath he hadn't realized he'd been holding, and scurried off to the west of the dragon's lair seconds before Glomgurgle appeared.

In mere seconds, Dylock's vision began to blur and soon he could see nothing but swirls of dark, dull blacks, browns, and grays. Staring at the swirling shapes, he suddenly felt extremely light, as though he were floating, and impulsively dived into the vortex of color. Seconds later, he saw Natalie, her expression solemn, as she sat at her marble vanity table, combing her beautiful auburn hair. Looking over her shoulder, he eyed the vanity mirror only to find that it wasn't a mirror at all, but a window into her hopes and dreams for the future. He saw her walking toward someone he vaguely recognized.

It could only be her childhood friend Blaine, who, despite being all grown up, still sat in a wheelchair. Smiling, the princess approached her friend in a sparkling white dress as the entire kingdom of Cinder's Edge watched. Then, as she continued to daydream, the vision changed. Blaine, who was just slightly older, read a book to a young toddler, who was his spitting image. Next to Blaine, Natalie rocked a younger baby girl to sleep.

What's happening? Dylock wondered. As the princess finished combing her hair, she settled in at her desk and began writing. As she put quill to parchment, words appeared in thin layers of smoke above her head, secretly revealing her thoughts to Dylock... *I haven't heard anything from Blaine about the book yet, but I still think it was the best way for me to express my feelings. My birthday wish is simple. I want him to apologize to me as well, so we can move on from our fight and figure out a way to be together.*

Dylock pondered on what he had heard... *It seems the princess knows what she wants for her future, but isn't sure if the object of her affection wants the same.* Just then, another swirl of color, this time consisting of dark greens and deep blues clouded his vision. *No, I'm not ready to stop listening to her yet.* Closing his eyes, he wished for the colors to go away. But he wasn't strong enough to control what was happening and, instead, found himself looking at a different scene.

Well, this is not exactly what I meant, but I suppose this will be interesting too, he thought upon seeing that he was no longer in Natalie's room, but instead on the path to the castle in the Forest of Wishes. Blaine was trying out what looked to be a magic pair of pants. But it wasn't the pants that drew Dylock's attention, Blaine was staring at something. *What is he staring at?* Dylock wondered, seeing that Blaine was eyeing something at the end of the path, instead of focusing on the pants he was about to wear. Following the young man's gaze, Dylock saw that he was longingly staring at what looked to be a mirage of Natalie, which Dylock realized had to be Blaine daydreaming of the princess. The young man was smiling from ear to ear. *Ugh... I guess the princess's feelings are reciprocated.* Shaking his head in disgust, Dylock started to walk away, but turned back as Blaine cleared his throat.

"Okay, Mama... please let this work. If this is what it takes for Natalie and I to be happy together in the kingdom, then work whatever magic you can up there in heaven."

Oh, now we're getting somewhere... could it be the two had a lover's quarrel surrounding Blaine's disability? Just as Dylock pondered that thought another swirl of colors, this time a mixture of burnt orange and dark crimson, clouded his vision. Opening his eyes as wide as possible, he tried his best to stay present in the hopes of seeing what would come next, but the colors soon became so bright that it forced him to shut his eyes. Blinking at the sight of the Tree of Friendship, somewhere that he and the other trolls had once gone to find peace and camaraderie, he hung his head.

What good is being here going to do me? He wondered angrily. *I already know that treasure trolls are suckers who believe in light magic. Oh, here are a couple of the suckers now,* he smirked as Rosie and Murlyn approached the tree. "Hey suckers, have ya missed me?" He taunted, waving his tiny hands in the air to get their attention. "I stole the black diamond from ya'll once and I'm gonna do it again," he let out a roar of evil laughter. *It's not as fun to taunt them when they can't see or hear me. I guess I should listen to whatever it is that they are going to whine about,* he sighed.

"Sweetheart, I know I said I wanted to focus on us and let those two figure things out for themselves, but can't we just nudge them in the right direction?" Murlyn questioned solemnly.

Shaking her head, Rosie answered in her tiny squeaky voice, coated in love and understanding. "We're dealing with matters of the heart, it wouldn't be right for us to push them in one direction or another. They trust us, so we have to trust them, too, and have faith that they will work things out."

Yuck, they are so sweet. I think I'm gonna hurl, Dylock felt relieved when color, this time a swirl of black and brown, once again clouded his vision. *Where am I going to end up next?* Letting out a breath, he shut his eyes again. He smirked, realizing he was back at Mount Wishnik. *Oh, thank god. Now all I have to do is execute my plan to capture the princess and the black diamond will be mine.*

DYLOCK RETURNED to the present almost as quickly as he'd left it when he once again heard footsteps approaching. Holding his breath, he stayed completely still as Natalie opened the small window of the hut. *It's over*, he thought. *How will I explain all of this?*

A moment later, he heard Blaine say, "There, we should be more comfortable now."

Whew. Dylock let out a breath. *This spell is going to take years off of my life. What was I thinking?*

As if on que, something his grandfather, Artemis, who'd raised him had always said popped into his head. *A spell is only worth doing if you see it through, kiddo.*

"Okay grandpa. I'll see this one through," he whispered. Smiling briefly at the thought of his beloved grandfather, he turned his attention to Blaine who was describing the resistance he'd once had to Natalie's writing.

BLAINE LOOKED at the thick stack of parchment in his hands. *I can't believe Natalie sent Rosie here with an apology letter the length of War and Peace, but wouldn't come here herself to apologize,* Blaine thought, tossing the stack onto his cot without a second thought.

"What's that on your cot?" Murlyn asked as he walked in and spotted it. "Did you finally find a way to get a new book without making a wish?" He chuckled.

Shrugging his shoulders, Blaine dismissed the idea. "Nah it's just something from Natalie that Rosie dropped off this morning."

"Rosie was here?" Murlyn questioned, smiling from pointy ear to pointy ear. "Why didn't you tell her to stop by my tree and say hi?"

"She said something about needing to get back and make sure the princess didn't have a kink in her neck," Blaine explained.

"Have you at least read what she dropped off? It looks pretty important."

"Nah, I don't care what Natalie has to say at this point," Blaine stated angrily.

"Well, then I guess you won't mind if I read it then." Hopping enthusiastically onto the cot, Murlyn gathered the parchment and began to read. An hour later, the treasure troll hadn't looked up from the story, not even once.

What could she have written that has Murlyn that enthralled? Blaine wondered. By the time another half hour had passed, he could no longer stand it. "What did she write that has you so interested?" Blaine asked, his voice still thick with anger. "I thought it was just an apology letter... what could be that exciting?"

"This is far from an apology letter," the troll answered after a moment, still not taking his eyes off the pages he was reading "I'm pretty sure it's about you or was at least inspired by you."

"What makes you say that?"

Still reading, Murlyn wordlessly pushed the portion of the stack he'd already read toward Blaine.

"Oh, all right," letting out a huff, Blaine reluctantly picked up the pieces of parchment and began reading.

Oh, my god. Blaine thought, smiling as her read the book, titled *Only You.* He read the foreword of the book and was taken aback. It was a story about a prince in a wheelchair, who is given the ability to walk after granting an evil sorcerer asylum in his kingdom. Blaine stopped reading and smiled to himself. *She gets it,* he thought and carried on reading the book about the prince's efforts to romance a princess of a neighboring kingdom. *She totally gets it,* he realized as he read that, in the end, despite the reversal of the spell, the prince and princess still find love.

"I was so wrong," he said after a long moment, his voice full of pure regret. "I have to go apologize. I have to tell her how much I love her."

Murlyn nodded. "I couldn't agree more. Hop to it and tell both of the girls 'hello' for me," he urged, handing Blaine the new invisibility cloak.

Nodding, the young man offered the troll reassurance, threw the invisibility cloak over himself as well as his wheelchair, and headed out of the hut, determined to make things right with Natalie.

~

"*Only You*... Where have I heard that before?" Isabel mumbled under her breath. "Wait a minute, Nana, are you..." Shaking her head, she trailed off. "No, it can't be."

"But it has to be," Rosie insisted, her eyes lit up with excitement. "Blaine just described the book."

Chuckling, Natalie nodded. "The secret's out. You girls are right. I wrote *Only You.* It was published a couple of years later under the penname Natasha Bonnett."

"Oh, my gosh! I knew it," Missy exclaimed, her voice full of a mixture of vindication and amazement.

Wide-eyed, Isabel stared at her grandmother. "That's amazing. Why didn't you tell me? Why all the secrecy?"

"Sweetheart, as queen, my duty to this kingdom was second to my duties as a wife and mother," Natalie explained. "I didn't want any of the praise or criticism I might have received as an author to get in the way of that. I love to write so I never wanted it to feel like work. Besides, I like being the elusive third Bonnett sister. Before today, I thought I may go my entire lifetime without anyone finding out that Natasha Bonnett and I are one in the same," she said wistfully.

Isabel hugged her grandmother. "You're so awesome, Nana. Don't worry, your secret is safe with me."

"Same here," Missy agreed.

Tears formed behind Natalie's eyes, and she flashed a weak smile. "Thank you, girls. I appreciate your loyalty so much. It's not easy to keep a secret, but sometimes it's important."

Nodding, Murlyn chuckled. "Dylock should be the one speaking to all of us about secrets."

"What do you mean by that, Daddy?" Missy asked. "What sort of secret did Dylock keep from you guys?"

With that, Missy and Isabel settled into their seats again as Murlyn answered their question, giving the girls yet another glimpse into the history of Cinder's Edge.

CHAPTER 16

I can't listen to this. I just can't. It's too shameful. Shaking his head, Dylock covered his ears and ran away from the hut and into the trees of the forest. Just before making it to the lime green fern he called home, he heard his grandfather's voice again. *You can't run away from this kid. You said you were going to face your past. And you conjured up a spell to do it, so you're going to face it.*

Looking up to the sky, he addressed his grandfather. "I can't do this, grandpa. I'm not strong enough."

Sure, you are. You can do this. You just need courage and a little magic, his grandpa encouraged.

Before Dylock could even think to utter more resistance, a cloud of green smoke formed around him. When the smoke disappeared, he found himself back in Mount Wishnik about to perform the spell that would help him capture the princess.

Here goes nothing," Dylock whispered, smiling down at his restored gemstone.

Rubbing the spider gemstone in the center of his stomach,

Dylock grinned as a cloud of thick, dark, blue smoke formed around him. Moments later, the dark black-haired troll closed his eyes and said with a voice full of disgust:

"Today I wish to trick the princess of Cinder's Edge, whom I despise.
May the dark magic within me provide the perfect disguise,
so I may lead her and the kingdom of Cinder's Edge to their ultimate demise."

Looking down at his belly, Dylock saw a pink, half-star-shaped gemstone as well as light-brown soot-free skin and smirked. Pulling on his dishelved hair, he noted the dark-blue color and grinned. *It worked*, he thought, his heart suddenly pounding in his chest. *Now, I just have to make sure I sound like that blue-haired loser Murlyn*, he grimaced, cringing at the thought. After a long moment, he closed his eyes and said:

"Make my voice match my disguise,
so I can easily lure the princess without her realizing
that she is one of the people I most despise."

Dylock once again stroked the gemstone in the center of his belly. Within seconds, a dark blue smoke cloud, just like the one that had engulfed him moments before, surrounded him. Taking a deep breath, Dylock inhaled as much of the smoke as he could. *Ewww... it smells like Roses. No wonder that loser's voice is so calming*, Dylock thought as he breathed in every last vapor of smoke. "That was just plain gross. This had better be worth it." Jumping at the sound of his voice, Dylock realized that what had once been deep and scratchy was now smooth and calming.

"Dark magic has done the trick yet again." he yelled excitedly.

Suddenly, a loud rumble made Dylock jump again. *It's about time that stupid drake woke up*, he smirked thinking of his future plans. Taking another breath, he calmed himself and slowly walked to the other end of the volcano, careful not to step into any of the lava-filled craters or onto a razor-sharp stalagmite, as he made his way to the dragon's lair. *Just act scared so the overgrown idiot doesn't suspect anything*, he told himself before stepping directly in front of the giant creature.

"Well, well, well. I never thought I'd see the day that a treasure troll would step into my lair willingly." Glomgurgle eyed the troll, his menacing voice laced with anticipation. "What should I do with you? Turn you into another lackey, perhaps? Or just kill you now and get it over with?"

Ha... I've tricked him just as I'd hoped. He's falling right into my trap. This is going to work perfectly. Dylock grimaced to disguise his happiness.

As Glomgurgle's eyes turned from coal black to fiery orange, Dylock finally spoke, his disguised voice full of not-so-feigned anxiety. "No, Master... it's Dylock. This is the disguise I'm going to lure the princess with."

A low growl escaped the dragon's throat as his eyes returned back to a less-menacing black. "Ah, yes. Brilliant... Cinder's Edge will undoubtedly meet its demise in no time and the black diamond will be mine," the dragon said, his voice full of dark excitement.

Ha ha... yeah, that's what you think. Dylock feigned attention as the dragon continued to lecture him.

"Do what you have to, but do it quick," Glomgurgle growled.

Letting out a breath, Dylock looked up at the dragon. "Thank you, Master. I won't disappoint you."

If he only knew, the troll thought, scurrying out of Glomgurgle's lair. *There's one last thing to do*, he thought, rubbing the disguised gemstone in the center of his belly as hard as he could. Taking a deep breath, he said:

> "Write the apology letter the princess seeks to go with my
>   new look,
> so I can gain her trust before she realizes what's in store and
>   she's hooked."

Within seconds, blue smoke covered both of the troll's tiny hands. "This is going to be perfect," Dylock whispered, reading the letter that appeared in his hands moments later. *I will have the black diamond in no time. I will be able to transform not only Cinder's Edge, but the entire world with dark magic. It's going to—*

"Go and find the princess before I do it myself," Glomgurgle growled interrupting the troll's thoughts. "And bring her to me the moment that you return."

"Yes, Master. Right away, Master," Dylock called out, his voice artificially fretful. *I better hurry.* Dylock looked down at his gemstone, ensuring his disguise was still intact. *Here goes nothing.*

Armed with Murlyn's look and the apology letter desired by Natalie, Dylock let out another evil laugh as he left the volcano, determined to find the young royal and lure her to the dragon's lair.

"Caw, caww, caww," the sudden screech of a crow as black as coal startled Dylock back to the present. *What was I thinking? How could I do something so deceitful to someone as sweet as Natalie?* A single tear rolled down his left cheek. "Toughen up," he whispered to himself, wiping it away.

At that moment, Dylock's grandpa offered him advice once again. *You can do this. You are strong and although you strayed at one time, you are the treasure troll I raised. Be brave. Show your friends who you truly are.*

Grandpa's right, Dylock thought, suddenly more determined to make the spell work. *I will find a way to show them who I am. I must,* he thought, turning his attention to Natalie, who was describing how he lured her to Mount Wishnik.

"Murlyn, what are you doing all the way out here?" Natalie questioned, having spotted him just outside of the castle. Quickly looking from her right to her left, the princess made sure they were alone. "You could get in so much trouble being this close to the castle. What're you thinking?" Her hushed voice was coated in confusion.

"Oh, I know dear, but I'm here on a very important mission," the troll explained. "Blaine asked that I give you this as soon as possible." Dylock, disguised as Murlyn, handed her the apology letter.

Accepting the letter, Natalie read it and instantly begun to tear up. "I don't understand," she sniffled. "Why did he chance you getting in trouble by sending you with the letter? Why not just come and apologize himself?"

"Well, my dear, Blaine is nervous to see you after the way he acted the other day, so I told him I'd bring the letter on his behalf."

Something is up. Murlyn never calls me dear. Shifting her weight from one side to the other, she studied him. "What's really going on? I mean, I know my twenty-fifth birthday is tomorrow and all, but that's really not that old and you never call me dear."

"Oh, all right. You caught me," Dylock admitted, his eyes suddenly full of anxiety. "Blaine not only asked me to give you the apology letter, but also to bring you to a picnic he planned for your birthday."

"Awww… he planned a picnic?"

"Yes, he thought it would be a sweet way to apologize and celebrate your birthday. But don't tell him or Rosie that I told you," he said fretfully. "I set up a little picnic for me and Rosie as well."

"Don't worry," Natalie smiled. "Your secret is safe with me. Lead the way."

Smiling, Dylock obliged, but to Natalie's surprise the two were still walking hours later. "This is a bit of a hike, isn't it?" She questioned.

"Yes, you're quite right princess," the woodland creature chuckled. "Blaine wanted to make sure the two of you had some privacy but, don't worry, I know a short cut and we're almost there."

Uh oh... I should've trusted my initial instinct that something was wrong. We're approaching Mount Wishnik. Natalie's heart practically jumped into her throat. *I have to get out of here and find Blaine fast.* The princess quickly started backing away as she saw the volcano up ahead.

Dylock spotted her shadow moving. "Where are you going? Don't you want to go to the picnic?"

Just be brave, she told herself. "I know you're not Murlyn," the princess admitted, her voice full of fear. "As the princess of Cinder's Edge, I forbid you from being within five hundred miles of the kingdom. Now, leave before I alert the royal guard," she shouted, a mixture of the authority her mother had tried to teach her in queen lessons and fear of the unknown in her voice.

"What are you talking about?" Dylock questioned, his voice coated in insincere surprise. "Of course, I'm—"

I banished him and he's still trying to trick me... what kind of creature is this?

Suddenly, Natalie felt as angry as she was terrified. "No, you're not Murlyn," she shouted, trembling as she looked at the woodland creature. "There is no way that Murlyn would bring me this close to Mount Wishnik knowing who is in there. Now, do as I said and leave me be or face dire consequences!" She shouted, folding her arms across her chest.

Suddenly, the troll laughed so hard that the pink half-star-shaped gemstone in the center of his belly fell off to reveal a spider-shaped gemstone in its place. "You're smarter than I thought, princess. Guess we're going to do this differently than I planned."

Uh oh... that laugh sounded evil and that gemstone doesn't look like any I've ever seen before. He's not like any other troll either. I'm in real trouble, she realized her stomach suddenly queasy. *You can do this,* the princess told herself. *You have to be brave for yourself and your kingdom.* "I don't care what you have planned. It's not going to— ouch!" Natalie exclaimed, surprised as the troll jumped up and yanked a few strands of hair from her head.

Before the young royal could even question what was

happening, the troll rubbed the strands of hair against his gemstone. After a tense moment, he said:

"I took these strands of hair from the Cinder's Edge heir.
Now make this young woman who is so fair
succumb to magic, so I can bring her into Glomgurgle's
lair."

Within moments, a cloud of blue smoke surrounded both of them. "Whatever you're trying to do isn't going to work. I'm stronger than—" Natalie begun before everything went black.

THE SMELL of sulfur assaulted Natalie's nostrils as she awoke to find herself sitting up against cold hard stone. *Where am I?* Standing up, she shook her head, blinking. Moments later, as her eyes adjusted, she gasped at the sight of Glomgurgle's tail. *Oh, my God.* Scanning her surroundings, she noted the numerous stalactites above her head and craters of bubbling lava just inches away from her feet. *I'm inside a freaking volcano.*

"Sounds like sleeping beauty is awake." the dragon growled, swinging his tail around. He eyed her. "Hello, princess."

Throwing a stone at his head, Natalie eyed the dragon. "Don't 'hello' me, you two-ton bully!" She shouted angrily. "What do you have against Cinder's Edge? Why did you bring me here?" She tried her best to sound tough despite the fact that she was shaking more than a rattle snake's tail.

Glomgurgle let out a loud growl from deep within his throat. "She's a feisty one, all right." The dragon's eyes instantly turned fiery orange. "Let's just kill her. It'll make things a lot more interesting," he inhaled deeply, still staring straight at her.

"No, Master!" A black-haired troll with a spider-shaped gemstone shouted, stopping Glomgurgle from letting out his breath. "If we kill her now, we won't have anything to bargain with.

It'll be ten times harder to retrieve the black diamond," the troll said, his voice shaking slightly.

Oh, my God. They are going after the black diamond and using me as bait!

Glomgurgle huffed, small puffs of smoke emitting from his nostrils. "Fine. Then I'll hurt her just enough." he took another breath and blew a cloud of black smoke at her.

The smoke smelled of rotten eggs and nearly knocked Natalie to her knees. After mere moments, moments that felt like an eternity, the smoke and odor dissipated. "Is that all you— AAAAAAHHHHHHH!" The princess's relief was short lived as a burning sensation one thousand times worse than any sun burn she'd ever felt radiated through all her limbs.

Glomgurgle chuckled, but it sounded more like the crackle of lightening than amusement. "Oh, this is going to be real fun." he bellowed, the fire in his eyes intensifying.

Letting out another breath, he blew a cloud of purple smoke in her face. Seconds later, her still-burning legs were covered in scorpions. Pulling one from her right leg, Natalie threw it at the dragon with all the strength she could muster. *What kind of magic is this fire-breathing loser using on me?* She wondered, wide-eyed, watching the scorpion bounce off his wing before disintegrating into thin air. A cloud of green smoke overwhelmed her senses, making her cry out as her shoulder blade shattered. Collapsing to her knees, Natalie hung her head. *No matter what happens, I can't let this monster see me cry*, she told herself. *I have to be strong. The future of my family, my kingdom, and magic depend on it.*

"Ready to give up yet, princess?" Glomgurgle growled, his fiery eyes more intense than ever as he watched her roll around in pain.

"Never!" She shouted angrily. "You can do whatever you want to me, I'll never give up. I'll never let you hurt my kingdom!"

"I'm afraid you have no choice, princess!" Glomgurgle bellowed, his voice more menacing than ever before. "I'm far more powerful than you!" He took another breath, letting it out and this time he blew three multi-colored rings of smoke in Natalie's direction.

Holding her breath, the princess closed her eyes, bracing herself for whatever may happen next. Moments later, she was surprised to hear the troll cry out, and she opened her eyes. "I'm sorry, Master!" The troll cried. "It's just that she has to be in one piece if we want to distract them long enough to get the black diamond, remember?" He urged, his voice trembling.

"Fine! But you better be right about all of this, Dylock. If this plan of yours doesn't work, you'll pay the price!" The dragon warned, small puffs of smoke once again coming out of his nostrils, as he walked away.

Dylock? Why does that name sound familiar... Oh, my God, that's the treasure troll that Blaine told me Glomgurgle made into his minion. Glomgurgle must've asked him to lure me here. I wish there was some way I could let Blaine know what's going on. I'm sure if he knew what was happening he'd be here to rescue me by now, wouldn't he? As she pondered, doubt crept into her mind. *What if he doesn't come? What if no one comes? What if they all decide to sacrifice me for the sake of the black diamond?*

Suddenly, in the midst of her overwhelming thoughts, Natalie heard a calming voice that was familiar and unfamiliar all at once. *Don't worry, sweetheart. My Blaine has everything he needs to save you and he's coming. Just stay strong.*

She's right, whoever she may be. I need to just hang in there until Blaine comes and everything will be just fine, the princess told herself, finally feeling more confident that everything would be okay despite the excruciating pain in her shoulder.

CHAPTER 17

Uh oh... Maybe I'm not the only one who needs to apologize for something. Once certain that there were no other humans around, Blaine removed the invisibility cloak he'd hid under. He was surprised to see a sobbing Rosie just outside of the castle. "What's wrong? Why are you crying?" He asked with genuine concern.

Still sobbing, the pink glittery-haired troll handed him a piece of paper.

"Oh, my god... Glomgurg—" Blaine begun, his voice full of a mixture of fear and anger.

A still tearful Rosie reached up and put her tiny hand over Blaine's mouth. "Shhh... King Frederick hasn't made the official announcement yet. He doesn't want to frighten the public."

"I don't care about the public right now. Why isn't anyone out there looking for her? The whole kingdom should be up in arms. What's going on?"

"This is going to be distributed throughout the kingdom within the hour." Rosie explained, handing him another piece of paper.

"What the heck is this?" he asked, his voice just above a whisper but full of anger. "Natalie's been kidnapped and he's more worried about finding her a husband? This is complete garbage." Crumpling up the paper, he whipped his wheelchair around and wheeled himself away from the castle.

"Where are you going?" Rosie shouted after him.

"To talk to Murlyn. I'd love to go and kill Glomgurgle right now, but I know I can't go into Mount Wishnik without a plan."

Pushing his wheelchair as hard as he could, Blaine made it from the castle to the hut in under thirty minutes, busting through the door.

"Whoa, watch the door there, son," Benjamin warned. "I just put that door back on its hinges the other day."

"Sorry, Papa, this is an emergency. I need to talk to Murlyn. Have you seen him?"

Rosie grabbed onto the armrest of Blaine's wheelchair, having finally caught up with him. "I made it," she said, struggling to catch her breath.

"I'm right here." Murlyn poked his head out from behind Benjamin. "What's going on?" Wide-eyed, he rushed to Rosie's side. "Are you okay sweetheart?"

Shaking her head, the pink glittery-haired troll handed him copies of the pieces of papers she had shown Blaine.

"Oh no..." Murlyn whispered, suddenly ghostly-white as he dropped the papers to the floor.

"What? What is it?" Benjamin asked, his voice coated in concern as he spotted the woodland creature's loss of color.

Blaine quickly told his father about how the princess had been kidnapped by Glomgurgle and how Frederick had decided to turn her rescue into a competition to find her a husband.

"I'm so sorry, my boy," Benjamin said, his voice solemn and quiet. "But at least now you can wear the pants that Natalie helped sew to go save her." Smiling, he held up the silver pants, proudly presenting them to his son.

Scoffing, Blaine shook his head. "I've got more important things to worry about right now, Papa."

"But, son, I really think these pants will give you the edge ya need in the compet—"

Cutting his father off, Blaine turned his attention to Murlyn. "Tell me everything you know about that stupid fire breather, Murl. I need a plan."

"Believe it or not, I agree with your father on this one." Murlyn admitted. "I think the first thing you need to do is see if you're able to walk in those pants or not. Mount Wishnik is a scary place. You're going to need to be as physically and psychologically fit as possible if you plan to go up against Glomgurgle."

"What are you saying?" Blaine shouted, his eyes widened in disbelief. "You don't think I can go up against Glomgurgle in my wheelchair?"

The troll sighed. "That's not what I'm saying. It's just that Glomgurgle is no ordinary dragon. We can't let him see any weakness on your part."

Shaking his head, Blaine looked from his father to Murlyn. "You're crazy… you're both crazy."

"I agree with them Blaine." Rosie admitted after a moment, her squeaky, high-pitched voice full of apprehension. "There's no telling how many men will plead their case to the king and queen once word of a competition for the princess's hand spreads through Cinder's Edge."

"Plead their case… what do you mean?" Blaine asked, confused.

"Oh, did I not mention that part earlier? Every man who wants a chance to save the princess must go to the king and explain why he's qualified to rescue the princess and prove that he is strong enough." Rosie explained.

Sighing, Blaine hung his head. "Okay. I'll try on the pants."

"Ya won't regret it, my boy. I have a great feelin' about these." Benjamin smiled from ear to ear. "After all, the woman you love helped to sew them."

"Yes, she did and I'm going to save her if it is the last thing I do," Blaine said determinedly. With that, he, his father, Murlyn, and

Rosie left the hut and gathered around the Tree of Friendship. They were soon joined by the other trolls.

Smiling, Benjamin laid the magic carpet down in front of Blaine's wheelchair "Whenever you're ready, son." he encouraged, carefully laying the pants onto the magic carpet.

Examining the pants, Blaine eyed them questioningly. "Okay, Mama… please let this work. If this is what it takes for Natalie and me to be happy together, then work whatever magic you can up there in heaven," he said in the quietest of whispers, tapping his knee three times. "Love." he declared after a moment.

Suddenly, Blaine heard a voice that seemed strangely familiar to him even though he'd never heard it before. A voice he instantly knew belonged to his mother. *Everything will work as it should, sweet boy. Just remember, as you begin this journey love is the most powerful magic there is, and the capability to love is within all of us.*

Benjamin and the trolls watched in awe as the pants floated over Blaine and onto him in mere seconds. "I don't understand, son. You were supposed to use the word 'Alakazam'. Why did you say love?" He asked, holding his hands out to his son.

"Love was sewn into these pants, so I figured I should use that word to activate their magic." Smiling, Blaine shook his head. "Thanks, Papa, but I'm going to try and stand up on my own. I actually have a very good feeling about these pants."

Reveling in the confidence his mother had given him, Blaine took a breath. "Okay, Mama… stay with me." Blaine whispered, carefully swinging the footrests of his wheelchair out of the way.

"You can do this, son." Benjamin encouraged. "One step at a time."

Taking another breath, Blaine took a step forward and then another. *I definitely feel differently than I have before when trying to walk in the past*, he thought. *More secure. Whoa… so this is what the ground feels like underneath your feet*, he realized after taking a few steps on the magic carpet as the trolls begun to cheer.

"Oh, my God… son, you're walking! You're actually walking. I can't believe it! I've waited for this day for so long, my boy!" Benjamin exclaimed, rushing over to hug him.

Giving his father a quick hug, Blaine looked over his shoulder to the trolls. "We can celebrate later. I have another challenge to conquer first," he said resolutely, before starting his way down the path between the forest and the castle.

THE LINE of men looking for a chance to compete for Natalie's hand begun outside of the castle walls. *Wow, Rosie was right. Look at all these men. How am I ever going to prove that I deserve a chance to save Natalie?* Blaine eyed the long line of men ahead of him.

"Don't worry Blaine. We can—"

Blaine jumped at the unexpected sound of Murlyn's voice. "Oh, my God Murl, what are you doing here?"

"I'm here to help. I know I haven't seen Frederick or Alexandria in years, but I figured I can at least help gauge their moods for you."

Throwing his head back, Blaine chuckled. "No offense, Murl, but their daughter is being held for ransom. It doesn't take a rocket scientist to know that they are likely to be very angry and frantic right now." He looked the woodland creature straight in the eye, his tone suddenly more serious. "Thanks for trying to help, but I'm going to prove that I am man enough to save Natalie myself. I need to do this on my own."

"Are you sure?"

Uh oh, glancing around, Blaine noticed some of the other men in line were shooting questioning glances at Murlyn. "Yes, please go before too many people see you. Go make sure Rosie is okay. I'll be fine. Besides, I'm not alone. Mama is watching over me; I can feel it."

The troll smiled, "I told you she would be there for you if you just let her in. Best of luck, Blaine. I have the utmost confidence in you," he encouraged, before hesitantly heading back to the forest.

How am I ever going to get a shot at this? How am I going to convince them that I am strong enough? Blaine watched man after man go into the castle with grenades, guns, and bows and arrows.

You don't need a weapon to convince them, sweet boy. Just be honest about how much you love Natalie, and Alexandria will give you a shot at saving her daughter. His mother's voice advised after a moment. *Just be confident.*

Armed with his mother's advice, in time, Blaine walked confidently into the throne room of the castle. Clearing his throat, he approached Frederick and Alexandria who sat in jewel encrusted thrones, with the pillar that held the black diamond between them. "Good evening, your majesties. My name is Blaine Benson and I would like the opportunity to save your daughter from Glomgurgle," he flashed them a confident smile.

"Benson... I thought I knew everyone in the kingdom, but I don't recognize you. Who are you, young man?" Alexandria questioned, looking him straight in the eye.

"I'm Blaine—" he begun.

Anger flashed across Frederick's face. "How dare you walk in here and ask for a chance to rescue my daughter?" Frederick, a now plumper man with thinning gray hair stood up from his throne, his face bright red. "I put you and your crazy father into exile twenty years ago and just because his cockamamie pants actually worked, you think you—"

"Frederick, shut up!" Alexandria bellowed.

Wide-eyed, a shocked Frederick sat back on his throne.

"Our daughter has been taken by a fire breathing dragon that has been after our kingdom for years and instead of going after her full force, I let you talk me into this ludicrous decision to find her a future husband. The least you could do is not attack each one of the potential suitors that come in here."

Letting out a huff, Frederick turned toward Alexandria and shook his head. "But, Alexandria, he's a cripple—"

Shaking her head, the queen cut him off once again "I have listened to you long enough," she said defiantly. "The future of Cinder's Edge and, more importantly, the life of our only child is at stake, so I'm going to start following my instincts like I should have done years ago." Before her husband even had a chance to respond, the queen turned her attention to Blaine. "Come with me," she urged.

Wow this place hasn't changed at all since Rosie gave me my safety gear, Blaine thought, noting the sleek, professionally designed kitchen with granite counters, stainless steel appliances, spotlessly scrubbed utensils on hooks, and the gentle swish of the dishwasher as he walked in.

"Have a cookie." Alexandria suggested, her voice kind and calm as she sat a plate of chocolate chip cookies on the granite counter.

"Thank you." Blaine smiled, taking a cookie from the platter.

"You're welcome. Now, while you enjoy it, tell me what my husband was shouting about."

"Oh, with all due respect, your majesty, it's not my place to—"

"Young man, do you want the chance to save my daughter from Glomgurgle or not?" The queen questioned pointedly.

Uh oh. I better start explaining myself, Blaine thought, taking a bite of the cookie.

Swallowing, he shook his head vehemently. "Yes, yes of course. I love Natalie very much. It's just that everything else is so complicated." he explained before taking another bite of his cookie.

"Young man, that's no excuse. Life is complicated. Tell me what you know that I don't."

Why am I always the one who has to tell people about things Frederick did in the past? Blaine wondered.

Everything will be all right, sweet boy. Just be honest, the voice of his mother reminded him after a moment.

Sighing, Blaine proceeded to tell the queen about how she and his mother had been best friends until her untimely death.

"I-I don't understand. Why do I not remember anything about her or you?" Alexandria queried, shock coloring her voice.

Shifting his weight from one side to the other, Blaine told her about the deal that had been made at her wedding, his disability, and his father's obsession.

"Well, clearly, your father did not hold up his end of the bargain." The queen let out a curt laugh.

"No, he didn't. Well, not in time anyway. That's why Frederick sentenced me, my father, and the trolls into exile."

"Trolls?" The queen questioned, her right eyebrow raised.

Chuckling, Blaine told her about Murlyn, Rosie, and the other trolls.

"You, my friend, are a wealth of knowledge." Alexandria smiled. "Why do you love my daughter?"

Whoa... I should've seen that question coming. Laughing, Blaine's cheeks grew hot as he considered his answer. "There are so many reasons that it's hard to narrow them down. Your daughter is wonderful. She is brilliant, but humble at the same time. She accepts me for who I am now, but, at the same time, makes me want to be better. For those reasons and so many more, I love her and would love nothing more to try and save her if you'll let me."

"Frederick has picked four others, but my money is on you," the queen smiled. "Know why that is young man?"

Shaking his head, Blaine bit into another cookie.

"When you spoke about my daughter just now, you had the look of a man in love. There was a sense of adoration in your voice that I have longed to hear in my husband's voice for as long as I can remember, yet never have." she admitted wistfully. "As I said, four other suitors have been chosen. If the gentleman sent tomorrow morning does not succeed, the next gentleman will be sent tomorrow afternoon. If he does not succeed, two more suitors will be sent the following day. Finally, if neither of those gentlemen conquer Glomgurgle, you will be sent the following day so be ready to face that fire breathing tyrant in three days."

As Alexandria's words registered, Blaine dropped his cookie to the floor. "Oh, thank you your majesty. Thank you so much. You won't regret this."

"I better not," she said, her voice full of authority. "Feel free to take the cookies with you. Now, if you will excuse me, I need to have a serious discussion with my husband."

"Oh yes, of course. Thank you so much for the cookies. They're delicious. I'll be going. I've got a princess to save," Blaine said, before he left the castle feeling happier than he had in days.

~

THE ANXIOUS EYES of several trolls landed on Blaine as he opened the door of the hut, practically bursting with excitement. "Alexandria gave me a shot." Blaine shouted. "I can't believe it! I'm going to get to save Natalie!"

"Oh, I'm so relieved," Rosie said as the other woodland creatures begun to cheer.

"Way to go, son." Slinging his arm around Blaine's neck, Benjamin smiled. "I knew you could convince her."

"Really?" Blaine questioned. "I wasn't sure. I'm still not even sure how I'm going to save Natalie, but I'm sure glad I've got the opportunity."

"That's it son, focus on the positive. Don't worry about going up against that fire-breather, you'll be fine."

OH MY GOD... Papa's right. I have to go up against a fire breathing dragon. How am I gonna make sure he doesn't blow me to smithereens, let alone save Natalie? Suddenly, feeling nauseous, Blaine held his stomach and looked to Murlyn. "You know me better than anyone, old friend. Can I really pull this off?" He asked, his voice quiet and full of doubt.

Looking from one end of the hut to the other, the dark blue-haired woodland creature spoke for the first time that evening, addressing the other trolls. "Okay everyone, I know this is all very exciting, but I'm going to have to ask you to move the celebration outside so that Blaine can strategize."

"I am staying right here," Rosie said firmly. "I've been through way too much with that girl to start minding my own business now."

"Strategize all you want Blaine." Bernie encouraged, walking toward the door. "Just defeat the stupid dragon once and for all," he said excitedly before closing the door behind him and his fellow woodland creatures.

Oh great. Just what I need... more pressure. As the enormity of the task that lay ahead of him continued to sink in, Blaine's stomach churned.

"Take a seat on the cot, bud. You're ghostly white." Murlyn said.

"Eat this," Rosie suggested, holding a blueberry out to him.

Eyebrows furrowed, Blaine shot Murlyn a questioning look. "That's not just any blueberry is it?"

Murlyn reassured Blaine. "That berry was picked from the Tree of Friendship. It should help settle your stomach."

Accepting the berry from Rosie, Blaine bit into it. "Thanks, but I think I'm gonna need more than a magic blueberry to help with this." he chomped into the berry again, finishing it. "I don't know what I'm going to do. I mean, I should've thought this through before going to the castle. How is a guy like me, who has barely even been around people for twenty years, going to kill a monster like Glomgurgle?"

"You got Alexandria's approval. Trust me, that's half the battle," Murlyn chuckled.

"Murl, this is no time for jokes. I need a plan," Blaine insisted, his tone desperate.

"I know, bud. Just take a breath."

Rolling his eyes, Blaine did as instructed.

"Okay, now... you said something about having three days to prepare. What do you mean?" Murlyn asked, sitting on the cot next to Blaine, as Rosie sat at the table across from them.

"I'm going at the end of the week, if the others have failed their rescue attempts. Although, all that means is that I have the most time to sit and worry," Blaine sighed.

"Au contraire, mon frère. it puts you at an advantage. It means that you can avoid making the mistakes of your competitors and develop an ironclad defense to vanquish Glomgurgle," Murlyn declared, his eyes suddenly glittering with excitement.

If only this were really that simple, Blaine chuckled to himself. "You seem to have skipped a couple of steps ahead of Rosie and I. Care to catch us up?"

"I'm going to use my invisibility cloak to spy on our competition," Murlyn grinned. "Hopefully I'll discover a way to finally defeat that overgrown lizard."

"No, Murlyn! You mustn't!" Rosie cried, standing up from the table. "That's a death sentence!"

Waving a dismissive hand, Murlyn stood and closed the space between him and his love. "Nonsense, no one will even see me." Leaning down ever so slightly, he kissed her on the forehead. "I'll be fine."

"Yeah, Rosie," Blaine agreed. "Everything will be fine, and this may be our only shot at discovering a way to defeat Glomgurgle."

Rosie's eyes filled with tears. "How can you be so sure?"

"Sweetheart, do you remember what I said before? Our love is strong enough to conquer anything."

Tears flowing down her cheeks, Rosie nodded. "Once we are past all of this, you better keep your promise to me and focus on us, once and for all time."

"I plan to do nothing less," he said, embracing her tightly.

With that, Murlyn and Blaine planned to meet at the Tree of Friendship at dusk for the next two days and then he and the woodland creatures bid each other good night.

Be with Murlyn over the next few days please, Mama. Protect him with whatever magic you have up there in heaven, because he's definitely going to need it. In fact, we could all use a little heavenly magic right now, Blaine thought as he laid down on his cot that evening.

Tossing and turning for most of the next couple of hours, Blaine struggled to find sleep. *What was I thinking?* He wondered. *I can't sleep at a time like this. I need to focus on the competition. I can't let that power-hungry dragon or anyone take Natalie from me. I won't. I love her too much.* Pulling his wheelchair over to the cot, he carefully transferred into it and ventured outside. The late hour meant that it was cold enough for the wind to hurt Blaine's face, but he didn't care. *Poor Natalie is probably in far greater pain than I am right now. I have to save her, but how? How is a guy like me going to defeat a 20-foot-tall dragon?* As Blaine thought about the reality of the task ahead of him, his chest tightened, making it hard to breathe. Not knowing what else to do, he looked up to the star-studded sky and said whispered. "I don't know what to do, Mama. Please tell me what to do. Please tell me how to defeat him."

You're going to be okay, sweet boy. Just take a breath and think about not only who you are protecting, but what you're protecting. Ask yourself what the dragon is truly after, Lizzie's spirit advised.

Blaine's eyebrow's furrowed. "C'mon, Ma. We all know he's after the black diamond."

Exactly. Give him what he was after and you'll have a chance to save Natalie, sweet boy. You can do this. I'll be watching over you the entire time.

Chuckling, Blaine addressed Lizzie again, his voice sarcastic. "Thanks Ma, but something tells me, just giving that fiery-eyed monster the black diamond is not a good idea. Besides, even if I wanted to, I couldn't shrink the black diamond. When I was a kid Murlyn said that Dylock shrunk down the black diamond years ago in order to capture it and, as we all know, spells preformed through dark magic can never be replicated by light magic."

After a long moment, Lizzie responded. *Even the dirtiest of rocks can shine as much as the black diamond with a little magic.*

"Oh my God…that's brilliant!" Blaine exclaimed, bending down to grab a small rock from underneath the wheel of his chair. Looking up to the sky again, he smiled. "Thanks for your help, Mama."

Energized by his mother's tip, he pushed his wheelchair to the Tree of Friendship as quickly as his arms would allow. Placing the small stone he'd found onto his right leg, Blaine squeezed a magical blueberry onto the rock and said:

"Turn this rock into my secret weapon.
Let the magic in this berry allow it to sparkle black,
so Glomgurgle won't suspect deception,
when I take the princess back."

Moments later a bright blue glittering light formed around the rock, making it glow incandescently. Blaine grinned as it disappeared in seconds, leaving a smooth, shiny, black stone in its wake.

"Yes, it worked! This will make a fantastic decoy. *I just hope that Glomgurgle is enough of an idiot to fall for it. I guess time will tell. I only hope Natalie has that time.*

Remember what I said, sweet boy. You can do this. You and Natalie will be just fine. You just have to have faith in yourself, Lizzie reminded him.

Blaine once again looked up to the twinkling stars in the sky above. "Don't worry, Ma, as long as you are watching over me, I'll have faith in us," he said sweetly before making his way back to the hut.

CHAPTER 18

Somehow, this place seems even creepier than it did twenty years ago. A chill traveled up Murlyn's back as he tip-toed into Mount Wishnik under the cover of his invisibility cloak and spotted a half-eaten snail inching its way along the soot covered ground. *My ankle has never been the same since I stepped into that lava,* he thought as he came up on the craters once again. *I better* —"AAAAHHHHH!!!!" Suddenly, a scream in the distance interrupted Murlyn's thoughts. *Oh no, am I too late?* He wondered, running toward the sound.

Murlyn skidded around the corner and stopped suddenly. *What the heck is that guy doing?* Murlyn watched as a man with curly black hair and dark green eyes attempted to strike the dragon with a bow and arrow. Instead of finding its mark, the arrow clipped the sleeve of the red lace dress the princess wore, missing her hand by inches.

Fighting fire with a bow and arrow... real husband material right there. Holding his breath, Murlyn watched as the potential suitor loaded another arrow into his bow.

"Where's the black diamond?" Glomgurgle demanded.

"I-I-I'm h-here for the princess," the curly-haired suitor admitted, shooting another arrow at the dragon.

Lunging at the flying arrow, Glomgurgle caught it and crushed it between his razor-sharp teeth and spat it out.

"You can have her as soon as I have the black diamond," the dragon bellowed.

The suitor let out a nervous chuckle. "I w-will n-never give you the black diamond. T-t-turn over the princess now." the potential suitor shouted meekly, shooting off yet another arrow.

Expanding his wings, the dragon easily dodged the arrow and flew directly above the suitor. "Don't you get it?" Glomgurgle growled, puffs of smoke emitting from his nose. "These arrows are useless against me. Give me the black diamond," the dragon insisted as his eyes turned from coal black to an intense, fiery red.

"N-Never," the suitor insisted, his voice trembling.

"We'll do this the hard way then," Glomgurgle growled, taking a deep breath.

Well, this potential husband is definitely a goner, Murlyn cringed as the dragon open his mouth as if to unleash fire. *If only I cou—Oh NO!* Biting down on his lip, the dark-blue troll fought the urge to scream out as Glomgurgle turned toward the princess at the last second, unleashing his fiery breath right in her direction. *Oh my...* the troll's mouth dropped open as the suitor threw himself in front of the princess.

Well would you look at that? The curly-haired goon actually did something right. Maybe if I say a spell as quiet as possible, I could make sure he gets out of here alive. Sighing, Murlyn opened his mouth to say a spell but stopped as the fire that escaped from Glomgurgle's mouth turned into nothing more than a gust of wind.

Shock flashed through the dragon's eyes for a moment then quickly turned to anger as his pupils remained fiery red. "I knew I smelt the stench of that troll," he growled. Where are you? Come out and face me, you miserable little goody two-shoes. You are a traitor and now you must pay!" The giant-winged creature bellowed.

Oh My God. It's Dylock! Murlyn spotted his fellow troll crouched in a corner to the left of the princess. *After all of these years, Dylock used magic to save Natalie.* But *wait a minute, he's still black. That means he's using dark magic.* Murlyn's smile fell at the thought. *If he used dark magic to save the princess then something is up, but what?* He wondered, studying the woodland creature. *Maybe there is some sort of spell I can do to read his thoughts right now. Oh, I know.* "Dark magic is at play so—" Murlyn started to whisper.

Lizzie's sweet voice interrupted his train of thought. *Remember what you've always told my Benjamin, dear friend. Magic cannot be used to manipulate fate or destiny.*

Letting out a huff, he looked up. "Okay, Lizzie. I get it. No spells." *But there has to be some other way to—*

"Leave the princess and the filthy troll alone. You're about to meet your doom!"

A futile insult from the suitor stunned Murlyn out of his thoughts. Taking his eyes off Dylock, the woodland creature turned to see the potential rescuer make another fruitless attempt at shooting an arrow toward Glomgurgle.

Apparently, I underestimated this guy's intelligence even more than I realized. Murlyn watched the suitor shoot his last arrow, only to miss and hit a stalactite about three feet above the dragon's head.

Thunder rolled through the volcano as Glomgurgle erupted in laughter. "What did I tell you?" He asked as fire once again shaded his eyes. "Those arrows are useless against me. Now get out of here and tell the next one to bring the black diamond." he shouted before shooting fire at the suitor's feet.

"S-sorry, princess. I t-tried my best." The curly haired guy cried, his eyes full of terror as he ran out of the volcano mere moments before the dragon's fiery breath hit him.

That actually ended better than I thought it might. Now, if only I could figure out what's up with Dylock, Murlyn rushed out of Mount Wishnik, still under the cover of his invisibility cloak.

~

OH, my God... this cannot be happening. The princess wriggled, struggling to free herself from the stalactite Dylock had tied her to the night before. "This is not happening. I must be seeing things," Natalie whispered to herself as the very arrogant Sir Blackford, whom she'd last seen with Caesar salad dressing dripping from his chin, came storming into the volcano with a grenade.

Craning his neck, he stared up at the dragon, his eyes full of determination. "I'm here for the princess. Hand her over to me or I'll blow this place to smithereens." he shouted, his voice laced with the authority his title afforded him.

Letting out a roar of laughter that made the entire volcano shake, Glomgurgle stared at Sir Blackford as though he were nothing more than a cockroach that needed to be squashed for invading his territory. "You're even more of an idiot than the last guy." the dragon snarled. "Your little grenade has nothing on me! The sound of thunder intensified as Glomgurgle continued to laugh. You're more likely to kill yourself and the princess than you are to actually save her. Give me the black diamond before I show you what it really means to be blown to smithereens!"

"I'll never give you the black diamond!" Sir Blackford shouted. "No one in the kingdom ever will."

"Well then, no one in the kingdom will ever see Natalie again!" Whipping his tail around, Glomgurgle turned to face the princess, who had been watching the exchange while still attempting to break free from the stalactite.

Oh, lord... he looks angry. He's gonna—"Eeeeewwwww!" Natalie exclaimed, her thoughts interrupted, not by the burning sensation she'd expected to feel on her skin, but the stickiness of slimy, green snot.

"Dylock!" Glomgurgle growled, as he took his eyes off the royal and thumped his way toward the dark troll.

Peeling snot from her cheek, the young majestic took the opportunity to address her latest rescuer whose color had completely disappeared from his face. "Sir Blackford, please don't take this the wrong way, but what on earth are you doing here?"

"When word got to Stalagmiteville that whoever saves you gets to marry you, I knew I had to try."

Eyebrows scrunched in confusion, Natalie studied him. "What're you talking about?"

The gentleman shook his head. "With all due respect your majesty, I wish you the best of luck, but this is too much for me. I'm getting out of here while I still have a chance." Looking to the right and then to the left, Sir Blackford made sure the dragon was still occupied, then rushed out of Mount Wishnik, grenade still in hand.

Oh My Gosh... did he say what I think he just said? The man who rescues me from Glomgurgle gets to marry me? That must be why strange men keep coming to try and save me. Lord knows who I am supposed to end up married to. That's if I manage to make it out of here alive. Natalie sighed as she heard the dragon's footsteps approaching in the distance.

"What is it with the idiots of your kingdom?" He growled.

"For your information, the majority of citizens in Cinder's Edge have an above-average IQ!" Natalie shouted.

"Then why haven't any of the clowns that have come through here brought the black diamond with them?"

"How many times do you have to hear that it doesn't matter what you do to me, no one is ever going to give you the black diamond!"

The dragon studied the princess, his eyes coal black for once. "Perhaps you're right," he said after a long moment. "Maybe no one cares what happens to you, so they aren't going to bring the black diamond." He let out a chuckle that sounded more like a clap of thunder. "Maybe I should give up now and just kill you."

As soon as the words escaped from Glomgurgle's mouth, the dark, black-haired troll scurried over and put himself between them. "Let's not be hasty, Master. Only two men have come so far. Perhaps the next will be bright enough to bring the diamond. Do we really want to take a chance by killing her?

Even if no one else in the kingdom cares about me, at least Dylock seems to want to keep me alive. That's the second time he's kept me from being dragon food. But why? She wondered, having barely any time to register the thought before an explosion stole her and the dragon's attention.

CHAPTER 19

Oh, my lord... I'm glad Blaine helped me convince Rosie that doing some recon was a smart idea. I cannot believe another guy is going to try to fight fire with fire. What in the name of wishes are these men thinking? Murlyn wondered as he watched the princess's eyes grow wide at the sound of a stick of dynamite that was thrown at the dragon by the latest suitor, a man by the name of Fred Michaelson. He was a skinny man with salt and pepper hair, olive green eyes, and a slightly crooked smile. Murlyn knew Fred to be a well-known coal miner in Cinder's Edge.

"Come face me, you coward!" Glomgurgle growled angrily.

"I'm anything but a coward," Fred announced, stepping into the volcano. "You're the coward for holding a princess for ransom and you've held Natalie long enough. Hand her over!" The miner ordered, his voice laced with the confidence of a man who had spent more than his fair share of time in caves.

"I will as soon as I get the black diamond and not a moment before," the dragon shouted. "Where is it?"

Fred let out a curt chuckle. "Nowhere that you and your spiky scales can get a hold of it."

Whoa, his eyes changed colors in record time! Poor Fred is in for it now.

Murlyn cringed, as the dragon opened his mouth wider than Murlyn had ever seen before.

"Your fiery breath doesn't scare me. I'm a coal miner. I've been around dynamite for the last thirty years."

The volcano shook as Glomgurgle erupted with laughter. "Dynamite is no match for me," he snarled. "Your precious princess isn't going anywhere."

"We'll see about that," Fred smirked.

"Sir, please." Natalie begged. "I know you're an experienced coal miner, but Glomgurgle is stronger than you think. Don't do anything rash."

Turning to face the princess, Glomgurgle growled angrily, thick smoke rings escaping his nostrils. "Shut your pretty little mouth before I shut it for you," he bellowed, his voice as thick and raspy as ever.

Natalie's been so brave, Murlyn thought. *She is going to make a fine queen someday. That is if Blaine and I can come up with a plan to get her out of this mess.*

"Don't worry, princess." Fred assured her, his voice still full of confidence as he seized his opportunity and threw dynamite at the distracted dragon's back. "I know exactly what I'm doing. We'll be out of here in no time and then you and I are going to have a wonderful life together."

This guy is way too confident for his own good, Murlyn rolled his eyes, having spotted dynamite on the dragon's back. *Real smart move there, buddy. Plant dynamite on a fire breathing monster.*

"You want to know what makes me smarter than you, fire breather?" Fred asked, his tone confident yet smug. "I know when to watch my back."

"How dare you insult me?" Glomgurgle bellowed, turning to face the suitor. "No human has ever dared to enter this cave or come close to being as smart as me." He opened his wings to show off his full size.

Oh no, it's never good when he exp—"AAAAAAHHHHHHHH!!!" A

piercing scream escaped from Natalie's lips, jarring Murlyn from his thoughts yet again.

Oh lord. Lizzie, please be with us. Please help us out of this, Murlyn thought, following the gaze of a wide-eyed, terrified Natalie, who spotted the stick of dynamite that had been on Glomgurgle's back in a crater of bubbling lava a mere three feet away from her.

"There is no reason to be frightened princess. Like I said, we'll be—"

"Fred, p-please." she cried, still struggling to break free of the stalactite, seconds before an explosion erupted around him.

Oh no, what's the spell to put flames out? Suddenly sweating in spite of being under the cover of his invisibility cloak, Murlyn shook off his nerves focused on the flame and whispered quietly. "Flames be gone..." he begun, watching the flames inch closer and closer to the princess by the second. "Flames to—" *Oh, thank God.* Relief washed over Murlyn as he watched the flames turn to water before he could even finish the spell. *I still don't know why Dylock's protecting Natalie. But I sure am grateful. That was a close one.*

"Nooooo!" Natalie cried, eyeing the spot where the coal miner had stood but was now reduced to ashes. Her eyes welled up with tears. "Why did he have to die?" She screamed at the dragon, tears streaming down her face. "No one was supposed to die! The others were fine. Why did he have to die?"

Practically slapping her in the face with his tail, Glomgurgle growled. "The others got out of here by the skin of their teeth. You better get used to seeing people die because if I don't get the black diamond soon, I'll kill every citizen in Cinder's Edge before finally putting an end to you and your family."

Natalie scowled at Glomgurgle, anger etched into her still tear-stained face. "Do what you will to me, but leave my family and the citizens of my kingdom alone!"

Leaning forward, Glomgurgle left mere inches between himself and Natalie. "Your wish... is my command." He growled, taking a deep breath.

"Killing me will only make it harder for you to get the black diamond," she urged, her voice full of anger and anxiety as the dragon opened his mouth. "My family will hate you so much that there's no way you will ever get your claws on the black diamond."

That's my girl, Murlyn smiled at Natalie's self-defense strategy. *Throw him off of*—Murlyn's thoughts were interrupted by yet another suitor walking into the cave. *Uh, oh it looks like someone else thinks he knows how to throw the dragon off of his game.* Wide-eyed, mouth agape, the troll watched, his eyes peeled to the dragon, as the next suitor burst into the cave and stuck a sword into Glomgurgle's back, making him lunge straight into the princess.

WELL AT LEAST this guy is smart enough not to fight fire with fire, Natalie thought as Dylock pulled the suitor's sword out of Glomgurgle's back. While the giant creature was temporarily stunned, it only took him a few seconds to recover.

Expanding his wings, Glomgurgle turned to face the suitor, an overweight, forty-something year old man with mud-colored eyes and a wrinkly neck.

What the heck was Daddy thinking sending him to rescue me? Natalie cringed as the dragon sent flames in his direction. *I can't even remember his name, but I'm pretty sure he's failed royal guard training three times,* she sighed. *Hey, he must've stolen that from the castle,* she thought as he lifted the shield with the letters CE on it.

"You're even dumber than the last guy," the dragon said. "Where's the black diamond?" He towered over the suitor, leaving mere inches between their noses.

"Where is what? I'm here for the princess." The suitor explained.

Oh, good lord. Just because the dragon called him dumb doesn't mean he should play stupid. I'm never going to get out of here alive. Why can't Mama and Daddy just understand that I love Blaine and send him to rescue me? As that question crossed Natalie's mind, she saw the wrinkly-necked suitor attempt to sneak behind Glomgurgle. "Oh my god... are you nuts?" The princess shouted, eyes widened in disbelief, as she continued to watch the man climb onto the dragon's back as though it was nothing more than an angry horse.

Before the suitor could even utter a response, the dragon let out the loudest growl that Natalie had ever heard and spread his wings yet again, knocking the man off of his back and straight into the rocks that were piled up in the cave.

Without missing a beat, Glomgurgle turned to face the princess's suitor, his mouth wide open.

"No, stop! Please don't hurt him," Natalie shouted. "I'm the one you want. Kill me," she pleaded.

Whipping his head to the left, the dragon growled at Natalie, bright red and orange colors flickering in his eyes. "Don't push your luck, princess. I have no problem turning you both into ash in a split second." Glomgurgle turned his attention back to the suitor. "I'm going to kill both of you anyway."

"Dylock! Please do something!" Natalie shouted, her eyes darting from the dragon to the troll, who was cowering in the corner watching the dragon intently.

Eyes widened in disbelief, Dylock let out a curt chuckle, his stare still fixed on the dragon. "It's better him than either of us. Now shut your trap before he makes good on his threat," the troll cautioned.

Something is definitely up. Dylock will stick his neck out to protect me, but won't do anything for an innocent citizen? Well, not me... she used her new-found determination and all of the strength she could muster to break free of the stalactite. "I won't stand for you killing another innocent citizen of Cinder's Edge." The princess cried, running directly in front of the citizen just as the dragon opened his mouth wider.

No citizen should have to die rescuing me. I just hope that Mama, Daddy, and Blaine believe that my death was noble because this is apparently the only chance I'll get to be the type of queen Mama has taught me to be. I only hope the pain is momentary. Holding her breath, the princess braced herself for pure agony.

Just when I thought nothing could be more gross than snot, he pukes dead snails all over me, the princess let out a breath, relieved yet disgusted all at once at the fact that she was still alive.

Wiping the puke from her eyes, the princess saw that Glomgurgle had turned his attention to Dylock. *Oh, good. There is still a chance.* She looked to her middle-aged rescuer. "Quick, save yourself, sir. Get out while you still can," she urged, a mixture of terror and relief in her eyes.

"Thank you," the man said, his voice full of anxiety.

"This is not the time for gratitude. Get out of here."

Without another moment of hesitation, the suitor ran out of the volcano as though he were covered in flames instead of dead snails. *Well, at least he got out of here alive,* Natalie sighed, watching him leave.

The moment the middle-aged man was out of her line of sight, the princess turned her attention to Glomgurgle, who looked like he was about ready to gobble up Dylock in one bite.

"Leave Dylock alone!" She shouted angrily, gaining the dragon's attention.

Wipping his body around to face her, Glomgurgle growled. "Why do you keep trying to play hero? No one cares about you. None of these idiots your father sent, not this troll, and especially not me! All I care about is the black diamond! Why aren't any of the idiots coming to rescue you bringing it with them?"

"I can't believe the dragon said such despicable things and tried to make you think that no one cared about you. How could such an awful creature have ever lived near Cinder's Edge?" Isabel questioned, suddenly bringing Natalie back to the present.

"I know that all of this seems a bit unbelievable to you Isabel, but it happened. To be honest, I am glad it did," the silver-haired grandmother said. "In a strange way, I'm grateful for everything Glomgurgle put all of us through because it made us who we are today. My arm only took six weeks to heal, but the pain of having to watch an innocent citizen die has stayed with me. I am not sure I'd be as compassionate a person or appreciative of life as I am today had I not witnessed that," she explained, a single tear rolling down her right cheek.

"Awww…Nana don't cry," Isabel said. "You're amazing. I don't know how you managed to stay so brave in the face of the dragon."

Wiping away the tear from her cheek, Natalie managed to smile. "I knew that if I hung tough your papaw would come to rescue me and eventually he did. I will never forget the look of sheer determination I saw in his eyes as he charged into the volcano," she explained, her voice wistful as her thoughts drifted back to that day.

CHAPTER 20

As Natalie continued to describe how he rescued her from Mount Wishnik, Blaine could tell that she was immersed in the memory and couldn't help but become absorbed in his own recollection of it. Within moments, the white-haired man was once again his twenty-five-year-old self, standing outside Mount Wishnik, wearing the pants Natalie had sewn love into, ready and determined to save her and conquer Glomgurgle once and for all. "You want the black diamond then let the princess go!" he shouted, leering straight at the dragon as he rushed into the volcanic cave, with the small shiny black stone meant to be a black diamond tucked safely into the pocket of his magic pants.

"Where is it?" Glomgurgle growled. "Where's the black diamond?"

"Let Natalie go!" Blaine insisted, turning his head as the stench of Glomgurgle's breath filled his senses. Holding his breath, he looked past the dragon and straight at the young royal. "Don't worry, sweetheart. I'm going to get you out of here," he said before turning his attention back to Glomgurgle. "Let her go or there will be dire consequences!"

"Sweetheart, huh?" The dragon smirked. "Dylock, I want you to do a black diamond locating spell. I've got a funny feeling about this one."

"You can't have the black diamond until I get the—" Blaine begun.

Ignoring him, Dylock nodded, cleared his throat and said:

> *"The black diamond is the key to all magical power.*
> *It's so powerful it could change an entire kingdom's fate.*
> *In fact, it has the power to make Cinder's Edge a clean slate.*
> *Let the black diamond prove its power by showing its*
>   *location at this crucial hour."*

A puff of black smoke surrounded Blaine in seconds. *Yes, my spell worked. Now let's just hope it fools the dragon.* Blaine held his breath, waiting for the smoke to dissipate.

"There it is," Dylock declared, as the smoke begun to disappear.

"What?" Glomgurgle growled, his raspy voice colored by outrage. "You've been eating too many mushrooms you useless little berry lover. The black diamond is gigantic. It would never fit in his pants you idiot!"

Shaking his head, Blaine eyed the dragon. "Not anymore. The treasure trolls snuck into the castle and performed a spell to shrink it after hearing that you were holding the princess for ransom," the lie spilt quickly out of his mouth. *Here goes nothing.* Without giving it a second thought. Blaine reached into his pocket and grabbed the decoy diamond. "Ma, please be with me now. Please don't let Glomgurgle get the real black diamond. Our future and the future of Cinder's Edge is at stake. Please help us." Blaine begged in a whisper, throwing the shiny stone as far as he could.

Blaine smiled, as he watched Natalie lunge for the stone and catch it just moments before it could fall into a crater of bubbling lava.

"I have had enough of these little heroic games of yours, princess." Glomgurgle expanded his wings towering over the young royal. "Hand over the black diamond."

"There is only one way you're getting this black diamond and that's if you pry it out of my cold dead hands," her voice once again full of the royal authority she'd been trying to find for months, but had only harnessed since being in the volcano.

"With pleasure." the dragon growled, bright red and orange colors once again in his eyes.

Oh God. We need you now more than ever, Ma. Please protect Natalie. I have to save her. I must. Please help me. Please tell me what to do, Blaine pleaded inwardly, his eyes glued to the dragon who was staring at Natalie as she said:

> *"This black diamond holds the power to make the future of*
> *Cinder's Edge sweet or sour.*
> *Its radiance will surely protect us from near or far.*
> *Let light magic allow it to land beyond the dragon's radar,*
> *so the future of my kingdom remains as beautiful as a*
> *flower."*

After her incantation, she threw the decoy diamond with all her might, the magic carrying it farther than anything she had ever thrown.

"There won't be any flowers in your future once I find that black diamond." Glomgurgle growled, before turning his attention to Dylock, who was once again watching everything play out. "Dylock, watch them until I come back with the diamond!" He bellowed before quickly making his way out of the volcano.

I'm always watching over you, sweet boy, Lizzie's voice reassured Blaine as he watched the dragon make his way out of the volcano. *Just remember that love is the most powerful form of magic there is.*

Love... that's it. Murlyn said that thinking about those he loves has got him out of predicaments time and time again. Maybe it will help us out of this. Comforted by his mother's words and new-found hope, Blaine eyed the dragon. *Oh my God... I can't believe I never noticed the similarity before,* he thought as his mind's eye transposed the dragon's tail for the ramps in his treehouse. Taking a deep breath,

Blaine took a step toward Glomgurgle only to fall straight to the ground. *That's strange*, he thought after a moment. *I must've tripped over my shoe.* Shaking his head, Blaine sat up and tried to push himself up into a standing position only to fall over again. *Oh, my God. The pants aren't working anymore. I can't walk. What am I supposed to do? Ma, how am I supposed to save Natalie?*

Lizzie's voice filled his mind. *You don't need working legs to save her, my sweet boy. Like I said, love is the most powerful form of magic in the world.*

As Lizzie's word rang through Blaine's mind and heart, Murlyn appeared at his side, having thrown off his invisibility cloak and shouted out his own magic:

> *"This man's destiny is yet unfulfilled.*
> *The woman who's heart he holds is about to be killed.*
> *To help him avoid a future he doesn't want to see;*
> *use light magic to return him to where he was always meant*
>   *to be."*

Moments later, a cloud of blue smoke formed around Blaine and disappeared in seconds, leaving only his magic carpet in its wake. *Woah... what's happening?* Suddenly he saw his wheelchair floating over as the carpet lowered him, floating away the moment he was safely in his wheelchair. "Thanks, Murlyn, I owe you big time, but first I need your help." Leaning forward, Blaine whispered his plan into Murlyn's ear.

"That's brilliant. Just brilliant," Murlyn said, excitement apparent in his little voice despite its equally low volume. "You can use my invisibility cloak as the source of magic."

"Thanks. It'll only be a brilliant plan if—"

"What are you guys doing? How can you be so calm?" Natalie exclaimed, looking from Blaine to Murlyn. "Glomgurgle is gone for cryin' out loud. This is our chance." she exclaimed, gesturing toward the edge of the volcano.

Throwing his head back, Dylock let out an evil chuckle. "Dream on, no one is going anywhere until I—I mean Glomgurgle gets the black diamond."

Rolling his eyes, Murlyn looked to Blaine. "You take care of her and I'll take care of the dark lord over there," he mumbled, his voice full of sarcasm.

"Seriously, what's up with you two?" Natalie exclaimed. "If you don't tell me right now, I'm goin—"

Gosh, even covered in soot and grime she's really cute when she's angry. Leaning forward, Blaine embraced the princess and cut her off with a kiss.

"Sorry, I just couldn't wait another moment to kiss you," he explained, reluctantly parting after a long moment.

The princess winced as his embrace caused pain to radiate through her shoulder.

"What's wrong?" Blaine asked as he saw the pain in her eyes. "Are you okay? Did the dragon hurt you?" He asked, his voice full of concern.

"I'm fine. It's just my shoulder," she explained. "We have more important things to worry about. What are we going to do about Glomgurgle?"

"Don't worry. I am here now. Everything is going to be fine," he assured her before filling her in on the plan.

"I can't believe that none of the other suitors thought to fight him with ice," the princess said after a moment. "It's genius and yet so obvious."

Blaine frowned. "I just hope it isn't so obvious that it won't work," he said, his meek voice full of nervousness.

Natalie shook her head. "I didn't mean to make you doubt the plan. It really is an amazing idea and it's going to work. We're going to need all of the light magic we can get so tell Murlyn that I am letting your father and the other woodland creatures out of exile, okay?" The princess laughed at Blaine's shocked expression. It's going to be okay. This plan will work. I can feel it," she encouraged, her eyes and voice full of hope. "It's the beginning of a new era.

Smiling, Blaine kissed her again. "I hope you're right."

Blaine's smile transformed to the stern look of a man ready for battle as he watched Murlyn and Dylock approached one another wearing similar expressions.

~

Under the influence of dark magic or not, I can't believe Dylock has lived here for so many years, Murlyn thought as he glanced around the dark, drafty cave and cringed at the sight of a spider crawling next to a hot, bubbling lava puddle.

Following his gaze, Dylock smirked. "Don't worry Murlyn, being cooked in lava makes the spiders nice and juicy."

"Huh?" Murlyn looked at Dylock. "No, never mind. That's not important." *Stay on task, be strong, and hope that the real Dylock is still in there somewhere,* he told himself. Clearing his throat, Murlyn begun, his voice serious and quiet. "Dylock, we have to talk."

"Can we just skip the stupid little heart to heart and get the heck out of this volcano?"

"This is serious, Dylock. Blaine has a plan, but we need to know if you're going to foil it for us or, more importantly, for the people of Cinder's Edge?"

The black-haired troll let out an evil chuckle. "I would never dream of ruining such an important day for Cinder's Edge."

Okay, apparently kindness is getting me nowhere. It's time for a little cold, hard, honest truth. Murlyn grabbed both of Dylock's shoulders and leaned in so their noses were mere inches apart. "I don't have time for your antics. I'm going to be straight with you. You slipped up earlier and I noticed. I know you want the black diamond for yourself."

"I don't know what you're talk—" Dylock begun angrily, squirming as he struggled to free himself from Murlyn's grasp.

Tightening his grip, Murlyn glared at Dylock. "Stop! I don't care to hear any more of your lies. You've been under Glomgurgle's influence for so long you're as despicable as he is!" He shouted, his heart pounding in his chest as he tried unsuccessfully to keep his frustration at bay. Shaking his head, he continued. "C'mon Dylock, this isn't who you are. You guarded the black diamond for years and now suddenly you want it all to yourself? So you can do what? Take over the kingdom or destroy it and kill innocent people as well as all of your old friends in the process?"

"Friends? What friends? You mean the trolls who practically let me rot here for the past twenty years?!"

Oh, my God... it's no wonder he wants to destroy the kingdom, kill us all, and be alone. He's been alone for years. He probably thinks power is the only comfort he needs. How did I not see this before? Murlyn's anger dissipated only to be replaced by a profound sense of sadness for his fellow woodland troll. Biting his lip, Murlyn fought back tears. *Hold it together.* "Dylock, I'm so sorry. I realize now that you wish to turn to the ultimate source of magical power to fill the void of loneliness. But you know what? You're not alone. I'm your friend and though I can't speak for the other trolls, I'd venture to say that if you choose the right side in the fight, between good and evil and help defeat Glomgurgle, then they will do more than be a friend to you; they will love, admire and respect you." Pausing momentarily, Murlyn allowed what he'd said to sink in, then continued. "Despite being under Glomgurgle's influence for many years, I know that the real you is still in there, somewhere. The real you must remember that love is the most powerful form of magic in this world. Is possessing the black diamond really worth not being admired, respected, and loved by potentially every person and woodland creature in Cinder's Edge?"

"Weren't you guys exiled after I took the diamond the first time?" Dylock asked.

Murlyn waved a dismissive hand, "Natalie will fix that. Are you going to help us or not?"

"Let's just say I won't get in the way," the black-haired troll answered after a long moment.

"I'll take that. Please... just think about what I said."

Looking up to the sky, Murlyn did the only thing he could think of to ease his worries in the moment and prayed to Lizzie. *Oh Lizzie, please watch over us as we prepare to defeat Glomgurgle. Please help Dylock's heart to do the right thing. Please help us all to do the right thing and save Cinder's Edge.*

Lizzie immediately responded. *I'm here with you now. Watching over all of you.*

Comforted by the presence of his dear friend, Murlyn led Dylock back over to Blaine and Natalie and took a deep breath before the four left the volcano to face Glomgurgle.

CHAPTER 21

"Oh, no!" Blaine exclaimed, looking to the princess, having spotted Glomgurgle soaring through the sky, about twenty miles shy of her home. "Sweetheart, he must've already realized that wasn't the real black diamond. He's headed straight for the castle. "I'll hold him off, but you need to get your family out of the castle as quick as you can with as many people and trolls as you can find, okay?"

The princess nodded, her eyes full of terror. *She looks so scared. I wish I had the right words to calm her.*

Just assure her that no matter what happens you guys will get through it together, Lizzie's voice advised him after a moment.

Following his mother's advice, Blaine stopped and looked the princess straight in the eye. "I know you're scared, sweetheart. I am too. But we are going to get through this together."

Blaine looked to Murlyn. "Hey Murl, did you grab the magic carpet after you cast that spell earlier?"

The blue hair troll shook his head, smirking slightly. "No, I did something even better. I tossed the invisibility cloak over the carpet. I am pretty sure that the magic I used is still active because both magical materials followed us out of the volcano," Murlyn explained, lifting the cloak from the air beside him to reveal its shiny black exterior as well as the magic carpet.

Nodding Blaine looked to Natalie. Use the cloak and magic carpet to get to the castle quickly and unnoticed," he urged. Then, he smiled and added, "The magic carpet and cloak have kept me safe for years, just as they will now keep you safe. The carpet will take you to safety as soon as you climb onto it."

"You're right. We can do this together," Natalie agreed. "Especially if the entire kingdom helps." Bending down, she kissed him as he sat in his wheelchair, and then climbed upon the floating carpet and held on tightly. Murlyn then threw the invisibility cloak over her allowing her to escape unnoticed as the carpet sped to the safety of the castle.

AFTER THE MAGIC carpet lowered her safely onto the castle grounds, Natalie stepped inside. *I sure hope we can all face this together*, she thought before walking into the throne room. Clearing her throat, she gained the attention of her mother, who was surrounded by various members of the castle staff.

"Glomgurgle is closing in on the castle. Blaine has a plan, but we need to hurry," she said anxiously.

"Oh, thank the heavens, Blaine did it!" Alexandria breathed, bursting into tears as she rushed toward her daughter.

The princess turned her body instinctively to guard her injured shoulder from her mother's touch.

Following his wife's gaze, Frederick's eyes lit up with excitement. "Sweetie! I can't believe you're home," he exclaimed, throwing his arms around her neck. "How did you get away?"

"There will be time for explanations later. We have to face Glomgurgle, right now."

Frederick studied his daughter. "Natalie, sweetheart, what are you talking about?"

"You're here. You're safe now," Alexandria pointed out, embracing her daughter once again.

Shrugging free of her mother's embrace, Natalie shouted. "No, you need to listen to me! Glomgurgle is right outside. Blaine is holding him off, but I need reinforcements!"

Looking at one another, Frederick and Alexandria nodded. "I'll deploy the royal guard right now," Frederick assured Natalie.

Ugh, they are still not listening, the princess thought angrily.

This is no time to let anger over come you, sweet girl, the voice of Blaine's departed mother reminded her after a moment. *Remember that this is going to be your kingdom someday soon. You have authority. Use it. Make them listen to you. The future of the kingdom depends on it.* Feeling both a sense of comfort and an urgency to get her parents attention, Natalie screamed "Listen!"

Shaking his head, Frederick eyed his daughter. "Sweetheart, I understand that time is of the essence here, but that sounds a bit crazy. I mean, we don't want to endanger every citizen of the kingdom," he cautioned, his voice full of a mixture of parental and royal authority.

"This is not up for discussion! Glomgurgle is closing in on the castle and the future of this kingdom is a stake. Either do as I say or face the evil that is Glomgurgle all on your own."

Frederick sat on his throne with his eyes bulging out of his head. Natalie knew that he wasn't used to being spoken to in this way, but she needed him to know that she was no longer a child and was ready to be a queen. When he had gotten over his shock, a small smile played across his lips. "Point taken, sweetheart, what do you need us to do?"

Struck by a feeling of empowerment, Natalie looked to Lorenzo, the head of the royal guard, who'd been watching her address her father. The heavyset, forty-something-year-old man looked at her to tell him what to do next. "Have the rest of the royal guard gather up every citizen in the kingdom and bring them here as soon as possible. Go through the back way so Glomgurgle doesn't suspect anything. You and I are going to handle the black diamond."

"Your highness, are you sure you want to—" Lorenzo begun, his usually authoritative voice, meek and nervous.

"This is no time to question me, Lorenzo," she said curtly. "Like I said, join me or face Glomgurgle yourself."

The guardsman's flashed a nervous smile. "I'm with you."

"Good. Now help me get this pedestal and black diamond outside."

Shaking his head, Lorenzo eyed the black diamond and its pedestal warily. "We're definitely going to need more manpower."

"Ok, yes, assemble the royal guard, gather up the citizens, and go find a hand cart. I'll go find us some additional manpower," she explained before rushing off to find help. *Oh, my goodness*, Natalie thought, stopping in her tracks, as she spotted a few royal guardsmen sneaking people into the castle through the back door. *I always knew there were a lot of people in the kingdom, but to see so many gathered in one place is amazing.*

"Hey there, princess," a burly, blacksmith named Bruce said. "Care to tell me what we are all doing here inside the castle when we should be out there helping that man beat Glomgurgle to a pulp?"

Oh, my God. Bruce is as strong as twenty men... why didn't I think to get his help before?

Natalie smiled. "Come with me and I'll explain everything."

Natalie got Bruce to help move the black diamond and its pedestal. He made it look so easy and gave her the confidence that they could defeat Glomgurgle. Smiling, she tried to hold on to that confidence as she led her citizens and the black diamond outside to face the dragon.

"Leave Natalie alone and come face me like the monster you are!" Blaine shouted.

Whipping his head around, Glomgurgle spotted Blaine. "I

figured you would be inside with your beloved," he snarled, hovering above the castle.

Panic gripped Blaine at that moment. His throat was closing, making it hard to breathe, yet he still needed to face the monster.

Just breathe, sweet boy. Just breathe. I'm here with you. You are not in this fight alone, Lizzie's sweet voice assured him.

Comforted by the support of his mother, Blaine managed to take a breath. "Face me like the monster you are Glomgurgle!"

Growling, the dragon flew down to the ground in front of Blaine, landing so hard that soot flew up around the two of them. Coughing, Blaine covered his mouth to keep from inhaling.

"Am I supposed to be intimidated by a man who can't even handle a little soot?" The dragon's laughter imitated crackling thunder, making the ground shake. "Something tells me that you are going to be an easy one to kill."

You can do this, Blaine told himself after a moment. *Just stay foc—*

"Master, the black diamond is behind you. Turn around now!" Dylock suddenly shouted.

Peering behind the dragon as he turned around in search of the diamond, Blaine tried not to smile at the vast number of people surrounding Natalie. Next to Natalie stood Rosie who quickly threw him her invisibility cloak. "Okay, Ma." Blaine whispered. "Natalie has done her part. Now I must do mine. Please be with me."

I have watched over you and protected you every time you did a jump in your treehouse and now will be no different. Just do your best.

Fueled by the knowledge that his mother had confidence in him and always had, Blaine took a deep breath, threw Rosie's invisibility cloak over himself and in the quietest of whispers, said:

> *"May the light magic in this cloak allow me to answer the*
> *ultimate call.*
> *Cover the wheels of my chair with ice,*
> *so that with the help of his only vice,*
> *I can defeat Glomgurgle once and for all."*

Moments later, Blaine felt a gust of cold air and smiled. *Yes, it's working. It's ice cold*, he thought, his heart suddenly pounding inside of his chest. Yanking off the invisibility cloak, he tossed it to the side and took a deep breath. "Here goes nothing." he whispered, quickly pushing his wheelchair up Glomgurgle's tail and onto his back.

I can't believe I am actually doing this. This is crazy. Blaine thought, his heart pounding louder in his chest as the dragon growled louder than ever before, expanding his wings. Holding on tightly to the wheels of his chair, Blaine waited until the dragon was about ten feet up in the air before jumping off of his right wing. *Yes, my timing was perfect*, Blaine smiled, noting that the dragon was also on the ground, his tail and right wing frozen over. Still smiling, Blaine joined the crowd of people surrounding the princess. Scanning the crowd, he addressed them. "Is everyone ready?"

The dragon snarled angrily, furiously attempting to flap his wings despite not being able to get up off the ground. "Whatever you and the rest of the citizens of this useless castle have planned, it won't work. You found my weakness, but you didn't kill me. You'll never kill me," he growled his menacing voice full of arrogance. "I am going to destroy all of you and this kingdom!"

"You don't scare any of us anymore," Blaine shouted. "We are going to stand here in front of the castle together, no matter what you do to us because we love one another and this kingdom."

Smiling, Natalie grabbed Blaine's hand and squeezed. "That's right and we know that love is the most powerful form of magic in the entire world."

Suddenly, as the dragon laughed yet again, it sounded as though a thunderstorm was mere moments from breaking out. "That's ridiculous. Nothing is more powerful than the black diamond."

This is your moment, sweet boy. *I'm here with you. Shining love on all of you*, Lizzie's voice assured him sweetly.

Smiling, he looked to Natalie. "Now, sweetie."

I hope you're right, Mama. I really hope you are right, Blaine thought as the crowd of people parted, revealing King Frederick and the black diamond which had been placed on the hand cart along with its pedestal and brought outside.

"I still can't believe how many people and woodland creatures are helping us," Blaine whispered to himself as people and creatures gathered around the king, placing their hands on the diamond.

Keeping hold of Natalie's hand, he moved close enough to place both of their hands onto the diamond, too.

"Aww that's so cute," the dragon snarled sarcastically. "But it doesn't matter how many of you idiots try to shield the black diamond from me, I will get it and then I will destroy this kingdom."

"Even if you destroy the entire kingdom, we'll still love you just as we love one another," Blaine said as kindly as he could.

"What did you just say?" The dragon asked.

"Say it with me," Blaine urged, once again addressing the crowd.

"We love him," the people and trolls shouted even louder this time.

"Shut up... shut up, you idiots!" The dragon growled, his voice suddenly full of more fear than arrogance.

"No, Glomgurgle. Don't you get it? We will never stop because we love you!" Blaine insisted.

"Yeah, we love you!" The crowd shouted again.

"Say it even louder," Blaine shouted. "Say it as loud as you can."

Following the young man's urging, the crowd shouted, "We love Glomgurgle," at the top of their lungs.

Yes, yes. It's working. Glomgurgle's powers are bound to be sucked out of him any second now, Blaine thought, smiling as the black diamond begun to shake on its pedestal. *Is it just me or is his tail getting smaller?* He wondered as he eyed the dragon, who seemed to be recoiling in fear more and more each time the word love was spoken.

"Oh, no!" Natalie screamed suddenly, her voice just loud enough to be heard over the crowd. Blaine turned and watched the black diamond fall off of the pedestal and then heard a collective gasp escape from the crowd the moment the diamond hit the ground, shattering into pieces before Natalie or anyone else could catch it.

CHAPTER 22

"Is everyone okay?" Natalie questioned after a moment.

"Yes, my beautiful daughter. Everyone is all right. Thanks to you and Blaine. Thanks to the two of you, all of Cinder's Edge is going to be just fine forevermore, because we no longer have to worry about Glomgurgle."

"What are you talking about, Daddy?" She asked, her attention still on the shattered black diamond.

"Sweetheart, don't you see? The dragon has turned to stone."

Wide-eyed, mouth agape, Natalie turned to see that the dragon had indeed become a statue. "Well, would you look at that?" Tracing the statue delicately with her fingers, she examined it. "I don't get it. How did this happen? We expected the black diamond to absorb Glomgurgle's dark magic, not turn him to stone."

Making his way up to the statue, Murlyn eyed it. "I have never seen anything like this either, Miss Natalie, but I have a theory. I think we forgot to take into account that dark magic is very different from light magic. As my dear friend Lizzie has reminded me time and time again over the years, love is the most powerful form of magic in the entire world. And as we all know, Glomgurgle had some of the darkest magic around. When two powerful forms of magic collide, one is bound to eventually overpower the other. We're just lucky that today good overpowered evil."

～

"Wow!" Isabel exclaimed. "Glomgurgle actually turned to stone? Why didn't you tell me? I always thought that statue was built as a reminder of the evil our kingdom has faced and beaten or something," the newly-crowned queen admitted sheepishly.

Placing a hand on Isabel, Natalie squeezed gently and met her granddaughter's gaze. "Sweetie, that statue isn't just a reminder of what this kingdom has prevailed against. It's a reminder of how we all came together that day for a common cause and succeeded. It's a reminder of how powerful love is."

Blaine nodded. "I couldn't agree with you more. The statue is a powerful reminder. But, I have to say, I think Dylock is an even more powerful example and reminder of its power."

Chuckling, Isabel looked to her grandparents, "What else have you guys not told us about him?"

"Something happened to him that day. Something changed him forever," Murlyn drifted back into a sad memory as he spoke. Within moments, he was at Dylock's side as the spider-adorned troll gasped for air.

～

"Blaine, Natalie, everyone! Come here… it's Dylock!" Murlyn cried.

Oh, no. We forgot to take Dylock's dark magic into account, Natalie realized as she, Blaine, and the other woodland creatures rushed toward the sound of Murlyn's voice. They found him kneeling over the black-haired woodland creature who lay on the ground clutching his chest.

"I think he's having a heart attack… we have to do something!" Murlyn said.

Making her way through the crowd of trolls and people, Natalie watched Rosie kneel next to Murlyn. "Sweetheart, you and I both know that if he has been under the influence of dark magic long enough there is nothing we can do," she said sweetly.

Shaking his head, Murlyn disagreed. "No, I refuse to accept that. He may have been under Glomgurgle's influence for years and he may have even planned to kill us, but, in the end, he decided to help us by making the dragon turn around so that Blaine could wheel onto his back. That act of goodness is worth something." He looked into Dylock's dark eyes.

"It's okay, Murlyn," Dylock managed, his voice barely audible. "Just knowing that you care, is all I need—" he begun before his eyes closed and his breathing shallowed.

"I'm afraid Rosie is right, Bud," Bernie said solemnly. "We have to let him go."

"No! When I was stripped of my magic, Rosie was kind enough to share her gemstone with me, so now I'm going to return the favor and if you are the trolls and people that I think you are, you'll join me in saying the spell."

Murlyn is right. We have to do something. Glomgurgle would've killed me four times over if it hadn't been for Dylock. Regardless of his motive, I owe him my life, Natalie cleared her throat and addressed the crowd. "Murlyn is right. If it weren't for Dylock, I wouldn't be standing here in front of you right now. We can't let him go without a fight. It's like we told Glomgurgle, here in Cinder's Edge we stick together because we love each other." She turned back to Murlyn, "We'll repeat after you."

Taking a deep breath, Murlyn looked from the crowd to Dylock before saying:

> *"Despite dark magic lingering inside him,*
> *Dylock helped the kingdom in its greatest need.*
> *Now his chances of survival look slim,*
> *let our light magic heal him with great speed."*

Awestruck, Natalie watched as swirls of red, blue, purple,

orange, yellow, and pink colored smoke floated over Dylock's chest and then entered the troll's nostrils, restoring his normal breathing pattern.

The crowd gasped as Dylock took a couple of breaths and green smoke traveled from his nose to the center of his belly, instantly transforming his black spider-shaped gemstone back into a green four-leafed clover, while his coal black hair and eyes were restored to their former dark green glory as well.

I knew there was something different about him. He was a treasure troll under the influence of dark magic. Why did I not see it before? The princess wondered as Dylock sat up slowly and looked to the crowd.

"Thank you," he exclaimed, his voiced laced with gratitude. "Thank you all so much!"

Smiling, Natalie shook her head. "No need to thank us. In Cinder's Edge, we take care of our own."

"Wait a minute," Missy exclaimed, stunning Natalie back to the present as she looked to Murlyn, wide-eyed. "If Dylock's light magic was restored, why wasn't your magic restored too?"

Tilting his head to the left, Murlyn considered his response then answered. "That's a good question sweetheart. As you know, trolls are told practically from the day we're born that magic cannot be used to manipulate fate or destiny. Despite that I knowingly used put my needs and the needs of the trolls ahead of the kingdom. There is no excuse for my actions," Murlyn said, his tone matter-of-fact. "I should've known better. Dylock, on the other hand, only tried to manipulate destiny while under the influence of dark magic. Moreover, despite being under the influence of darkness for a number of years, he ultimately decided to help us defeat Glomgurgle and benefited the greater good. Our green-haired friend deserved to have his magic restored whereas I did not," he admitted. Pausing for a moment, he allowed his words to sink in then continued. "Besides," he flashed Rosie a smile than looked back to his daughter. "I love sharing magic with your mama and wouldn't change that even if I could."

"Awww...you're so sweet Daddy," Missy said, her tiny, high-pitched voice full of adoration for her father.

Murlyn's cheeks turned slightly crimson. "Thank you sweetie. I am just glad that your mama loves me enough to share her gemstone with me and that Natalie was kind enough to allow me back into the kingdom."

"For me, there was never any question of whether or not to let trolls back into Cinder's Edge," the retired queen said sweetly. Within moments, the silver-haired woman's thoughts drifted back to the day the kingdom had defeated Glomgurgle and she once again found herself standing with the woodland creatures as they assured the newly-restored, very grateful, Dylock that he was still one of them.

"The sentiment that those in Cinder's Edge take care of their own is really sweet, Miss Natalie, but you seem to have forgotten one tiny thing," Murlyn said, finally tearing his attention away from Dylock.

"What might that be?" The princess queried, eyebrows furrowed.

"Your father exiled the other woodland creatures and I from the kingdom."

"Don't be silly," the princess scoffed, waving a dismissive hand. "When this is my kingdom that's the first thing I'll fix."

Marching over to his daughter with the authority only a father could have, Frederick eyed Natalie. "Whoa there, sweetie, I know you're eager, but don't go making decisions that Blaine should be making. This is about the *king*dom after all." He declared, emphasizing the word 'King'.

"Sir, about that, I—" Blaine begun, then stopped when he heard what Frederick was implying.

"Don't you worry about a thing, young man." Frederick slapped Blaine on the back in a friendly fashion. "I have the finest event planners in the kingdom planning your coronation as we speak. It'll be great." Frederick flashed a toothy smile. "Trust me, it'll be nothing but the best for the mighty slayer of Glomgurgle."

Slayer of Glomgurgle or not, Blaine has no idea what he's in for, Natalie laughed to herself as her father continued to drone on, detailing his plans for Blaine's coronation.

CHAPTER 23

This is crazy. I never knew there were so many different shades of white, Natalie rolled her eyes at Blaine as her mother held up fabric swatches.

"Do you prefer the eggshell or cream?" Alexandria queried pointedly, eyeing the eggshell sample.

Sighing, Blaine hung his head momentarily then looked back at the swatches. "Really, your majesty, whichever you and Natalie like is fine. This really isn't my kind of thing."

Letting out a huff, Alexandria dropped the swatches on the handcrafted table where they all sat and looked around the place Blaine had called home. "Yes, I see that your life has been..." the queen eyed his bookshelf, biting her lips. "Lackluster," she finished after a moment.

"Mother!" Natalie yelled.

"But," Alexandria said pointedly. "That's about to change. You won't need to read books to get a thrill anymore, young man, because you'll soon be living a life of excitement and luxury. Now, let's do this and remember we can't pick the same shade of white for the coronation reception as we do for your wedding linens. We need to make sure that the shades are distinctly different."

Glancing at the table then at Natalie, Blaine said yet again, "I'm sorry. Pick whatever you like. I can't do this now." And he turned to leave.

"Blaine, wait… where're you going?" Natalie called out, standing up from the table.

"You'll see soon enough. I'll see you at the coronation." Leaning forward, he opened the door of the hut, exiting slowly.

Sitting down, Natalie shot her mother a look. "Mama, must you be so rude to Blaine?"

"I didn't mean to be sweetheart. I was only trying to make his new life sound more enticing." Frowning, the older woman scanned the hut again. "I know Lizzie would have wanted more for her boy than this."

"Don't you get it, Mama? This is who Blaine is. This is all he has ever known, and he still grew up to be an amazing man, whom I love very much."

"I understand that, sweetie, and I'm happy for you." pursing her lips, the queen looked her daughter straight in the eye.

Natalie sighed. "I sense a 'but' coming."

"Despite having heard your feelings for Blaine I'm beginning to question his motives. He somehow manages to change the subject and/or leave every time the coronation or the two of you getting married is brought up. Does that not bother you, sweetheart?"

I'd hoped that I'd imagined Blaine's pre-wedding jitters, but Mama's noticed it too. What does this mean? Whatever is going on I can't let her see me sweat. Looking down at her hands, she avoided her mother's gaze. *Be confident. You love Blaine and you know he loves you too, even if he is a little nervous about getting married and reigning over the kingdom.*

Taking a deep breath, Natalie looked at her mother. "No, Mama, it doesn't bother me. He's probably a little nervous. I mean, c'mon, I'm nervous and I wasn't even exiled from the kingdom for twenty years."

"Point taken," Alexandria nodded. "Now back to planning. Do you like the china with the hummingbird pattern or the rose pattern?"

Natalie spent the rest of the afternoon huddled in the place Blaine called home, with her mother, making one mundane decision after another for the upcoming wedding and coronation.

How am I supposed to worry about chair covers and cake, when I'm not even sure Blaine wants to marry me? Is all of this for nothing? Did Blaine save me just to be able to come back into the kingdom? Suddenly overwhelmed by her thoughts, Natalie shook her head and stood up from the table. "I can't take this anymore!"

"What… what's wrong, Natalie? Do you prefer the coral chair covers over the lavender?"

"No, mother. This has nothing to do with chair covers. I just need a little break. I'm going to take a walk and meet you at the castle for supper, okay?"

Before the queen could even finish uttering words of agreement, Natalie ran out of the hut and headed straight for the Tree of Friendship. *This is where the trolls come to find clarity, right? Why isn't it working for me?* Still overwhelmed by her thoughts and on the brink of tears, Natalie heard a familiar voice. The same voice that had given her hope while she was stuck in the volcano.

Don't cry sweet girl. Blaine has your best interests at heart. All will make sense in due time.

Comforted yet again by the words of Blaine's mother and guardian angel, Natalie smiled and walked toward the castle to meet her mother. *I'm going to put on the best coronation ceremony Cinder's Edge has ever seen*, she thought, suddenly determined to do just that.

OH, my god. I can't believe it. I just can't believe it. Blaine looked at a newly remodeled castle, wide-eyed.

"What do you think?" Natalie asked, her voice full of excitement. "Isn't it great? It's granite so it'll last and now you can get into the castle for the coronation ceremony. C'mon, come and see how beautiful the thrones look."

Flashing a smile, he followed her up the newly installed ramp and into the throne room. "Someone definitely gave this place a makeover." Blaine's mouth dropped open as he looked around the room and noticed that the old burgundy curtains had been replaced by new dark purple draperies.

"Wow... new thrones too?" He queried unable to hide the surprise in his voice when he saw that the jewel encrusted throne chairs, that Natalie had admired so much as a child, had been replaced by even taller thrones upholstered in a dark purple that matched the drapes.

"Do you like them?" She asked. "I know the purple makes them slightly feminine, but they will be a lot softer than the old ones, which I figured is important considering how much time we will be spending in here for years to come."

"Sweetheart, the thrones are fine, but we need to talk. I should t—"

Placing a hand on his shoulder, Natalie squeezed gently. "We can talk after the coronation," she assured him in a whisper. "People are coming in."

Has the number of people in the kingdom doubled since we defeated Glomgurgle? Blaine wondered as people begun to file into the throne room.

"Are you two ready to get started?" Alexandria asked, her voice full of the pride that only a mother could have on such a special day.

"I'd really like the chance to talk to Natalie first." Blaine said.

Shaking his head vehemently as he approached, Frederick disagreed. "Talk later son. Right now, we got a coronation ceremony to get through."

Ugh... why won't they listen to me? What am I gonna do? He wondered, beads of sweat suddenly trickling down his forehead. *How am I just now seeing that? Could things get any worse? I can't wear that for the rest of my life.* He spotted a gold crown adorned with sapphires, emeralds, and rubies resting on the pillar that had once been the home of the black diamond. *That thing is worth more than everything I'll ever own. How am I supposed to do this? I know I'm not the right person to reign over this kingdom, but I don't know what I am supposed to do about it.* Overwhelmed by his thoughts and the magnitude of what was about to happened, Blaine felt dizzy and nauseous. Taking a deep breath, he struggled to keep his queasy stomach at bay and focus on the kingdom as he turned to address the crowd.

Frederick stood up and addressed the crowd. "Ladies and gentlemen of Cinder's Edge, today is a very special occasion. Today marks a new chapter in the history of our kingdom. A chapter free of Glomgurgle and the threat of his dark magic. Thanks to the bravery of one man we will never have to worry about such threats ever again. Let's all take a moment to applaud that brave man and express our debt of gratitude."

A chorus of gratefulness exploded through the room causing Blaine's cheeks to turn bright red in seconds.

Great... now I not only have to worry about disappointing Natalie, but all of the wonderful people in the kingdom as well. Ma, I know you're here now, just as you were when we defeated Glomgurgle, so please help me. Please tell me what to do. Blaine waited patiently for Lizzie to respond and he wasn't disappointed.

Just do what your heart tells you, sweet boy. Everything will be fine. Natalie knows you have her best interests at heart.

Reassured by the words, Blaine focused on the king's speech just in time to hear the leader ask him to step forward.

Here goes nothing, he thought and turned to face the crowd. Clearing his throat, Frederick looked at Blaine. "Do you, Blaine Benson, promise to lead the fine realm of Cinder's Edge in accordance to the decrees drafted by those whom ruled before you and, in doing so, protect the land and its people from any and all potential threats?"

Feeling even more nauseous than moments before, Blaine looked up to the cathedral ceiling. "Give me the right words to get through this without hurting anyone, Ma," he whispered.

Taking yet another deep breath, Blaine looked from the crowd to the king. "I'm so thankful for the gratitude that each and every one of you have expressed to me here today, but I don't deserve it. The entire kingdom worked to defeat Glomgurgle, and each and every one of you fine people had a part in that. Governing you fine people would undoubtedly be one of the greatest honors of my life. However, I must decline. I must decline be...wait Natalie, where are you going?" He called out as she ran out of the throne room and the castle.

CHAPTER 24

How could he do that? How could he abdicate the throne in front of the entire kingdom without even giving me so much as a heads up? Does this mean Mama was right? Does Blaine not want to marry me? Mind racing, the princess once again ran to the Forest of Wishes in search of solace. However, this time when she reached the Tree of Friendship the treasure trolls were gathered around it.

Uh oh... something must be going on. She made her way to Rosie, who was under the pink sapling that she had always considered home, looking at the Tree of Friendship with a longing expression on her face. "What's going on Rosie?" She questioned, approaching slowly.

"Nothing," Rosie sniffled, still looking the Tree of Friendship.

Kneeling, so she was at the same level as Rosie, Natalie looked into the troll's eyes. "What's wrong? Why aren't you over there with the others?"

"They don't need me. Murlyn practically shooed me away," Rosie cried. "We treasure trolls have planned and celebrated ever major event in our lives around that tree and now, all of the sudden, they don't need me," she wiped away her tears.

"Well, that doesn't seem fair," Natalie said, her forehead wrinkled with worry. "Murlyn loves you. I'm sure you just misunderstood. I'll go talk to him and see what I can find out."

"Yes," the pink glittery-haired troll's eyes lit up with excitement. "That's a good idea. He'll have to tell you something because this is your kingdom, right?"

Natalie chuckled. "I wish it worked liked that," she whispered under her breath.

Rosie looked at the princess, her nose scrunched in confusion. "Hmm?"

"Nothing. I'll see what I can do," she smiled as she walked toward the Tree of Friendship.

"What are you doing here?" Murlyn questioned as he spotted the princess walking toward the special sapling.

"The better question is what are *you* doing here and why can't Rosie be a part of it?" She asked pointedly.

Sighing, Murlyn shot her a look. "Must you be so nosey?"

Natalie let out a huff, placing a hand on her right hip. "This is my kingdom. Nosey or not, I demand to know what's going on."

Shaking his head, the troll let out a huff. "The Forest of Wishes is not technically in your kingdom, Miss Natalie… and you aren't even supposed to be here until nightfall. Blaine said—"

"Wait a minute—" Natalie yelled, cutting him off. "What do you mean I am not supposed to be here until nightfall? And what does Blaine have to do with any of this?"

"I've said too much. Please don't be angry with me. Rosie is already mad, and I just couldn't bear it to have upset you both on a day like this."

"Why shouldn't I be upset?" The princess snapped. "What's so special about today?"

"All I can tell you is that it's nothing bad and I'm quite sure you'll be pleased with the end result. Now if you could just do me one small favor and occupy Rosie until you both can come at nightfall, I promise you will not be sorry." Falling to his tiny knees, the troll begged. "Please, please. Just do this one little thing for me… for Rosie… please."

Wow... I doubt Murlyn has ever begged for anything before. Whatever is going on must be big, she chuckled despite her anger. "You're just lucky I love you." The princess shook her head and walked back toward Rosie's tree.

"I got shooed away too," Natalie frowned before her pink glittery-haired friend could even question the outcome. "But... hey, I don't feel like going to the castle so what do you say we take a walk and clear our heads?" The princess flashed an encouraging smile.

Rosie let out a huff, "Oh, all right, but I don't like this one bit."

"If I promise to style your hair for tonight after our walk, will that make you happy?" Natalie asked sweetly.

"I should be the one worried about making you happy not the other way around. I'm an awful friend."

Shaking her head vehemently, Natalie disagreed. "Nonsense. You have always been, and continue to be, a great friend. Now, let's get out of here."

With that, the two friends took a leisurely walk through the kingdom, then proceeded to help one another get ready for the much-anticipated evening, perfecting their looks from head to toe, until it was finally time to head to the forest.

"So, what do you think everyone is doing at the Tree of Friendship right now?" Natalie asked a few minutes into their walk.

"I don't know, but they better have a good reason for leaving me out."

"I agree. After what Blaine did this afternoon, he better have a good reason for being involved."

"What did Blaine do this afternoon?"

Taking a deep breath, the princess proceeded to tell Rosie about how Blaine had relinquished the throne without any warning.

"Oh, sweetheart. I'm so sorry." Rosie said. "But I know that Blaine would never deliberately disappoint you. I'm sure he has a good reason."

"I hope so. I just don't know what his reasons could be."

"I don't know either, but I think we are about to find out," Rosie pointed toward a bright light leading into the forest.

Walking toward the light, Natalie and Rosie saw it was coming from the Tree of Friendship which the other trolls were still all gathered around. "What's going on guys? Why is the tree illuminated?" Rosie asked.

"More importantly, where are Murlyn and Blaine? It's dark and they asked us to be here at nightfall. Where could they be?" Natalie asked.

Rosie's fellow trolls looked at one another and nodded.

Natalie let out a huff, "C'mon guys, seriously, where are they? What's going on?"

Grinning, the woodland creatures formed a line and linked hands. Within seconds, each of the gemstones that adorned the center of their bellies begun to glow their corresponding color and grew in size until each of the trolls' stomachs were completely covered.

"Oh, my goodness," Natalie exclaimed, putting a hand over her mouth as a letter appeared on each of the gemstones, beautifully illuminating and spelling out the words 'will you marry... *Am I reading what I think I'm reading?* Natalie watched as each of the letters lit up.

"Me," Blaine and Murlyn finished simultaneously as they came out from behind the special sapling, holding a ring and bracelet respectively.

Oh, my God. Is this actually happening? Smiling from ear to ear, Natalie looked to Rosie. After a moment, they answered simultaneously, "Yes."

The trolls cheered as Blaine slipped a ring onto the princess's finger and Murlyn slipped a bracelet onto Rosie's wrist.

As the trolls admired Rosie's bracelet, a dainty, silver bangle adorned with beads of genuine tiger's eye and a small prism charm in the center they offered the woodland couple congratulations. Natalie and Blaine snuck away to the hut.

"Hi Papa," Blaine said by way of greeting, holding the door open for Natalie. "She said yes."

"That's wonderful," Benjamin smiled pulling her into an

embrace. "Welcome to the family, little lady. Take care of my boy and that ring he gave you. The band was my Lizzie's great grandmother's.

"Oh, my gosh," Natalie exclaimed, taking a seat at the table. "I haven't even taken a close look at the ring." Wide-eyed, her chin dropped as she examined the white gold band with a heart-shaped black diamond in the center and a smaller white gold, diamond-studded heart on each side. "Is the black stone in the middle, what I think it is?" She questioned, eyes still focused on the ring.

Flashing a proud smile, Blaine nodded. "Yes, I managed to grab it after the explosion and I carved it into a heart myself. I thought someone as special as you deserved a true piece of magic in a ring she is going to wear for the rest of her life," he said, his voice quiet and full of love.

"I don't understand," Natalie mumbled after a moment, her eyes filling up with tears.

Benjamin shot his son a nervous look. "Uh, I'm just going to give you two some privacy. I'll be in my workshop if you need me."

"What's wrong sweetie? Are you not happy with the ring?" He queried sweetly as his father closed the door to the hut.

"I love it. It's perfect. You're perfect. It's just that I wasn't sure if you wanted to marry me."

Pushing his wheelchair up to his now fiancé, Blaine leaned forward, looking her straight in the eye. "Sweetheart, what made you question my intentions?"

"C'mon Blaine, every time anyone has brought up the idea of marriage you've changed the subject, and you renounced the throne without even telling me. What was I supposed to think?"

Chuckling softly, Blaine placed his hand on her knee and squeezed gently. "Sweetheart, I wish you had stayed at the coronation today. I had intended to explain that I didn't like the reason why I had been given the opportunity to reign over the kingdom. You, Natalie Nordstrom, are neither a prize nor a trophy. I didn't like the idea of marrying you as some sort of reward." He squeezed her knee again and continued. "I love you. I wanted to make sure that we were taking our relationship to the next level for the right reasons. That's why today, at the coronation, I told the people of Cinder's Edge that you are fully capable of reigning over the Kingdom independently and I wouldn't have it any other way."

"What-wh—" She begun, her nose scrunched in confusion.

Blaine gently placed a finger to her lips. "Shhh… please let me finish."

Smiling sweetly, Natalie nodded.

"After the shock wore off, I asked your father if I still had his blessing to have your hand in marriage. Initially, he was reluctant to let someone who did not wish to rule over the kingdom marry his daughter, but, thankfully, your mother convinced him that someone who believes in you as much as I do, was worthy of marrying you."

"Oh my gosh. Why didn't you tell me any of this?"

"That's not very romantic, now is it? I wanted you to have a surprise. A fairy-tale proposal because that's what you deserve. That's why I wanted to use a little magic from the Tree of Friendship, as well as help from the trolls."

"Do you really love and believe in me that much?" Natalie asked, fresh tears welling up in her eyes.

"Yes, sweetheart, I do. I know that we are going to have a wonderful life together whether you choose to reign over the kingdom, write books, or do something else entirely."

"Well then, I guess we've officially got a wedding to plan, but let's go celebrate with our friends first."

With that, the two went back out into the forest and danced the night away with the woodland creatures.

CHAPTER 25

A knock at the door startled them out of the past and back into the present. "Hey bud, what're you doing here?" Blaine asked, opening the door for a tall man named Byron. He was a forty-something-year-old with the same shade of blonde hair Blaine once had and Natalie's emerald-green eyes.

"Hi, Daddy," Isabel said, her voice full of excited happiness as she walked over and kissed her father on the cheek.

"Don't 'hi Daddy' me young lady. I've been looking everywhere for you. People and trolls are piling into the throne room. I just ran into Dylock outside and sent him on his way. He was sitting by the window just listening to all of you. It was odd."

Blaine's eyebrows furrowed. "That is odd, how did he seem?"

"The little guy was scared at first, but when I told him a little bit about the importance of the decree and sent him off to the castle he got real excited and said it was going to fix everything."

Isabel flashed a smile. "Well, at least one creature will be happy with the decree."

Byron sighed. "Sweetie, everyone will love the decree as long as you actually sign it into effect. I spoke to your aunt Marie last night. She sends her love and says she couldn't be prouder of you. She loves the idea and said they may consider signing something like it into effect in Embersville."

"Really?" Isabel queried, her eyes widened in disbelief.

Byron nodded. "Trust me, your aunt is ecstatic and wishes that she, your Uncle James, and your cousins could be here today, but it just so happens to be the day of Embersville's annual debutante ball."

Natalie smiled. "Marie and James can't help it if royal duty calls. They will just have to bring my other grandbabies for a visit after you sign the decree so that they can see all the wonderful changes in the kingdom."

Nodding, Byron looked to his daughter. "There won't be any changes for them to see unless you sign the decree. Now, c'mon, it's almost time."

"But Daddy, Nana and Papaw have to finish their story first. It's about—"

Shaking his head, Byron disagreed. "Sweetheart, they can tell you stories anytime. Your first royal decree is important. Especially this one. It'll go down in history," he yanked at her sleeve and looked toward the door.

"Not so fast, son." Blaine warned, his voice full of authority. "You're right. This royal decree will go down in history, which is why my beautiful granddaughter needs to know the history of her kingdom. So, take a seat and let us finish our story."

Rolling his eyes, Byron looked to his mother. "Ma, the throne room is full of people and—"

The silver-haired woman shot her son a look. "Retired king or not, you're not too old to mind your parents. Take a seat and do as your father says," she ordered, eyeing the empty chair across from Isabel.

Sighing, Byron took the seat.

Leaning forward, Blaine patted his arm. "Don't worry, my boy. Every royal person in the kingdom is here. They can't start without us." Smiling, the elderly man looked to his wife. "Go on, sweetheart."

Natalie kissed her husband on the cheek, "Now, where was I?

Ah, yes. Naturally, my first royal decree was to let my fiancé, future father-in-law, and the trolls out of exile. Our wedding took place about six months later, on an unseasonably warm October day. It was the best day of my life." She looked to Byron and smiled sweetly. "Aside from the day I gave birth to you of course."

"It was a wonderful day," Blaine agreed. "And you were a beautiful bride."

Shaking his head, Murlyn disagreed. "With all due respect, dear friends, I have to say, Rosie was by far the most gorgeous bride." Murlyn looked to his wife and winked.

Rosie giggled and looked to Natalie. "Let's just say it was a tie between us."

The silver-haired woman chuckled, "Works for me."

As the four of them continued to reminisce about their wedding, Natalie went back in time and was once again not the silver-haired grandmother who sat with them, but the jittery bride who walked toward the Tree of Friendship in her mother's wedding dress. She tried not to cry, as she prepared to spend the rest of her life with Blaine.

"You look magnificent, sweetheart. I love you," he whispered as they and their fellow woodland bride and groom, joined hands, and turned to face her father.

"Ladies, gentlemen, and treasure trolls of Cinder's Edge, we are gathered here tonight, to join these two couples in holy matrimony. These four have all faced, not only the greatest evil our kingdom has ever known, but also years of separation from their respective soulmates. I cannot apologize enough for being responsible for that separation."

"Daddy..."

"Okay, okay... what is joined here today, let no man separate." Frederick finished.

After a moment, Blaine looked to Natalie, cleared his throat, and said, "You Natalie Nordstrom are, and always have been, my best friend. Today, I vow to never let that change. I vow to support you in good times and in bad. I vow to help you achieve your every dream and live the happiest life possible, because, by marrying me, you are ensuring that I'll live the most joyful life I can imagine."

With tears in her eyes, Natalie nodded and recited her vows. "Blaine, you literally saved my life, but not in the way you think. You saved me by believing in me more than anyone ever has so I vow, from this day forward, to do the same for you. I love and accept you just as you are, and I vow to spend the rest of my life proving that to you and everyone else in this kingdom, day in and day out until they accept, love, and embrace you, because you deserve nothing less and I can't imagine spending our joyful life any other way." Wiping tears from her eyes, she turned and nodded to Rosie.

Smiling, Rosie looked to her future husband, "It's hard to know where to begin," she admitted, her small, high-pitched voice full of love. "I never thought this day would come. We all know that love is the most powerful form of magic in the world. The love you and I share is precious. We were forced to be apart for years, but our love was strong enough to endure the separation. From this day forward, I pledge to nurture the love we share and be the best wife and partner any troll has ever been."

Taking a deep breath, Murlyn took Rosie's hand and squeezed gently. "You're exactly right, sweetheart. The love between us is special. I spent years putting my duty to this kingdom ahead of our love, even after I promised you I wouldn't. Well, no more. From this day forward, I vow to always put you and our love first and be the best husband I can be," he declared, his voice brimming with a mixture of pride and happiness.

Moments after the dark blue-haired woodland creature finished his vows, the couples exchanged rings and bracelets respectively and turned to face Frederick, who tearfully declared each couple husband and wife.

～

"Awww.... that's so sweet," Isabel exclaimed, bringing Natalie back to the present.

"Yes, that was the first time I saw my Daddy cry. The second time was at my coronation. Silly me thought that life was going to go back to normal after we got married and I became queen," Natalie chuckled softly.

"What a minute," Isabel's eyebrows scrunched in confusion. "Didn't it?"

Giggling again, Natalie looked to Blaine. "Sweetie, I think you should tell them the rest of the story.

The moment the words left his wife's mouth, Blaine found himself back in the castle, after returning with Natalie from their honeymoon in Embersville.

I can't believe the honeymoon ended so quickly. On to a brand-new reality now, Blaine thought as he started up the newly-installed ramp to the castle with Natalie in tow.

Opening the front door, she smiled. "It's good to be home, isn't it sweetie?"

Blaine sighed, "Does the honeymoon have to be over?" He whined, kissing her sweetly on the lips.

"No, of course not," she whispered, kissing him back.

Clearing her throat, Alexandria approached, startling both of them.

"Sorry, Mama," Natalie said quickly, her cheeks bright crimson. "We didn't see you there. Do you need something?"

"Yes, in fact, I need you. You're needed for a ribbon cutting ceremony at the new hospital in thirty minutes. After that, you're needed at a debutante ball rehearsal and finally tonight you're expected at dinner with the duke of Stalagmiteville."

"But Mama, we just got home. No one told me that I had at so many events today. I need—" Natalie began.

"Newlywed or not, you're still queen. It's your responsibility to know and keep track of your schedule from now on. People expect a lot out of you as the ruler of the realm. You must hold yourself to a higher standard. Come along now," she urged.

Natalie turned to Blaine and frowned. "Sorry sweetheart. Looks like my day is full. Are you going to be okay?"

"I'll be fine. I'll just head to the forest and catch up with Papa and the trolls."

"Okay." she kissed him on the cheek. "Please remind your father how much we want him back in the kingdom." she called out as he started back down the ramp.

As Blaine started down the path toward the Forest of Wishes, he heard chanting in the distance, "All kids deserve to enjoy Frederick Hall; make magic accessible to all. All kids deserve to enjoy Frederick Hall; make magic accessible to all…"

What in the world? Blaine wondered, heading toward the sound. "What's going on?" He approached a crowd of people surrounding a beaten down, weathered brick building that looked much older than those surrounding it.

"Oh, hello… I can't believe you're here!" A golden-haired man with a crooked smile exclaimed, having spotted Blaine. "Hey everyone, we have a shot at this one, Blaine is here!"

Suddenly, the crowd stopped chanting and begun to cheer.

"I'm glad everyone is happy to see me." Blaine shouted, struggling to be heard above the crowd. "But will you please tell me what's going on?"

"Sorry, I got so caught up in the protest. I didn't even think to introduce myself," the golden-haired man explained. "I'm Roger Richardson, the man who organized this protest." he extended his hand.

"I guess you already know who I am. Nice to meet you, Roger," shaking his hand, Blaine smiled. "Tell me… why did you start the protest?"

Roger chuckled, "Sorry, I keep getting ahead of myself. My son, Kevin, is nine and in a wheelchair. He's been into magic for a couple of years and was real excited that Magnificent Melvin, a magician from Embersville was coming here for a show. That is until we found out that show was going to be at Frederick Hall." Gesturing toward the building, Roger shook his head.

"Obviously, he and other kids with disabilities can't get in there. Needless to say, when I told Kev, he was crushed. So, I called in some reinforcements and put together a protest."

Wow... he's so supportive of his son. I can't believe it. Maybe Papa was wrong about the people of Cinder's Edge, Blaine smiled at Roger, "How can I help?"

Grinning, Roger handed him a sign with the words 'Make Magic Accessible', and the two turned their attention back to the protest.

"Hey everyone, Blaine's agreed to join us. Blaine, this is Mike, Karen, Suzie, and Suzie's twins, Jim and Jill," Roger explained.

"Thanks so much for helping us out today." Karen, an elderly woman in her eighties with curly white hair and silver glasses held out her hand toward Blaine. "My granddaughter was paralyzed years ago after she fell during a ballet routine. After three surgeries, she's remained in remarkably good spirits and wants to support her fellow dancers. Unfortunately, she can't attend their recitals because each are performed in inaccessible venues like Frederick Hall. It's not right," she shook her head. "It's just not right."

"I couldn't agree more. My father used to be a magician and I never—"

"I knew you looked familiar. Your father was the Amazing Benjamin Benson, wasn't he? You look just like him."

Grinning, Blaine nodded, "Yep. That's the one."

"Oh, it's a shame he's not out here with you today. He was always so great at making kids laugh."

"Wait a minute. How'd you know my father?" Blaine asked.

"Years ago, your father and his lovely female assistant, whom I can only assume was your mother, put on magic shows for the kids like my granddaughter, who couldn't make it out to see their shows around the kingdom."

That must be why Papa thinks the people of Cinder's Edge would never accept me. I always thought he was just being paranoid. Little did I know that the kingdom wasn't accessible enough for all the kids to see his magic shows.

"Yeah," Mike, a man who walked with a wobbly gate and wore crutches under both of his arms, agreed. "I went to a couple of those shows as a kid and they were great. It'd be awesome to have him out here right now."

I wish Papa were here right now to see this and hear people singing his praises. Then he'd see that some people do care about and accept people like me.

His mother's voice drifted into his mind. *If you can't bring your father to the people, sweet boy. Bring the people to your father.*

That's it, Blaine thought excitedly, turning toward Suzie and her twins. "What about you? Have you ever heard of the Amazing Benjamin Benson?"

"Yes, of course," Suzie said. "I saw one of his shows in the auditorium as a kid." Smiling, she looked to her twins who were asleep in their double stroller, "I just wish they had the access and the opportunity to see one now."

"What if I told you they could?" Blaine's voice was full of excitement.

"What… how?"

"Come with me," Blaine urged. "Everyone else can handle the protest for a while, right?" He questioned, addressing the group.

"Yeah, take your little ones and go have some fun. We've got this," Roger assured.

With that, Blaine rolled toward the Forest of Wishes with Suzie and her twins in tow.

"HEY PAPA, I'm back. How did you and the trolls survive without me?" He questioned, pushing the door of the hut open for Suzie and the twins. "I see they helped you with the cleaning as always," he chuckled, looking around the immaculately-kept hut complete with a "Welcome Home Blaine & Natalie" sign.

"My boy!" Benjamin shouted excitedly, rushing to the front door. "I missed ya. It's so good to see you, but... wait, who are these people?" He eyed Suzie and the twins, his forehead wrinkled with worry.

Blaine chuckled, "Papa, don't worry. My beautiful wife will be by later. She's busy with royal duties today." Smiling, he pointed his head toward the woman standing behind him, "This is my friend Suzie and her twins, Jim and Jill. I met them at the protest at Frederick Hall today. They and some friends are—"

"A protest?" Benjamin eyed Blaine. "Son, you and Natalie just tied the knot. Don't ya think you are pushin' your luck by already getting' in trouble with a protest?"

"Papa, I'm not in trouble and, even if I do get into some hot water, it'll be worth it. Some people with disabilities and parents of kids with disabilities are trying to make Cinder's Edge a better place."

Letting out a huff, the loving father rolled his eyes.

Suddenly, Jill cried reminding Blaine of Suzie's presence. Sighing, he hung his head. "Please forgive me, Suzie. I didn't mean to be rude by starting an argument in front of you and your children."

Pushing the double stroller up to the table, Suzie took a seat and looked from Blaine to his father and back. "It's okay," she said kindly. "Equal access is something we are all passionate about."

Letting out a huff, Benjamin looked her straight in the eye. "With all due respect, I want nothing to do with this, which is why I told my son not to go back into Cinder's Edge in the first place," he said, his voice laced with aggravation.

"But Mr. Benson, I've heard that you're such a—" Suzie begun, her voice timid and quiet.

"Like I said, I want nothin' to do with any of this. Leave me out of it," Benjamin said.

"Is that why you didn't fight the day we defeated Glomgurgle? Are you so against the realm of Cinder's Edge that you can't accept anything positive happening there?" Blaine's voice was cautious yet deliberate. "I've been wanting to ask why you didn't fight for a while, but I've been afraid to do so." A silence settled between the young man and his father until he decided to speak again. "Let me tell you, Papa, that defeating Glomgurgle was a wonderful thing and I'm confident that the outcome of this protest will be wonderful too. You could be a part of all the amazingly positive things happening in Cinder's Edge right now Papa. All you have to do is be okay with being a part of the kingdom."

Shaking his head vehemently, Benjamin disagreed, "I stopped carin' about that dragon and that kingdom a real long time ago. That's why I didn't see any reason to fight. I made a new pair of pants for you instead. I still can't believe that the last pair stopped working, but I'm really confident I worked out all the kinks this time. Wanna come try 'em on? We can show Suzie and the kiddos."

"No, Papa. The protest is far more important," Blaine insisted. "I wish you'd come." *Why doesn't Papa get how important this is?* He wondered. *I wish I knew what's going through his head so I could make sense of it.*

Lizzie's spirit reassured him at that moment. *Your father is a complicated man, sweet boy. I am certain he loves you more than life itself. But he's carried a heavy burden for your entire life. It may help for you to give him permission to let go of that burden. If you give him permission to let it go, then he may give himself permission to let it go.*

Of course... why didn't I think of that years ago? It was like a light bulb had gone off in Blaine's mind.

Turning his attention to Suzie, whom he'd forgotten was there until his father mentioned her, Blaine flashed a polite smile. "I apologize for our continued rudeness. If you'd be so kind as to take the twins outside and give us a moment alone, I would really appreciate it."

As the door to the hut closed behind Suzie and her twins, the loving father quietly reiterated, "I love ya, son, but I'm not going anywhere with you and your friend."

"I know you love me. I love you, too, and it's okay, Papa."

Nodding, Benjamin smiled. "Thank you, my boy. I just don't want to go back into that kingdom."

Shaking his head, Blaine disagreed, "No, Papa, that's not what I mean. What I mean is, it's okay. I turned out okay. Heck, I conquered one of the evilest creatures around. I'd say I turned out more than okay. Don't you see? I might not have been able to conquer Glomgurgle if I wasn't who I am, and I wouldn't be who I am if it weren't for my disability." Taking a deep breath, Blaine looked his father straight in the eye before continuing, "I guess what I'm tryin' to say is, I don't blame you for Mama's accident. Most of the time, I want to thank you for allowing her to ride horseback that day, because, if it weren't for that, I may not be who I am or have the amazing wife I have now. Pausing, Blaine took a deep breath then continued to explain himself. The pants stopped working because treasure troll magic only grants the wish that is in your heart of hearts. My wish was not to walk with the pants. It never has been. Initially I wanted to please you, so the pants worked, but once I entered that volcano all I wanted to do was save Natalie and, as a result, the wish within my heart of hearts changed and the pants stopped working."

"What are you babblin' about, my boy?"

"I don't blame you for Ma's accident or for my disability. I know you blame yourself, but you don't have to, Papa. You can let go of that burden. I'm giving you permission." Pausing for another moment, Blaine let his words sink in and then continued. "More importantly, you need to give yourself permission to let go of your guilt. I've realized my purpose. I am living the life I was destined to live now. The kind of life I always wanted. And I am happily living my life as a man with Cerebral Palsy, so please allow yourself to finally be freed from the guilt that you've held onto for all of these years. It's what I want, and it is what Ma would have wanted." *Uh oh, maybe I went too far*, Blaine thought as his father stared at him for a long moment. "Please say something, Papa," he said when he could no longer stand his father's silence.

"Thank you," Benjamin whispered.

"Hmm?"

"Thank you. Nothing's gonna happen overnight, but it's nice to hear you say that, my boy. I know things haven't been easy for ya over the years, but I hope you understand that I've only ever wanted to do right by ya and your mother."

Closing the space between himself and his father, Blaine put a hand on his shoulder.

"I know Papa," he squeezed gently. "You have. Granted you got a little fixated on the wrong thing, but you've always done right by Ma and me. You are a good father and a good man."

Benjamin embraced his son, "Thank you, my boy. Hearin' you say that makes me feel so darn good. Ya know what? You're right, I am a good man and as a good man I'm gonna go to that protest, like your Ma would have wanted," he nodded, still grinning. "Now, take me with you before I change my mind."

Ma's wisdom saved the day yet again, Blaine smiled as they left the hut and headed toward the protest with their new friends in tow.

CHAPTER 26

"What in the world?" Natalie wondered aloud as she walked into the castle to find half of the staff, looking out the window.

"So sorry, your majesty," Clarence, the castle grounds keeper said, as the rest of the staff scattered.

"It's okay, Clarence. What's everyone staring at?"

"Well, I… um…" the grounds keeper flashed her a nervous smile.

"Clarence, please just spit it out," Natalie insisted. "I've had a long day."

"Okay, Okay, no one wanted you to find out this way, but there is a protest going on at Frederick Hall. Both your father and Blaine's father are there now and, well, it's not pretty."

Nodding, the queen thanked Clarence for his honesty and ran out of the castle toward the protest.

"Daddy, Stop! What do you think you're doing?" She shouted upon seeing him rip a sign that read *All Kids Need magic'* from the hands of a crying, red-headed toddler.

"Stopping this ridiculous protest! I can't even believe you let it go on. Frederick Hall is my namesake building for crying out loud!"

"Daddy… please calm down. I'm—" Natalie began.

276

"Calm down...? Calm down...? How do you expect me to calm down? This building has been around since before I was born. Who cares if it's accessible or not? It's historic!" The former king turned to address the crowd. "No one is to touch a single brick of this building. Is that understood?"

Throwing his head back, Benjamin let out a curt chuckle, "C'mon, Frederick, get with the times. Historic or not, these kiddos, and all people like them, deserve to see the magic shows, plays, musicians, and other great events that happen here."

"Oh, how would you know?" Frederick's voice full of disdain. "You've been in exile for twenty years and your cripple son suddenly has you brain washed."

In an instant, Benjamin's hands became fists and his face turned bright red. "How dare you call my—" he began, his voice brimming with anger of a protective father.

"Stop!" Natalie shouted. Taking a deep breath, she looked from her father to her father-in-law. "With all due respect to both of you, last I checked this is my kingdom. I'll make this decision."

Smiling, Blaine wheeled though the crowd and up to his wife. "That's right, my wife will have this place accessible in no time."

Natalie eyed Blaine as the crowd begun to cheer. "You said I was capable of reigning over this kingdom myself, so let me," she whispered through gritted teeth.

"Yeah, but that's when I thought you were going to always do the right thing. I didn't think—" Blaine began.

"Oh, so my decisions will only be right if you agree with them? We'll see about that," Natalie quipped, her voice full of disgust.

Clearing her throat, she turned to address the crowd once again. "Anyone who wishes to know the fate of Frederick Hall should be in the throne room at noon tomorrow. Until then, please disperse and enjoy the rest of your day."

UGH NO MATTER *what I do someone is going to be upset,* Natalie realized as she contemplated what to do in the privacy of the throne room. *I hate being torn between my dad and my husband. What am I going to do?* She wondered as she heard a knock at the door.

"Sweetheart, may I come in?" Blaine asked as he hesitantly pushed the door open.

Natalie looked down at her feet, avoiding eye contact, "What do you want?"

"I just came to say that I'm sorry and you're right. I am going to let you decide whether to renovate Frederick Hall or not and I'll respect whatever decision you make," he said kindly.

Natalie smiled, "Thanks sweetheart, I am so happy to hear you say that. I can't tell you what I'm going to do yet because I haven't decided. But I can promise you whatever I do will be in the best interests of the kingdom."

Blaine flashed a nervous smile. "I am glad to hear you say that, because I brought some people here with me who can tell you about what's best for the kingdom."

Looking down at his watch, Byron cleared his throat bringing Natalie back to the present. "Ma, I don't mean to be rude, but the ceremony is fast approaching. Can we wrap this up, please?" He glanced at his watched again, his forehead wrinkled with worry.

"Son, how do you expect me to finish the story if you keep interrupting?" She asked pointedly.

Byron threw up his hands, "Okay, okay. Just please continue."

Smiling, the silver-haired grandmother continued, "Initially, I was angry at your Papaw for bringing citizens to the throne room to talk to me, but by the time the citizens were finished with their testimonies, I could no longer be mad. I was shocked when your great grandpa gave the first testimony. He was nervous and awkward, but still somewhat convincing nonetheless, she chuckled at the thought. Within moments, it was as though she had once again been transported through time and was back in the throne room, wide-eyed as her father-in law approached.

"Oh… Hi, Benjamin. It's great to see you," she gushed, pulling him into a hug. "I didn't expect to see you today. Do you need something before I listen to the testimonies of a few citizens?

Returning her embrace, he squeezed her tightly. "It's good to see you too, sweetheart. I'm here to give ya my testimony."

"You're going to give a testimony?" She queried, her voice full of skepticism.

Freeing her from his embrace, he flashed a grin, "You betcha, sweetie."

This should be interesting, Natalie thought, offering him a smile. "Okay. Begin your testimony whenever you are ready," she encouraged, her voice slightly more formal than it had been just moments before as she readied herself for royal duty.

"Well, uh, it's hard for me ta be here right now. Ya know that I ain't been into the kingdom for years, but I came here with my new friends today to tell ya why Frederick Hall should be changed for those kiddos," he smiled briefly at Suzie and her twins who were standing off to the side along with Blaine and other protestors listening to his testimony then continued.

Ya know I don't buy into the whole magic can't be used to manipulate destiny thing. If were up to me, magic would be used to cure disabilities, but the trolls swear that magic can't be used like that. The way I see it, if magic can't be used to help fix kids with disabilities, it should at least be used to make 'em happy. As a former magician, I can tell ya how happy magic makes kids. Heck, if I am bein' honest, magic makes a lot of adults happy too. I imagine that fixin' up a building like Frederick Hall would be mighty expensive, but do ya really want money to get in the way of a lifetime of happiness for those little guys?" He pointed toward Jim and Jill as he asked the question.

~

"Great grandpa made a valid point," Isabel said. "But if he wasn't the one who convinced you then who did?" The lovely granddaughter queried, bringing Natalie back to present day.

"A man by the name of Roger, who'd been the mastermind behind the protest gave a testimony after your great grandfather about how, if Frederick Hall was renovated, Cinder's Edge would be seen as innovative and on the cutting edge, but it was the testimony of a woman by the name of Suzie that had the biggest impact. To this day, I still remember exactly what she said," Natalie explained, smiling wistfully. She allowed the vivid memory to overtake her and within seconds found herself back in the throne room, ready to listen to Suzie's testimony.

~

"Hello, your majesty. I'm Suzie Ferguson." Smiling, the young woman held out her hand.

Accepting the gesture, Natalie shook her hand and forced a smile, "Let's get straight to the point, miss. Please just tell me whether you think Frederick Hall should be renovated or not and why."

It was Suzie's turn to force a smile as tears welled up in her eyes, "I wish it were that simple. But, to be perfectly honest with you, nothing about life has been right since the day my twins, Jim and Jill, were born. They each were diagnosed with Cerebral Palsy at about eight months old. I'm telling you this, not to get sympathy nor even empathy from you, but to explain why I participated in the protest today. For me, it wasn't about making a building accessible. It was about something far more important. Participating in that protest was a way of helping to secure a better future for my kids." Dabbing at her eyes, Suzie took a deep breath and continued, "I am an advocate for my children and will continue to be until I take my last breath. With all due respect to our new friend, Benjamin, I hope that in the future no one will want to cure my children with magic because they will be accepted for who they are. My children shouldn't have to change for the world. Instead, I will change the world for them. I envision a future where protesting won't be needed because Jim, Jill, and other people like them will have the same rights and level of access as everyone else in Cinder's Edge. Your majesty, I know this is not an easy decision for you to make and that you likely feel torn between your father and your husband, so I am going to leave you with this: what sort of future do you want for your children? Do you want your children to see a future where a man, like their father, who was brave enough to defeat Glomgurgle, has to fight for his rights or do you want them to see a future of equality?"

Thank you for that powerful testimony, Natalie said after a long moment, "I will take it under advisement. Turning, she addressed the group, "I will take all of your testimonies into account when making my decision. I appreciate each and every one of you for coming. Now, if you'll excuse me, I have some thinking to do."

"W-wait a minute," Benjamin stammered.

"Did you forget part of your testimony?" Natalie queried sweetly.

Benjamin shook his head, "No not exactly. But I got somethin' to say."

Having stopped to watch Natalie's exchange with his father, Blaine and the other protestors listened intently.

Shifting his weight from one foot to the other, Benjamin made brief eye contact with each person in the room then spoke, "I want ya'll to know that Suzie's testimony touched my heart. I've been goin' 'bout this all wrong. I should've been changin' my boy's environment instead of tryin' to change him. I dunno why it took me so long to catch on. But I'm not gonna be makin' anymore pants. Instead, I'll be going back to my magical roots," he declared, grinning happily.

"That's so wonderful to hear, Papa," Blaine's voice brimmed with happiness as he embraced his father. Benjamin's new friends cheered for him, celebrating his revelation.

Natalie remained speechless, taking in the happiness around her. *Well, would you look at that. The idea of renovating Frederick Hall is already bringing about positive change in the kingdom. Renovating it definitely seems like the right thing to do,* she realized, suddenly as happy as the others and very confident in her decision.

～

"Awww... Nana, don't cry," Isabel soothed, once again bringing Natalie back to the present.

Flashing a smile, she reached for her granddaughter's hand, "It's okay, sweetheart. I was just remembering how hard Suzie's questions and your great grandfather's reaction to her testimony hit me, because no one knew at the time, but I was already pregnant with your father." She smiled at Byron then looked back to her granddaughter. "You are going to do great things for the kingdom, sweet girl, and I am sure it's a sign of even greater things to come."

Blaine shook his head, grinning, "I'd agree with you, but I can't think of anything greater than what our wonderful granddaughter is about to do."

Sighing, Isabel stood up from the table and began to pace around the small hut, "I'm glad that you guys are so confident. But I'm still really apprehensive. How can you be so sure that the citizens of Cinder's Edge will support this? I mean, c'mon guys, not everyone is going to be happy about this decree or even understand it."

Byron looked to his daughter. The worry lines in his forehead were even deeper than moments before, "Sweetie, I've told you before that royal decrees are about what's best for the kingdom, not about making every citizen happy. Sit back down before you work yourself into a frenzy," he urged.

"Daddy, this isn't just about the royal decree," Isabel retorted. "It's about the future of Cinder's Edge. The entire kingdom is about to change forever, for crying out loud!"

Practically standing up in his wheelchair, Blaine shot his granddaughter a look, "Isabel, don't yell at your father."

"Sweetheart, don't get in the middle of—" Natalie began.

Blaine shook his head vehemently, "This is our family. I'll get in the middle of whatever I please."

The trolls, who had been listening to the interaction, yelled simultaneously, "Quiet!" As silence fell over the hut, Rosie and Murlyn looked to Missy and nodded encouragingly.

Taking a deep breath, the purple glittery-haired troll looked to Isabel, "Girlie, ready or not, the kingdom is in your hands now. As your best friend and confidant, I suggest that you trust your grandmother when she says that both you and the kingdom are ready for this. I know that I was a bit apprehensive earlier, but after hearing the history of this kingdom, I couldn't be more certain that she's right. You just have to trust your instincts," Missy encouraged, her voice quiet and sweet.

Isabel sighed, "I know you're right. And after that story, I definitely do trust my instincts. I'm just so nervous about the impact the decree will make. I really hope it's big enough to make a positive, lasting impact, like we're all hoping it will."

Chuckling softly, Natalie looked her granddaughter straight in the eye, "Of course, it will. Don't you see sweetheart? I may have made an impact by renovating a few buildings over the years, but the impact you will make today is so much greater and one that will last forever. I am sorry that I didn't think of it sooner, but I'm so proud that you have. Everything this family has achieved has led to this moment, so I want you to take a deep breath, hold your head up high, lead us back to the castle and the throne room, and sign that decree."

CHAPTER 27

"$\mathcal{I}$ wish my parents and Madison could be here to see this," Blaine whispered, amazed at the number of citizens who were there as Isabel, he, Natalie, Byron, and their woodland friends entered the room. "Wow, this place looks amazing… just amazing." He looked around, wide-eyed at the room which was adorned with pictures of not only the protest at Frederick Hall, but also a protest at Cinder's Edge Cinema, and a sit-in on the ground floor of Samuel Crawford Academy, all of which were eventually renovated to be wheelchair accessible, thanks to the efforts of Blaine, Roger, Suzie, and other advocates like them. Smiling, he spotted in empty space in the front row set up a few feet from Isabel's throne for the ceremony.

"They are here." Murlyn whispered as he settled in a chair to the left of Blaine.

"Of course they are," Natalie agreed as she sat down in a chair to her husband's right. "And I'll bet they are just as happy about this royal decree as we are," she whispered as Isabel approached the podium.

Clearing her throat, she began to speak, "Ladies, gentlemen, and woodland creatures of Cinder's Edge, thank you all so much for being here today. As you can see, I decided to give the throne room a bit of a makeover. If you ask me, it was *well* overdue. No offense, Nana," she chuckled nervously. "The point is, I chose to spruce up the room with photos of the protests that have taken place in Cinder's Edge over the years as a reminder. The pictures show the strides that have been made in the struggle for equality for all people and creatures in our kingdom. Today marks another very significant stride in the struggle. For, today, I am ordering by royal decree that people with disabilities are granted not only equal access to *all* public buildings, but also equal treatment in all other areas, including employment, education, forms of transportation, and all other aspects of public life, which will be defined in the Cinder's Edge Doctrine of Equality."

Looking down at the document on the podium, she smiled and lifted the quill next to it, then hesitated, "I'd be thrilled to exercise the right that my new position as the Queen of Cinder's Edge affords me, but I can't."

What's that girl have up her sleeve now? Blaine wondered, as he and Natalie exchanged worried glances.

Isabel looked to her grandfather, tears welling up in her eyes, "I can't because signing this doctrine is not a right. It's an honor. It is an honor that should be bestowed upon those who held up signs at protest after protest, year after year; those who were arrested after staging a sit-in at the school named for my great-great grandfather, Samuel Crawford; and those who fought to give people with disabilities in Cinder's Edge, who were silenced for years, a voice." Tears rolling down her cheeks, the newly-crowned queen's voice broke.

Awww...my sweet girl's emotions are catching up with her, Blaine thought worriedly.

It's okay, my sweet boy. Sometimes we can become overwhelmed even in moments of great joy such as this, the sweet voice of his mother reassured. *Isabel will be just fine.* Comforted by the ever-present familial guardian angel, Blaine smiled encouragingly at his granddaughter.

Smiling back, she nodded, took a breath, wiped away her tears, and addressed her people once again, "With that said, I call my grandfather and his fellow disability rights advocates, Roger Richardson and Suzie Ferguson, without whom the kingdom would not be what it is today to the podium. Papaw, please join me up here with your friends and do me the honor of being the first to sign the Cinder's Edge Doctrine of Equality," she urged, holding the quill out toward Blaine as he and his friends approached.

Smiling from ear to ear, Blaine accepted the quill as Roger pushed him around the podium and stood next to his granddaughter.

This is what being overwhelmed with joy feels like. Enjoy it, Lizzie's voice encouraged.

Placing the quill on the podium, Blaine turned to face his granddaughter and embraced her tightly, "I love you, sweetheart. Thank you so much for this," he whispered.

A moment later, he let go, turned back to the podium, and with tears in his eyes signed the doctrine. As Roger and Suzie took their turns signing, Blaine addressed the crowd, smiling despite the moisture in his eyes, "I'm overwhelmed with joy, thanks to the great honor my wonderful granddaughter has granted my friends and myself. In fact, I'm so overwhelmed with gratitude that I feel the only thing I can do is spread my happiness. With that in mind, I invite every person and woodland creature who believes in the purpose of the Cinder's Edge Doctrine of Equality, equal treatment of all people and woodland creatures in this kingdom, to sign as well be—"

Clearing his throat, Dylock cut Blaine off, gaining the attention of everyone in the room. "I'm sorry to interrupt you, Blaine," he begun, his voice coated in nervousness, as countless eyes settled on him. "I just wanted to ask if I could be the first woodland creature to sign. As everyone here most likely knows, I haven't always been on the right side of the fight between good and evil and… well, I hope that signing will show my fellow woodland creatures and the people of Cinder's Edge that I really have changed."

Studying the green-haired troll, Blaine chuckled softly. *Has Dylock forgotten how he ultimately helped us defeat Glomgurgle?*

Sometimes even treasure trolls don't give themselves enough credit. Sometimes even they forget about the magic within all of us. Perhaps you should remind him and everyone what the most powerful form of magic is, Lizzie's spirit advised after a moment.

"Dylock, I'd be honored to have you be the first woodland creature to sign this doctrine," Blaine said, his tone kind and thoughtful. "But, know this: you never have to prove to anyone that you're on the right side of the fight between good and evil. We will always remember that because of you the fight is no more. For, when faced with the greatest evil to ever threaten this kingdom, you chose to help us defeat him using the most powerful form of magic in the world: love."

Fresh tears blurring his vision, Blaine gestured for Dylock to approach the podium and once again addressed the crowd, his voice light and hopeful despite the moisture behind his eyes. "As you join me, Dylock, and my other friends up here to sign this life changing doctrine, remember that while this ruling is a great thing, it's ultimately just a piece of parchment. We may have to wait years for the accessible buildings it promises, but we don't have to wait years for equality because the ability to love and treat one another equally is within all us. We just have to spread a little of that magic within all of us from time to time."

With that, every remaining person and treasure troll in the realm was moved to sign the Cinder's Edge Doctrine of Equality. Despite it taking them three years to finish the renovations set forth by the ruling, from that day forward the people and woodland creatures lived happily and equally ever after.

ABOUT THE AUTHOR

Allison M. Boot, otherwise known as the Wheelin' Wordsmith, wrote this story to spread a message of self-acceptance to young adults and children traveling paths similar to hers. She earned a Master of Arts in Mass Communication from the University of Dayton and currently resides in Urbana, Illinois with her husband, Dylan. She is also the owner of an extensive troll doll collection, started at the tender age of three, after being told that they bring good luck. To this day, it continues to grow and do just that.

WANT TO CONNECT WITH THE WHEELIN' WORDSMITH?

Join her mailing list by visiting www.allisonmbootauthor.com, where you can learn more about her and her books today! Also, don't forget to "like" her on Facebook and Pinterest as well as follow her on Twitter at @WheelNWordsmith and Instagram at @Wheelin_Wordsmith!